Rachel Dove is a tutor and romance/romcom author from West Yorkshire in the UK. She lives with her husband and two sons, and dreams of a life where housework is done by fairies and she can have as many pets as she wants. When she is not writing or reading she can be found dreaming of her next research trip away with the family.

Deanne Anders was reading romance while her friends were still reading Nancy Drew, and she knew she'd hit the jackpot when she found a shelf of Harlequin Presents in her local library. Years later she discovered the fun of writing her own. Deanne lives in Florida, with her husband and their spoiled Pomeranian. During the day she works as a nursing supervisor. With her love of everything medical and romance, writing for Mills & Boon Medical Romance is a dream come true.

A MIDWIFE, HER BEST FRIEND, THEIR FAMILY

RACHEL DOVE

FLIGHT NURSE'S FLORIDA FAIRY TALE

DEANNE ANDERS

MILLS & BOON

First published in Great Britain 2023
by Mills & Boon, an imprint of HarperCollins*Publishers* Ltd,
1 London Bridge Street, London, SE1 9GF

www.harpercollins.co.uk

HarperCollins*Publishers*, Macken House, 39/40 Mayor Street Upper,
Dublin 1, D01 C9W8, Ireland

ISBN: 978-0-263-30604-0

04/23

A MIDWIFE,
HER BEST FRIEND,
THEIR FAMILY

RACHEL DOVE

MILLS & BOON

For Auntie Dale Walker

With love

CHAPTER ONE

'YOU HAVE GOT to be kidding me.' Molly couldn't believe her ears.

The sign for Ashford Birthing Centre loomed in the windshield, looking resplendent even in the dull January weather. It was freezing outside, and she pulled her black parka tighter around her at the thought. She was glad she'd plumped for her thicker winter tights today. Even in the delivery rooms, where the temperature was controlled centrally, she always felt the cold in winter. A remnant from her childhood, no doubt. Her mother had warmed herself with vodka, and had often forgotten about the needs of her daughter. Sometimes, she still experienced that cold feeling, even when she was wrapped up snug in her adult life.

'What?' Matt looked across at her as he pulled into the car park of their workplace. His dark brow was raised. 'I only said she wasn't that bad. It was a short ride.'

'Seriously?' Her brows were so far up into her hairline, her whole face tightened. She couldn't help feeling a bit ratty. She hadn't slept well and having company in the car pool with Matt had been a shock, and not a good one. Of all the mornings, and before she'd even managed to get a drop of caffeine into her system. Her flatmate, Amy, had forgotten to buy coffee. 'Next time you give me a lift to work, give me a heads up if you've got someone with you, so I can skip it.' She didn't look at him, but she knew that he was smirking.

'I thought she had some interesting opinions, myself.'

'She was talking about medicine, and the only relevant medical experience that woman has is having a smear test.' She clenched her jaw. 'It was exhausting.' Plus, she never usually saw the women he dated. Not that there were many. Her best friend was not the relationship type. Everyone knew that. 'It just surprised me she was there.'

Matt's tone changed. 'She put me on the spot, and I didn't think. She was moaning about how late she was for work and I had my car parked outside her place. You know I never sleep over normally, but I crashed out. It was a mistake, an oversight. I thought I was being gallant.'

He had a fair point. What was he supposed to do, say no to giving her a lift? He wasn't cruel to women. Or a player.

'Fair enough. Next time though, I'll get the bus.' She shot him a smile, but he didn't match it.

'No, don't start taking the bus. It's too cold, and you hate the winter. Besides, I like taking you to work. It starts my day off right.' He reached for her hand across the gear stick. 'Forgiven me yet?'

She pretended to seriously consider it. He groaned.

'Mol, come on! You're making me feel like a playboy. I met a woman; we spent the night together. I don't do it all the time. Hardly ever, in fact. It's no different from the dating you do. I just…keep it short.'

'How short?' she quipped.

'Steady,' he warned. 'You know what I mean. Every-one needs a little company sometimes. Even me.' His jaw tightened, and the urge to tease him left her.

She understood that. Throughout her childhood, the one thing she'd encountered was loneliness. It was easier not to trust people, let them in. Relying on herself was the only sure thing. She knew Matt felt the same way. It was one of the reasons she'd let *him* in. Trusted him. She pushed away her intrusive thoughts and focused on her friend.

'I don't think you're a playboy, Matt. I get it. Sorry, grumpy morning.' A phrase he'd coined. He'd learned early on in their friendship that she wasn't a happy little early bird.

He didn't get attached to people, and that's how he lived his life. He didn't lie to the women he spent time with; he was honest about not wanting a relationship. He wasn't like the many men her own mother had dredged up over the years. Or Matt's own father for that matter. The doctor turned lawyer was a world away from him. He was devoted to his job, like her. He had no desire for anything other than what he had.

To be fair, the women all knew the score, even if they sometimes thought they would be the one to finally land Matt Loren, the hot legendary baby doctor. The bachelor with the big family name. His father's work in medical law had seen to that, even before Matt ever picked up a textbook. A high-flying doctor who'd become a medical-professional-suing shark was a difficult act to follow, whether he wanted to or not. The tabloids made sure of that. Some of his colleagues had even judged him for it over the years, afraid he might tell dear old Dad something that would land them in court on a malpractice charge. His dad's record didn't exactly scream trust, and Matt was tarred by association. The things parents inflicted upon their offspring always surprised Molly, even knowing what she knew.

Matt Loren was the obstetrician with a reputation for being cut-throat, at the top of his game. People travelled miles to have their high-risk pregnancies overseen by him.

Women loved all that. You put a baby into the arms of a good-looking man, and it was game over. Ovaries and hearts went all aflutter. If he ever chose to, he could have a woman's company every night of the week. The Loren name was known for producing ladykillers. That little moniker had followed him around in life, even longer than it had at work. Add to it an air of unattainability, and there he was. *Her bestie.*

That's how it usually ended too. The pair of them hanging out. She dated, he had his occasional sleepover, but they always ended up being back to just them. Being confronted by one of his lovers grinning at her from the passenger seat? That felt new, and slightly unpleasant to witness.

'It's fine.' She patted his hand. 'I just wish you had a bit more respect for yourself sometimes.' He cast her a sheepish look. 'You're a smart guy, Matt. You literally save mothers and babies every day.'

She refrained from adding that his father turning on his original profession and being a player wasn't his fault, and shouldn't mean he be treated the same way. It was true, but he wouldn't hear it. She understood that too. Sometimes, the shadows of their parents blocked out the light of their adulthood. When things grew in the dark, sometimes they grew differently. Harder, stronger. Reaching out for the light with every limb.

She tried not to be mad, but her best friend could be his own worst enemy. 'The least you deserve is a woman who sees that.' She let the smirk she was holding back play across her lips. 'And one who can spell *vagina*.'

'Fair point,' he conceded as they got out of his sleek red Lexus. They headed to the front doors of the workplace they had shared for so long that she couldn't remember a time when he hadn't worked there. 'But I don't exactly ask for a list of qualifications beforehand, Mol. It was only one night.' The second they walked through the foyer, all talk of hookups stopped.

'Busy day today?' Molly asked as they headed to their respective changing rooms.

'Not bad. Liam Evans-Shaw's out for his wedding and honeymoon still, so I have his cases to cover. You?'

'Three inductions booked in. All low-risk.' Molly smiled. She loved the labours that came walking through the doors, but there was something about inductions that she enjoyed more. Probably because the women often came in fed up, their baby overdue, or anxious as hell because they needed to be induced early for one reason or another. Seeing the faces of the parents when their baby was born into the world safely was an amazing high. She had never been one to try drugs or enjoy the buzz of alcohol, but she was addicted to the feeling of creating families. 'Remember the twins I told you about, gestational diabetes? That's today.'

Her patient Emma had had a rough time of it, but today was the day she got to meet her twins. Everything was on track for a double dose of delivery joy, and even the vapid passenger this morning couldn't dull Molly's mood now. She knew her best friend got it. Matt worked the major cases; despite his relatively young age, he was one of the most respected obstetricians out there. He loved the thrill of new life as much as she did.

'Looks like you're buying the first round at Neville's tonight then,' Matt said.

Neville's was the place to be after a long shift, probably because it was near work and the train station. Not too far from where they each lived. Matt had a house of his own, Molly a flat she shared with nurse Amy.

The women were like ships passing in the night though, so it wasn't too bad for Molly. She couldn't afford a place on her own—her disposable income would take too much of a hit. Who wanted to live alone anyway? It worked for them. Amy worked nights exclusively and stayed at her boyfriend Anton's place more than she did at theirs. It was like Molly had her own home, without the crippling expense. It had been a while since Amy was around long enough to hang out with her. She couldn't remember their last night out. Still, flatsharing was perfect for her plan to save some money and pay off her student debt. She'd only had a few months of payments left. Or so she'd thought.

Till she'd woken up to a letter on the kitchen table, kicking her terrible morning off. Amy was sorry to leave Molly in the lurch, but Anton had asked her to move in with him. Marry him. She was leaving at the end of the month.

Since then, Molly had felt the familiar feeling in her gut. The one from her girlhood. Feeling unsettled, askew. Insecure. It was a feeling she despised but could never quite get rid of. Being the only child of a single mum who struggled to be alone, letting anyone and everyone into their lives, who took what they wanted from her and left Molly to pick up the pieces. Not knowing when her next hot meal was coming or when the lights would go back on in the worst weeks. There was never enough money, and her mother had frequently escaped into the arms of a man or a bottle whilst Molly sat at home, planning a future in her head to cope with her reality.

She'd wanted a different life. Her mother never knew her own worth. Molly prioritised hers. She was not someone to be used, cast aside. Those days, those dark memories, they were all fuel for her drive forward. She shunned the shadows and stayed in the light. Her story was not her mother's. She would make sure of it. Having her home life threatened was a trigger she could never cope with easily. Trauma ran deep, no matter how much work she did on herself to combat it. It was in her, part of her DNA.

Even as her stomach lurched, Molly knew it made sense for Amy to leave, and Molly was happy for the friend she loved dearly. She didn't trust easily, kept her circle small. They'd bonded while training and stayed close. Amy and Anton were head over heels for each other. It was the logical next stage for them. As stressed as she felt over the development, she couldn't be mad. Molly would have done the same if she'd been the one lucky enough to be with a man she could spend the rest of her life with. Given her latest dating efforts, finding Mr Right was a million miles away. She would be single and ready to flatshare instead. The whole thing depressed her. She hadn't even had the heart to tell Matt yet.

She probably would have if they'd been alone; he'd have known something was up. Bugged her on the drive to work till she caved. His surprise guest had put paid to that possibility. Besides, she already knew what he would do. What he always did: try to help and cheer her up. She found herself wanting to wallow alone, just a little.

It wasn't only the fact that Amy was leaving. It was the wedding too. A tinge of envy was hidden in her happiness for her friend. She couldn't help thinking of that old saying 'Why not me?'

Money would be a bit tighter now, that was for sure. She needed to look for another flatmate, but the thought depressed her too much to think about it. By her calculations, even without her flatmate woes, she was still two years off from being able to buy her own place. Put down roots properly. Plus, she had that date tonight. God, she wished she'd never agreed to it in the first place.

She rolled her eyes at Matt as they walked together. 'I can't go to Neville's tonight. Date, remember?'

They headed out of the foyer and stopped outside the doctors' lounge. They did this every morning, usually planning their shifts together and car pool. They were a good team, having started only a week after each other, and the management were more than aware of their skills. They'd become the best of friends. People didn't always get it, but it worked for them. They'd learned to tune the attention on them out. Blur it into the background.

'Date?'

'Yep.'

'Which one is this again?' Matt nodded distractedly at Shirley, one of the nurses. She simpered back at him.

God, Shirley had been happily married for the past forty years. Everyone in the building either fawned over Matt or declared him the Antichrist. It was like none of them saw the real him. The one that she saw. She brushed the feeling of watching eyes away and focused on picturing her date's face.

'You know which one. The vet.' She blushed at the

thought of the evening ahead. Dating wasn't one of her favourite things. It took her a while to warm up to others, and she could spot a red flag from a mile away. Her friends said she was too picky, but she knew what she was looking for. Waiting for it to show up was the problem. In short, she was getting annoyed.

Is it too late to cancel?

No, she thought. He seemed nice. Animal lover, good job. Nice smile. Besides, she'd already cancelled on him twice. Oncc because an emergency had come in at work, the other time because Matt had dragged her off to watch stock-car racing instead with last-minute tickets. He'd practically hijacked her, but she hadn't been that excited for her date in the first place. To be honest, she'd had a great time with Matt. They'd laughed most of the night. Stuffed their faces with hot dogs and drunk beer from plastic cups. Sat on the sidelines, the roar of the cars and the scent of engine oil all around them. That was a good night, she mused.

She would have to go tonight though. She'd only wallow at home anyway. He *was* nice. She'd bumped into him at the hospital next door. He'd chatted with her, given her his number, asked her out then and there. That never happened! Not to Molly. She wasn't exactly a femme fatale. She didn't think she was ugly, but when she looked at the other confident women out there, she knew it wasn't her thing to get dressed up all the time. She was comfortable just being her, and when she was growing up, her priorities had been different from those of her peers.

With her long blond hair and sparkling blue eyes, she was hardly a Plain Jane, but she was the girl next door type, she guessed. She was more at home in sweats than heels, and that suited her fine. Not every blonde was a bombshell. She was good in her own skin. She just wished, for once, that a man would look at her and think that she was the beginning and ending of his world. When she settled down, she wanted a man who couldn't bear the thought of not being with her.

Hmm, maybe I am a little picky.

She felt a jab in her side and came back out of her head. Matt was leaning against the wall next to her, one brow raised quizzically.

'Earth to Molly. Date? Details? Tell me it's not the guy from Essex.' Matt's voice was flat. 'Tell me it's not Dr Dolittle.'

'Well, he's from Essex, but—'

'Oh, not him—come on! He sounds like such a drip. He puts his hands up cows' backsides for a living. Not sexy. Don't take him back to your place, whatever you do. You'll end up adopting a menagerie.'

'Take him home? On a first date? I'm not you, Matt.' Dating was one thing. Getting naked on the first night? Hell to the no. She was far too nervous for that. She waited till the feelings were there, strong in her gut. Not lower down and regretted later. She crossed her arms huffily.

'Besides, he's a city vet. He deals with dogs, cats, little kids' bunnies. No livestock.' She had no idea why she'd felt the need to defend a date she was suddenly dreading. 'It's only a dinner date.'

Matt shrugged, then pushed himself off the wall and dropped a kiss on her cheek.

'Just be careful, okay? Ring me when you get home like always. Lift after work?'

She nodded at him. He was always playing big brother

when she was on a date. They said their goodbyes and got to work. She had babies to deliver, and that always gave her joy. She'd worry about the date later.

CHAPTER TWO

MATT PICKED UP on the first ring.

'Hey! I was just thinking about you. How did it go? Did he bore you to death about animals? It's still pretty early.'

Molly shoved her phone into the crook of her neck, kicking her heels off and flicking them across the wood floor of the hallway. She could hear the TV in the background behind Matt's voice.

'To be honest, boring me about animals would have been preferable to sitting alone in a ridiculously overpriced restaurant. The wine I drank cost more than a full shift at work.'

'He didn't show up? No way.'

'Way,' she huffed, flouncing down onto the sofa. 'And his phone was off. I sat there like an idiot.'

'Are you okay?' His voice was full of concern. 'Want me to knock his head off?' He said it in a mock Essex accent. It sounded comical, but Molly didn't laugh.

'No, no. What's the point? I did cancel on him a couple of times too.'

'Mol, you didn't leave him sitting at a table on his own. What a total fool.'

'Yeah,' she sighed, her eyes taking in the living room for the first time. There were boxes in the corner. Amy had started packing already. Which reminded her of the fact that not only had she been stood up, but she was also about to be minus a flatmate. 'Well, that's my last date. I'm going to buy a house cat and have done.'

Matt's deep laugh reverberated down the line. 'Don't give up, Mol. It's not you; it's him.'

'Is it though, really? I mean, it happens a lot. It can't all be them.'

'It absolutely can.'

'Yeah well, I have enough going on right now. I'm going to give the frog kissing a wide berth for a while. I'll speak to you later, okay?'

'Mol—'

She sighed heavily. 'Matt, I'm fine. Don't worry.'

'What do you mean you have enough going on? What's up?'

'Nothing,' she lied.

Just a bit of impending poverty, or homelessness.

She didn't want to burden him. She didn't rely on anyone. That was her way. Just because she wanted to find someone to share her life with didn't mean she intended to be any less independent.

'Liar. Spill it, or I'm coming over.'

She could hear his TV click off through the phone, and she knew he was already getting off the couch.

'Sit back down! I'll tell you tomorrow. It's nothing major.' Another lie. She was glad he wasn't in front of her. He could always tell her moods the second he looked at her face. It was extremely annoying. Helpful at work though. Their shorthand with each other was second to none. 'I just want to get showered and get to bed.'

Wash off the stink of rejection.

Matt hesitated, but she knew she'd won. 'If you're sure. Listen, Saturday night. We have the day off together. Let's go out, let our hair down, eh? Bust some of that stress.'

Molly nodded. It did sound good. Matt was a hoot to go out with.

'You're nodding, right?'

She rolled her eyes. 'Yeah. I'm nodding. Night, Matt.'

'Night, Molly Moo. Sleep tight.'

The minute Matt clicked off, she checked her phone for grovelling messages from the vet. Nothing. She threw it onto the couch in disgust. What a night.

Going out on Saturday would help though. She never could handle stress very well. It made her blood fizz like a shaken bottle of soda. She needed to be occupied. Matt knew that better than anyone. He matched her energy. She guessed that was one of the root reasons their friendship had evolved so quickly. Since the first day they'd started working together, his humour had matched hers. Something about him had shattered the ice shield she protected herself with.

She was herself around him. Why couldn't she find that in a guy who wanted to rip her clothes off, make her his one and only? Amy had that. Everyone had that, or it so seemed like it to Molly. Even Matt's dates always showed up.

Sure, he wasn't marrying any of them, but he was still out there. Making connections. At this rate, the only connection she was going to come home to would be one that came with a litter tray and a pooper scooper.

'You should just move in with me,' Matt said.

Molly was grumpy already, but this wasn't helping. 'Not a chance in hell.'

'What?' Matt stopped the delivery trolley she was pushing with an outstretched hand. The loud squeak it made reverberated down the corridor. 'Why?'

She looked at the clock fob on her uniform pointedly, then crossed her arms with a huff.

He tilted his head. 'Why?' he repeated. 'Just till you get sorted. Renting's not cheap.'

Tell me something I don't know.

'Listen, we need to get ready for the incoming patient. The answer is no, but thanks. I'll be fine.'

'We'll be ready on time. You know that.' He didn't look impressed with her deflection. He was right too. They were like an octopus when they set up together on shift. Fast hands, the two of them working as one and knowing what move the other was going to make every time. A lot of colleagues assumed they were dating when they first saw them together because of how close they were. Matt was a man of few words normally. When they saw him talking away to her, it looked like something was going on. Some of their patients had thought it too.

So they laughed it off. Made a joke of it. Which made everyone else laugh it off too. Sometimes, a little too hard for Molly's liking. As if it was just so alien a notion it was hilarious. Whenever she dared look across at Matt, he didn't look thrilled either.

A bit like now. He was positively pouting.

'It makes sense though. I have the room. You need to keep saving money, and we get on. I don't want you ending up living with some weirdo stranger, and it's expensive to live alone.'

'You manage.'

'Yeah, but it's not cheap.'

Molly rolled her eyes. One thing Matt wasn't short of was money. His expensive car was just one indicator of that. He wasn't showy, but he had his life sorted. The things he did have were high-quality. Built to last. He took care of what belonged to him. 'No, I still have time to figure things out. I will take your brawn if I have to move though. You can help me with that. I'm quite glad actually; I'll be able to get a lot of boxes moved in your penis extension.'

'It's a sports car.'

'Yeah, that's what I said. The phallus you drive.'

'Hey! It's not a phallus. It's special. My dad hated those cars. It's the reason I bought it.'

'Your dad's not dead, and you bought it to spite him because he hates them. Buy a new car.'

Matt puffed his lips together but dissolved into laughter. Only Molly could joke about his dad like that and get away with it. She was the only one Matt ever talked with about him. The Loren publicity machine didn't need his help. His father had sued enough hospital trusts to be notorious in his own right. It had even cost Matt jobs in the past, which had hardened him further. As rigidly as Molly stuck to her independence, her stubbornness and unwavering plan for her perfect future, he stuck to his. His self-imposed isolation from people, hiding the real him behind a seemingly arrogant façade, was a huge part of that.

He wasn't known for being subtle at work. He was used to getting his way. Molly was the exception, and she knew it was frustrating the heck out of him right now.

'Fine but think about it. And don't mock my vehicle. It will be moving all your bits and pieces later. I wasn't kidding though. You could stay with me till you get another place sorted. Like I said, I have the space; you wouldn't even need a storage unit.'

'Oh, yeah, I forgot you lived in a mansion.'

She'd been to his house before, many times. It was a nice detached three-bedroomed house, around twenty minutes from the hospital by car. It was a grown-up house, but that was Matt. He was a goofy guy with a grounded soul. Not that he showed his lighter side to many people.

'It's more than big enough for both of us. Be cheaper than living with Amy, so you could put more aside towards a house of your own. It might be time, with Amy moving on, you know? I know a good mortgage broker, who helped me when Mum… Well, you know. He's a good guy,' Matt pressed.

The prospect of buying a house on her own suddenly seemed like too much work. Something other people managed to do, not girls like her who grew up with nothing. Who were expected to amount to nothing, as if the poor didn't have dreams, or grit. Now it was a goal even further away. A deposit big enough wasn't something she had in the bank right now. She'd only just paid off another chunk of her massive student loans.

She already felt very off-kilter. She needed time to think. Refocus. Not having the most stable childhood really made a difference with credit, and finances. Now that it was all up in smoke, a girl needed a minute. Not to mention the fact that she was still single, with no prospects.

The vet standing her up was just the straw that broke the camel's back. Sure, she didn't need a man to buy a house with, but it didn't mean that she didn't want to one day. She'd always wanted that. The man, the house, the kids perhaps eventually. Once the house was how they wanted it, when they had money in the bank. When their careers were secure for both of them. If she had kids, she wanted to work too, not lose herself. That was important. Her independence couldn't be diminished. Ever.

'Hello? I said are you in?' Matt asked. 'After shift, I could take you to mine so you can check out the spare room? I use the smallest bedroom as my office, but the guest bedroom's pretty big. You can store your stuff in my garage too. It would be cool to have a bit of company.' She was still looking at him agog. He frowned. 'You trust me, right?'

That was never in question. 'Always.'

'Right, so stay with me, okay?' He gave her one last firm 'think about it' look before turning to get to work. 'Till you save up, at least.'

'Why are you so worked up about this? I looked after myself before I lived with Amy, you know.'

'Yeah, but I know you. Living with some random person would bother you. Better go.' He flashed her a smile.

'I'll think about it,' she yelled after him. He ignored her. He always ignored her. He thought it won him the argument. It probably did, to be fair. She always gave up in the end. Who had time to be mad? She moved on swiftly, didn't dwell on things too long, but always made her decisions carefully. The alternative led to chaos.

'Did I just hear that right?' Adina, one of the other midwives, was just coming out of a patient's room. 'You're moving in with Matt?'

'No. He thinks it's a good idea because Amy's leaving.' The two women fell into step as Molly pushed the trolley towards the other end of the ward. 'Did you speak to your mate from the neonatal ward, the one who was looking for a room?'

Adina shook her head, a rueful smile on her pretty features. 'Sorry. She decided to move back in with her parents in the short-term.'

'Damn it,' Molly said under her breath. She'd asked all of her friends now, having fired off texts to everyone she knew, but no joy. 'I think I'm just going to have to move somewhere smaller, cheaper.'

Adina stopped her before they got to the nurses' station. 'Why? I hate the idea of you being alone in some pokey place. Especially coming off a late shift. Come on, Matt's your best friend and it's better than sharing with some stranger. What's the harm?'

Molly shrugged. 'I don't know. Sharing with a stranger is the opposite of what I want. Unfortunately, I'm stubborn. I just want to stand on my own two feet. Matt will mother me.'

Adina burst into laughter. 'Matt, mothering a woman? That's a first.'

Molly's smile faded. Even her friends didn't understand Matt. It was getting tiring.

'Adina, he's not as bad as you think he is.' Adina's eye-roll told her that her objections were futile.

'Mol, I know you two get on, but you can't convince me that he's not a bit of a tyrant.' The call button went off, and both midwives ran to the sound. Molly never got the chance to refute Adina's claim, and the shift ran on like that all day. None of them had a chance to think about anything else. Mothers came in thick and fast, and she soon found herself happily immersed in her work.

She loved seeing the expectant mothers, seeing their

excitement at hearing their babies for the first time. It was the same on clinic days, when she was on that service. Discussing due dates, prenatal care. The joy always rubbed off on her, rejuvenating her from the inside out.

So what if she wasn't one of them yet? She'd meet someone when the time was right. It wasn't over yet. Not till the pregnant lady sang, and she had expectant mothers far past her age who were all doing amazingly well and were equally thrilled to become parents. They had their careers in order, houses, partners. Or so it seemed to her. She supposed most people kept their real fears hidden, just like their aspirations.

Molly just needed to get more ducks in a row, and finding somewhere to call home was the main thing on her mind. It needed sorting, and fast. Before Matt asked her again. And again, and again. Before she caved and moved in with Matt. He was pretty insistent when he had a bee in his bonnet about something and he'd get this little worried furrow on his brow. Become distracted. He always did when she was going through something, which wasn't often.

But she felt his pain too. Usually when his father was in the news. Another high-profile case. Another triumphant press conference. She hated the look on Matt's face whenever that happened. It stirred something, deep in her gut.

As the shift drew to a close and she headed to the staffroom with the other midwives, Adina's words came back into her mind. She sat down on the bench in front of their lockers and gave her friend the side-eye.

'Adina, you know, what you said about Matt earlier wasn't exactly fair.' Molly bit her tongue. She always got this sort of hot rage burning through her when someone dissed her bestie. Even Liam Evans-Shaw sometimes made the odd joke, and he was Matt's friend.

One glare from Matt and Liam always stopped, but she did pick up on an odd kind of tension sometimes, when they socialised together. From Matt mostly. Like he was afraid of Liam saying something to Molly. It was odd. She'd asked him about it once, and he'd brushed it off.

She sighed, looking at Adina and shrugging her shoulders. 'I don't want to make it a thing, but it's just getting old.'

'What did I say?' Adina thought for a moment. 'The tyrant thing?' She blushed. 'It was a little mean, sure, but he doesn't have the best reputation around here. You must know that. People do talk.'

Molly couldn't deny it. Matt could be surly at work, focusing on his job a little too much perhaps, especially with Liam being off on leave, but he was one of the best too. That didn't come from always being nice and people pleasing.

The tide had turned against him more when an agency midwife had come to cover a couple shifts a few months ago. She'd been one of his conquests, and her criticism of him had got around the centre pretty quickly. Matt hadn't promised her a thing, but when he didn't call her after their one night together... Suffice to say, the old adage about a woman scorned still had legs. And big flapping mouths too.

'Sure, as long as people have tongues in their mouths, they'll talk. But you just don't know him that well.'

Adina raised her brows. 'None of us do. That's the point. The last few weeks he's been downright cold and he was hardly friendly before.'

'Who's hardly friendly?' George walked in, pulling off his ID card from his uniform and using the key on it to open his locker.

'Dr Loren.'

'Oh.' George looked at Molly. 'Well, she has a point.' He clocked Molly's incensed expression. 'Sorry, honey. I say it with love, but Adina's only saying what we're all thinking. The apple doesn't fall far from the tree. Sure, he doesn't sue the pants off people, but he sure scares them off his colleagues.' He smirked. 'And drops a few panties for other reasons.'

'Guys!' Molly shook her head at them, slamming her own locker door and throwing her bag over her shoulder. 'He's not like that, not really. Can we not?'

'Can *he* not?' George wasn't going to back down. 'Don't you remember the Christmas party?'

Molly pulled her jacket off the peg near the door and turned to face them both.

'You mean the Christmas party when he donated all of those toys, out of his own pocket, I might add, and dressed up as Santa?'

Adina had the grace to blush, and Molly turned her glare to George.

'Sure, he did that, but then he didn't speak to anyone but you and Dr Evans-Shaw. He's not a team player, Molly. And we've all heard the rumours about that night.'

'Oh, yeah?' Molly was feeling really angry now. She had heard the rumours. Hell, she'd met a couple of the 'rumours' before. The other morning's car pool debacle sprang into her head, but she pushed it right back out again. 'Enlighten me.'

George sighed, coming over to take her by the shoulders.

'Come on, Mol, we know you two are best friends, but he's a ladykiller, a true Loren; he's arrogant by birth. He gets people's backs up. That's all we're saying. His dad is always in the tabloids. It has to have affected him.'

Ugh. There they go again. Judging.

That was a trigger for her too, and bringing Matt into it sent her heart racing and made her feel increasingly indignant on his behalf.

Molly had had just about enough of people saying things about Matt. They didn't see him outside of work. The Santa thing wasn't a stunt to impress anyone; he didn't even want people to know what he'd done. He was always doing things like that, for Molly, for Liam Evans-Shaw and for his mother, Sarah. If Sarah knew what people thought about her son, she would be so upset.

'I get it, George. He likes the ladies sometimes, sure. What are you, a monk? He doesn't speak to people much, granted.' She looked across at Adina, and she could tell that they'd both made their minds up a while ago. 'Fine, I'm not going to waste my breath. Matt is a good man; you just don't get him. That's your loss. Bye.'

'Molly!'

'Mols, don't go!'

The two of them tried to block her exit, and she plastered on a smile to keep herself from snapping at her friends.

'Look, I get it. You don't like him, but I do, okay? No point in falling out about it.'

George reached for her hand. 'Sorry, we did gang up on you a bit.'

Molly nodded. 'Yeah, you did. I get it, like I said. I just don't agree with you. If you knew why...' She bit her lip, cutting her own words off. It wasn't for her to say any of that, and Matt would leave work and never come back if he thought anyone knew about his past.

She smiled at her colleagues instead, choosing yet again to take the high road. Sometimes, her friends really were small-minded.

'Listen, I love you both. Matt is not what you think, and he's my best friend, okay?'

Adina raised her brows. 'So, you going to move in with him then?'

Molly let the slamming door be her only response.

Not if I can help it, she replied in her head.

No, she could do this on her own. She headed off down the corridor, knowing the others wouldn't be far behind. She wanted to get out of there.

Matt was waiting for her at the main doors, like he always did when they were on shift together if he wasn't operating or she hadn't been called into a delivery. They always let the other know. Matt had learned she didn't have a car early on and the car pool thing had started not long after. It was about the only bit of help she was glad to accept.

She assumed her best smile to greet him. Seeing him there instantly eased the tension in her shoulders.

'Hey,' he called to her, pushing his muscular body off the stone pillar that was one of two forming the centre's foyer entrance. 'Fancy going for something to eat?' His open smile dropped the second their eyes locked. 'What's wrong?'

She shrugged, irrationally irritated that he'd read her once again.

How did he do that?

'Nothing. Food sounds good.'

His brows were knitted together. The second she reached him, he pulled her in for a hug, drawing attention from their other departing colleagues. She caught sight of George heading to his car, throwing them an intrigued look that he didn't try hard enough to hide. Molly scrunched her eyes at him, trying to pull out of Matt's embrace. If he noticed, he didn't release her from his arms or acknowledge her actions.

'Matt, come on. People are looking. They talk enough about us already.'

He released her so fast she teetered on her feet. He steadied her, then took a step away and looked around them. His face was like thunder rolling through the clouds.

'Forget about the food, actually. I have to be somewhere.' He was halfway across the car park, keys tight in his fist, before she caught up with him.

'Hey!' She reached for his arm, but he shrugged her off. His phone rang in his pocket, and he grabbed it without looking at her.

'It's fine, Mol. I get it.'

He got it; they both did. It didn't mean that it was any less hard to see him get upset by it. Over time, the speculative looks had died down, but she couldn't move in with him. It wouldn't work. Matt always looked out for her, but she wanted to do things her way. She needed to. It might ruin their friendship, though the pair of them were protective of it. Fiercely. His circle of trust was small too and entwined with hers. They each knew what had shaped the other into the adults they were. Her response was to do things on her own, have control. His was not becoming what everyone assumed he was. Both made life impossible at times.

He understood all that, she knew, but it didn't stop him from trying to help her anyway. That was who he was; he fought fiercely for the people he cared about.

Standing in the car park, she could still see the hurt on his face, even as he spoke into the phone in his hand. He always got angry when people speculated on their relationship. He didn't take kindly to gossip, and with good reason. It was in the air around him so often it choked him.

'Hey, Mum,' he said softly, his gaze looking everywhere now but at Molly. 'Yeah, just got off work.'

He locked eyes with her, and she linked her arms with his, leading him over to his car. He made no attempt to pull away. Their little spat was already forgotten.

'Yeah, Molly's with me.' Molly couldn't make out what his mother was saying, but his frown lines had deepened on his chiselled face. 'Tonight?' He shifted from foot to foot. 'I don't know, I...'

His mother spoke again, faster this time, and Matt seemed to hunch over by a full foot, a deep sigh reverberating in his chest.

'Fine, I'll ask her. Well, she might have plans, Mum—what's the big deal? Okay, okay.' He squeezed Molly's hand into his side tighter. 'We'll be there in half an hour. Love you too.'

CHAPTER THREE

BLOODY GEORGE. On the way to his mother's house, Matt couldn't shake the look the midwife had thrown their way. Even as he thought about how weird it was that his mother had summoned them both to her house at a moment's notice.

He hated that people stuck their noses into his business. Their business. Molly was too nice to see the looks half the time, or she chose to ignore them better than he did. When it got to her too though, he wanted to punch something.

He was well aware of what people thought of him in the workplace, and out of it, and that was all well and good. He liked it that way. Minding their own business, getting on with the job. What they said behind his back he couldn't control, and he'd learned to tune the noise out. They did it whether he reacted or not. These days he tried not to. He didn't need them to like him. He needed them to do their jobs to the best of their abilities. When they didn't, he told them.

Molly was off-limits though, beyond reproach, and he would be having words with George if he carried on like that. He'd be having words with all of them. Couldn't a guy and a girl be just good friends in this day and age? He and Molly had never been more than that. Sure, they were physical with each other—they hugged and often touched each other in some way. That was their friendship. They were like brother and sister.

No, nothing like brother and sister. Ugh. No.

Best friends then. Closer than best friends. Which was what people just didn't get. She was his ride or die. He felt his jaw clench, and Molly's hand covered his on the gear stick.

'Are you going to tell me why we've been summoned to see Sarah tonight, or give me the silent treatment the whole way there?' She squeezed his hand, and he opened his fingers and wrapped them around hers.

'She just said she wanted to see us both. It's probably nothing.'

He almost went through a red light, growling under his breath at the traffic lights.

'Really. That why you're speeding to get there?' She pulled her hand out of his grasp. 'Slow down.' He headed to the large housing estate his mother lived on, turning onto her street practically on two wheels. 'Matt. She's not sick, is she?'

Matt let his heart start beating again before he answered. The thought of his mum being sick had stopped it momentarily. He'd considered that scenario himself. Her tone of voice had seemed different, off somehow. She never summoned her only child to come over, and asking to see Molly too? His mum loved Molly, but she'd practically demanded he bring her along tonight. Did she know he'd need the support?

'No,' he answered, just to get the look of worry off Molly's face. He'd seen it too much of late. He hated it every single time and battled to keep it at bay. It physically pained him when Molly wasn't happy. His stomach was roiling as he pulled onto his mother's neat driveway. 'Don't worry. It's nothing like that.'

Still, he raced around to Molly's door to open it, then half pulled her out of the car in his haste.

'Okay,' Molly laughed.' I'm coming. I can walk, you know.'

He'd practically carried her to the door in the nook of his arm. She smoothed his shirt collar down before they walked in.

'Mum?' he called. The house was tidy, like always. He could smell his mother's perfume, and the scent that seemed to be around whenever he was here. The fragrance of home, he mused.

'Hi, you two. Come on in!'

Molly's shoulders dropped to match his as they sagged with relief.

'Well, she sounds happy enough,' Molly murmured. They walked through the hallway to the lounge, and the words of reply died in Matt's throat.

It wasn't the happy engagement banner he saw first, or the group of people who had been his mother's friends for years. It wasn't even the neighbour she'd lived across from for the last twenty, ever since his dad had left them both, and they'd had to downsize to this house to survive.

It wasn't any of that, or the champagne that was being thrust into their hands. It was his mother's face, as she stood there in the arms of her neighbour. With a rather large rock on her finger. For what seemed like an age, the two parties were motionless and stared awkwardly at each other.

'Oh, my God, Sarah! Congratulations!' Molly had been

holding his hand, and as she rushed forward, his hand followed her for a moment. She tried to tug him along behind her, but he felt rooted to the spot. The whole room was all smiles and chatter, Molly exclaiming over the ring and hugging the happy couple. Matt felt like his face was on fire. He felt Molly come back over to his side, linking her arm in his. It broke him from his stupor.

'Wow,' he said through barely unclenched teeth. 'Congratulations.'

He managed to sit through the niceties. The neighbours and friends around them kept up the chatter. Molly thrust a plate of food into his hand at one point, and he ate reluctantly. He would much rather have gone for a curry with her like he'd originally wanted to instead of being trapped in this nightmare. He had managed to move away from the crowd and was staring at the wall of photos up in the conservatory when Duncan found him.

'There you are,' he said jovially.

Matt took his time looking away from the smiling faces behind the frames to acknowledge the interloper. 'Here I am,' he retorted. 'Standing in my mother's house, wondering why I was the last to know about you two.'

He finally turned to face the man who had been his mother's friend for years. When the scandal had hit and his father had left them for the secret family Matt and his mother had no clue about, they were broken. And broke. He'd stripped the accounts, and knowing the law, he'd been sneaky about hiding his assets too. Taking him to court wouldn't have done them any good. Not even if they could have afforded it. Mutual friends had shunned them. Crossed the street to avoid them, either not knowing what to say to them, or being too much in Mr Loren senior's thrall to break ranks and check on the family he'd left behind. It was astonishing to Matt, even now, how people with money could do whatever they liked. His father's PR firm had handled it like a dream, burying the bad news. His other woman was introduced to the media like a new date, and they ate it up. The 'new' family were made respectable overnight. His first one cast out, left to fend for themselves.

They'd moved out of the area from unwarranted shame and financial necessity. He'd never forgotten how shattered his mother was. How long it had taken for her to crack a smile again.

When they'd first moved here, to Kent, to this decent, understated street, Duncan had been the one to show them kindness. Now Matt felt like that kindness might all have been a ploy. Had it?

Duncan, to his credit, didn't bite. He walked over to the drinks trolley in the corner and poured two stiff Scotches into crystal-cut tumblers. Matt felt his jaw flex. Those tumblers were one of the few things from their old life that they'd managed to hold on to. Seeing them in the other man's hands made him feel a pang of grief. Duncan was standing in front of him now, offering one of them. He took it, nodding once towards the comfortable overstuffed sofa, and the two men sat.

'I didn't want to keep this a secret from you. I know how close you and your mother are, but it was her decision. I had to respect that. Tonight's celebration was sprung on us really. You know what your mother's friends are like. They got a bit excited.' He looked sheepish as he said the next part. 'I understand that you're protective over your mother, and why.'

Matt felt his anger rise, but it wasn't at Duncan. It was at the last man she'd got engaged to. Married.

He wasn't a man. An amoeba, more like.

'It was a shock, that's all.' Matt looked across the room at the man who had made his mum happy again. He wasn't oblivious. 'I know she's been a lot happier lately. I guess I just didn't think too hard about why.' He had been distracted by work, been busier than usual. Molly's flatmate moving out was worrying him too. Molly still hadn't sorted anything out, and he knew she was stressing about it. 'How long?'

Duncan didn't look away. Matt respected him for that. 'It was purely friendship at first. When you guys first moved in across the street, I just wanted to help. You were only small. You had to grow up a lot faster than the other kids in the neighbourhood. I hated seeing that. I wanted to be there, for both of you. It was company for me too.'

Matt knew all that already, but he let his impatience fade. Let Duncan finish. He was a good man. Before tonight, he'd always really liked him. Duncan had taught him to fasten his first tie. Even given him driving lessons in the supermarket car park after it was closed. He'd taught him many things that his own father had never been there to do. He'd been glad that his mother had company when he'd moved out, to go away to study to become a doctor. It had always given him comfort. He didn't want her to be alone. So why did he have such an issue with this now? Why did everything seem like it was changing? He suddenly felt out of his depth.

There was movement near the doorway. Matt saw a

flash of material. Molly's light blue dress. He looked up, and could see that she was hovering, out of sight. Or so she thought. It made his lip twitch.

'I get that you've been there for Mum as friends, but this is something else entirely. I never had a problem with you being part of our lives.'

'But you do now?' There was a noise in the corridor. A little cough. 'Matt, your mother is a grown woman. She knows what she wants, and I love her. Dearly. That woman is all I care about. My sole purpose in life is to put a smile on Sarah's face. Without her, I just don't function.'

Matt heard an 'Aw...' from outside the door, clear as a bell.

Duncan kept his face straight, but Matt could see his eyes flick towards where Molly was hiding. 'I think you might understand that too, not that you'd say as much,' Duncan continued. 'Take a few days—that's all I'm saying. Let it sit. You know where I am when you want to talk. If you need to. Just know that I will never come between you and your mother. You can count on that.'

Matt stood, and Duncan stood with him. 'I love my mother, and of course I want the best for her.' He ran his free hand down his face before offering it to Duncan in the form of a handshake. 'Congratulations, Duncan. I know you'll make her happy. I just might need a minute to process.'

Duncan's whole body relaxed, and the two men shook hands.

'The offer's there. Just knock on my door, anytime. Your mother is my life. I was put on this earth for her. I know it in my gut.'

Matt's mind threw an old childhood memory at him, when

he'd had trouble with his bike. He'd knocked on Duncan's door then. They'd fixed it together on his driveway. He owed the man respect, even if the news was still jarring. Before Matt turned to leave, Duncan said something that ran circles in his brain for hours after they'd left the party.

'I think you'd have your own reason to exist if you'd only let it happen, Matthew.'

The two men patted each other awkwardly on the back before Duncan slipped out to find Sarah.

'Come in here, earwigger,' Matt said, loud enough for Molly to hear. She poked her head around the door a half second later.

'Oh, hi!' She looked around as if she'd just been dropped from nowhere. 'I didn't see you there.'

Matt rolled his eyes. 'You are a terrible liar. You came in case I knocked him out.' Her lips twitched with amusement, making the corners of his own mouth turn up.

'Well, that or bundled him into the boot of your car, never to be seen again.' She came to give him a hug, and the tension in his shoulders dropped away as he wrapped his arms around her. He drained the rest of his glass and dumped it onto a side table. 'He's a good bloke, you know. Sarah's always singing his praises.'

He pulled away to look her square in the eye. 'Did you know?'

She shrugged, her nose scrunching up in her signature way. She looked cute when she did that. He bopped her on the tip with his finger, and she wiggled it back at him.

'I've had a feeling about them for a while.' She waved her hand towards the photos. 'They're in a lot of photos together. They go on days out. They're always together, they hang out, go shopping. They don't date anyone else.'

'You just described us,' he pointed out, and it made him think of Duncan's final words.

Molly looked away. 'Yeah, but I don't date much because I'm broke and have no social life, and you don't date because the big C-word terrifies you.' Looking back at Matt, she said, 'It's a bit different.' She hugged him tighter, and he lifted her off the ground till she laughed out loud. 'We're best friends. Nothing will change that, will it?'

She wriggled out of his grasp, flashing him her best smile before heading off to say goodbye to Sarah and Duncan. As Matt followed her out, he couldn't help the feeling of unease that sizzled in his gut. He was never good with change; it always made him feel out of control. Trapped even. He couldn't shake the feeling that something momentous was about to happen, and he once again wasn't in a position to stop it. The boulder was already rolling towards him, and he had no option but to wait to be crushed.

'Hey.' Molly's blond head bobbed back around the door. 'You coming, or what? I'm still hungry. Let's get a burger on the way home.'

Matt smiled, letting her pull him along by the arm. Anything for Molly. Ride or die.

CHAPTER FOUR

IT HAD BEEN a week from hell, and Molly could not wait to let her hair down. Work had been hectic, she'd had no joy in looking for a flatmate, or a cheaper place to live, and she was starting to panic. Every time she went home, Amy had boxed up more of her stuff, and the place was starting to look derelict.

She'd never had much, never needed much really. She'd left her mother's house with the clothes she'd been wearing and hadn't looked back. Her mother's parade of boyfriends was not something she'd missed. Once she'd got into university digs, even having three flatmates had made for a much less chaotic household than the one she'd left. Now, after she'd found Amy and had such a nice, easy time with her, the uncertainty of where she was going to live, and with whom, made her really anxious.

She'd spent the day looking through listings, ringing around the rest of her friends to see if she could get lucky, but things were not looking good. When it came time to get ready to meet Matt, Molly was already a stiff glass of Merlot in and itching to go somewhere.

They normally ended up hanging out on their time off. Movies, nights on the town. Bowling. It had been a while since their last proper night out. Too long. She'd been so busy saving up, and with Liam off work getting hitched, Matt had been pulling a lot of extra hours. A good party for the pair of them was long overdue.

She took her time on her make-up, and even raided Amy's wardrobe for a dress with a little bit more zing than she usually wore. Since she was in her uniform at work and in her sweats when she wasn't, this felt like an opportunity to really go all out. Give the old confidence a boost after the vet debacle. She wanted to feel hot for a change. Kick her heels off and have some fun.

She chose to go smoky-eyed, red-lipped and skilfully applied eyeliner to make her blue eyes stand out all the more. She surveyed herself in the mirror. The look was dramatic against the blond of her hair, which she'd curled for a change. She looked like a different woman. It was eerie what a bit of make-up could do to a person.

'New make-up, new hair.' She smiled into the mirror. Amy was normally a lot more daring in her wardrobe choices than Molly was. Growing up, Molly'd always had rent to pay, books to save for. She didn't spend her student loans on going out, or fancy things. She had neither the spare money nor the inclination to waste what she *did* have. She felt like that plan was faltering, and the young girl who'd had no control was screaming at her from the inside. Warning her to keep working harder. Rise over the speed bumps. It was exhausting worrying about it all. Worrying that she was heading for a disaster.

Tonight, she wanted to feel different. After thumbing through the dresses Amy hadn't packed yet, she'd selected a gold dress, one that shimmered like silk and clung to her curves. She'd never been a skinny girl; she'd always been a little voluptuous with curvy hips. Her mother called it her hourglass figure. She'd mostly hidden it under her uniform and comfortable baggy clothes that served a purpose. She'd always been so conservative, so functional. In contrast, her mother had used her looks to get what she wanted till they faded with vodka and the passing of time. Molly had learned early on to dull her shine. It wouldn't do to out-shine the narcissistic woman who'd birthed her. Trauma was an education, and some lessons were hard to unlearn.

She'd realised since Amy had told her she was getting married that she'd been holding her own life back. She was so used to playing it safe, wanting a life so far away from her upbringing. Striving to get it at the expense of living sometimes. She envied how settled Matt was despite the family dynamic he'd grown up in. Having one awesome parent was something she'd never experienced first hand.

He had a home ready for the family she wanted to have one day. She was still trying to make her home, and the irony that he didn't want any of that for himself wasn't lost on her either. She was sick of watching other people live their lives whilst she just tried to plan hers and hope nothing derailed it.

Well, tonight she was going to forget her troubles, and just live in the moment. Matt was the perfect drinking partner for that. All he did was live in the moment. He worked hard, played hard. Kept life fun. Looked out for himself. That was what she needed to do. Perhaps tonight she'd ask him how to do it.

Pushing her tired feet into the nude heels she'd splurged on, she checked her reflection in the full-length mirror in the hallway next to the front door. Still her, just more. It gave her a thrill to see how great she looked. She might even turn a few heads in the club tonight. She took a photo on her cell phone and sent it to Amy, who was already at work for her night shift. She'd be starting soon, but she texted back right away.

Wow! You should dress like that more often! Have fun, babe! Love ya!

Amy was one to tell it straight. If she said that Molly looked good, she could trust it. Everything was set for a great night out.

'Wow, Mol, you look…'

Matt's face was a picture when he came to pick her up in the taxi. She jumped in, shut the door behind her and shoved her clutch purse onto the seat between them.

'Different? Sexy?' she offered, laughing at his expression. He was like a fish out of water, gasping for breath.

'Very sexy,' the taxi driver butted in, leaning back over the seat.

Matt snarled the address of the first bar at him, and the driver concentrated on pulling away from her flat at speed and heading towards town.

'Well, he approves. What do you think?' Molly giggled, shimmying her shoulders at him.

Matt's scowl deepened.'I think you need a jacket.' He turned to gaze out his window, moving his body away from her.

'Wow, well thanks, Matt.' Molly flinched and shrank back into her seat. 'I thought I looked good.'

She instantly felt his hand under her chin, holding it between his fingers and pulling her to him.

'Sorry, Mol. You look great. It was just a bit of a shock,

that's all.' He lowered his gaze, and she could feel his eyes appraise every inch of her. 'You look amazing. That's a dress and a half.'

She grinned; his odd response forgotten instantly.

'Excited for tonight?' he asked, changing the subject. 'I must admit, I can already taste my first pint.'

'I can't wait.' She smiled back. 'A night out with the doctor—just what I ordered!'

The first bar was already pretty busy. The outdoor seating area was lit up by lanterns and electric heaters around the tables. Matt was at her door before she had a chance to open it, and she heard a wolf-whistle as she stepped out onto the street in front. Matt took her hand in his, and walked her in.

'I see we're in for an interesting night, with you wearing that,' he said, his face paling slightly as he fully took her in. 'I might just start on the whisky instead.'

She swatted at him playfully with her clutch, heading to the bar. Secretly liking his protective streak, which seemed to have sharpened with her outfit choice. 'Come on, grumpy. First one's on me.'

Four drinks in, they were sitting in a booth at the back of a small bar called Passion. They'd spent most of the night messing about, dancing to the music, making each other laugh. It's how they were whenever they went out. They had so much fun on their own, they didn't need anyone else. Molly was feeling buzzed from the drinks, and Matt had steered them to a quieter place to catch their breaths before hitting the clubs.

'So what's with the different look tonight anyway?' Matt looked at her over his glass.

'I felt like a change, that's all.'

A little bit of rebellion against my anxiety.

'Well, you accomplished that. It feels like everyone's changing these days.' He looked like he wanted to add more, but he took a sip of his drink instead.

She changed the subject, though she didn't throw it far. 'Including your mother getting remarried?'

'Touché.' Matt's lip twitched. 'Yeah, in a way. Liam's married now, Amy's getting married. Mum and Duncan— I mean, I didn't see it coming but I can hardly stop it. I don't think I would if I could. I don't have to like it. I just worry about the fallout, I guess. Old habits. I want her to be happy.'

'You always want your mother to be happy. Who says there's going to be a fallout?'

Matt drained his whisky, eyeing the bar.

'Not so fast.' She knew him too well. He was wanting to escape the conversation. She'd seen him pull that move a lot over the years. 'No more drinks till you tell me what's happening. Is it because of your father? Do you think he knows? About your mother I mean.'

Molly watched Matt change from mildly irritated to downright shut-off in the space of thirty seconds.

'I couldn't care less what he knows. It's none of his business. He gave up that right years ago. It's everyone watching him, us. Getting picked over by the gossip mill. I just worry for her, that's all. I need another drink.'

She reached for his hand, but he was already gone. Stalking off to the bar, glass in hand. She watched him walk away, his shoulders up around his ears, and found herself hating the man who had abandoned him. The legendary Phillip J. Loren. Matt had always felt like he was in his shadow, but Matt just didn't get that he already surpassed him in every way. She wished more people could see what he did at work. How good he was with his patients, with her. His mother. Liam, who had pulled strings to land him the job despite Matt's infamous surname.

He was special, but the front he put up often made him look and sound like a jerk. People saw his chiselled appearance, so close to his father's, heard his surname, and connected the two. Combined with his aloof attitude and thanks to that loose-lipped agency nurse, everyone thought he had a rotating door of girls on his arm. They assumed he was cut from the same Loren cloth. Treated him as such. No matter how much Matt differed in reality.

Scandals had a habit of sticking to people. Even the rich who could pay the best spin doctors. His father's two daughters and second wife were never dragged through the papers. Matt was incensed at the fact that people compared him to his parent. Wrote him off before they knew him in person.

He could never live like that. Two families, two homes. It had changed Matt for ever. Molly could see the tension in his shoulders when he walked away, the pressures getting to him. He was twice the man his father was, but he just didn't see it. Which made him almost as stupid as everyone else who thought badly of him.

Even her own colleagues had denounced him, and they did know her. Why would they think she would hang out with the man they described? They made him sound like a cross between Scrooge and Mr Darcy. They thought she was foolish for being his best friend, but Molly was loyal.

Fiercely. Especially when it came to Matt. She knew from her own experiences not to judge people on rumours and hearsay, or what their parents did or didn't do. If people associated her with her mother in such a public way, she knew she'd fare just as poorly. Anonymity had a lot of comfort hidden within.

She was so busy stressing about her own situation, she'd barely thought about how Matt might be feeling. She wanted to make it right. Reclaim the fun of the night. She was about to follow him, to have it out with him and clear the air, when her line of sight was blocked.

'Hey, gorgeous,' a man drawled, his words slurred. 'Having a bad night?'

'No, and I'm waiting for someone.' Molly was trying to look over his shoulder to track Matt, but the guy wasn't having any of it. He moved closer, leaning over the table and knocking into the glasses. She pulled one back along the table before it got smashed to the floor. She hated drunk people like this. It reminded her of the good-for-nothings her mother would bring home sometimes late at night.

'Oops,' he said, laughing like a hyena. 'I saw your guy. Seemed a bit moody to me.' He leered, looking her up and down in a way that made Molly feel decidedly uncomfortable. She could see his mates, all three sheets to the wind themselves, egging him on from a distance. 'I could treat you better.'

'No thank you.' Molly went to get out of the booth, purse in hand, when the man blocked her exit, sitting down next to her.

'Aww, come on. Play nice, eh?'

She wiggled as fast as she could to the other end of

the booth. It was getting pretty busy now, and she looked around for someone to claim the moron. His friends just grinned at her.

'Sorry, love. He's harmless. He just got dumped,' one of them, probably the least drunk of the party, shouted across at her. 'He fancies you, blondie!'

'Wonderful,' she shouted back in a retort, before putting her purse in between herself and the man. 'Go enjoy your night with your friends. I'm not interested.' She might as well have saved her breath. He wasn't listening to a word she said.

'Come with us! You'll have a much better night with me, eh?'

His hands were already lifting from his sides as if to grab for her.

'Hey!' she shouted, but then she saw Matt loom behind him. He put the drinks he was holding down on the table, fixing the man with a cold glare.

'You heard her. Move. Now.' The bloke stood up and pirouetted on his unsteady feet, turning to look up at Matt, and Molly used the opportunity to squeeze by him. Drunk and Dumped's friends came over like flies round garbage, surrounding Matt. He tucked Molly into his side, shielding her with his body.

'Hey, man, what's your problem?' one of them asked, and Drunk and Dumped kept talking to Molly like nothing had happened.

'So, you coming with us? We're going to Shooters next.' Shooters was a bit of a dive bar. Patrons could play pool there after hours, if they didn't mind their feet sticking to the decades-old carpeting. She'd dragged her mother out of there enough times to know never to set foot in the place ever again.

'I said no. Matt, let's go.'

Matt shook his head, pointing to the drinks he'd just bought. 'No need. These guys are leaving, and we're going to finish our drinks.'

He fixed the men with a look that Molly hadn't seen often. He was shaking with suppressed anger, she realised. She could feel it reverberating through his arm as she slipped her hand into his. He squeezed it tight.

Drunk and Dumped followed her arm movement, his face turning from hopeful and tipsy to sozzled and bitter in an instant.

'Oh, I see. Like that is it?' He thumbed in the direction of the doors, missing by a mile. 'Come on, lads. She looks like a bit of a ho anyway.'

One second, the man was standing there. Well, swaying. The next, he was barrelling backwards, right into his friends. He felled his mates like bowling pins, drinks flying up into the air and smashing down around them. Molly saw Matt uncurl his fist, leaning forwards and pointing his finger right into the man's face.

'Don't you ever speak to her like that again,' he growled, his other hand still in hers. She tried to pull away, but he gripped her tighter. He turned to her, looking her up and down. 'Are you okay? You get hit?'

She shook her head mutely, not quite believing what had happened. Matt scowled back at the men, who were busy picking each other up off the floor.

'Come on, Matt. People are looking. We need to go.'

She managed to pull him away, and soon they were

heading through the bar and out onto the street. The second they were outside, she pulled away. He let her go this time.

'Molly, stop.'

She kept walking, away from the crowds, towards the top of the street where the taxi rank was. Her heels were pinching the hell out of her feet, but she kept on. The night air was hitting her, making her feel the alcohol in her system. She was never normally a big drinker. A couple of shots and she was tipsy, but her anger was fuelling her on.

'Molly, stop!' he repeated.

'No,' she spat back. 'Why did you hit him? If he calls the police, that's it for you. No more job, no more career. What the hell was going through your head?'

'He was going to put his hands on you! That's what was going through my head. He had no right to talk to you like that. I just lost it!'

She huffed and kept walking.

'Molly, stop please. I can't fall out with you. I hate it. Stop. Please.'

She'd already started to slow but hearing the plea in his voice stopped her dead. She turned to face him, and he strode over. Took her into his arms. She went willingly but gave him a tap on the arm to express that she was still irritated with him.

'Ow!' He rubbed his arm, though she knew he didn't even feel it through his muscle. He was in the gym far too much to be hurt by a slap.

'You deserved it. You keep playing into people's hands. He was just drunk.'

'Who needed a good telling off.'

'Yeah,' she retorted huffily. 'Not a punch in the face.'

He grunted in response. 'I mean it. I defend you all the time, but sometimes...'

He sighed heavily, and she felt his chest rise and fall under her cheek. She listened to his heartbeat, still racing fast from the adrenaline of the past half hour.

'I know, I know. I'm sorry. I just didn't like it. I didn't think.'

'You were in a mood even before that when you walked off.' She felt him tense in her arms.

'I wasn't.'

'You were,' she rebutted. 'That's why you flipped, isn't it?'

He sighed. 'I know that it was my fault the creep got near you in the first place. That's why I got so mad. I shouldn't have walked away.'

'Fair enough.' She could see what he was saying. He was her best friend. If anyone had done that to him, she'd have probably wanted to let her fists fly too. 'It's not down to you to protect me or stay glued to my side but I get it. It's over now.'

'It won't happen again because I won't be walking off next time.'

Molly puffed out her cheeks. 'I don't think dressing like this is going to be something I repeat.'

'Yeah?' He kissed the top of her head. 'Well, that's a shame. I kind of like it. You were confident, more than I've ever seen you before. Don't let those idiots tonight spoil it for you.' He pulled away to look her in the eye. 'You deserve to be looked at, looked after. I just didn't want you to get hurt. The thought of that man touching you...'

She shushed him and pushed her finger against his lips. 'Come on. I'm fine. It's over. Let's just go home.'

'Oh, no!' Matt tried to pull her back up the street towards the clubs, but Molly dug her heels in. Literally. She planted her stilettoes against the kerb and crossed her arms. 'Mol, don't let my stupidity ruin our night. We don't have to go to a club. We could try Jenkinson's—it's normally pretty dead at this time.' He checked his watch, waggling his brows at her by way of challenge. 'You never told me how the housemate hunt was going.'

She waved him off. 'You didn't miss much. I'm still searching, but it's looking like I might have to move instead.' She shivered. 'I don't want to talk about it right now.'

He tapped his shoulder. 'Broad, you see? Problem shared…problem halved.'

She bit her lip, wondering how much she could tell him. Even with Matt, she kept some things close to her chest. He knew that she and her mother didn't speak any more, that they didn't have the best relationship even before that. She didn't know herself why Amy's leaving and getting married had stirred her up quite so much, but it was really doing a number on her. Leaving her anxious, unsettled. Antsy to change her life in ways she had never thought about before, and frustrated because she couldn't.

'My heels are killing me,' she said instead. That was a truth she could willingly share. He looked down at her nude stilettoes, nodding once. 'I'm not really in the mood to party after that.'

'Right. My place it is then. I have a liquor cabinet ready to be pilfered.'

She shook her head. 'I should get home.'

'To an empty place?' His brow raised theatrically. 'Amy's

out for the night. You'll just sit and stew about things. Come on, we can stick one of your favourite films on.'

'*Predator?*' she checked. She was never one for romance movies. In her mind, *Predator* was more likely to happen than some of those romcoms ever were. She could never see anyone running through an airport to declare their love for her or standing up in a wedding chapel to stop the ceremony going ahead. Hell, even in her thirties she'd never been lucky enough to date a guy she'd even consider going up the aisle with.

He groaned at her request. They'd already watched it. A lot. '*Predator*, really? How about we compromise with *Die Hard*?'

Molly thought for a moment. She'd already made him watch the Bruce Willis movie last month at Christmas, but she didn't remind him of that. 'Throw in a takeaway pizza, and you have a deal.'

Matt scoffed, but she knew from his smile that she'd already won. They headed to their favourite pizza place on the way, and as they ate the slices, sitting on a bench waiting for their cab, Molly realised something. That whatever she was going through, heck, whatever the two of them were going through, they at least had each other. Nothing would change that. It was about the only thing besides her job that she could bank on.

'I love you to bits. You know that, right?'

Matt smiled, his lips glistening with the grease from the pepperoni under the street lights. 'I know. I love you too, Mol. You and I against the world, right?'

She bumped her arm against his playfully. 'Right.' She grinned at him. 'Always. At home, at work. Everywhere.'

'That's good to hear.' Matt's jaw clenched, a sombre expression dulling his features. 'I think George hates me, and the others aren't exactly friendly these days. I know I've been extra moody lately. I've been overdoing it covering all Liam's work and it's made things worse.' He smiled at her, but it fell flat. Molly's heart clenched, like it always did when she saw her friend looking sad or lost. He was like a boy when he looked like that, not the arrogant man he projected to everyone else.

She had a sudden thought as she sat there eating, and it grew to take over all the other thoughts in her head. Maybe it was the alcohol talking. She never drank much, and she was feeling the effects a little now, even with the food in her stomach. She felt brave. Naughty, perhaps. She had just had a man defend her honour against an unsuitable suitor. That was hot, even if Matt was the one doing the defending, wasn't it?

Whether it was the adrenaline or the dress, she didn't know, but she didn't stop herself from talking for once.

'You know, when you first started at the centre, I said something to George about you.' Matt's eye-roll made her laugh. 'Don't roll your eyes at me. It was nice, I promise.'

'Yeah, well, it didn't work. I don't think he's my biggest fan.'

Molly finished her last slice and wiped her hands on one of the napkins she'd snagged from the restaurant counter. 'He's harmless. A bit judgemental maybe, but harmless. No, it was when you first started. I was new too, of course. I'd been there a week, and everyone was excited about the new doctor coming.'

Matt rolled his eyes again, but his lips bore a slight smile. There was no arrogance on his features; he was almost bashful about how good a doctor he was behind closed doors. The rest was bravado, and skill never let him down. Never made him a liar. She and Matt were both young, ambitious and at the top of their game.

'Is there a point to this, or are you just blowing smoke?' He took a napkin from the bench between them and wiped at his mouth.

'Yes, there is. Let me talk, okay? No more eye-rolls.' He blinked to stop himself and fell silent.

'Well, I was a bit frazzled that day, and when I walked into reception, I walked right into you.' She didn't expect any recognition to cross his features. He hadn't taken any notice of her then. He'd never seen her that way. Not like she'd first seen him. She hadn't always looked at the man and automatically thought 'best friend' material. 'I remember we were busy that day. Loads of little things needed to be done. We were in a flap. I was taking some donations from the local library up to the wards, a bunch of—'

'Knitted hats,' he finished for her, his tone quiet. 'I remember. They fell all over the floor. The box crushed right up between us.'

Molly's voice gave out on her for a second.

He remembers? Well, he remembers the clumsy oaf with the hats. Of course. Not the slightly erratic blonde behind them.

'That's right. Anyway, you helped me to scoop them up, put them back in the box. You were wearing that dark grey suit I used to love on you.' He was staring right at her, their thighs close enough to touch. She felt a little awkward now she'd started her story, but she wanted him to know. She'd come this far. She could take a little embarrassment to cheer her friend up. 'Well, George was at the nurses' station when I got back. He asked me why I was so flustered, so I told him. I'd just met the man of my dreams, right in the foyer.'

She looked away, feeling the blush hit her all over again. 'I swear, I gushed about you for half an hour straight. Me!' She was laughing now, recalling how she'd talked and talked about the jolt she'd felt when their fingers touched, how cute she thought he was. Something about him had told her that he was special, and Molly wasn't the kind to tell anyone her feelings. She usually made it a habit not to have them.

'I was such a lovesick puppy, George was jumping up and down on the spot, and then you walked round the corner. Doctor's jacket on, Liam showing you around, and I realised who you were.' She shook her head at her own stupidity for declaring all her feelings out loud back then. 'I never told George it was you to this day. I was too mortified, and I would never have heard the end of it.' She giggled again. 'Can you imagine if he'd known it was actually *you* I fancied?'

When she glanced back at him, she expected him to be laughing too. Ready to take the mickey out of her, like he always did. He wasn't laughing. He'd gone pale. His eyes were fixed on hers, as if he was searching for something.

'Oh, come on,' she mumbled, suddenly feeling awkward. 'It's not that bad, is it?' He looked positively downcast. It stung her. A lot. She might not be his usual type of woman, but she was good enough to be his best friend, right? Was the thought of her fancying him that repellent?

She brushed off her dress, getting to her feet. 'You don't have to worry. It passed pretty quickly.' She turned away from him, buying time for the sting of humiliation to fade from her features, when she set eyes on him again. Even her outfit felt stupid. Wrong.

Who am I trying to kid? I'm the friend, the girl next door. Not the one that men would set their world on fire for.

'Come on, there's a taxi just pulled up.'

'Why didn't you tell me?' He was closer than she thought. Standing right behind her. She turned to face him. He was inches away from her. She felt his warm breath on her cheek. His expression was incredulous. 'Why didn't you tell me you liked me? I didn't have a clue.'

Molly played it off, the embarrassment having burned away the rest of the alcohol buzz.

'What, so you could get a big head and tease me for ever? No chance. I only told you tonight so you'd know that not everyone hated you on sight.' She slammed those shutters right back up. 'I need to go home. My heels are killing me. See me to the taxi?' She wanted to go back to her flat, get rid of the awkward moment between them. With a bit of luck, he'll forget this by morning. Things would snap back to normality. She didn't get to the taxi before his arm was linked through hers.

'Bruce Willis, remember? You're coming to mine.' They were both in the cab before she could protest, and he fired off his address to the driver before Molly could blink. The taxi pulled out onto the road and drove off into the night.

'Are you going to be weird about this?' she asked, talking to the back of his head. He'd been looking out of his window as if he wanted to climb through it. 'I only told you to make you feel better. I thought you'd laugh. George never knew it was you, if that's—'

He whirled around in the back seat, his eyes pinning hers.

'I don't give a damn what George knows. That's...that's not it.' He was coiled, she noticed. Tensed up tight.

'Well, what is it then? I told you; it was a passing thing. That's all. I wish I'd never said a word now!'

'But why now?' He was raising his voice with every sentence. 'Why wait all this time? I've... Oh, God, Mol. I...' His face was pale, as if he was running their entire friendship through his mind with this filter of new information layered over it. 'I really wish you'd told me.'

'Yeah, well, I wish I never had!' Her shields intensified around her. 'Forget it. Just take me home.' She tried to look away, but he stopped her.

Matt's hands were on her face, his fingers gripping her gently. 'I can't forget it, Molly.'

'Yeah?' she breathed, trying and failing not to feel the tension between them. The shocking frisson of sexual charge that filled the back of the cab and crackled around them. 'Well, I'm asking you to forget it. I'm telling you to. It was—'

'Don't.' He stopped her, a warning tone in his voice. 'Don't pretend it's something I can ever forget, Molly.' His gaze dropped to her lips, and she felt the pull of him like she never had before.

Tonight had been different from the first moment he'd seen her... She'd felt this before now, she realised. It wasn't the first time he'd watched her this evening. While her mouth wrapped around her straw, when she laughed. She took him in, removing the best friend label from him. Just for a second. To see...

All the touches, the hugs, the up-close dancing. It had never felt like this between them, except when there had been a crushed cardboard box of knitted hats between their bodies. Somehow, they were so close in the taxi that not even that box would have squeezed through. His chest was warm, his breathing hard. Matt, the man. The man she'd fallen for in the foyer years ago. It was as if he was suddenly right before her. Like the first time she'd seen his face. She'd shut those feelings off, but they were back in full force now. Screaming at her through every nerve ending. She felt like she was on fire. He inched even closer.

'Try,' she said, but it sounded feeble to her own ears. 'Forget everything I said tonight.'

A half second before his lips crushed down on hers, she heard the growled response reverberate from him. 'I will, if you can forget this.'

She didn't answer. She kissed him back, and they clung to each other.

CHAPTER FIVE

THE AIR HAD changed around them. Even when they were out of the cab, she could still sense it. Fizzing anticipation. Matt paid the driver, passing him too many notes and not bothering to wait for change. He took her by the hand, saying nothing till his front door closed shut behind them. Molly could feel the electricity as he dipped his head to hers once more. Walked her into his house with his lips. For a half second, before he pushed her against the wall of his living room, she swore she saw a spark jump from his flesh to hers.

This is Matt, Molly. Your best friend. Get a grip!

'Matt,' she breathed, half a question. Half a plea. 'What are we...?'

'Don't think, Molly.' His gruff voice cut the rest of her objection short. 'Let me kiss you.'

She could do nothing but look back at him. His expression was something she'd never witnessed before. Not first hand. Not even second hand, come to think of it. He was looking at her like he wanted to absorb her into himself. Her lips went dry.

'Let me,' he said, so slowly, so deeply it felt like a low rumble reverberating across her skin. Her whole body felt hot. The dress she'd worn for her night out was tight, but now it was uncomfortable. Restricting. She could feel her nipples harden painfully against the balconette bra she'd scaffolded them into earlier. She wanted to rip it off, relieve the pressure. 'Molly, let me make you feel good.'

'Matt...'

She wanted to tell him he always did that, that he didn't need to do it this way. Not for her. Even if she did feel like she might burst if she didn't escape his grasp. Hell, she wanted to run home and furiously pleasure herself.

It wouldn't be the first time.

Right now, she needed to leave. Go home. Purge the urge to ride her best friend like a rodeo bull. She was tipsy, but not drunk enough to be able to play it off afterwards. She had to stop it now.

'Can I kiss you?' he rasped.

This was a bad idea wrapped in a pulsing bag of nerve endings, and *oh, oh, oh...* He was kissing her face now. She realised she'd whispered yes at him. He'd wasted no time, a ghost of a smile crossing his lips before he put them to work on better things. Dropping seductive kisses on her cheeks, trailing his five o'clock shadow along her skin.

'Molly, tell me what you want.' His voice was husky and utterly sexy. She wanted to record it, to save it for ever. Replay it every day for the rest of her life. He stopped kissing her, fixing her with the eyes she knew as well as her own.

She tried to look away, pretend she didn't know exactly what he was talking about. And what she wanted her answer to be.

Matt was having none of it. One hand on her hip, he held her steady against the wall. She could feel his body shaking against hers, his groin pushed against hers so deliciously it made her eyelids flutter. His other hand reached up to grip her chin between his fingers, his eyes devouring her like he had been waiting to do this since the moment they met.

'Matt, I think…'

His whole body went rigid the second she spoke. He didn't draw a breath. He was waiting for her. This was her opening. She needed to shut this down, now. While she still had control of her faculties and her sexual urges, while their friendship was still intact enough to laugh this off. She should say something, anything.

She parted her lips and spoke the truth. 'I want you to kiss me.'

His full mouth sealed onto hers, and her thoughts vanished. Everything vanished. The Earth fell away around them, and Molly didn't think to mourn the loss of any of it. What she had in front of her now was worth the loss. God, it was worth it. Every coherent, independent thought fell straight out of her head, replaced by a surge of lust that roared through her. Her moan was stolen by his mouth, and he growled in response.

Is this what Matt was like with those other women?

She pulled at his shirt.

'Do you want me to stop?' he half panted, his eyelids hooded. The black lashes she'd always coveted fanned around his piercing blue eyes. 'Molly—'

'No,' she sighed. 'Don't stop.'

She shut down any thoughts of other women feeling this, feeling him, when his hand curled into her hair. He wrapped her locks around his fingers and pulled, gently but insistently. Her neck tilted to one side, willingly, hungry for him. Hungry to get the full Matt experience.

My Matt.

His tongue glided down the line of her jaw, and he nibbled at her earlobe, sending a hot shiver running through her.

'Need more,' he mumbled, dipping his head to suck at her collarbone while she wrapped her fingers tighter around his shirt, pulling him closer. He grunted in frustration, not able to lift her dress higher than an inch around her thighs. 'Hold tight.'

She was in the air, his arms around her waist as he turned and strode towards his stairs. He lifted her till she was straddling him, his large, masculine hands strong around her as they ascended. He kicked his bedroom door open, then slammed it shut again with his foot and deposited her on her feet. She was here, in his bedroom. She'd been in here before, so many times, but in this moment the atmosphere crackled like wildfire. She stood before him, feeling oddly naked and exposed. Her whole body burned with anticipation and incredulous shock as she met his gaze. Saw his eyes rove over every inch of her. How was this happening? She'd never felt so sexy in front of a man in her life. She was soaked, and desperate for her best friend to put his hands on her.

'Tell me to kiss you again, Mol.' He leaned in, touching the zip fastener at the side of her tight dress. It made a tinkling sound against the thick gold ring on his thumb. She'd bought it for him one birthday. 'Tell me what you want me to do.' Again he waited for her response.

'Take it off,' she demanded.

He gripped the fastener between his fingers and whooshed it down to the bottom. The fabric pooled like a shimmering gold rose around her bare feet, and she felt a slight chill from the air in the room. She didn't remember when she'd lost her heels. Her nipples squeezed painfully tighter, so aroused now she knew that Matt would be able to see it. Feel it.

'Hell,' he muttered. His face lit up at the sight of her skimpy matching underwear set, and she was suddenly glad she'd made the effort tonight. 'How did you go out like that? If I'd known...'

He kneeled before her. She watched him take her in, his sky blue eyes roving lower till he'd run over every inch of the scant fabric covering the last of her modesty. He drifted a finger along the edge of the lace, making her breath hiss in through her teeth.

'Tell me you don't wear these in my presence at work,' he said hoarsely. 'I would never have got a thing done had I known.' He lifted his gaze, locking his eyes on to hers as his index finger dipped under the seam of her thong, branding a hot line of sensation right against her sex.

Oh, my God. Now I'm imagining him in the OR, bending down over me, taking off his scrubs and...

He hooked his fingers under each side of the thong and pulled till the scrap of soaked material was at her feet. She went to step out of them, and he stilled her. Standing, he slowly walked her backwards till the backs of her legs hit the edge of the bed. The panties stayed where they were, and her bra soon followed its partner to the floor.

She waited, watching him as he watched her. Both of them standing there, her naked, his chest rising and falling sharply as he took in her nude form. She should feel embarrassed, self-conscious. This was Matt. Her friend Matt. It should feel strange, but she couldn't stop staring at his rapt expression. He looked like he'd always wanted this with her.

Had he?

She did, she knew. She'd buried it well, sure, but she couldn't deny it. Not while standing naked before him. She wanted him badly.

'You are stunning,' he exclaimed, a happy little smile playing across his intent face. 'I always knew you would be. Tortured myself with it.' She wanted to ask what he meant, but his eyes had grown dark, less soft. He dipped his head to drop a kiss onto her lips, and that's when all hell broke loose. It was as if everything had sped up. Fast, so fast. So hot. She kissed him back, just as hard. They were a mess of teeth and tongues, lips and hands. He went to lift her into his arms, but she put both hands on his chest and pushed.

'No,' she said, breaking the kiss. He stopped immediately, looking stricken. His face turned so bleak at the loss of her touch, it thrilled her. Surprised her and totally turned her on.

'No?' he echoed, breathing hard. 'Molly, I—'

'You have too many clothes on.' She smiled at him devilishly, enjoying the look of intense relief on his face. It soon turned to lust when she put her fingers on the buttons of his shirt. 'Let me help you, Doctor.' His lips twitched. 'I feel like we need to even things up.'

He stood there, watching her intently as she went from the bottom of his shirt to the top. One pearly-white button at a time. She reached the top of his chest, pushing the material aside, and he gasped as her fingers ran down his muscular front. She'd always known he was ripped; she'd seen him in both boxers and swim shorts before. They were always comfortable around each other, but now she was touching his body in ways she never had. Running her fingertips down the contours of his abs, enjoying the feel of his taut skin, the way he stilled under her touch. He was holding himself back; she could feel the sexual tension within him. He felt so good, so—

Matt growled. An honest to goodness throaty, wolf-like growl. The second she'd touched the waistband of his trousers, reaching for the belt buckle, the sound had come out of him. Dragged from his throat as if she'd pressed a button on his groin. His lips crashed down on hers again, and she hopped up to wrap her legs around his waist this time. He took her in his arms as if she weighed nothing, pulling her to him tight, and then lowered her onto the bed. He stepped back only to finish what she'd started. He removed his belt, threw it to the floor and kicked his trousers aside.

Desperate for him, she watched him with a hungry gaze. He was hard, and he'd gone commando. Having sprung free of his pants, his shaft grazed his belly. It was swollen, and he pumped it a couple of times as if he couldn't bear the pain of his desire. She expected him to join her on the bed fast, quick. He surprised her by lying down slowly, hovering over her and caging her between his arms and legs. She could feel his length press against her stomach as he kissed her. This time, it was slow. Much slower, tender even. He took her face between his hands and kissed her like a man who'd arrived safely back from battle would kiss his true love. She kissed him as long as she could before the want of him became too much.

'Matt,' she panted. 'I want you.'

She still couldn't believe that this was happening. They'd been drinking, but they were far from drunk. She knew what she was doing, and the reality of it felt far away.

Something to think about later. All she could think about now was him being inside her. Feeling every inch of him.

He pulled back, sitting up and taking her with him.

'Are you sure?' he asked, his eyes intent on hers.

'Yes,' she breathed. 'God, yes.'

He went to say something else, then bit his lip. A habit when he was thinking something over, but she didn't want him to think. She wanted action, and she knew that Matt could deliver.

She reached for him, and took him in her hand, running up and down his length. He hissed, releasing his lip and reaching shakily into the nightstand. A moment later, he was ripping the wrapper off a condom. He didn't take his eyes from hers as he sheathed himself. She moved for him again, and he kissed her back down to the mattress.

'You're so beautiful, Mol. My Mol.' He was whispering to her between kisses, moving from her lips to her jaw, dipping down to kiss her nipples. One at a time, slowly. Taking one into his mouth while gently pinching the other. She was writhing beneath him on the sheets, trying to touch him, but he kept moving away. Teasing her.

'Let me touch you,' she begged. He shook his head, coming back to cage her with his limbs again.

'I need a minute,' he confessed, and she realised he was shaking. 'I want this to last. I need this to last.' He looked a little sad for a moment, and she wanted to ask why but he silenced her question by sliding his hand down between their bodies. He ran his finger along her centre, triggering what felt like lightning against her nub. He moaned, almost as loud as she did.

'God, Mol, you're so wet,' he breathed as he moved his thumb in circles around her core. 'So soft.' He was touching her with the rest of his fingers, gliding them from side to side, as his thumb moved in every direction. It was delicious and dirty in equal measure. Molly was beside herself with lust, her eyes so lidded she could barely see straight. 'I can't stop touching you.'

'So don't,' she whispered, pulling him down to kiss his face off. She wanted to get her fill while she could. Before reality and the morning kicked in. Before the last of the alcohol burned out of their systems. 'Touch me, Matt. I want you so badly.'

He groaned again and shifted his weight. Molly could feel the tension in his muscles and wondered how it would feel if he let go. Really unleashed the power he was holding back. She wanted it all. Every little bit of it. She could feel the tip of him now against her. Ready to push in, to take her, and she couldn't bear it. She needed him now. She grabbed his firm butt cheeks with both hands, pulling him closer.

'Mol, wait— I—'

'What?' She stopped, her hands stationary on his body. 'What's wrong?'

He was looking down at her. The light from the street lamp outside was coming through the open blinds. It shone in slants across them both, across the sheets. She could see the conflict in his features, and her blood went cold.

Is he regretting this already?

She went to move, to leave, but his hands were around her in an instant.

'Nothing's wrong.' He shifted back, just a fraction of an inch, giving their bodies the tiniest bit of space from each other. Fixing his baby blues on hers, he smiled. 'I'm just glad you're here. With me.' He pushed a lock of hair back from her face, and then there was no more space between them. He moved slowly, the tip of his hardness resting against her entrance, before he thrust forward. They groaned together at the sensation as he slowly filled her. Inch by wildly sexy inch.

'Holy hell,' he growled. 'Can you feel that?'

'Well, if I said no, I'd be lying.' He stopped to look at her, and they both laughed.

'I didn't mean that,' he said, before thrusting again. Molly moaned, wrapping her arms around his shoulders. 'I meant how it feels.' He pulled back, teasing her with his hips before entering her again. 'Can you feel that? Tell me, Mol. Tell me how good it feels.'

He was almost needy, his intent gaze watching her every movement. He slowly built up the pressure, touching her all over, kissing her, stopping to tease her and suck at her neck. Molly's whole body was on high alert. She felt so seen. Worshipped. His eyes roved over every little centimetre of her. His hands couldn't stop touching her.

'Tell me, please. I need to know,' he begged.

She could feel herself melting. She felt like she was turning to liquid in his arms, her pleasure growing and threatening to take her and everything around them with it in a gigantic explosion. She had *never* been so turned on. Her head felt hot, white-hot. She was starting to shake with the force of her feelings.

'So good,' she said, gasping out a feeble description. 'You feel so good. So hard. I can't take it.'

'Yes, you can,' Matt rumbled back, his voice coming from deep in his chest. 'I want you to feel everything. All of it.' He thrust, harder, his movements becoming less defined. More erratic, ragged. She could tell from the strain on his face that he was trying to hold himself back, and it turned her on all the more.

'Why haven't we done this before?' she asked, pulling him tighter as her orgasm built. She could feel it, on the cusp of overflowing within her. His thumb came between them, pushing and twirling, his hips thrusting and his lips claiming hers, and she came in that instant. Hard and fast. She came with such force she bit down on his shoulder to stop herself from screaming out loud.

'God, Mol, you're so damn hot. Molly, I—'

Her orgasm still ripping through her, she clamped down on him. Her hands gripping his body, pushing him into her firmly and giving her everything. Hell, she didn't think that she would ever get enough, and she wanted him right there with her. Always.

He came within seconds of her, a low, almost visceral groan rumbling through him as he shuddered inside her. Deep and needy. 'Molly. God, Molly. Damn.' One of his hands was clutching the cover, knuckles white. She'd heard a rip of material somewhere along the way to their bliss.

They were both breathing heavily, the aftershocks still running through them both. He kept kissing her, not stopping till they were both down off their cloud. Till their wildly pumping hearts settled into a normal rhythm again. Till they stopped feeling the other's beat against their chest. The room grew silent.

Matt kissed her nose and propped himself up on his elbows. 'Beautiful.' He had a look on his face Molly hadn't seen before. Like he'd finally figured out the key to life.

His post-sex face looks like that? No wonder no woman ever wanted him to leave.

She could see the attraction now. She would find it hard

to forget this, she knew. To go back to being just his friend. It was like seeing the other side of life, just once, before moving back to the grey normality of the day to day.

'Wait right there. Don't move,' he said, and she watched his retreating naked form as he left the bedroom. A moment later she heard the bathroom door open, the toilet flush. His feet padding down the carpeted stairs. Him moving around, the soles of his feet hitting the tiled kitchen floor. Before she could regain her senses, he was back in the room. He had two cold bottles of water in his hands, and he offered her one. He pulled the soft navy blue comforter from its folded position at the bottom of the bed, covering them. He made no move to dress, check the time. They both drank, and Molly found she was thirsty.

Her lips felt swollen, bee-stung. They'd been kissing for what felt like hours, but she knew from the light of the street lamp that it wasn't yet morning. She felt like days had passed and they were only two people in the world. Like time and work were all irrelevant now. Only this was what mattered. Being here, together. In the afterglow of what they'd just done.

The water drunk, he took the bottles and put them on his bedside table. Reaching for her, he lay on his back, tucking her into his side. Pulled her close, kissing the top of her head over and over. His arm kept squeezing her tightly to him, and she laid hers on his chest. Running her fingers over the lines of his body lazily.

'I should go, let you get some sleep.' She knew he was playing football in a few hours. He played for his local team when he was off shift. She often went to see him play. The other lads had thought she was his girlfriend at first. She wondered what they'd think now if they saw her again.

'Don't be daft,' he murmured in the dark. Beneath her ear. 'Sleep here. Stay with me.'

'We didn't watch the film.'

'Who cares? What we did was better than any film, Mol.'

She thought of all the times they'd been in his house. Not one of them had been like this. Next time she was here, would she be able to stop the feeling of disappointment? When he hugged her to him, would she want more? She knew what *more* meant now. What it felt like. A line had been crossed tonight. She was one of his groupies. She'd told him as much, how she'd fawned over him the first time she'd met him. Then this had happened.

She'd seen her mother do it often enough. Fawn over a man, get him into bed. They never stuck around. She was always alone, or worse. Broke. Dependent on the next man who smiled at her. Now Matt was more than a friend. She'd broken her own rule. It was going to be messy. So messy. He was the one man she did trust, but this was well out of best friend territory.

She felt him shift, moving closer and turning to face her, both of them sharing the same pillow. Her head lay on his arm as he cradled her. He twined his legs through hers.

'You're quiet.' He was running his fingers up and down her arm. Tiny little touches. It was very distracting. 'Are you okay?'

'Tired,' she lied.

'Really?' he pressed, his brow cocked. 'That's it?'

'Shocked,' she admitted. 'I didn't see this coming.'

'Me neither,' he replied. His face had that expression again. He looked serene…at peace. Like he'd figured something out. 'I didn't expect it at all. Listen.' His hand stilled in its movements. 'Molly...'

'I really am pretty tired,' she said, yawning. She needed time to process things. She knew the score. Matt didn't do attachments. She wasn't under any illusions. She'd messed up. She was looking for the man to father her children, to share her life with. Matt wasn't interested in doing that with anyone. Nothing could come of tonight, and now the consequences of their actions had started to hit home.

She knew the score but had chosen to ignore it for those few glorious hours. She wasn't ready yet for him to give her the speech. It was a one-off. She was in agreement on that one at least.

The alcohol and adrenaline of the night were catching up with her, and she felt her eyelids grow heavy. 'Let's get some sleep, eh?'

Something flashed over Matt's face.

How will our friendship survive this?

She felt sick just thinking about it.

After a long moment, he nodded his head. 'Turn over?' he asked, and she rolled away from him. Her back to his front, she felt his arms encircle her again. Caging her with his arms and legs and warmth.

She felt safe, and cosy, like she always did in his embrace. But she also felt like she was going to cry. What the hell was she going to do? Everything was messed-up. She'd opened her big mouth, and out had wriggled a huge can of worms.

'I'm glad you're here, Mol.'

She didn't answer. She didn't know what to say, so she kept her eyes closed, choosing not to fight the tiredness.

CHAPTER SIX

'I'M GLAD YOU'RE HERE, Mol,' he said to her in the darkness. He found he couldn't stop the words from coming out now. She was naked and warm, wrapped in his arms and legs. His limbs were all around her, keeping her safe.

She didn't answer him, but she shifted slightly in his embrace. Closer. He took it as a sign to continue on. He felt like a sap, but the floodgates were open now. All along she'd liked him. The first time she'd met him, she'd deemed him worthy to be with her. He still couldn't believe his ears. He'd wanted to shake her, demand why she'd never told him before now. All those times they'd been close, and he'd thought he'd spotted a glimpse of something between them, only to brush it off. Everyone seemed to have a comment on the two of them. His patients thought that they were together all the time. Molly would just roll her eyes and make light of it. He did too. It still hurt like a dagger though. He'd never imagined he'd be good enough for her.

When they'd finished making love, he'd felt cheated. Like he'd had a taste of something sweeter than he'd ever dreamed, and it was already over. When she'd turned over like he'd asked, it was easier to tell her. Hide, without her eyes focused on his. He'd always lost himself in her gaze.

'I wish you'd told me.' Once he started, he didn't stop speaking. He had to get it out. Had to speak his truth into the dark of the night. Chase the shadows of unsaid things away for once. 'I remember that first day. You crashed into me, and I was just…hooked. You took my breath away. Winded me too.' He smiled at the memory.

She had been dressed in her midwife's uniform, tiny woollen hats all around her. Her blond hair was tied back, functional for work. The dark shade of her uniform brought out the blue of her eyes. When he'd first set his sights on them, he'd forgotten everything else. That blue had been his favourite colour ever since. The cardboard box was smashed between them, the integrity of it crumpled. A bit like his heart, which had cracked open a little that day too, just enough to let her wiggle her way inside. She'd never left since.

'I wanted to talk to you, but I was already late. It was my first day, and I was due to meet Liam and the rest of the team.' Molly stayed quiet. He could hear her breathing. Even, relaxed. Secure in the embrace of his body. 'I wish I'd just asked you out there and then.' He'd wanted to. Badly. Even if his brain told him that this woman wasn't a one-time thing.

'By the time we talked next, it felt like a bad idea. I didn't want to make work complicated.' He sighed, mad at himself again just remembering his reluctance. He was always so driven, so focused on work. 'I figured I would keep my distance. Get on with the job.' He'd tried, but that had lasted about half a day. She was too friendly, too much a part of the place to avoid. 'We became friends, and I figured that was the next best thing.' He kissed the back of her head, pulling her closer even though they were already wound together. He could never be too close to her after this.

'Till tonight. I still can't believe it, to be honest.' He chuckled to himself. 'Maybe Duncan had a point. I think he hinted at this the other night.' She didn't answer. 'What do you think?' She didn't move. He leaned over, looking down at her face. She was fast asleep. 'Mol?' She didn't stir.

'Damn it,' he muttered. He'd poured his heart out, and she'd missed the whole thing. After dropping another kiss onto her cheek, he settled down next to her. 'Never mind. There's plenty of time.' He smiled to himself in the dark, his best friend in his bed, in his arms. 'All the time in the world.' He thought of all the ways he could deserve this woman. To keep her. He thought of his mother, starting out again. Happy. In love. Perhaps things changing weren't so bad after all. He fell asleep, holding Molly tight. After tonight, he was starting to think that it might be worth a try. His Loren heart had hope for the first time, and he wasn't in a rush to let it go.

Matt was still smiling when he woke up. The sunlight streamed through the open blinds, casting shadows on his face and making him squint. It took him a moment to realise that something was amiss. He'd been dreaming, him and Molly together as always. Laughing, messing about. Kissing. His arms were empty. He looked around him, but he was alone in bed.

'Molly?' he called. 'Do you fancy going to breakfast? I'll skip the footy.'

He pulled himself out of bed, eager to see her. As he put some boxer shorts on, he noticed that Molly's clothes were missing from his bedroom floor. Well, he could hardly expect her to walk around naked. He pulled his robe off the back of the door, stuck his arms through it and headed down the stairs. 'Molly?'

The house was quiet as always. Too quiet. He went into the kitchen but stopped dead when he saw it empty. 'Mol?' he shouted, listening intently. She wasn't here. He turned and ran back up the stairs two at a time. His mobile phone was still in his trouser pocket from the night before. Maybe she'd nipped home to get changed.

Why didn't she wake me? I'd have driven her.

He went into his bedroom and was just bending to pick up his trousers when he saw it. He'd missed it before, but he couldn't take his eyes off it now. An ominous feeling ran through him. Crawled up his spine. He picked up the folded piece of paper from the bedside table. His name was written on it in Molly's familiar swirly handwriting. He opened it with trepidation. Molly wasn't usually one for notes. But she'd left without waking him. He wasn't stupid. He'd left a few sleeping sexual partners himself. No notes, but still. He held his breath, hoping she was just telling him she'd be back soon. She'd gone to get coffee, breakfast. When he read the note, all hope left him.

Matt,
Thanks for last night! It was fun! See you at work, mate.
Molly x

Mate. She'd friend zoned him in a note. She'd skulked out before he woke up, dashed off a quick scribble. *Fun! It was fun?* He sank down onto the bed, reading it over and over. It was so…offhand. Banal. Cold even. Not his Molly. It didn't sound like her. She'd acted like it was just one of their usual nights out together. It was anything but. She'd told him about her crush. He'd opened up to her. She'd been asleep, but still…

He thought of them last night, him kissing her like his life depended on it. Holding her. Making love to her for the first time. For the first time with her, and the first time ever. He'd never had sex like that. Never wanted a woman so badly, and not just with his body.

Did she really not feel any of that?

Her actions said it all. He'd said it himself.

Let me make you feel good.

He'd offered himself to her like some kind of happy pill. She'd taken it that way. He thought back to their conversations. She'd never said anything back, had she? She'd never heard what he'd said to her after they'd made love. She'd just taken it as a friend helping out another friend. Scratching an itch.

He balled the note up and threw it onto the floor. She'd gone home, satisfied and satiated. Feeling happy. And he felt like he'd almost ripped his heart out of his chest and shown it to her. If she'd been awake, she'd have heard it. Him spilling his guts, for nothing. The minute she'd told him she fancied him, all sense had gone out of his mind. It was back now with a vengeance.

It was the 'mate' that did it.

Cheers, mate. Thanks for the mind-blowing sex, pal.

Not a sign of anything significant. He'd taken her home, shown her a good time, just like he always did. Of course she thought it meant nothing to him.

He'd shown her time and time again what he thought of

relationships, of being attached to another person. Hell, she didn't even want to live with him as a housemate. She'd told him as much. He was his father's son, all right. He'd gone and done exactly what he always did. Messed things up by getting too involved. It was why he never bothered with relationships. At first, with his past hanging over him, he hadn't wanted to ruin another's life. Then he'd learned to live without them.

He had sex when he needed it. Easy, superficial. No harm done. Not this time. This time he'd done it with his best friend, the one person he loved and respected other than his mother. He'd blown it. He couldn't go back to how it was before now that he'd had a taste of her, but she wasn't his to have. She was only a friend. A *mate*. He thought of everyone at work—if they found out what had happened between them. What they'd think of Molly. They already teased her for being friends with him. He felt his fists clench. He didn't want her tarnished like that. Not his Mol.

He couldn't let them know. He'd just have to forget it. Protect Molly's reputation, and their friendship. If that was all they had left, then so be it. He looked at the rumpled sheets on the bed. The only evidence that last night had happened. He went to rip them off when the phone rang in his trousers.

He scrambled for it despite himself.

'Molly?' He didn't even look at the screen before hitting the answer button.

'No, it's me,' Liam laughed. 'You coming to football today? We could use you.'

Matt sighed, chucking his trousers back on the floor. 'Yeah, why not. I've nothing else to do. You back now then?'

'Yeah.' Matt could tell Liam was smiling through the

phone. He sounded so happy. Well, he would, just return-ing from his honeymoon. Matt almost hated him for it. He hoped he wasn't too euphoric at the match. 'It was amazing.'

'Fantastic,' Matt replied a little too sarcastically. 'I'm thrilled for you.'

'Yeah?' Liam's tone changed. 'What's crawled up your behind? Last night's conquest still hanging around, is she?'

'Nothing, no conquest,' he muttered. 'I'll meet you there.'

'Don't you want a lift? What's up with you?'

'Nothing.' He tried to shake off his bad mood. 'I'm good. Pick me up in twenty.'

'Cool. Breakfast first, on me.'

'I'm not hungry.' He wasn't in the mood to hear about how happy Liam was this morning. He was still reeling from the night before.

'Yeah, well I am.' Liam's mood couldn't be dulled, it seemed. 'And you can tell me what's going on with you, before you take someone's head off on the pitch. Be ready. Be in a better mood when I come.'

Liam rang off without waiting for a response. Matt stared at the phone for a moment, and turning, he swiped the lamp off the side table. It smashed on the floor, and he stared at the broken pieces before stomping off to get a shower. He needed to wash the scent of Molly off his body. It would drive him mad otherwise.

The Eureka Café was busy that morning. Liam was look-ing, nay simpering, at a cute toddler being fed in a high chair at the next table. Matt looked away, concentrating on his full English. He ripped a slice of toast in half and dipped it in his beans before shovelling it down.

'Are you going to eat your food or not?'

Liam turned from the family. 'I'm eating it. I missed you too, by the way. Are you going to tell me what's up?'

Matt shoved another forkful of food into his mouth, grunting back at his friend and colleague.

'I need words, Matthew.' Liam raised a brow. 'You and Molly fallen out?'

Matt's fork dropped to his plate with a clatter. He picked it up, gingerly. 'What makes you say that?'

'You thought I was her when I rang. You sounded upset, and you've been a grumpy so-and-so all morning. Spill it.'

'I slept with her.'

'Molly?' His loud voice startled half the café. The toddler made a whimpering noise. Liam nodded his apology to the father, and focused his green eyes back on Matt. 'What the hell are you playing at? It's Molly!'

'I know,' Matt growled. He sighed in frustration, shoving his cutlery back down onto his plate. His appetite was gone. 'I didn't plan it. It just…happened.'

'Well.' Liam wasn't going to let it drop. 'No wonder you're in a sulk. What happened? Eh? You run out of random discreet women to sleep with?'

'It's not like that!' Matt said loudly. He saw people looking and lowered his voice. 'We went out last night, the usual drinks. We went to Passion. Some sleazebag hit on her in the bar. I stepped in, she got mad. It went from there.'

Liam furrowed his brow. 'You got jealous.'

Matt nodded, thinking of how angry he'd felt when he'd come back to find her being hit on. Pure green-tinted rage.

'She told me she liked me. Liam, she liked me that first day. The first day we met. But she never said anything.'

Liam digested that piece of information. They'd spoken about that day before, many times.

'It went from there. I didn't mean for it to happen.' Matt bit his lip. 'Not like this.'

His mate was quiet, taking it in. 'She liked you too? When you first met, the thing with the box?'

Matt nodded, a stricken look on his face. 'Yeah. She never told me, but she said she did. What was I supposed to do? Just say thanks and let her go home? She stayed over at mine, but when I woke up this morning, she was just...gone.'

Liam scooped another bite into his mouth, taking what seemed like an age to chew.

'Now you eat? Tell me what to do!'

Liam swallowed. 'Well, why did she leave? Have you called her?'

'Of course I've called her. Her phone's switched off.' He scraped the rest of the food off his plate, eating it for something to do. His stomach was in knots, and he felt wildly out of control. Like he was pushed so far out of his comfort zone he was on another continent. Without Molly, what would he do? 'She left because she didn't want an awkward morning, probably. She left a note.'

'Saying what?'

Matt swallowed. 'Thanks for the good night. See you soon, mate.' Liam's face said it all. 'I know, I know. You don't have to say it. I messed up.'

Liam threw some bills down on the table, draining his coffee-cup. 'I will anyway, ma pal. You need to think seriously about this. Right now, it's just one night.'

'You weren't there,' Matt protested. 'It wasn't a hookup, Liam. You know how much I care about her.'

'I know it wasn't. It's Molly. She is the best thing in your life. That's why I'm worried. Do you realise what will happen if you screw this up? Everyone at work will hate you.'

'They hate me now.'

'They tolerate you because of Molly. Without her, that's it. It will be impossible to work with her. I don't want that—do you?'

Matt shook his head, his eyes focusing on the tiled floor. 'I like her, Liam. You know that.' When he looked back at his friend, he had to blink to keep the tear that was threatening to escape. Liam brushed his dark brown hair away from his face, the new wedding ring glinting on his finger. Matt couldn't look at it for long. 'I just don't think she feels the same way about me. I'd made peace with it. You know what she wants.'

Liam's lips pursed. 'She wants the whole life. Marriage, kids…'

'Exactly. What do I do?' He pinched the top of his nose between his fingers. 'After last night… I don't know how to go back to just being her friend. I'm not sure I even want to. Do I try this with Molly?'

Matt watched his friend's expression slowly change, and he steeled himself for some hard truths. He knew he had a lot to change, a lot to prove.

'I think you should let it go.'

'What?'

Liam nodded once at him, steepling his fingers with his elbows on the table.

'Let her go. You said it yourself—she thinks it was just a friendship thing. A one-off. Can you really offer

Molly what she wants? It's no secret that she wants the whole white picket fence and you don't. I can't see how this won't end in tears. You have a reputation at work already for being aloof, and Molly is the one thing that redeems you there.'

'You think that little of me?' Matt countered. 'Really? Am I that bad?'

Liam sighed heavily. 'No, you're not. Come on. You know I get it, but you and Molly…you're just on different paths. Of course you're not like your dad, but you have to be honest. It's left you more than gun-shy when it comes to commitment. I know your story. So does Molly, but it doesn't change the fact that you want different things from life. Your dad leaving like that, living in his shadow…'

'This isn't about him,' Matt growled. 'I would never hurt Molly like that.'

'I know that, but this *is* about him. Your dad cheated with other women behind your mum's back. He left you both with no money, about to lose the house while he swanned off to his other family with wads of secret cash in his pockets. I don't think you're like him at all.'

'Get to the point, Liam. Tell me why I'm not good enough for Molly.'

'Fine,' Liam sighed. 'You've spent so much time keeping people at bay, you don't know how to let people in. You've spent so much time not being your father, looking after your mother, that you've forgotten to ask yourself what you want in life. Molly is the closest thing to a heart you have. If you mess that up, I just don't know how you'll turn out. She thinks it was a one-off. A friend helping a friend. If I were you, I'd leave it that way. For all your sakes. If you lose Molly, mate, I just don't see it ending well. You need her in your life.' His features softened when he focused on his friend. 'I think you and Molly are great together. We've talked enough about it. I just didn't see it happening. All I'm saying is, if you decide to go with this, with her—you need to be sure it's what you really want or you could do a lot of damage.'

Matt stood up from the table first, putting his napkin down, and then headed for the door. He was almost at Liam's car when his friend caught him up.

'Matt, you know what I'm saying makes sense.' The car beeped as Liam unlocked it. 'I know you're a good man. You took care of your mother, worked your tail off to get where you are. Despite your dad. You love Molly to bits, and she's good for you. Hell, she's the only thing apart from work that makes you human. Having her makes you happy. Are you really going to risk losing that? Can you honestly say you could give her what she wants? What she deserves? Is it even what you want?'

'I don't know,' he muttered. 'It happened last night, Liam. Her side of the bed is still warm. I haven't had a chance to think. I got up, and she'd gone, leaving me a Dear Mate letter.'

'Exactly,' Liam reminded. 'She gave you an out, Matt. All I'm saying is think about it. She's ready, but I don't think you are. You haven't even got over me getting married! Can you honestly say that you'd ever make that commitment, down the line?'

Matt wanted to scream at his friend. Trust Liam to bring him back down to Earth with a well-meaning pep talk. Even if it was true, it was still a bitter pill to swallow.

He could try. God knows he wanted to, but Liam's words were already seeping into his psyche. He knew what Molly deserved. He'd chased off enough reprobates over the years to know what she didn't too. Men like him.

George and Matt's other friends and colleagues all loved Molly, felt protective of her. Almost as much as he did. He wasn't Mr White Picket Fence. He'd seen behind the veil growing up. Those fences held lies, and secrets. His mother had been a broken shell afterwards. People stared at them, whispered at the school gates. He'd decided a long time ago that wasn't the life for him. Any children bearing his name would no doubt bear scrutiny. Could he honestly have a son, and see him go through that?

Could he even be the man Molly wanted? If not, how long would it be till she realised he wasn't? If it went wrong, he didn't want to think about what his life would look like. She was the only woman he'd ever considered having in his life permanently. If he lost her, he would lose everything. But that was only if he could convince her to give him a shot in the first place.

'I don't know, Liam. I just don't know.' He huffed out a breath. 'I can't lose her.'

Liam walked to the driver-side and opened the door, motioning for his friend to get in. 'I know. I get it. You need Molly, and right now, you can pull this back. I just don't want you to be alone, that's all. We're going to be late to the game.'

They sat in silence for the rest of the journey. Twenty minutes into the match, Matt was red-carded for an aggressive tackle, and stormed off to the changing room to cool off. It didn't work, so after Liam drove him home, he shut the blinds and ignored the world. When he called Molly again, she still didn't pick up. He was losing her already. He could feel it. He'd got closer to her than he'd ever hoped, but it had come at a cost. The house wasn't right without her now. After one night, she'd shattered his bachelor pad's status. And that's when he had the idea. A way to stay close, and not lose her. It wasn't perfect, but Matt already knew when it came to Molly, he would take what he could get.

CHAPTER SEVEN

MOLLY'S TOE SLAMMED painfully into a pile of boxes right by her bedroom door.

'Amy, damn it! Can you move your stuff?' She flounced into the kitchen and flicked the coffee maker on. 'That's the third time this week I've nearly taken myself out.'

'Sorry!' Amy shouted from her bedroom. A second later her hairdryer turned off, and she padded through wearing her old ratty dressing gown.

Molly scowled at it. 'I hope that's not making the move. It's seen better days. You look grubby.'

Amy ignored her, reaching for the teabags in the cupboard. 'I see the cat has its claws out again.'

'Yeah,' Molly retorted. 'And she's liable to scratch you without her coffee.'

Amy took her cup of tea over to the island and went to sit on the stool next to Molly. 'Are you going to tell me what's up with you?' She looked rueful. 'Listen, if it's because of this—' she waved her hand around the flat '—I told you I could pay rent for a bit, till you get sorted. I don't want to leave you in the lurch.'

Molly felt Amy's hand over hers and cracked. 'Don't be daft—you need that money. Sorry. I know I've been a little grumpy. I'm just tired. It's not about the flat. Really.'

'Have you not got anywhere sorted yet?'

Molly shook her head. 'Everything's either too expensive or too much of a rathole to consider. No one's in the market for a roommate.'

'What about Matt?' Amy asked.

'What about him?' She'd barely seen him in the last two weeks. She'd been picking up extra shifts, but only when he wasn't on the rota. She needed the money, and the distraction.

'He offered to let you move in, didn't he? It makes sense to me. He's got a big place, plenty of room.'

'So?'

'Wow, Molly.' Amy threw her an indignant look. 'Can you stop biting my head off? I just want you to be settled, that's all. I feel so bad leaving you like this. Like, it's my fault. I told Anton we could wait a bit longer for the wedding, but I practically live at his place as it is, with all the shifts we've been doing.'

Molly sighed, 'Amy, I don't blame you. How could I? I'm so happy for you both, really. I've just been working a lot lately. It's not your fault, I promise.' She hugged her friend to her. 'Ugh, have you bought a new perfume?' She scrunched her nose up against the smell.

Amy swiped at her playfully as they pulled away from each other. 'Hey! No, I always wear this.' Molly frowned. 'You love it normally. Don't you remember, we got it from that little place in Brighton?'

She took another sniff, but her stomach roiled.

Weird.

'Sorry, I feel a bit off lately. Overtired maybe.' She pulled away from the smell, willing her stomach to stop churning.

'And stressed,' Amy said pointedly. 'This is not just

about work. I've not seen Matt around here lately. Is he avoiding your moody face too?'

Molly couldn't look Amy in the eye. 'Something like that.' She held her breath to hug her friend. 'I'm going to get dressed.' She plastered on a smile. 'I am happy for you, Amy. I really am.'

Her friend hugged her tight. 'Thank you. I know it will come right for you, Molly. You deserve it.'

Molly nodded, heading to her room.

I do deserve it, she thought to herself as she dressed for work.

The thing was, she'd learned early on that not everyone got their happy-ever-after, no matter how hard they wished for it.

Molly was still thinking about what Amy had said that morning whenever she had a spare moment at work. She'd never answered her about Matt, just dismissed it as them both being busy. Hardly a lie. She'd lived and breathed work since the night they'd spent together, and judging from the rota, so had he. She noticed that even though Liam was back at work, Matt was still picking up extra shifts, mostly on the night shifts that she never worked.

Is he avoiding me too?

'How are things coming along?' she said cheerily as she entered delivery suite four. They were all named after trees, this one being the Sycamore Suite. Liz Masters was sitting on a birthing ball, bouncing away and puffing out steady breaths.

'Not bad, but she's been complaining of a fair bit of pain though.' Billy, her partner, was squatting next to her, a cup of water in his hand, which Liz kept trying to swat away.

'Fair bit of pain? Fair bit? I feel like I'm being squeezed in a vice down there.' Molly and Billy helped her back over to the bed to be examined properly.

After washing her hands and donning a pair of gloves, Molly checked the dilation of Liz's cervix and winced. 'Sorry, guys, we're still only at four centimetres. It might be a while before the little one starts to show.'

Liz groaned, and Billy offered her the water again. 'Billy, I don't want a drink of water. Will you buzz off already?'

'Darling,' he soothed, trying to placate his very pregnant and irritated girlfriend. 'Please, you need to keep your fluids up. The book says—'

Another contraction started to take hold, and Liz snarled something about shoving the book somewhere unpleasant, before the pain started to grip. Molly passed her the gas and air, and she sucked on it till the pain subsided. Molly put the Doppler wand onto her stomach and was satisfied when she heard the baby's strong heartbeat. Everything was on track for their first baby to arrive and make this couple a family.

'Better?' Billy tenderly stroked Liz's hair, leaning in to give her a kiss.

She kissed him back, starting to sob a little. 'Sorry. I can't help it. I'm scared. What if we can't do this?'

Molly kept herself busy, updating the charts, checking everything was in order, but she listened in. It was hard not to.

Billy shushed his girlfriend immediately. 'You're doing great. I told you; we got this, baby.'

'I know, but we don't even live together. We don't have a schedule.'

'So?' Billy laughed, taking Liz's hands in his and sitting down on the bed next to her. 'None of this was on schedule. We'd been on five dates; I didn't even meet your friends! You didn't know my middle name was Eugene.' Liz laughed through her tears, and Billy's whole face lit up. The way he was looking at her reminded Molly of Matt. She had to look away.

'Exactly,' Liz said, her laughter dissolving into fear once more. 'A baby isn't easy. I've got work, and you're trying to make partner at the firm… It's…impossible.'

'Nothing is impossible,' Billy refuted, taking her face between his hands and kissing her forehead. 'I know I love you, Liz, and our baby. Sure, it's fast, but we're not exactly strangers. I fancied you at work for so long, I still can't believe you looked twice at me.'

Molly should have left the room, but when he'd started speaking, she couldn't stop listening. The pair of them didn't even notice that she was there any more. They only had eyes for each other.

'Don't be daft.' Liz was laughing again. 'I liked you too. I just thought we'd have a bit more time together as a couple, you know?' She rubbed her bump affectionately, and Billy leaned down to kiss it.

'I don't regret a thing, baby. Sure, it's going to be hard, but we'll make it work. You and me, remember? That's all we need.'

Molly left the room then, slipping out of the door before she intruded on their moment any further. The next contraction would hit soon, but Liz was going to be a while yet before she delivered. She turned to check on the next patient and barrelled straight into a wall of muscle.

Hands closed tight around her. She bounced right back

off the person and was heading to the floor when they caught her. 'Sorry, Doctor!' She'd pushed out a rushed apology to the flash of white coat before realising who it was. Matt's eyes locked on to hers.

'Are you okay?' He searched her face, and she found herself looking away.

She was far too close to him. It was sending her body into overdrive. Aftershocks of their night together were flaming up her face. She was worried this might happen. Her body seemed to refuse to forget his touch. *Traitor*, she chided herself, trying to act normal when she felt anything but. *I was sure he wasn't on shift.*

'Yeah, of course!' She trilled, making the mistake of putting her hands on his chest to put some distance between them. She could feel the warmth of him through his scrub top. Pulling her hands away as though she'd been burned, she tried to recover herself. 'Thanks for... you know, catching me.'

'Always,' he muttered. 'You've not been around lately.'

'Are you kidding?' She tried to laugh but it fell flat. 'I've practically lived here.' *You have too*, she wanted to add, but then he'd know she'd been stalking his rota like a lovesick groupie. Not very well either, since she hadn't foreseen this happening.

'I don't mean at work.' The blue of his eyes looked duller today. Like a watered-down version of their usual brilliance. The dark circles under his eyes were hard to miss too. Even his hair was mussed up. 'Are you...' He looked up and down the corridor. 'Are you avoiding me?' His voice was low, a pleading tone running through it. 'I know that we—'

'Matt, come on. I know the score.'

'Really.' His brows were furrowed, deep. 'You know, huh?' He took a step back from her, cleared his throat.

Over his shoulder she could see George walking down the corridor towards them, pushing a patient in a wheelchair. 'Yes, of course. We're fine,' she said breezily. 'Listen, I need to get on. Catch you later, okay?' She went to leave but felt Matt's fingers brush against hers.

'I miss you, Molly. I don't like how we've been lately. We're both on the same shift today, so I'll take you home afterwards. We can go for some food.'

Did he plan this?

She looked for telltale signs, but he seemed like he did any other day.

Stop being paranoid. He takes you home all the time.

'Wait for me in our usual spot, okay?'

Before she could answer, he was heading down the corridor. Liz's call button went off, and the moment to get out of Matt's offer was gone. *I miss you too*, she thought. Looking at his retreating back, how straight and tense he was, she knew he'd changed. He was less relaxed, less the happy-go-lucky Matt she was used to. She should never have told him she fancied him, or let him think of her that way. They'd crossed the line, and now he felt awkward and she felt gutted. Gutted that they had to go back to the friendship she loved, knowing that was all it was. All it was ever going to be again. He'd already moved on. He hadn't changed his pattern; she'd just become woven into the fabric.

When she'd woken up that Sunday morning in his arms, she'd panicked. He was still coiled around her, and she'd loved it. Too much. She wanted to wake him up and do it all over again. Several times. She wanted to go to his football match with him, cheer him on from the sidelines like she always did.

The knowledge of how that muscular body had made her come so hard just hours earlier had been roiling inside her. She'd never experienced anything like that before. She wasn't some virgin, but she knew that no other man had come remotely close to giving her the pleasure he had that night. She doubted that anyone would again, and that thought depressed the hell out of her. She needed to feel it again, feel him.

'Everything okay?' she said jovially as she entered the birthing suite. A second later, she was dashing across the room and hitting the emergency button on the back of the wall.

Billy was shouting, panic evident in his voice. 'What's wrong with her? She was fine, and then she couldn't breathe!'

Liz was pale, gasping for breath. Clutching at her stomach. Lifting the sheet covering her legs, Molly saw the unmistakable sign of blood.

'It's the pain. It hurts so much! Something's wrong!'

The doors to the delivery suite banged open, and there was Matt, George and Ella, one of the other midwives. Ella ran over to Billy, telling him everything was okay, that they were there to help. She ushered him out of the room, telling him his family was in the best place. The atmosphere in the room intensified the second they were outside the suite.

'Elizabeth Masters, twenty-eight. Suspected placental abruption. First child. No health issues. Patient is forty plus four, normal pregnancy, no issues.'

Liz was screaming in pain, asking over and over what

was wrong with her baby as Molly fired off her patient information. Matt moved into action the second he got the update.

'I'm Dr Loren, Liz. We need to get you into theatre. Your placenta has detached, and it's causing the baby some distress. We need to move fast to get the baby delivered safely, and I need you to trust me. Okay?' Molly and George were already prepping her to move, throwing the bed sides up, putting a monitor on the baby. The fetus was doing well so far, but that would soon change. Liz started to nod, a panicked look on her face. Matt took her hand. 'We've got you,' he said confidently, before flicking his gaze to Molly. 'Let's move.'

The second they hit the operating room, it was all systems go. Matt was gowned and gloved, Liz was given sedation and Ella was comforting Billy in the family room. They could hear him crying as they ran past with Liz on the gurney.

'She's lost a lot of blood. Hang O neg now. Let's get her ready to be transfused. Call the blood bank.' Matt checked the field was ready, iodine tinging the flesh of Liz's extended stomach. 'Scalpel.'

He got to work, no time for screens, as there was no need. Molly sat on the monitor, checking the baby's vitals.

'Status,' he barked at her in his usual shorthand.

'Heart rate is starting to deteriorate. Move fast.'

Matt nodded once, his hands moving effortlessly to perform the Caesarean. After what felt like only several long minutes later, he was lifting the baby free, into the waiting arms of George. The midwife wrapped the baby in a towel, taking it over to the other side of the room. Molly ran to help, and they suctioned the nose and mouth, rubbing the blood and mucus off the baby and checking her over. They were rewarded seconds later with a very healthy and lusty cry from the newborn girl.

'Fantastic. All good?' Matt called over, working on Liz. 'Mum is stable, but we need to monitor her. She lost a lot of blood. Transfusing well.'

Molly was clamping the placenta and cutting the spongy cord that connected mother to child, checking it was intact. 'Baby girl, all good,' she reported. 'Vitals are good. No need for oxygen.'

'Nice colour too.' George smiled, running a gloved finger along one of her little fists.

'Excellent,' Matt replied. 'George, can you let the father know please? He'll be worried.'

George raised a surprised brow. 'Er, yeah. Sure. Of course. Molly, you got her?' He nodded towards the baby, and Molly smiled back.

'Of course. You go.'

George gave a nod to Matt, something he didn't usually do.

'Careful,' Molly said when they were alone with mother and baby. Matt was just closing Liz's operation site up; the nurses would already be en route to wheel her through to recovery. She'd be awake soon, and no doubt eager to meet her child. 'George might think you have a heart if you show your humanity like that.' She was teasing, but as he pulled off his mask, she could see that he didn't like the comment. 'Matt, I was only joking.'

Two of the nurses came in and took Liz and the baby away, leaving Matt and Molly in the room. It suddenly felt so large, and the distance between them so far.

'I know,' he said, shrugging. 'Figured I could try harder to be a bit nicer, that's all. See you tonight.' He was gone with a swish of the doors before she could even open her mouth to stop him. Not for the first time that day, she felt sick to her stomach. The can of worms was wriggling, making its presence known again.

The rest of the shift passed without event. Liz was sore, shell-shocked but recovering well. Billy had done nothing but cry and kiss her since the second they were reunited. It seemed that all their previous fears were forgotten. They were just thrilled to be a family. They'd already faced a nightmare, and now their little girl was here. They'd called her Isabella, and the pair of them couldn't stop looking at each other.

Molly was still high from being around them when she got into Matt's waiting car. 'Hi,' she said, leaning in to drop a kiss on his cheek like she always did. His brows raised, his head half turning towards her.

'Hi.' He smiled. 'Liz is doing well. I checked in on them before I left.'

'I know. they're such a cute couple. They met at work you know. I think it was a bit of a surprise, whirlwind romance.' Matt was pulling out of the car park, and she noticed he'd turned in the direction of his house. 'We not eating out?'

'Not tonight.' He looked distracted. 'They met at work?'

'Yeah.' Molly nodded, grateful that the tension from before seemed to be easing. It was still a bit awkward, but that was understandable. They'd seen each other naked, after all. Worshipped each other's bodies. It was bound to be odd for a while. She could get a handle on it. The next time he was with one of his hookups was what she was dreading. It would happen eventually. She knew that would make it easier to forget what they'd done together though. Make it less special. Allow her to see it for what it was, once and for all. A one-off. A mistake. 'I love the two of them together.'

Matt said nothing. Molly waited, but after two turns of silence, she pressed the radio on. Anything to fill the space between them.

'You got anywhere to live yet?' His eyes were firmly on the road.

'No,' she sighed. 'Nothing. I rang another letting agency at lunch, but everything in my price range already has a waiting list.' She pulled a face. 'Amy's offered to pay the rent a bit longer, but I can't let her do that.'

'The offer's still there, to move in with me.'

She was saved from answering by his phone. He clicked the answer button just as he pulled onto his drive.

He took me to his house.

'Hi, Mum, you okay? You're on speaker-phone.'

'Hello, darling. I just wanted to check you got the wedding invitation.'

He looked across at Molly, seizing his lip between his teeth. 'Yeah, I got it. You didn't need to send me one though, surely? I am walking you down the aisle.'

'I know. Is Molly with you?'

Matt blushed. Molly spotted it a mile off.

'Yes, Sarah, I'm here. I didn't get an invitation! What's up with that?'

Sarah laughed. 'Yes, you did. I put you on Matt's.' She paused. 'Didn't he tell you?'

Matt was firmly eyes front, as though he wanted the conversation to be over.

'Oh, we've both been busy working lately. I can't wait until your big day, thank you.'

'Well, as long as you're both there, that's all I care about. Have you decided whether you're going to move in with Matt yet?'

Oh, God, he'd told his mother. What else had he told her?

She felt her cheeks redden. 'Er…well…'

Matt cut in. 'Yes, actually. We're just talking about the logistics of it.'

'Matt—' Molly started. 'We—'

'Mum, I'm sorry. Can I call you back? We just pulled up.'

'Yes, love, of course. Night, Molly!'

The second the call ended; Matt turned to her. 'Look, I know it's been weird between us. We've both been avoiding each other.'

'No, I haven't.'

'Yes, you have.' He fixed her with his stern stare. It silenced her. 'I have too. It's been weird.'

Weird is an understatement. How the hell am I going to set foot in his house again tonight, let alone live there? Not. A. Chance.

'Listen, we're friends. Best friends. That can never, ever change. I want you to live with me. You need somewhere to live. What's the point in looking for a housemate or another flat? You know me better than anyone.'

'True, but…'

'Molly, I'm tired of this. It's not charity. You'd pay rent, get your own food. I have the space, and I could use the company. I don't want you to live with some stranger. You know as well as I do that you like your space. Just say yes and do us both a favour.' There it was again. That bleak expression. 'I know you need to feel safe in your own home.' He levelled her with a look so sure, she wanted to take him into her arms. She didn't. 'I make you feel safe. Right?'

'Right. Always,' she acknowledged. 'I do feel safe with you.'

His triumphant grin said it all. 'Good. That's that then. We'll go get your things on our next day off. Come on.' He jerked his head towards his house. 'Let's go home. I'm ordering extra spring rolls tonight from your favourite place. I feel like celebrating.'

Molly grinned back in relief before pulling him in for a hug. Finally, this was her Matt, happy again. Taking care of her in his own special little way. Their friendship was back. Perhaps living with him wouldn't be so bad after all. He was so set on it. Perhaps the other night was already fading into their past. She didn't know whether to be sad or happy, but this way, she at least had Matt in her life.

'Just for a little while,' she relented. 'Till I get sorted.'

Matt's smile was dazzling. 'As long as you need.' He gave her a squeeze, and she sank into his arms. 'No rush,' he muttered into her hair. 'Welcome home, roomie.'

CHAPTER EIGHT

IT WAS CLINIC DAY, and Molly was on shift with Matt. He had a full roster of patients, and the schedule was so full she hadn't stopped all morning. Which would be great, except the pancakes he'd made them that morning were lying heavy in her stomach. She'd been living with Matt a little over three weeks. For the most part, it had been fine.

Awkward at first. She remembered the first night. Going to bed at the same time. Him saying goodnight to her on the stairs, then leaning down to kiss her. She'd turned in panic at the last minute, wondering if he was going for the lips, half hoping, half dreading that he was. She couldn't survive another night of the Loren experience. She'd catch more feelings than butterflies with a net, and they were already flying around in the pit of her stomach. He'd simply pecked her cheek.

Today she felt like something was wiggling around inside her, but it felt more like worms this time. She got to the cafeteria, and George waved her over.

'Hey, come sit with me.' He was tucking into avocado on toast, and Molly wrinkled her nose up at it.

'Er, just let me get some coffee first.'

George indicated his full mug. 'Take mine. I have a juice as well.'

Molly took a seat next to him. She raised the cup to her lips, but the smell repelled her. 'Yuck.' She pushed it away from her. 'I think the milk's off.'

'Don't drink it then. How's clinic going? The labour ward is steady, not many in so far. No planned C-sections.'

They worked it that way the best they could alongside the clinic days, freeing up at least one doctor per day to work with the patients, monitor their pregnancies.

'Good. Rammed though. This is the first chance I've had to breathe all day.'

George offered her one of his slices of buttered toast. She waved it away.

'Not hungry?' he asked.

'Nope. I feel a bit sick. Matt made pancakes.'

George's eyebrows hit the ceiling. 'Really? Was he half-naked when he did it?' Typical George. He might not be Matt's biggest fan, but he could appreciate a good-looking man when he saw one.

'What? No.' Molly blushed at the thought. Matt had only been wearing a robe and boxer shorts, come to think of it. The robe was open too, hence the reason she knew he wore black silky-looking boxers. The night they'd spent together he'd slept naked. They both had. She snapped the image of Matt and his naked body out of her head.

'I told you—it's only temporary. Us living together, I mean.' She pushed George's coffee-cup further away with her hand. She could still smell it. 'I'm going back to work. See you.'

She headed back to the clinic area, checking everything was good at the nurses' station. Saying hello to a couple of colleagues as she passed them. She noticed a few odd glances, but given she was feeling a bit ropy, she knew her face probably looked a little pale. But it was more than that.

Her stomach was really off. With the move, she'd been burning the candle at both ends. She felt so out of sorts lately. Different. She just wanted to get the day over with. Get home and sink her tired, aching body into a bubble bath. She had a sudden image of Matt covered in suds, and blinked it away.

At reception, she picked up the next three patient records from the basket. Pasting on her best grin for the people sat on chairs in the waiting-room, she focused on the tasks ahead.

'Miss Pinkman?'

CHAPTER NINE

'WELL, MISS PINKMAN.' Matt smiled. 'Everything looks perfectly healthy.' He looked away from the file of charts and scans in front of him, steepling his fingers, elbows on his desk. 'I see no reason why we can't proceed as arranged.'

'Oh, thank God.' The relief on Ellie Pinkman's face was palpable. 'I can't wait to tell Eric. It's been so scary.'

'I know,' Matt said earnestly. 'Third trimester now, and everything looks great. Keep doing what you are doing, and your baby will be here before you know it.'

He reached over to the other side of his desk to select a pamphlet from a stack he kept. 'I know we've discussed this before, but I do think that speaking to someone about what you've been through would be beneficial. When you're ready, of course. We're here to support you.'

He pushed the pamphlet for the miscarriage support group across the table, just as Molly came back into the room. She'd been called out to assist with a birth, and Matt's whole body vibrated when she entered.

It had been so hard living with her. Seeing her every morning, every night. A kind of beautiful torture he couldn't get enough of or give up. He knew she'd been looking for somewhere else to live still. He'd seen the circled newspaper listings she'd left on the coffee table. She'd shoved them out of the way whenever he entered the room, but he wasn't stupid.

He had been thinking about how to get her to stay with him ever since. Liam thought he was daft, 'asking for trouble' as he'd put it. One night, when Matt had come home to Molly doing yoga in the front room in tight-fitting pink yoga pants that Matt wanted to rip off with his bare teeth, he'd barely got out of there alive. He'd called Liam, begging him to leave his new wife for the night and come out and have a drink with him. He'd had so many cold showers, he didn't know how he had any skin left. Even Molly had commented on the amount of empty shower gel bottles in the recycling bin. He'd changed to soap to throw her off the scent, no pun intended.

He realised that he'd spaced out at the worst possible time and scowled at himself. Molly caught his look, her face falling, and he flushed.

Damn it, now she thinks I'm mad at her again. I can't help it; I'm mad at the situation. So mad. I'm in a prison of my own making.

'You really think I need a support group?' Miss Pinkman asked. 'Everything's fine now.'

Matt nodded, smiling. 'Everything is great. Your baby is healthy and on track for a textbook delivery.' He patted the file. 'We've been extra cautious with your care. But given what you've been through...'

'The miscarriages,' she supplied glumly. She looked down at the pamphlet again and tucked it into her handbag. 'I'll call them. I know you're right, doctor. My family have been saying the same.' She sighed heavily.

Behind him, Molly was listening but looking through

the patient records. Discreet and caring as always. She looked a little pale under the harsh strip lighting of the room. Come to think of it, she'd been a bit off in general lately. Perhaps she was feeling awkward about their living arrangements too, just without the cold showers and the dirty dreams.

'Thank you, Dr Loren. I mean it—you've really been there for us both through all this.'

'No problem,' he said gently. 'Happy to help. Let's see you again in a week, ten days. Okay?' He signed the appointment request form, filling in the timescale, and passed it to her with a flourish of his wrist. 'Remember, plenty of rest and hydrate.'

Miss Pinkman nodded with a happy, watery smile. She squeezed Molly's shoulder as she left. 'Thank you. Both.'

Molly picked up the next file from the pile and deposited it onto his desk.

'Ready for the next one?'

'In a minute. I have lunch coming. I got one of the nurses to bring it up, cut down the time a bit.' He sighed, rubbing his hands down his face. He could feel the day-old stubble. For a man who spent so much time in the shower, he really needed to up his shaving regime. 'Can you ask the next patient to wait a few minutes?' Molly nodded, looking like she wanted to say something. She was rubbish; she could never hide her feelings. They were always displayed on her face. He just wished he could read how she really felt about him. 'Tell me what's up.'

There was a knock at the door, and she held up a finger. 'Thanks, Josie,' she said to the woman outside, taking a package of sandwiches and drinks from her.

'Cheers. Can you tell reception the doctor is on a break please? I'll come for the next patient when he's ready.'

'No problem. I put some in for you too. Just ham and cheese.'

Molly didn't look happy about that, and Matt wondered what was going on. He took the package from her and spread it out on the table. He had hot beef and mustard, one of his favourite sandwiches from the new menu. He noticed that Molly had sat down at the other side of the desk but was sipping gingerly at one of the orange juices.

'You already ate?' He opened the brown paper bag and was about to take a bite of his sandwich when Molly turned green. 'Mol, what's wrong?'

'The mustard.' She managed to get the words out before gagging. 'It stinks.'

Matt's brow rose. 'What? You love mustard.' He sniffed at his lunch, and Molly heaved. She ran to the waste-paper basket in the corner and threw up violently. Matt hurried to her side.

'That's it, get it out,' he soothed, pulling a blond strand of hair back behind her ear. 'Hell. Are you okay?' He rubbed her back, his hand moving in slow circles as she retched.

'No,' she said finally, standing up slowly and reaching for a paper towel from the dispenser. 'I think you poisoned me with your pancakes.'

He grabbed her orange juice. 'Here, drink this. My pancakes are perfect too, cheeky.' His hand was on her cheek before he thought twice about it. 'Seriously, are you okay? You look awful.'

'Thanks,' she muttered, pushing his hand off when he

checked her forehead temperature. 'Love you too.' She went to leave, but he closed his hand around hers.

'Steady. Come and sit down. You can clean up in a minute.' He pulled her over to the chair, and she came with him willingly. He could see that she was shaking. 'Have you not eaten since breakfast?'

She shook her head, reaching over to the bowl he kept on his table and popping a mint imperial into her mouth. She sucked on it, and her colour returned. Just a little. He still didn't like the look of her though. 'I couldn't stomach it. I think I might have a bug.'

'Right.' Matt pointed to the juice in her hand. 'Drink that.' She glowered at him. 'Please.'

She rolled her eyes, but slowly sipped at it till it was empty. He was watching her, and something else clicked in his brain. 'What other symptoms do you have, other than the sense of smell being off, and the nausea.'

She thought for a moment. 'Nothing much. I've felt a bit tired, maybe. Nothing major. Why?'

Matt couldn't answer her. It was all clicking together in his mind, and he felt sick himself.

It couldn't be, could it?

This time he was the one shaking. He picked up the phone on his desk, then called through to reception.

'Jane? Yeah, listen. I've had an emergency come up. Can you rearrange the clinic and let Liam know? Yes. No, I don't think I'll be back in for the afternoon. Nurse Molly is coming with me too.' Molly was looking at him as if he'd gone mad. He grabbed his bag, flicking his answering machine on. 'Come on,' he commanded, standing before her and reaching out his hand. 'Let's go.'

'Matt, what the hell? We can't just leave work.'

'It's a one-off, and you're sick. You can't work like this.'

'So?' She shook her head. 'I'll be fine.'

'Molly, move your backside. We're going home, now. Either you walk out of here, or I'll carry you out.'

Her look was incredulous, but Matt ignored her. He needed to get her out of here. He needed to know. God, he needed to know right now. He wasn't going to be able to concentrate anyway. Molly looked so pale, he wanted to get her home. Look after her.

'Matt, you're being weird. It's just a bug. I'm fine. This overprotective side of you gets right on my wick.'

'Yeah?' he said, grabbing her bag from where she kept it under the counter and passing it to her. 'Well, get used to it,' he half growled. She huffed but got to her feet. They walked out together, and he was driving towards his house in minutes. When they reached the parade of shops near his place, he parked and rushed into the chemist, leaving Molly in the car looking bewildered.

'You think I'm pregnant?' Molly was laughing, but he didn't laugh back. Molly stared at him aghast, but she could almost feel the cogs turning in her brain. Clicking into place with a resounding thud. 'I'm not pregnant.' There was a lot less conviction in her voice the second time around.

They were standing in his kitchen, the contents of the bag from the chemist spilled out on the counter. Pregnancy tests, Pepto, bottles of water.

'Molly, put it together. Think of your symptoms. You love coffee and mustard on everything, but you've gone off them both. You threw up. You feel tired.'

'Oh, God…' She sagged against the counter, picking up one of the tests with a glazed expression. 'Oh, no.'

Matt's jaw flexed. 'It's okay.'

'Okay?' she echoed. 'How is this going to be okay?'

She felt his arms come around her, and she went to him. She could feel him kissing the top of her head, his arms encircling her tight.

'Let's just find out, okay? I'm here.'

He walked with her up the stairs, to the main bathroom. She could barely put one foot in front of the other her mind was racing so much. His steps were strong, sure and he kept her upright in his arms. She still had the box in her hands, and she looked down at it again. 'I can't believe I didn't think about it.' She laughed, but it was short-lived, hollow. 'I'm a midwife, and I never twigged. We used protection.'

Matt's face looked stricken, and she couldn't bear to look at it for long. What a mess. He didn't want this; she was sure of it. He looked as sick as she felt.

'Don't worry about any of that now. Let's just find out and take it from there.'

He went to follow her into the bathroom, but she put her hand on his chest. Stilling him.

'I think I've got it from here.' They both smiled wryly, realising that he was about to watch her pee onto a stick. 'I know we're close, but there's a limit. Even to our friendship.'

'Molly, if you are—'

'I won't be,' she lied, even to herself. 'Don't worry.'

'I'm not worried. I…' He nodded to the bathroom. 'I'll go downstairs. Make us a drink. Come find me?'

She nodded, watching him walk down the stairs. He'd

held her hand the whole way up, and his fingers were the last to leave her. She waited till she heard him moving around in the kitchen, and then closed the bathroom door behind her.

The fancy mirror in his bathroom was lit up from behind by a bright LED. It made the tinge of her skin look all the greener. 'You are an idiot,' she said to her reflection in the mirror. 'You are a total idiot.'

Once she'd ripped open the box, she looked at the stick. It wasn't like she needed to read the instructions. She'd been dealing with pregnancies for so long; she wasn't exactly a novice. It was the first time she'd had reason to take one though. They'd used a condom, but it didn't surprise her that it might not have worked. They weren't infallible. She'd delivered enough results of them failing to know that, but now it was her. Her and Matt. Hell, there was the nausea again. Things had only just got back to normal with him. Normalish anyway. They were living together, for God's sake. And now a baby?

Being a broke single mum was the opposite of everything she'd strived to become. It was her mother's life, minus the dead beat surrogate dads hanging around. The absent, erratic parenting. And Matt. He wasn't exactly Mr Commitment, was he? He'd probably already had another romantic encounter since their night. Yet he hadn't mentioned anything. She'd seen no signs. Especially not since moving in. She'd half expected to be alone on her nights off, but he was nearly always around, or very occasionally out with Liam. She knew he never had women in his house, so she was grateful for that rule.

What would he say knowing his bachelor pad might end up needing a nursery? He'd grow to resent her. Hate her even. She'd seen it before, on the faces of a few of the expectant fathers in the delivery rooms. The hookups that had resulted in a baby. Some couples were just not cut out to be parents together. Her own parents for one. Now she was possibly repeating history and dragging Matt along for the ride. She'd never be able to move out if that was the case.

'Mol?' A soft knock at the door. 'I brought you some water, if you need it.'

'No!' she half barked back. 'No, I'm good.' The orange juice was already doing the job. She just couldn't bring herself to take the test. Ear at the door, she heard shuffling movements. 'You still there?'

'Yeah.'

'Are you really going to listen to me pee?'

'I'm going.' She heard him on the stairs. He'd be back soon.

What am I going to do? Hide in the bathroom for ever?

Taking a deep breath, she ripped the wrapper off the test. This was it. One little bodily function would decide the rest of her life. Their lives.

The test sat on the closed toilet lid, resting on a piece of folded-up toilet roll. It was odd. She'd heard about so many other women's moments like these. Happy tears. Sad tears. The angst and excitement, the fear and trepidation they felt while waiting for those three long minutes to pass. To see the liquid soak into the litmus paper, illuminating one line or two. A cross or no cross. A word saying yay, or not today. When the result came up, it took her breath away. Ripped the air right out of her lungs for a moment. She tried to breathe deeper, but her windpipe wouldn't work. She clawed at the door handle, wanting to run down the stairs. To Matt. She needed Matt.

'Molly?' Matt was right there, the wooden door the only thing between them. He'd never left. 'Molly?'

His arms were around her, strong. Steadfast as always. She looked up at him, and the second she locked gazes with him, saw the striking blue of his eyes, she caught her breath. Found her voice.

'We're having a baby,' she said, and passed out in his arms. The last thing she remembered was Matt calling her name, telling her he was there for her. Always.

CHAPTER TEN

MATT PUT HER to sleep in his bed. He'd tell her tomorrow it was because she'd left her bed a mess that morning, clothes strewn across it, and he didn't want to disturb her stuff. Which was true to a certain degree, but the real truth was that he wanted her close to him. She was carrying his child. The shock of it had made her pass out. He'd managed to get some chicken soup and water into her when she came round, but she didn't say anything. She looked so tired, so drawn. He didn't trust himself to talk about it. So they didn't. He took care of her instead. Showed her with actions that he was there. There would be plenty of time for talking later.

Once he was sure she was settled for the night, he'd come back downstairs. Molly would need the day off work, he knew. He could arrange cover for her at the centre. But first, he needed a stiff Scotch. Plan his next move. Digest the news that he was going to be a father. His best friend was having his baby. After one night together. It was the stuff of his clients' stories. The reason why many of them ended up in his office and in the delivery rooms at the Ashford. Fleeting little moments that ended in permanence. That's what they were now, more than ever—permanence personified.

Sighing heavily, he picked up his phone.

'Mum? Yeah, it's me. I'm fine.' It was so good to hear her voice. Whenever he had a problem as a child, he'd always go to his mum over his father. Even before his father wasn't there to call on any more. It was as if he knew at a young age his dad couldn't be relied on.

'No work today?' she asked.

'I was earlier. Something came up.' He could hear her intake of breath. 'Molly's pregnant.'

Wow, saying it out loud makes it real. He couldn't stop the smile that came out. *Molly's having my baby. Wow.*

'She found out today. She's in bed resting. She's tired out.'

He heard his mother's footsteps, and he knew she was heading back up to the house. He could almost pinpoint how many steps she had left before she was back inside his childhood home.

'Is Molly okay?' she asked softly.

'She's shocked, I think.'

'Understandable, my love. Having a baby is an adjustment, no matter how prepared you are. What is she going to do? Is she keeping it?'

Matt's blood ran cold at the thought of Molly not having the baby. She'd always wanted one, but would she want it with him? He'd never considered that scenario.

'I…er…I don't know.' Another conversation that they needed to have when she woke up. He heard his mother pour a drink, the chink of ice as it hit glass.

'Bit early, isn't it?' he quipped, trying to lighten the mood and cancel out some of the dark thoughts swirling around his head. 'Brandy already?' His mother was a sucker for a brandy on the rocks.

'Well,' she retorted, her soft tinkly laugh like a balm to his jagged nerves, 'it's not every day your son tells you he's going to be a father.'

Matt could almost feel his ears bug out of his head. 'How did you know the baby's mine?'

'Oh, give over, I'm not old yet. Of course it's yours. I didn't realise you'd finally done something about it.'

'Done something about what?'

'About your friendship. God, son, we've all wanted to bang your heads together for the longest time. She's the best thing in your life.'

'Exactly,' he grumbled. 'And now look how that's turned out. I've ruined her life, Mum.'

'Don't be ridiculous! How can you say that? I never thought that when I had you. Never.'

'I don't mean it like that. I mean, I tanked her chances to be with someone she can love, Mum. You know Molly— she deserves better than…this.' He thought he heard a noise from the stairs, and he went quiet, listening. But all was silent.

'Matt,' his mother said firmly. 'You are not your father. What exactly do you think she's looking for that you can't give her?'

'Everything!' he exclaimed. 'Molly wants the whole white picket fence thing. She wants the husband, and the family. She wants a good, normal life. I can't do that. I don't even know how to! Don't you see? This baby…this baby changes everything. It's all…ruined.'

He turned his back, looking out of the window of the house he'd bought years ago. When everyone else was partying or spending money on rent or university functions, he'd stayed home with his mother. Saved every penny.

Worked every shift. Stayed up nights learning, studying. To be the doctor, the man he wanted to be. It didn't matter. None of it made a difference. When people heard the name Loren, their eyes narrowed. It had taken years for both him and his mother to come out from under the Loren curse, or the worst of it anyway.

Now his mother wasn't having it, telling him he was nothing like his father. He'd already tuned her out. He always did. She meant well. She loved the bones of him, but she was biased. She didn't know how damaged he was on the inside. He'd always kept it from her. Kept it from everyone.

Almost everyone.

He heard Molly coming down the stairs. 'Mum, Molly just woke up. I have to go. Call you later, okay?'

His mother went to say something else, but he cut the call.

'Hi.' He turned to face her. 'How are you feeling?'

She walked past him, and reached for a glass from the cupboard.

'Better, thanks. Sorry I scared you.'

'Don't be daft. You hungry?'

She nodded but stilled his arm when he started to go to the fridge.

'Let's just get takeout. Listen, I have something to say first. Will you sit?'

He waited till she'd taken a stool to be sure he could sit on the one next to her. He pulled her seat a little closer, and she let him. 'Mol, about—'

'I need to speak first.' She put her finger against his lips. 'I just want you to know that I'm keeping the baby. I want it. Her. Him. Whichever.'

He tried to say *good*, but she pushed her finger harder against his mouth.

'I just thought you should know.' She pulled her finger away. 'I know that this wasn't part of the plan, at all. For either of us. I don't expect anything from you. I just want you to know that too. I don't want to derail your life, any more than I already have.'

'What makes you think I won't want to be involved?' He felt sick. *She's living in my house, carrying my child, and she feels further away than ever.* 'It's my child too. I can help. I want to help. More than help. God, this is not coming out right at all.'

Damn it, I don't want to just help. I want to be a family. I wish I could do that. I wish it was in me. You see it too, don't you?

'We both know that us sleeping together was a mistake.' She was looking at a point over his shoulder now, then the floor. Anywhere but into his eyes. 'We got drunk, and it should never have happened. I was sad and feeling lost. I shouldn't have confused things.' She drew herself up to her full height. 'But I can do this on my own.'

'No,' he said, his fear and disappointment turning into anger. She'd not even considered him as a father. That they could do this together. Even Molly, his Molly, saw him as his father's son. Someone to love them and leave them. The only woman in Matt's life he'd ever had feelings for wasn't even giving him the choice of being involved.

'No?' She looked shocked. Pale, and beautiful.

She's really pregnant with my child.

The more he thought about it, the more protective of her he felt. Hell, he already was before this. He knew he was going to be a nightmare going forward. He felt like asking her not to leave the house till she'd given birth. He couldn't let her go, not now. He could just about cope with not having her before this, but now? What was he going to do? Watch her meet someone else, take his child with her? Hell no. He'd rather live the rest of his life taking cold showers and holding back the words he wanted to say to Molly than watch someone else live the life he was too messed-up to claim for himself.

Not for the first time, he found himself cursing both their upbringings. They were so busy trying to break the mould, they'd poured themselves right into it instead. He thought of the new life growing inside her, and he knew without a doubt he wanted to do better.

'You heard me. I know it's a shock, but my answer is no, Molly.'

Her head snapped back. 'What do you mean, no?'

'I mean no, you're not doing this on your own. *Mistake* or not.' His jaw clenched with the effort of forcing that word out. None of this was a mistake. His heritage was. 'You're having my baby. I have a say in this, whether you like it or not.'

'Okay,' she said slowly. He waited, knowing she needed to feel in control. 'What do you suggest we do then? What about working at the Ashford, and us living together?'

'Work is work. People will talk, but so what? They do anyway. I'll shut them all up. We can tell them when you're ready to, and not before. Us living together is perfect.'

'Perfect?' she echoed, looking him in the eye. God, he wanted to draw her to him. He put his hands on his thighs to suppress the urge, felt the pressure of his nails digging into his skin.

'Yes. I have the office but we can change it to be a

nursery. I barely use it.' *True. Since you moved in, I prefer to be where you are. On the couch, sitting in the garden. Cooking in the kitchen while listening to music.* 'We have the room.'

Molly was looking at him as if he had lost his mind. 'So, you want us to bring up a baby, together? Just like that?' She bit her lip. 'You need to think about this.'

'Why?' He waved his hands around. 'We already live together. We're best friends. We work together.'

She was already shaking her head. 'Exactly. Work colleagues, friends. You're talking about acting like a family! I can't ask that of you. It's not what you want.'

'You didn't ask, I'm offering and it's happening.' He tried to keep the edge from his voice, but it was there. It hung in the air between them. Stubborn? That was a normal day for Matt. When he truly wanted something, he didn't stop until he'd achieved it. He couldn't help but grind out through clenched teeth, 'Work colleagues.'

'Matt, why are you so angry?'

'I'm not angry. I just want to be there for you, Molly. This isn't some problem you can go off and deal with on your own.' He needed to box this off. To get her to agree. The panic at her turning him down was driving him mad. 'I'm all in.'

'In?' Her voice rose to match. 'In? This isn't like splitting a pizza, Matt, or even living together. Oh, God, what a mess. I had a plan.' She gripped the countertop. 'I had a plan. To save up, buy a house. Meet the guy, then have a family. The right way. This is… It's all such a mess.'

'I'm sorry,' Matt said, feeling the familiar dread in the pit of his stomach. 'I dragged you into this.'

'You didn't drag me, Matt. I knew what I was doing.'

She paused. 'At least, I thought I did.' Her face flashed with pain, and he wanted to root out the cause.

'What do you mean?'

Does she regret leaving that morning like she had?

His heart jumped into his mouth.

Does she want more? Oh, God, what would I do if she does? How can I resist? How can I ever be the man she deserves?

'Nothing. It's nothing.' She sighed heavily, and Matt closed the shutters on his heart once more. 'This is serious. It's a baby. It's not something that will just go away if it doesn't work out.'

'I know that. You do know I do this for a living, right? I get how babies work.'

'Yeah.' She pushed off the stool, moving away. He rose and went with her. The two stalked around each other like magnets, attracted and repelled. 'I know that, but what about later down the line? Two years, five years. Ten? Will you still think the same then?'

'Why wouldn't I? Don't you trust me?'

'It's not that—'

'Tell me then,' he urged. Demanded. He could hear the steely tone in his own voice. Could cut the charged tension in the air between them.

'Tell you what?'

He took a step closer. 'Tell me that you trust me.' His fingers ached to reach out, to take her hand, but she looked so scared, so unsure. It was breaking his heart, and it was already damaged. Tattered. Trying to keep beating through the scars of unsaid things. Love unspoken festered in the chambers. 'Tell me that you trust me to do this.' She didn't move when he stood right in front of her, reached for her hands. Taking one of them, he moved it over her stomach, held it there with his.

'This is our baby, Molly. I never dreamed that this would happen. I'm sorry it's not the way you wanted it, the way you deserve to be a mother. You are the most important person in my life, and now there will be two. I will do anything within my power to make sure that you and our baby will never want for anything. Trust that, okay? Trust me.'

'I do trust you; I always have.' She cupped his face with her free hand. 'You really want to do this together?'

'Always,' he said. 'I told you—I'm all in.'

'He's all in? Really?' Amy was sitting aghast on the couch, her mug of tea halfway to her lips. 'Wow, Molly. I mean, I'm still reeling from the fact you had mind-blowing sex with him. Now you're his baby mama?'

'Did I say mind-blowing?' Molly blushed.

Amy nodded emphatically. 'Yes, and from the way you described it, you were still selling it short. How do you feel about all this?'

Molly sipped at her tea. 'Scared. Excited. Terrified. Elated.'

'Well, that's not confusing at all.'

'Nope. Clear as crystal.'

Confusing was a good way to describe it. She'd woken up in his bed after passing out. He'd put her into his bed instead of her own. When she'd first woken up, she had thought it might have meant something. Since they'd moved in together, she'd seen some signs of him wanting more. Or she thought she had. Hoped. Even though she'd left that note, and his bed, the memory of their time together still kept her up at night. Wondering how something so good with Matt could be such a point of misery. Even if he came to her on bended knee right now, would she even say yes? She didn't know whether to cling to him or run for the hills.

When she'd left him that note to spare him giving her the speech, she'd been hopeful all the same. She had thought that their night had meant more to him as it did her. It was so tender, so hot. He'd been so loving. Telling her she was beautiful. Talking about her body as though he'd imagined it all this time.

They'd made a baby that night, so waking in his bed once again after discovering she was pregnant seemed right. Full circle. She'd gone down the stairs to talk to him and heard him on the phone with his mother. When she'd heard what he'd said, picked up the tone of his voice, all hopes were lost.

Nothing had changed for him. He didn't want the life she wanted. He'd described it as 'white picket fence,' which sounded so twee. She didn't want a perfect cookie cutter life. She just wanted a family that didn't fall apart. The opposite of what she'd had growing up. He didn't even want to try for any of that. His childhood had sent him the other direction. A life with no ties, or people to hurt. She'd ruined it. Their one night together had scuppered both their plans. As soon as she overheard that call, she'd known for sure. Matt was doing this because he was Matt, but it didn't mean he wanted it. She'd accidentally trapped him into playing family by default, and she couldn't bear it. He felt bad for her, that she'd conceived a baby with a man who didn't want to be a family man. Neither of them was going to get their wish, but her wish was for him too. Just not like this. Nothing like this.

'He doesn't want this, you know.'

Amy frowned. 'Well, he sounds like he does to me. He cares about you. Enough to sleep with you, move you in.'

'He was being a friend, Ames.'

'You don't generally have sex with your friends.'

'I basically got tipsy and told him I fancied him from the start. I caused this,' she said sulkily.

'Er, it takes two to tango,' Amy cut in. 'He took you back to his place. He kissed you first, right?'

Molly thought of the taxi. The intense gaze on his face before he'd swooped on her in the back of that car. 'Yes.'

'Exactly! Two dance partners! You make it sound like you threw yourself at him.'

'Yeah, well. Either way, he caught me and boy does he regret it now.' She splayed one palm across her flat stomach theatrically.

'I don't think so. You've been drunk plenty of times together. You're always touchy-feely with each other. I've seen it myself. We all have. That kind of closeness doesn't come from nothing.'

'Yes, it's because we're friends! Best friends! That's all.'

Amy snorted. 'We're friends too, but I don't hug you all the time, hold your hand, kiss your forehead. The way he looks at you sometimes, it's like a romance novel.'

Molly shook her head. 'Well, even if I believed any of that, it's ruined now.' She checked her watch. 'I should be going. I said I'd meet him at home at ten. We have to go and see his mother tomorrow, sort the planning out for the wedding.'

Amy smiled and looked around at the place, empty now

that their stuff was pretty much packed. 'I can't believe this is our last night here together. Look at us. I'm getting married; you're having a baby. We've come a long way.'

Molly also glanced around her, taking her old home in for the last time. 'We really have.'

Amy walked Molly to the door a short while later, where a cab was already waiting. 'Listen, cut Matt some slack. Have some faith. If he didn't want to do this, he'd tell you. He says he's all in. I for one believe him.'

Matt was waiting for her at the front door when the cab pulled up. He came down the path, then paid the driver and opened her door for her.

'Nice time? How's Amy?'

'Good. Surprised about the baby. Happy for us.'

He nodded, taking her arm in his and leading her up to the house. 'Excellent. Have you eaten?'

'Snacks. Tea.'

He frowned. 'That it?' His blue eyes looked luminescent even in the dark of the night. 'Sorry. I know, I'm fussing.' He led her inside, not letting go of her till they were both settled on the couch. She kicked off her flats, and he started to rub her feet.

'It's been two weeks since I passed out. I haven't fainted since. All the initial checks have been good. I have an excellent doctor.' That earned her a nip on the toe. 'Hey,' she laughed. 'Okay, Liam is excellent, but you're better.'

'Thank you. It doesn't stop me from worrying about you though. It's perfectly normal.' He kept saying things like that. When he took her to work, brought her lunch. Brought her folic acid and prenatal vitamins. Made her breakfast. To be fair, he'd always done most of those things. Add in the pregnancy stuff, and he was just being a good obstetrician. A great best friend. It was nice to be doted on. She felt loved, protected. Confused and horny too.

The pregnancy hormones were driving her mad, even though she knew she should have expected it. Having the knowledge and living the experience were very different, she'd realised. She could hardly be surprised either. She was living and working with Matt, knew him inside out. She knew what he looked like when he orgasmed, for God's sake! There were bound to be a few dirty thoughts on her part. He was the father. So what if she'd had the odd sexy dream about him since finding out about the baby? Like she said, hormones.

'I see you don't mind the foot rubs though,' he said teasingly.

She realised she *had* been groaning a little. Whimpering. *Oh, stop it.* She went to pull her foot away, but he held it fast.

'You ready for tomorrow?' he asked.

'The meal? Of course. I can't wait to see where Sarah's going to get married. Are you ready?' Matt scowled a little, making her laugh. 'Give over. I know you're happy for her. What's the deal with you and this wedding, really?'

He was the one to pull away this time. 'No deal. There's some leftover chilli—do you fancy some of that before bed?'

He was halfway to the kitchen already. She let him go. That was Matt. Not one to speak about his feelings, especially when it came to his mother, commitment or weddings. Fair enough. She did need to ask him one thing about Sarah's wedding though. She'd definitely be showing by then. Not easy to hide the fact she was pregnant.

'Are you taking a date with you on the day?' She heard a bowl clatter to the floor. 'Matt, you okay?'

'Yeah,' he called back after a string of expletives. 'Dropped a dish. Are you?'

'Am I what?'

He was back before she knew it, holding two steaming bowls of chilli. Grated cheese sitting on top, hunks of buttered bread on a side plate resting on his wrist.

'Taking a date to the wedding. I thought we'd go together.' He passed her a dish, then half slammed the plate of bread onto the coffee table.

Okay, that was weird.

'Well, I did too, but I just thought I'd ask because…you know.' She pointed to her stomach.

His face was blank. 'The baby?' He raised a brow. He was smiling, but it didn't reach his eyes. 'Well, I don't think the baby will take up much space, if you're worried about too many plus-ones on the invite. We were already going together. That's not changed for me.'

He spooned some chilli into his mouth, chewing like a lion on a gazelle leg.

'Me neither. It's just… Are you ready for the questions? Your mum's friends are all going to be there. Family too.'

He looked relieved. 'That's it? There's no problem with that. You know my mum already knows. I told her the day we found out.'

'Yes.' But she'd spoken to Sarah in the days since, and she'd never mentioned a word about it. Ever the diplomat. He was more like his mother than he realised, she mused with a smile. Shame he thought his father had a hold on him too. She knew that would be troubling him. Having a baby, especially like this.

She finally got the courage to ask, 'Don't you care what people will say? Us there together, me with a pregnant belly?'

'I'll never be ashamed or embarrassed by our child, Molly. We will be there together.' His jaw flexed. He swallowed before he answered. She heard it. 'No one will say a thing to you while I'm around.'

Molly's heart swelled. Ever the protector. The thought of being there together, watching his mother get married, their baby on the way... It was almost perfect. She thought of what Amy had said. God, she wished it was true, but she'd overheard that phone call he'd had with his mum. It was what she constantly came back to whenever she allowed herself to want more. She wished she could tell him she didn't long for the perfect life. The white picket fence wasn't it at all. She just wanted to feel the way he made her feel. Safe. Loved. Seen.

'What about you?' He brought her attention back with his soft probing voice.

'What about me? It's your family. I'm not embarrassed at all.'

'They're your family too,' he chided. 'You know my mum loves you. She's thrilled, by the way. She's been biting her tongue every time she spoke to you since she found out, in case you didn't want to discuss it with her yet. She's been hard to hold off, to be honest.'

Molly blushed. 'I'll talk to her tomorrow,' she promised. She thought he'd be happy, but his still-furrowed brow was unmistakable. 'That wasn't what you meant, was it?'

'No.' He looked away, focusing on anything but her. 'I don't want you to feel...bad.'

'Bad?'

'My reputation,' he supplied reluctantly. He looked like he wanted the ground to swallow him up. 'My mum's friends, they knew my father too. Some of them are still in touch with him. He deals with their cases. You know what that circle is like.'

She could feel the rage simmering in him. It came off him in waves whenever he talked about his dad. Without thinking about it, she went to him. The bowls sat discarded on the coffee table now, and she was up on the couch, on her knees. He turned to her, surprise registering on his face.

'Stop that. Now. I mean it, Matt.'

'Stop what?'

She took his face in her hands, was so close to him that she could just pucker up and they'd be kissing. He'd straightened his body, pushing himself even closer to her.

Magnets, she thought.

The proximity of him was intoxicating. They'd well and truly broken the touch barrier now. Again. She missed him. The way she used to fall asleep in his arms watching the TV. They were slowly getting it back, but it would never be enough now.

'Molly, what are you doing?'

'I hate it when you do that. I never knew your dad, sure. I never want to know him. I do know your mother though, and you are so like her. All the good things. This front you insist on putting up, it's infuriating. You don't have to worry about me feeling any kind of shame being seen out with you.' She took his hand, putting it back on her stomach before returning hers to cup his gorgeous face. She could feel the warmth of his touch through her top. Feel his fingers rub her tummy affectionately.

'This might not be the plan I had for my life,' she continued, 'but so what? I was hardly dating Prince Charming, was I? I was floundering, outside of work. This baby...' She smiled, thinking of the life growing inside her. 'Our baby, it's a good thing. I don't regret that.' She leaned in closer to touch her forehead to his. 'I don't regret you being the father. I'm grateful for it.'

Matt let out a breath, as though he'd been holding it the whole time. 'You mean that?' he half whispered, moving his hands to settle around her waist. She caught a whiff of his cologne, and the butterflies flew loose again. Fluttering around them both as they gazed at each other. 'You're glad it's me?'

'Matt,' she said, exasperated. 'Always.'

Is that it? Could that be it? He thinks he's his father's son?

Perhaps it wasn't the stupid white-fence scenario that scared him. Maybe, just maybe, it was the thought of not being able to keep it once he had it. Involving her and his child in the juggernaut of gossip that swirled around him until he feared she'd leave him. Fear. Fear of loss. Fear of not doing the right thing. Falling flat on his face in front of the people who had judged him all his life regardless. She could show him otherwise. Right now, she wanted to show him a lot of things.

His pupils dilated under her scrutiny. She was breathing harder, faster, and she could see his chest heaving under his clothes. Maybe it was the hormones, the smell of him. The feel of him pulling her closer with his muscular arms. Their talk. Or just...them. Whatever it was, she needed him.

'Kiss me,' she begged. His eyes widened. 'Kiss me, Matt. Please.'

He looked conflicted, and she made a bold move before he had a chance to think about it.

Her lips were on his before he finished saying her name. She kissed at his closed mouth, feeling him tense. Just before she pulled back, lost her nerve, his mouth opened. His tongue licked at her lips. She sent hers to meet it, deepening the kiss and moving closer. She ended up sitting astride him, her knees on the outside of his thighs. She could feel his ardour through his trousers, and it spurred her on.

He wants this. Wants me.

His arms were pulling her tighter now, hands roving under her top. One flick of his wrist and her bra clasp came loose. She mewled, not caring how obviously aroused she was. He seemed to love it, his hands coming around to the front. Cupping her breasts.

'God,' he almost roared, his voice deep. The gravel in his tone rumbled around her. 'Pregnancy agrees with you.'

He pulled back, and for a second she thought the mention of the baby had pulled him out of it.

'Don't stop,' she urged, pushing her chest towards him. He looked so turned on, yet so conflicted. 'Please, don't stop.'

'Are you sure? What about—'

'Doctor, I think you know the answer to that. It's fine. I want this.' She ground herself shamelessly onto his lap, and his responding moan thrilled her. 'I want you.'

Before she could catch her breath, she was up off the couch. His lips were back on hers, his strong arms under her backside, holding her in place as he walked towards the staircase. She grabbed on to him with her hands, her thighs. Cupping his face, kissing his sexy chiselled face off as he mounted the stairs. His stairs were in two parts, and when they got to the top of the landing, he pushed her against the wall, as if he couldn't bear to take the next little flight without getting more.

'My Molly,' he whispered, running his stubble down her neck as he kissed his way to her collarbone. He pulled back, but she felt solid, supported in his hands. He nudged his head towards her top.

'Take it off,' he commanded. She locked her blue eyes on to his, absentmindedly hoping for a second that the colours of their eyes would merge into their child's. She focused on the hue of his irises as she took the material between her fingers. His hands were clasped firmly on her bottom, her back leaning against the painted wall he'd pushed her up against. She slowly pulled the top over her head, taking her unstrapped bra with it. Matt made a deep, visceral noise from the back of his throat, burying his head between her pregnancy-swollen breasts. Kissing and licking the exposed skin between them.

'I like them like this.' He kissed one nipple, then made it pucker as he blew on it. 'They were perfect before, but now...' He kissed the other as she threw her clothing aside. It landed on the banister. 'Amazing,' he breathed. 'You take my breath away.'

He drew back, and they were on the move again. His motions pushed his groin into hers, making her eyes roll back in her head from the sensations. He kicked open his bedroom door, as if he'd never even considered taking her to her own bed. She felt a surge of fresh lust. She wanted to be back in his bed. Had wanted it every night since she'd moved her things in.

She expected him to put her down, lay her on his bed, but he turned. Sat down on the edge and took her with him. She went to grab his T-shirt from his back, and he pulled away just enough to let her remove it. He seemed disappointed at having to lift his hands from her body. The second she'd undressed his torso, he gripped her waist. Tight, possessive. Soft and tender. All at the same time. He gave her a look that made her libido spike off the chart. Like he wanted to utterly ruin her and worship her all at the same time. It was intoxicating. They looked at each other, as if time and space had stopped. Like it meant nothing, because they were here together. In this moment.

'You drive me crazy,' he muttered. 'I don't know what to do when I'm around you lately. I can't think straight. I don't want to lose you.' He looked a little sad about it, and she wanted to know why, what this beautiful man was thinking, but she didn't want him to pull away from her. Not now. Not ever.

'You won't.' He didn't look convinced. 'Matt, you could never lose me.' His half smile was a nice little reward, but she knew he needed to hear more. She couldn't shake off that phone call though, what he'd said to his mum when he thought she was sleeping. It wasn't the time. She couldn't say the words.

'Let me make you feel good,' she said instead. Using his own words to reach him, like he had her. A little code of theirs. She took charge. Reached down to cup him. To show him what she could do. 'I want this, Matt.' She was sailing so close to the truth now. To everything she wanted to say but wasn't ready to divulge yet. 'I want you.'

She touched her lips to his, the softest and tenderest of kisses. She put everything she wanted to say into that kiss.

Actions speaking far louder than the words she was holding back. There was no fear in her touch. No hesitation, or embarrassment. She could show him how she felt this way, and for now at least it would be enough. She would worry about the consequences later. She couldn't stay away from him. She'd already failed. The way he took her in his arms, kissed her back, she had an inkling that he couldn't either. He reached for her, discarding any clothing that got in his way, and she stopped herself from overthinking. From thinking at all. By the time he entered her, she was already about to climax again. She gripped his shoulders tight, whispering his name feverishly as he thrust into her, her name on his lips like a promise.

CHAPTER ELEVEN

MATT LOREN WAS a one-woman man. As they got out of his Lexus, hand in hand walking towards the fancy hotel his mother was getting married in later that year, the thought popped into his head.

That's a lie. His brain laughed back at him. *The thought didn't just pop into your head. It's always been there.*

True, he agreed with himself, grinning back at Molly as she smiled up at him.

Man, if my dad could see me now.

Matt liked to think it would irk him. That his son was trying to be the man he never was.

'You ready for this?'

'Are you?' he teased. 'You look a little tired.' Her smile turned from wholesome to sexy in half a second.

'Yeah, well. Someone kept me awake.'

He winked at her, which made her sexy smile all the brighter.

God almighty, she is stunning.

They'd woken up in his bed, naked. Limbs entwined around each other. Her little spoon bum making him hard as soon as she started to stir. He didn't tell her, but he'd been awake for a while. Watching her sleep. Wondering how he could be so close to having it all, and so undeserving. At times like this, he was jealous of his mother. Getting to shed the Loren name. He almost hoped that Molly would insist on their child taking her surname, but not enough to suggest it. He still needed that connection. He just wished her surname would be the same too. Possessive? Probably. He felt like a stud dog, wanting to mark his territory, chase off any other contenders.

He'd made love to her again that morning, a slow, leisurely push of his hips into her body. Her once-sleepy eyes rolling with pleasure as he rubbed his thumb against her clitoris, no need for talking. *Is this what a relationship is like? I could never go back to meaningless sex after this.* They'd spent half the night together like that. Touching each other, tasting. He literally could not get enough of her. Even now, walking into the hotel, he had to adjust himself, his erection painful against his tailored trousers.

'You okay?' She squeezed his fingers in hers. 'Where did you go then?'

Into you, he thought. *I was deep into you.*

'Nowhere,' he said, squeezing her hand back and willing his hard-on to go away. 'Just thinking about last night.'

Nice going, idiot. Now you're thinking about her naked breasts again. About how nice it would be to wake up next to her every morning. Not a wall apart.

She smirked, lifting onto the balls of her feet to whisper something into his ear. They were nearly at the entrance, and he didn't want to come in his boxers. He turned his head and dropped a quick peck onto her cheek. He hated himself for the look of disappointment on her face but needs must. She was driving him wild, and he couldn't shut himself off like he did with every other woman he'd been with.

'Let's find my mother, yes?'

She nodded, a faint flush colouring her cheeks.

Damn it, now she felt rejected.

He flexed his fingers, wrapping hers tighter in between them. He felt her relax as they headed inside.

'Hello, you two!' Duncan and Sarah were waiting in the foyer, a glass of champagne in each of their hands. 'What do you think? Beautiful grounds.'

Duncan looked nervous. Matt stepped forward without letting go of Molly, offering his free hand.

'Gorgeous,' he said, even though on the way in he hadn't paid much attention. 'Nice to see you again.' Duncan's nervous smile dissipated. Molly let go of his hand, and he mourned the loss.

'So.' He distracted himself by making small talk as he watched Molly walk across to the bar area with his mother. They were deep in conversation. His eyes never left Molly. 'How are the nerves? Getting cold feet yet?'

Duncan laughed. 'Not a chance. I wish it was sooner. Still a few weeks to wish away yet. What about you?'

'Me what?' His mother was embracing Molly now. The news of the baby was official, it seemed.

'Are you ready to walk your mother down the aisle?'

He turned to Duncan and realised that the man had been watching him watch Molly all along. 'No, no nerves here. Shall we get a drink?'

'Good idea,' Duncan agreed. 'Scotch, is it? Or too early?'

'Driving,' Matt replied. 'We have to get back tonight, as we're working tomorrow. I'll take a soft drink though.' He was hot on Duncan's heels, eager to follow Molly to the bar. His heartbeat raced when he saw her face light

up the minute she realised he was at her side again. He
wanted to reach out, wrap his arms around her, but there
was a little crowd at the bar. He wasn't sure how she would
react. She answered him by lacing her arm through his,
reaching up to drop a kiss on his cheek. When he looked
at his mother, he could see that she was positively vibrat-
ing with happiness.

'Thanks both of you for coming. They are pretty packed
here over the next few weeks, so I wanted to take the time
to do the planning, run through the day. Having lunch and
tasting the menu at the same time seemed perfect.'

A waiter appeared, pristine black and white uniform
denoting the character of the place. It was nice to see his
mother getting a touch of some opulence for once. It made
the years of struggling seem worth it somehow. 'Your table
is ready, if your party has all arrived?'

Lunch was perfect. Duncan's younger brother, Edward was
just like him. Kind, funny. It was annoying, if Matt was
honest. Edward loved Molly from the off, which wasn't
surprising. Everyone did.

She was glowing today. She'd put on a dress he'd not
seen before for the outing. A gorgeous blue that seemed
familiar to him somehow. The shade reminded him of
something. It brought out the darker blue in her eyes. Made
her blond hair almost ice-white. She was radiant. Flushed
from the pregnancy, and the morning sex. He was already
looking forward to them being alone again. After their
morning session, they'd drifted back to sleep. Had woken
in a panic, realising that they were late for the two-hour
drive to the venue his mother had picked for the wedding.

Duncan's family lived in the North, so they'd settled on

somewhere halfway in between. That was his mother, always thinking about everyone else. He'd already booked him and Molly a twin room for the event. He was tempted to ask them to change it to a double while he was here but he didn't want to presume, even after last night. They'd not discussed it. Molly had fallen asleep in the car pretty much the second they'd hit the road. He'd let her sleep. She was growing their child; she needed the rest. Talking about what came next could wait.

His mother had been watching them for most of the meal; he could feel her eyes on them. Every time Molly reached for him or gave him a little smile. Told the table one of their work stories, holding back the client details but keeping the humour and warmth of the situations they'd found themselves in. The baby wasn't mentioned, and he loved his mother for not putting him on the spot. He realised that Duncan knew as well, but he found he wasn't bothered by it. Far from it. Duncan seemed pleased too, and he felt an odd sense of pride. Was this what it was like to be in love, starting a family and sharing the news with your own parents?

Damn, just listen to yourself. You'll be calling Duncan Dad next. Simpering over Babygros and stuffed toys. Although... we do need to get going on that side of things.

The rest of the afternoon was relaxed, fun even. Matt felt as though something had eased. Being in public together like that had offered real insight into how things were on the other side of the track.

They were driving home now, having been waved off by his mother and Duncan. Molly had been quiet since they'd left, looking out of the window. Her hands were in her lap, and she kept picking at the skin on the sides of her manicured fingers. She'd had them done especially for today, he'd noted. Work called for short unpolished nails. He was absurdly happy that she'd made such an effort. As if she really cared.

'Well, that was a lot easier than I expected.' He tried to start up a conversation. All he got was a distracted smile and a nod, and her face was back at the window. 'Do you have anything planned for the rest of today?'

She looked at him then, intrigued. 'No, I was just planning to have a bath and an earlyish night. Back to work tomorrow.'

He nodded, noticing for the first time how tired she looked underneath her make-up. He felt bad for being the cause. 'No problem. We'll just go straight home.'

Her eyes didn't leave him. 'What did you have in mind?'

The place they stopped at, near to home, was like a baby superstore. Matt had never seen so much equipment, all seemingly put into three realms. Pink, blue and anything bland to pass for either. Gender neutrality hadn't quite caught up when it came to babies, it seemed. At the hospital, they didn't assign colours to any of the babies as such. Boy or girl, they were put in blankets and clothes of all colours. He was pleased to think about it. Not every girl wanted pink, nor every boy wanted blue. Even he knew that, from his limited experience of children.

'Wow,' Molly exclaimed from his side. 'Where the heck do we start?'

She'd readily agreed to look at baby things on the way home. All her tests had been normal, Molly was carrying well and the pregnancy was perfect so far. She was over two months, so it made sense. Plus, given the fact that she

was still looking for flat listings, Matt figured that showing her how the baby could fit in at his house was a good
idea. He hated the thought of Molly not being there when
he woke up. Even if she was in another room. He already
felt so protective over her and the baby. He needed them
to stay with him. Maybe she would agree to it if she saw
the baby's room all kitted-out. Ready for them to tackle
the challenge. Together.

Matt took a deep breath. 'Well, we'll need a cot, so
let's start there.' He took her hand in his, and she allowed
him to lead her over to the back wall. There was an array
of differently coloured wooden cots in various sizes and
styles. Some were dressed up already, cot bumper sets with
bunny rabbits or bears or hot-air balloons.

'Wow.' Molly's voice was flat, unimpressed. 'The ducks
are a bit scary, aren't they?' She poked a hanging duck
soft toy from one of the mobiles. 'They look dead-eyed.
I wouldn't fancy staring at them every night. Don't they
have anything else?'

Matt tore his gaze from a weird looking animal cot
bumper. It looked like a family of dead racoons from a
distance, pretending to be pretty little teddy bears.

'Like what?' he quipped. 'Little stethoscopes?' He
squeezed her hand. She squeezed it back.

This is nice. Domesticated.

'Hi there, can I be of any help?' The pair turned to see
a woman in staff uniform behind them. Her name badge
declared her to be a 'Baby Expert' called Priscilla. Matt
saw Molly's eyes narrow when she read the label. He re-
sisted the urge to laugh. He was pretty sure Molly had the
slight edge on the 'baby expert' tag. Maybe he'd make her
a joke one for work.

'Er...no, th—'

'Yes,' Matt cut Molly off. 'We do actually. We need to kit out a nursery.'

I need it to be enticing, homely. Somewhere Molly can picture laying our child to sleep.

The woman beamed. 'Well, you've come to the right place. Mr...?'

'Loren, but call me Matt, please. This is Molly.'

Molly was already smiling at her, but she looked uncomfortable. Luckily, the saleswoman had no issues in filling the silence.

'Matt, Molly, we have you covered. So, just so I have a guide...on budget, timescale? Is this your first baby?'

'Yes, my first,' Molly replied. 'I think we'll just start with some of the smaller things. Car seat, maybe? I would like one to fit into a pram. Maybe this one?' She was already off, heading to the area that housed the prams. The woman gave Matt a weird look, probably as confused as he was.

My *first. Not* our *first.*

It was probably nothing, a slip of the tongue, but it still stung him. His phone rang in his pocket, and he was in two minds. Did he go and stake his claim? Go over there and casually mention it was his baby too? Why did he feel so hurt that even a shop assistant didn't know the truth? He was trying to care for Molly, be protective of her, but it was clear she didn't want or need him. He answered the call.

'Hello, Dr Loren.'

It was the Ashford on the line, and he had to go immediately. An emergency.

'I'm on my way,' he answered grumpily. A young sales

assistant passed him, a stack of boxes in the lad's hand. Matt rushed over to him, no time to lose.

'Do me a favour.' He pointed over to the two women. 'Tell that blonde customer Matt had to leave for work. An emergency, okay? Tell her I'm sorry and ask her to take a cab home. She'll understand!'

He was already out of the door when the boy turned around, taking the ear bud out of his ear.

'What did you say? Sir?'

Molly.

He'd left her there, right in the middle of the stupid baby superstore. Looking like a total idiot. She'd called Matt's name, looked for him. She'd had to arrange a cab home and that was only after buying half the shop too out of sheer embarrassment. Her credit card was still smoking, unaccustomed to being used, never mind being taken on a spree.

One minute he was there, the next gone. No phone call, no text. He'd just walked right out of the place. She'd come home to find his car missing. His place in darkness.

The cab driver had taken pity on her and brought the boxes in for her. 'First baby, eh?'

'Er…yeah,' she said, raiding her purse for a tip. 'Thought I'd better make a start.' She passed him the money. 'Even as a midwife, I didn't realise that they needed so much.'

He chuckled. 'I remember. We only had a small flat when we started out.' He glanced at the photo on Matt's side table. It showed the two of them on New Year's Eve. It was one of her favourite photos. A guys-and-dolls party a friend had thrown. Matt had let his hair down that night for once, really laughing and having fun with the others, and not just her. His fake tommy gun rested under one of his arms, Molly held in his other. They were both laughing into the camera. She could still remember the moment. He'd seen the photographer coming and lunged for her.

Come here, he'd said, kissing her cheek as she squealed in his arms. *I can't have a photo without my girl.*

The driver saw her gaze at the photo. 'Well.' He smiled. 'You two just enjoy it. It goes so fast.'

'Oh, we're…' She should have put him straight, but she didn't. She didn't want to explain to anyone how they weren't together. Why they weren't. She didn't really understand it herself. The longer she was here with Matt, doing this, the more it would make her want it. She didn't know how they'd got here, but she couldn't bring herself to regret it. Not the nights together, and definitely not the baby.

Once she'd closed the door on the driver, she took a shower. Dressed in sweats, she came back down to the packages. She'd half expected Matt to be back by now, sitting in his chair reading, making something to eat in the kitchen. It was too quiet without him. She'd dialled his number, but only got his voicemail. His phone was only turned off for work. She rang the Ashford, asking if he was on shift.

'Dr Loren's here, dealing with an emergency, yes. Do you have a message you want to pass on?'

'No, no.' She got off the call as quickly as she could. The last thing she wanted getting round was that she'd phoned looking for him. She and Matt didn't do that. They normally knew, so didn't need to check in. He'd just walked out of that store without a second thought. For all she knew, he'd panicked in there, and left her. The emergency could have come after, saving him from having to explain. Why else would he just leave her there without a word?

Hell, now I'm trying to work out what was going on in his head.

She never had to do that before. He was the one man in her life whom she didn't need to be wary of or worry about.

She flicked on the television and made herself a sandwich. After she'd eaten and tried to distract herself with a reality show, she gave up. Pulling one of the large brown paper bags towards her, she started to unpack the tiny clothes she'd bought that day. She'd picked pretty trendy designs, nothing too cutesy. She could tell from Matt's face he'd thought the same as her about the flopsy bunnies and eerie-looking teddy bears. She didn't want to kit the baby out that way. Something simple, classic. Nothing too cute. She was pretty sure Matt had never been a baby anyway. He must have arrived into the world with a determined scowl on his face.

Maybe they'd make this work, maybe not. They'd had sex again. A lot of sex. Wow, it'd been even better than last time. It felt as though he'd wanted to be there, with her. Like she was the only person in the world. Like the first time, but that it meant even more. He'd held her tighter, whispered sweet nothings into her ear, as though his tongue had been loosened and now he couldn't stop telling her how he felt. In the morning though, nothing. He wasn't weird per se, but he wasn't exactly forthcoming either. He didn't mention anything that had happened, just spoke of their day. Which had gone well, until he took her to buy baby things and then bolted on her.

Molly made a stack of the clothes and went to write everything down. An inventory. After she'd moved around so much growing up, it was something she always did. Once that was done, she turned the notepad to a clean page. Started writing something else.

She'd always done well on her own. Before Matt, she firmly believed that people were just human beings she would have to encounter in life as she went about hers. Before the Ashford, before she grew to love Amy, before she met Matt, she was firmly of that resolve. Once it was meant to happen, it would. She'd find love. The one person she could trust beyond all reason, and love enough to let in. The small nugget of hope that she held, kept close to her chest. All of that felt so close now but altered. Imperfect. Like there was a crucial piece or two still missing. Molly didn't like feeling out of control, and she wanted to try taking it back. She couldn't talk to Matt about it, and Amy was busy. So she wrote to her child instead, using the nickname she'd formed for their unborn babe.

Little Resident,

I know it's a strange name to call you, but your daddy is a doctor, your mama is a midwife and you might be one day too. Since you're residing in me at the moment, it kinda fits.

I don't even know why I'm writing this. I think it's for me more than for you, my tiny peanut. You've caused all kinds of trouble already, but that's not your fault.

I know things are messed-up right now, but I want to make you a promise. Here and now. Reassure you of a few things too.

Your father is the best. Literally. My best friend. The best doctor I've ever known. He's the best son to your grandma, and he'll be the best dad. He doesn't think that, but that's your daddy. He never sees what I see, and maybe one day you can show him just how amazing he is.

Just bear with him. He might need a minute now and again to get on the same page.

Your dad and I didn't have the easiest start in life. Our parents were...complicated. It made me independent and your dad stubborn. Guarded. We won't always get it right, but the point is, little one, we will be here. For you. To love you. Fiercely. Unconditionally. For ever.

Whatever happens, my child, I can promise you two parents who will never stop doing everything they can to make you happy. To keep you safe. To keep each other safe. To love you fiercely, just as we love each other.

Always.

Love you, baby.

Mummy

She'd gone to bed right after stacking the baby's things up in her room. She left her notepad on top, figuring she could show the list to Matt later. Maybe he'd want to go back to the store with her, save the delivery driver bothering.

When she'd woken up, it was morning. Matt's car still wasn't there. His bed was still rumpled from the night they'd spent together. Her phone was devoid of messages. He'd not checked in, at home or on her phone.

Well, that's your answer.

He'd obviously not changed that much.

She headed to work in a fog, barely remembering the bus ride to the Ashford. She went to get changed, slamming her locker shut in frustration. The nausea was gone now, but she still felt sick to her stomach. She was desperate to see Matt this morning, but she hated herself for it. She'd already texted Amy, asking her if she fancied catching up after work. She didn't fancy an awkward night at Chez Loren.

She slammed her locker again, just for something to do. She had fifteen minutes till the beginning of her shift, but she wasn't in a rush to get to handover. She'd seen what life would be like living with Matt, raising a child together. They'd fallen at the first damned hurdle. Standing there holding a deformed stuffed dog in that store, she'd wondered whether Matt was really capable of being there for her.

She didn't like the feeling of going it alone now as much as she'd thought she would. She'd had her first glimpse of life as a single mother, doing things on her own. She could do it, she knew, but with Matt there? Wondering whether he resented them both? Wishing he was with someone else? She'd considered that too. She couldn't lie and say it hadn't crossed her mind. That he'd just leave them to go and hook up with someone. He was technically single, after all. Would still be single when the baby was here. She fixed an errant lock of hair that had escaped from her tight ponytail, checking herself over. Trying to bring some semblance of control to herself. She needed order, and work.

'Morning!' George trilled as she got to the nurses' station.

'Good morning,' Molly said, too busy looking at the

boards behind him to notice her friend gawking at her. 'What have we got today?'

'Well, we had quite the trauma last night,' Liam said from behind her. Molly turned to see he and Matt both standing there, looking exhausted. 'Room Three, Caroline Sellers. Had twins via Caesarean section last night. Both babies are doing well, thirty-four weeks and three days delivery.'

Matt came and stood at her side. She felt his fingers brush her hand, and she crossed her arms across her chest before she took them in hers. He frowned, moving a fraction closer. She moved back, away from him, pretending to look at the board with a little more scrutiny even though she already knew what it said. Liam was still talking to the rest of the team about the operation.

'Are you okay?' Matt grazed his side against hers, but she kept her arms folded. 'Sorry I didn't get a chance to call you after I left the shop. I tried, but my stupid phone had died. I forgot to charge it the night before.'

The fact that he hadn't put his phone on charge because he was too busy taking her to bed didn't need saying, but Molly was clicking the pieces into place. He'd been at work the whole time, and he'd tried to call her. She felt herself thaw a little, but the seed of doubt had already been sown there. In her head. She didn't want to be the one who was always calling the hospital to see if he was there. Sure, he was there for her now, attentive. What about when their baby was born—would the novelty wear off? He had needs, after all, and they weren't a couple.

'Molly?' He'd turned to her now. 'Are you angry with me?'

'Yes,' she half hissed. 'Not now, okay?'

'Yes now,' he retorted, not lowering his voice one iota. 'I'm sorry I didn't call you.'

'You left me in the shop!'

Liam looked their way, but Matt didn't even flinch. He reached for her hands, and she brushed him off. Checked to see if anyone was watching. They were all getting on with their work, which was just what she was supposed to be doing.

'I told the stock boy to tell you I had a work emergency and to catch a cab home; did he not tell you?' When Molly shook her head, Matt looked as if he wanted to go back and murder him. He cursed under his breath several times before visibly composing himself. 'Molly, I'm sorry. I did ask him to tell you. My phone is never usually dead, you know that. Did you get anything from the shop?'

She nodded stiffly. 'Yeah, I got a few things. They're in my room if you want to look. You don't have to be sorry,' she added, pretending that she didn't give a jot about where he'd been. 'You don't owe me an explanation for your whereabouts. We're not together. The baby's not here yet.'

She walked away and joined George while Liam and the head midwife on the night shift were discussing the patients on the ward, what procedures were scheduled for the day, what clinics were running. Matt went and stood beside Liam, but his eyes were locked on Molly the whole time.

'What's his deal?' George whispered out the side of his mouth. 'You two had a fight?'

'Something like that,' Molly half whispered back. George waved to Matt, who realised he'd been spotted and glanced away. 'Stop it!'

'Hey,' George countered. 'I'll have you know that over

the last few weeks, your man and I have got along a little better.'

'Really,' Molly dead-panned. 'Best buddies, eh?'

George stifled a laugh. 'No, but he has been a lot nicer.
All the staff have said the same thing.'

Matt was staring at her again, and she glared right back
this time. A smile tugged at his features, till he shut it
down and continued looking at her intently. As if he could
make her less mad by just staring her anger down. She ignored him. She was annoyed with him.

All the staff have said the same thing.

George's words pinballed around her skull.

'Really, he's been nice to everyone?'

'I know,' George murmured. 'We couldn't believe it either, but to be honest... I quite like him now.'

'You what?'

She said it a little too loud, and the surrounding conversations dropped from a low ebb to a pin-dropping silence.

'Something to share, Molly? Before we get to work?'
Liam's brow was raised, but she didn't get a sense of irri-
tation from him. More like mild amusement. At his side,
Matt was positively smirking. He couldn't have known
what they were talking about, but he'd probably worked
out it involved him.

As she glanced around her, the mood did seem quieter somehow. Calmer. Less tense, even with Matt looking every inch the surly doctor he normally was. 'No, no.
Nothing to add, Doctor.'

'Are you sure?' Matt's voice cut across the room. 'Nothing else?'

What is he doing?

She was about to shake her head, say no, when she saw his eyes dip to her stomach.

The baby? He wanted her to declare it to everyone, right here?

She raised her brows in question at him, but he raised them right back. Tilted his head with a tiny nod.

Is he...challenging me?

She thought about what his angle might be. He was wanting her to tell their news, here. With him there.

Maybe, just maybe, this was his way of being there for her. Everyone was looking at her like she was about to drop some truth bomb. The second truth bomb of the week.

He'd already told her that he'd notified HR about their relationship. He'd gone and declared them to be living together, with a baby on the way. They had to, given their working hours and HR requirements. The Ashford HR department apparently didn't even react. When Matt had relayed the conversation back to her, she'd read in between the lines. Although HR had these rules, either they highly valued the pair of them working together and wouldn't rock that boat—or they'd thought that the relationship was already there in some way or another.

George elbowed her in the side, bringing her back out of her head and into the room with all the tension.

'Sorry.' She smiled at everyone, looking at no one. 'It's nothing.'

She studied Matt, expecting him to be laughing or smirking, but his face...

She realised what he was doing under the bravado of his usual pushing. His challenge. He'd told HR, and now he wanted her to tell everyone. She thought of what George had said, about him making the effort at work. She'd not really noticed, already knowing the true, full picture of Matthew Loren.

That's what he's been showing them. Himself. He's been trying, this whole time.

She locked eyes with him, saw his tight, grim jawline clench, and the words came easily. The crowd had already started to disperse, to get to the day.

'I do have some news.' Molly stopped them all. She smiled as she thought of what she was about to tell them. It was good news. Exciting. 'I'm pregnant.' She moved from George's side, taking in his open mouth, and the faces of her other colleagues, as she went to stand next to Matt. The minute she was near him, he reached for her hand, pulling her to him. 'Matt and I are having a baby.' His hand gripped tighter when she spoke his name. She could see George's face, close to exploding with shock and surprise, and looked up at Matt.

This time, his expression was one she'd seen only a few times, and had searched for ever since. After they'd first lain in bed together. When they were sitting on the sofa, watching the television and talking about baby names. He looked down at her with such peace, his face was serene.

He'd begged her with his eyes to tell the people in their lives about their child, but this…this was like declaring they were together too. She just…had to test the theory. Do what she always did, match his stake and up the ante. What she was doing was dangerous, but she couldn't live in limbo. She had to know.

As if he knew what was going through her head, he finally reacted as people around them came out of their stupors to congratulate them. He brought their clasped hands up to his face, rubbing them against the hard stubble on his cheek, then kissed her hand. Just two soft, short little pecks. Comfortable, like they'd done it for ever. Pulling back, Molly managed to see his calm smile broaden before George was in her face.

'Molly! You're having a baby! Really?' He was stunned but beaming his head off. 'O-M-G, does Amy know? How do you feel? How many weeks?'

She laughed, feeling Matt's hand slide out of hers as George and a couple of her other colleagues took her off to dissect the news. When she looked back, he was already walking down the corridor, deep in conversation with Liam.

Before she knew it, they were back to the job. Everyone knew about the baby she was having with Matt, and she was working away as normal. After she delivered her second healthy baby of the day, she realised that she felt happy. Settled. Like a weight had been lifted off her shoulders. She couldn't wait to see what happened next. Maybe they really did have this thing all sorted out.

'Ready?' she asked, grinning, when she got to the main doors of the Ashford that evening. Matt was in his usual spot, leaning against one of the pillars like he was shooting a *GQ* cover. She felt her stomach flip at the sight of him.

'Not quite,' he returned, taking her into his arms and slipping the handbag off her shoulder to carry himself. 'I need to nip back in. Come with me?'

Her feet were killing her, but she nodded anyway. 'If you're quick, I had visions of a hot soapy bath in my near future.'

They walked towards the consultation rooms, and just before he opened the door to Room Four, he whispered into her ear. 'I have a vision of that too now. I might just have to get my loofah out.'

She chuckled, following him into the room. 'Promises, promises.' He motioned to the bed in the corner. 'What?'

He was smiling, but she could see his nerves hiding behind it.

'Don't be mad. I know you have an ultrasound booked, but I thought for the first time... Well, we have all these machines.' He pressed his lips together. 'I wanted it to be just us. What do you say?'

Molly was already heading towards the bed, his hand in hers.

'I think it's a great idea. Are you really ready?'

His smile dipped, and she hated herself for second-guessing him.

If he's not ready, he wouldn't be doing it, she chided herself.

'I'm ready,' he said. 'Let's meet the little one, eh?'

The gel on her belly was colder than she'd expected. She felt a pang of guilt for her patients; she'd never realised it was such a jolt. She only saw the joy of the scans, or the horror of finding something awful on the screen and having to break the news. It hit a lot differently when it was your stomach, your baby.

'I'm scared,' she admitted. 'Pathetic, eh?'

Matt shook his head, his hand holding the instrument an inch from contact. She noticed the slight shake and felt better.

'No, baby,' he soothed. 'Not at all.' He took her hand in his, around the instrument.

'No peeking,' she said urgently, realising that on the screen the baby might show them more than she wanted to know. 'At the sex, I mean. I know it's too early anyway, but—'

He laughed. 'Spoil-sport. But I'm not that good.'

Her sceptical brow raise had him chuckling again.

'Okay, fair point. No peeking.' He leaned down and spoke to her stomach. 'You listening in there, little peanut? Cross your legs.'

Her laughter made her tummy jiggle, the gel wobbling. 'Ready?'

Their eyes locked, both of them taking in the moment before pushing on.

Is this how every parent-to-be feels? It's worrying, terrifying, scary. Elating, exciting, daunting. I'd run out of adjectives to describe this moment and still not do it justice.

'Let's do it,' she said.

Together their hands pushed down, made contact with the gel. Matt had turned the screen away from her, like they always did for patients. She found herself holding her breath as Matt's eyes roved over it. When he broke out into a broad grin, she relaxed.

When the screen turned, Molly had to remind herself to breathe. The black and white image was clear. Healthy. Everything where it should be, right on track. Teeny, fragile, but there. A scrap of life, made from love. Molly felt like her throat was blocked off and she was unable to speak. A single tear rolled down her cheek.

'I can't believe that's our baby,' Matt uttered, his voice a half-cracked whisper. He reached up and pointed to the tiny little flutter on the screen. 'Strong heart, just like his mama,' he said, and she saw that face again. The serene look she'd grown to crave seeing. 'Hello, baby.' He leaned in and dropped a kiss right above the gel. 'I love you so much.' His smile dimmed when he saw Molly's face.

'What's wrong?' He pushed the screen closer to her line of vision. 'Everything's perfect, Mol. You're perfect.' He snapped a couple of photos, then wiped the gel away and took her into his arms. 'Don't worry, please. That's my job now.'

She managed to clear the slab of emotion crushing her chest, shaking her head with a watery smile. 'I'm not worried,' she reassured him, squeezing him tight to her. 'I'm happy.' She took the photos from the machine, and the pair of them sat on the bed, looking at every detail of the images. Enjoying the moment together.

That night, when they arrived home, Matt put both photos on his fridge, in pride of place. When he took Molly to his bed later in the evening, he grabbed the pictures and tucked them into the frame of a photo of them together on his nightstand.

'We're going to be a family,' he whispered to her before she drifted off, safe and warm in his strong, solid arms. 'I'm going to take care of you both, for ever.'

That was the last thing she heard before sleep claimed her.

We're going to be a family.

She was starting to believe it might all just work out.

After that day, their announcement spread like wildfire. Everyone hid their shock well, and congratulated the pair of them. Molly and Matt settled into life in their new roles. Went to sonograms together, him holding her hand and marvelling at the heartbeat like any new dad would. She found herself nesting at his house, spending any time off work together getting ready for the baby. Relaxing on the couch. Going to see Duncan and Sarah, watching them light up and Sarah get teary-eyed over the baby photos.

It was almost, almost perfect. Her bedroom was barely used; she spent her nights being held in his arms. She felt so close to having the life she'd always wanted, with a man she'd never dreamed of doing it with. As her belly grew, so did her feelings. She tried to ignore the warnings of her shields, make herself wait for the other shoe to drop.

When Amy had said she was moving out, Molly had worried she'd lost her home. Now she thanked God for Anton and his proposal. She and Matt never talked about themselves, their relationship—whatever it was at this point, they didn't make a label for it. She simply waited and hoped. Looked for a sign. But when it came in the form of a phone call the day before they were to leave for his mother's wedding, it was the last thing she'd been expecting. The other shoe suddenly felt like a boot on her neck. Crushing her windpipe, and her foolish misplaced heart.

The tutor running the birthing class that morning was a nice woman named Jessica Sims. Molly had met her a few times over the years, had referred her patients to Jessica's classes. She was one of those earth mother types, always cheerful, patient. Till today.

'Ahem…' She cleared her throat pointedly, and Matt sheepishly took the disposable nappy off his head. He'd been wearing it and pretending to be a toboggan driver, sitting on a foam mat with a rather pregnant Molly in between his legs, twisting their bodies from side to side as if they were heading down an icy slalom.

Molly had been too busy trying to laugh without peeing herself to tell him off. It felt like she had stuffed a bowling ball down her top sometimes, her growing stomach a marvel to them both. Matt couldn't stop touching it, talking to the baby. Touching her, telling her how beautiful she was. How radiant. Even when she developed a craving for pickled onions straight out of the jar, and moaned incessantly every time she tried to get comfortable on the couch, or slide her tired and heavy body into the bath, he'd been there for all of it. Pickled onion runs at midnight? No problem. He'd been there, the whole time…and they were still them. Friends who made each other laugh.

'Sorry.' Matt was contrite, but Molly could see the suppressed mirth in his eyes. 'Do continue.'

Nodding, Jessica resumed the breathing exercises. Matt's hands wrapped around Molly's, and the pair of them breathed and hee-hee-*hoo*-ed together in time with the tutor.

'This is some irony, you know,' he whispered. 'Us learning all this when we could probably teach the class.'

'I know,' Molly said out of the corner of her mouth as Jessica started to demonstrate panting for the head. 'But since you won't have a baby flying out of your hooha in a few weeks, maybe you should count yourself lucky.' Jessica shot him a look that could cut glass. 'Shh, we're going to get told off again.'

'Well, your panting leaves a lot to be desired,' he scoffed, his voice a low rumble in her ear. That rumble ran through her entire body, and she had to remind herself that they were in public. 'You sound constipated.' He made a grunting noise, pulling a face.

Her belly-laugh rang out loud in the room before she could stop it. Jessica was not impressed. Mercifully, they got through the rest of the exercises without further trouble, though she did see a couple of the other fathers crease up when they thought Jessica wasn't watching.

When it was time to practice swaddling the baby, Jessica gave Matt the only headless doll in the box. 'Sorry, Doctor,' she said. 'Budget cuts, you know. These things cost money.'

Matt took the headless babe without a word, waiting till Jessica was out of his proximity to roll his eyes at Molly.

She took the doll from him and swaddled it in seconds before passing it back to Matt. 'Congratulations, what shall we call him?'

Matt looked serious for a moment, taking in the space where a doll head should have been.

'Headless Hal,' he replied, putting the baby into the sling of his arm and cradling it close.

The fathers all laughed their heads off, the wives rolling their eyes but laughing too.

'Your husband is a handful,' one said to Molly, rubbing her own bump. 'I bet your labour will be hilarious!'

Molly giggled. 'Don't remind me. We're not married. He's…' She hesitated, just for a split second.

'We're best friends,' Matt said, putting the doll on the table and wrapping his arms around Molly from behind, cradling her bump with his hands. He kissed her on the cheek. 'And you're right.' Molly felt him squeeze her a little tighter. 'I am a handful, right, Mol?'

She was saved from answering. Jessica asked the class

to return their dolls and began handing out course feedback sheets for them to complete. She gave theirs to Molly, deliberately avoiding Matt's waiting hand. But all Molly could focus on was the look of surprise the pregnant woman had given her.

We're best friends, he'd said.

From the expression on the woman's face, Molly knew what she was thinking. For the first time in weeks, she felt the bubble walls thin around them. He'd only spoken the truth. It didn't mean she had to like it.

After the class, they'd gone out to lunch, and she'd almost forgotten that look. Matt was his usual self, talking about work, what they had left to do before the baby's arrival. He'd dropped her off at home, and gone to football practice, kissing her like he usually did before she waved him off. She was heading to the bath when she saw the blinking light on his answering machine. She pressed Play and headed for a drink from the fridge, listening to the message. After that, she couldn't stop seeing the pregnant woman's face in her head. *Best friends* rang out loud in her head on repeat.

She listened to the message four more times, and headed up the stairs, all thoughts of a hot bath forgotten.

The minute Matt walked through the door after football, he knew something was wrong. The air was different.

'Honey, I'm home,' he called, as he'd taken to doing whenever he entered the house. She didn't answer, but he heard movement from the second floor. Moving fast.

'Molly?' he called from the hallway. 'Hello?'

The second he headed up the stairs, towards the noise, and saw her standing in her bedroom, it felt like his breath was being sucked out of his lungs. Her bump was prominent now under her clothing. She looked beautiful, but the way she looked at him nearly knocked him off his feet.

'Molly, what's going on? Where are you going?'

'You don't want this,' Molly spat at him. 'You never did. You said so at the class today—we're best friends. Not some married couple having a kid. I knew I was trapping you by having this baby. I knew it, and God knows I didn't want to. Damn it, it was the last thing I ever wanted. Why would I?' She was crying, the tears streaming down her face. 'I loved my best friend, just as he was. I didn't want to change a thing about him, the same way he didn't want to change me. I should never have told you how I felt that first night.'

'Don't be ridiculous.' Matt took the clothes out of her suitcase as fast as she was putting them in. 'Where the hell is this coming from? I don't regret the baby; I love the baby. You love the baby. I'm glad you told me.'

'Why?' She rounded on him, throwing a pair of socks at him in frustration. 'Why? Why are you glad? You don't feel the same! You never did!' She spotted one of her tops in his hands and snatched it back. 'We should never have slept together. It ruined everything!' She threw the top into the case, then tried and failed to get it zipped up. He came over just as she sat down on it.

'Move,' he mumbled. 'Please,' he added when she glared at him. She went to stand, but at this stage in her pregnancy, it wasn't easy. She'd blossomed over the last few months. Bloomed. He'd loved every minute of watching his child grow. He put his hand out, but she slapped it away angrily.

'No. I can do this, on my own.' She flailed like a turtle

for what felt like hours, but Matt's hands finally encircled hers, and she was lifted up. He sat her at the edge of the bed, kicking the case underneath.

'I'm still leaving,' she sulked. 'Amy will come and help me pack.'

He was on his knees in front of her, but Molly couldn't bring herself to look at him. If she locked on to those troublesome baby blues, she'd never go. She'd never leave. And she had to. She just had to.

'I don't want you to leave. What's happened?' He sounded so desperate, so disbelieving. 'What don't I know? I left for football practice, and everything was fine!' He was looking around her room, his eyes searching for a reason for her change of heart. She watched him.

How could I have thought any differently?

She realised she was punishing him, but the pain was all hers.

A leopard can't change its spots. He's not to blame.

He'd always told her who he was. She was mad at herself as much as him.

'Victoria called for you today.'

She'd expected his face to fall, his cheeks to blush with embarrassment. A flinch at least but he just looked puzzled.

'Who?'

'Victoria. She left a message. I checked the machine while you were out.'

'Who?' Matt repeated, his brows furrowed over wide eyes.

'Don't,' she warned. 'I'm not stupid, Matt. Victoria. She sounded lovely, said she looked forward to seeing you again after the great day you'd had together.' She felt like a crazy woman, but this was how he made her feel. The minute she'd heard that sweet female voice on the machine, the bubble they'd hidden in for the last few months had popped. They'd slept together every night, but they hadn't had sex for a while. She'd thought his concern about hurting her was over the top, but she'd never considered that he'd been getting it elsewhere.

Stupid idiot.

She watched him, waited for realisation to take hold. It did, but he didn't crumple. He looked almost...relieved.

He is. Her heartbroken mind was talking to her. *It was never going to work. Pull the plug before he does it to you.*

Images of her mother crying flashed into her head. Every time she'd put all her eggs in one basket for a man who ultimately proved not to be worth it. Not to care. To find leaving all too easy. That voice on the answering machine had been a wake-up call for Molly. Amy had said she could stay with her and Anton, get sorted. She just needed to go, stop the cycle of this heartbreak. He was going to meet someone else, one day. Even if he didn't, he wouldn't be celibate for ever. If he even was now.

'That's why you're leaving?' His voice was a little less desperate. 'Because of a message from a woman?'

'Not just that. Earlier today, at the class!'

Matt frowned. 'The marriage thing?'

'Yes!'

His frown deepened, making him look tense. 'But...I just stepped in. It's no one's business what we are to each other, Mol. We are best friends—that wasn't a lie!'

Molly bit her lip. 'I know that, but the look—' She sighed. 'It doesn't matter anyway. Please, just let me go.'

Matt's hands were on her thighs now as he leaned close to her face, still on his knees.

'I don't want you to leave. And especially not because of some woman. I haven't done anything with anyone since before you moved in.'

'Oh.' Molly wanted to argue the other points, but his revelation had floored her. 'Why?'

His head snapped back in shock. 'Oh, I don't know. Maybe because I slept with my best friend. Had the best sex of my life. After that, I didn't feel the need to go elsewhere.'

He was speaking in sarcastic tones, as if she wasn't getting what he was trying to say. It irked her.

'You don't have to be flippant about it.'

'Flippant?' He laughed, a mirthless, hollow sound. 'I came home to find you packing, crying your eyes out. I'm upset. Why didn't you call me?' His gaze dropped to the full holdall next to her closet. 'Were you just going to leave without telling me first?'

'I—'

'What were you going to do? Leave another note?' He looked around. 'Where is it then?'

'What are you talking about?'

'The note!' He stood and started pacing the room. 'Telling me you're leaving without dealing with the serious stuff. Again.'

The memory of their first night together slammed back into her head. The note she'd left the morning after. She'd escaped then. The memory of it made her cheeks burn. She was escaping now too, but only to protect them both. Again.

'It's not like that.'

He was leaning against the door-jamb now, eyeing her from his cross-armed position. She noticed how bunched his forearm muscles were. He looked as if he was relaxed, but Molly knew he was taut with emotion. He bristled with anger, just below the surface.

'The woman, Victoria? She's the owner of that baby shop we went to the first time. She was ringing because I'd been in again. We still don't have the cot. So I sorted it today, and I asked her to call me when they had some more information about the custom cot bumpers I wanted.'

'It was her?' Molly's spine chilled as she replayed the voice in her head. It hadn't said anything about a date.

You assumed.

She cringed. Feeling foolish. 'I'm sorry. I jumped to conclusions.'

'I understand.' His jaw tightened. 'If I'd heard a message from a man asking for you, I wouldn't have liked it either. There really hasn't been anyone else, Mol. Not since the first time with you. I mean it.'

'Okay,' Molly said slowly, 'but maybe I should move out?'

This time I'd been wrong, she thought to herself. *But next time I might not be. Why wait for it to happen? When I have our child to explain it away to?*

She thought again of her mother, always off with some new love or another.

Will it be the same for us? Me waiting for him at home, dreading the beep of the machine? I can't, won't, live like that again.

Yes, she'd jumped to conclusions on this occasion. It didn't change the facts she would have to face down the line. Eventually, Matt would need to have his own life back, and so would she. This way, perhaps they could still try to salvage the friendship. Raise their child with love. She knew they both wanted that. She pushed down her feelings and brought her shields up high. 'It was only meant to be temporary, staying here with you. The baby and I will have to get our own place eventually anyway.'

'Yeah, well, I don't agree.' Matt was coldly angry. 'You can't just leave without telling me what's really going on. One message from a woman, that's it, and you're jumping ship?'

'I heard you.' This was it. Time to lay all her cards on the table. She needed to tell him as much as she could without revealing her feelings for him. That was what had got her here in the first place. She needed to get out from under all of this, before he ended up hating her. Driving him away was something she couldn't risk. Child or no child, she couldn't live without him in her life. 'The day we found out, about the baby, I heard you talking on the phone to your mum. I tried not to think about it too much, but you don't really want this life, Matt. You never have. The white picket fence idea has always felt like a prison to you.'

'That's…not true.'

'It is.' She reached across the bed for her handbag. Stood to leave. 'I know it is. I know you, Matt, and you will do the honourable thing. Always. I shouldn't have let you. You always do the right thing, and I love you for it—'

She heard him gasp and didn't trust herself to look anywhere near his eyeline. 'I think we had the best intentions, but living and working together, playing house, the baby— it's blurring lines that we just don't need to cross. Not any more.' She put the bag onto her shoulder, standing right in front of him. 'We both need our own lives. I think me moving in with Amy, till I find a place—it's for the best. You can still have your life; I can have mine. We can raise the baby together. Just like before. No courts, no stress. We can raise our child without the need for labels, right?'

'Is that what you really want?' He had moved out of the doorway now, but he was still so close. Searching her eyes, his baby blues roving all over her face. 'Molly, I don't want you to go, but if you're telling me that you really want this, I'll step back.'

'I do want this,' she said firmly, and watched as the light went out in Matt's eyes. He'd dulled visibly before her. She imagined it must have been him seeing the change in her.

We have to stop hurting each other like this.

He'd been looking like this for weeks, so upset at times. So drawn into himself, as if keeping in his truth was just too much for him. What about when the baby arrived? Would the novelty wear off in months, or years? She couldn't be so stupid as to think that he would turn into a monk until their child was eighteen. 'We need our old lives back, Matt, just a little. This way, we can both…breathe.'

She could stop the codependent feelings she'd been having. The fantasy that Matt would declare he loved her too. Like she loved him. As more than a best friend. As the woman, the only woman, he'd ever see his life playing out with. She needed to do this on her own, as she always should have done. Realise her own dream of being a mother, even if her life plan didn't look quite the same as the one she'd had in her head.

'You can't…breathe around me?' He moved aside, his movements clunky till he sank down onto her bed, his legs half collapsing beneath him. 'I never wanted this, Mol.'

'I know,' she said gently.

'Oh, you really don't. You don't have the first clue.' His dull eyes focused on a pink heeled shoe, abandoned on the floor where it had dropped out of her case. 'I'll have your things packed properly and sent to wherever you want. I'll let you get on.' He suddenly stood and walked right past her, his head firmly fixed forward. 'I'll head up to Mum's wedding venue early. Give you some time to move out. I'll pass on your excuses to her.'

She had expected him to go to his room, to go downstairs and pour a Scotch, but he was in and out of his room within moments. She watched as he headed down the stairs, suit bag and suitcase in his hands. The front door shut with a slam, and then she was alone in the house they'd shared.

She sank to the floor and cried her eyes out.

My mother gets married today.

He'd woken in a foul mood and had to keep reminding himself of the fact that it was a happy day. A happy day, which required smiling and pretending to be in a good mood. Even though his life had been completely blown apart and hung around him in tatters. The last thing he felt like doing was grinning at a camera. Watching true love against the odds as Duncan and Sarah promised themselves to each other for the rest of their lives. He hadn't been at his mother's first wedding, for obvious reasons, but he knew how it had ended. The fact Sarah was even looking forward to today was a testament to her strength and resilience, Matt knew. That she could be so happy and eager to live her life with Duncan after what his father did to her. It was maddening. He didn't know why anyone would willingly go through this again. It hurt too much.

Hence the mantra he kept repeating to himself, over and over. Anything to stop him from calling Molly, telling her that he would rather die than see her move out. That the office turned nursery was the best thing he'd ever put together. Better than any operation. Any life he'd saved. He'd loved every minute of the last few short months, and going back to an empty house was just...

He wanted to get in his car and drive straight down the motorway, turn up outside Amy's place and beg Molly to come back with him. To stay in his hotel room, in his bed, be there when he walked his mother down the aisle. To be there after too. Every day after.

It was barely dawn. He'd not done more than doze, despite the half bottle of whisky he'd ordered up to the room the instant he'd arrived. The rest of the night had been a mess of cold showers, unsent texts and angry conversations with his father inside his mind. Matt had declared him dead the minute he'd walked out on them, so why was he bothering to give him head space now? He was lying here, in the hotel room he'd booked to share with Molly, having imaginary discussions with his stupid father. Blaming him for how things had turned out. What was the point? His dad wouldn't give a fig even if Matt did actually tell him how his actions had changed his and Sarah's lives. He was a man who didn't believe in apologies. In looking back. In that last way the two men were similar.

Matt hauled himself out of bed, clad in last night's boxer shorts and feeling more than a little parched after the alcohol the night before. He might as well start getting ready for the day. Distract himself from his phone, the keys to his Lexus that taunted him from the coffee table. After taking a shower, he went over to his suit bag hanging in the wardrobe and pulled the zipper. The second he'd done it, his hands stilled. There was another hanger, a garment placed over the top of his suit jacket and shirt.

'Molly must have put it in there,' he whispered to himself. He reached up to thumb the soft cream cotton. It was a little Babygro with black writing embroidered onto the fabric.

'Grandma's Little Devil,' it said. Obviously a gift from her to his mother. To mark the day. She must have slipped it in there before everything had been so screwed up. Tugging the tiny little item of clothing off its fastener, he held it in his large hands.

Little devil, Sarah said. What if that was true though? After all, the baby was half him. A quarter his father. He went to fold the Babygro up, to tuck it into his suit jacket, but the second he moved the fabric, he heard it. The crinkle of paper.

Molly's note.

His breath rushed out of his lungs, as if she'd just walked into the room. It was a letter written by her, but not addressed to him. It was to their child. From Molly, talking about her and Matt. How they were imperfect but would be there for the baby. She believed in Matt, and the way she wrote about him cracked his heart wide open. The man she described in this letter, to the child they'd made together, stirred him. This man sounded nothing like his father. It did sound like him though.

He thought of everything from the last few months. Molly telling him how she'd seen him that first day they'd met had woken him up. Caused feelings that he'd pushed down and locked away to come knocking again. How had he been so blind? Having Molly as his best friend had brought his humanity back. Molly had been incensed when she'd heard the voicemail from Victoria.

She was jealous.

He'd thought at the time that it was just more proof they couldn't be together because she didn't trust him, but she was jealous. There was a difference. He thought of how he felt whenever he pictured another man in her life. Not just his baby's. Hell, he'd run off enough suitors of hers over the years.

He'd always told himself that he was protecting her. Had gained the skills from being the man of the house way before his time. He realised now why that protective streak towards her had been so ever-present, so strong.

I love her. I want no man touching her, because I already consider her mine. She belongs with me.

He'd cocked up. She'd probably already moved out of his place, but the letter, the Babygro—they were her way of showing him what she truly felt about him. Even though she'd left him, she'd still wanted him to know how much she trusted him. He hated himself for it. For being so weak he didn't just admit his feelings for her from the get-go. From the minute she'd told him how she'd felt about him that first day they'd met, he'd been running scared. Not from her, but from the words. From saying something he couldn't take back and then letting her down somehow. With the pressure of being so enamoured of her, of so much relying on their relationship now, he'd thought straightaway of his own father, like he always did. Took out the yardstick of his paternal influence, measuring himself against it. But Molly didn't see that. She didn't see *him* like that. The most important revelation that screamed out of the letter was something Matt hadn't expected.

He wasn't his father. Sure, he'd had to grow up in his shadow. People had prejudged him all his life. Assumed he was a bit of a flirt, a womaniser. When he was in medical school and his father was still making waves in the legal world, he'd tried to hide from the name Loren. Instead, he'd made the mistake of damn well living up to it.

'God, I'm an idiot.' He put on his suit, tucked the letter into his pocket and headed for the door. If he got on the road right now, he could still be there and back in time for the wedding. He checked his watch. It would be tight, and his mother would probably have a stroke, but...

He could tell his mum where he was going. To get Molly, to beg her to move back in with him. Into their house, their bed. He wanted to be the man he'd thought he could never be. Molly was the woman all along who saw it in him. Who understood just who he was. She made him *be* a better man. *Want* to be the best man. The version of Matthew Loren that he was when he was with her. He didn't need or want to stay away from her a second longer. He needed to stake his claim on his family in no uncertain terms. *For ever.*

He reached for his phone and dialled her number. After grabbing his keys, he yanked open the hotel door, and heard ringing. Molly was standing there in her maternity bridesmaid dress. She looked like a vision. Pretty in pink. She waggled her cell phone in her hand.

'You rang?'

Mascara, especially supposed waterproof mascara, was the biggest con women today were sold. Well, the second.

The first was that every girl would grow up to meet her Prince Charming. That was a huge pack of lies too. By the time Molly had turned up on the doorstep of where Amy and her fiancé lived, she was a huge snotty mess, streaked with make-up and sobbing into the bag of doughnuts she'd stopped to buy on the way over.

'Hi,' she keened when Amy opened her flat door. 'I brought you wine.' She waggled the bottle at Amy, who took it and brought her inside with a comforting arm. 'The doughnuts are for me, and the baby.' Thinking of her fatherless child made her even worse, and she burst into fresh tears.

They both sagged onto the couch and Amy poured the wine into a glass. 'Anton's working late,' she told her crying friend. 'He sends his love.'

Molly balanced the doughnut bag on her rather pronounced stomach. Amy took a large gulp of wine while Molly sucked the sugar off her fingers, one at a time. She offered a doughnut to Amy, who took it with a grateful smile.

'Where's Matt now?' she asked when they'd both finished scoffing, and Molly had filled her in on the drama.

Molly shook her head. 'Not sure. I think he went to the hotel. He took his suit. It was awful. I accused him of sleeping around!'

'You reacted,' Amy comforted. 'You're only human.'

'I just didn't recognise her voice. When I heard her, I lost it. I've been stupid to think that he wouldn't be with another woman eventually. I'd hoped...'

'You wanted to be with him, properly.'

Molly just about managed to nod. She needed a second to get over saying it out loud. 'Yep, I know. Because I'm in love with the father of my child, the best friend I have secretly fancied for years. Well, anyway, I made a big scene and started packing my bags. He said he didn't want me to move out, but I was just awful to him. I panicked. I was truly awful, and that was it. I left.'

'He said he didn't want you to leave?' Molly shrugged. 'What did he say about the woman on the machine?

'He knew straightaway who it was. He'd been to the store that day and ordered stuff for the baby. He was really upset, hurt…I think.'

'So, you love him, and by the sound of it he loves you too.'

'Matt doesn't do love. I overheard him talking ages ago. He said that my dream of a family life basically left him cold. I've already exploded his life.'

'Er yeah, and he ran with it.'

Molly looked at her friend, agog.

'Listen, I had my doubts about Matt. But even I can tell he loves you, and he never ran once from your news. He ran towards you, babe. *You're* the one who ran away. Go back. Right now.'

'What, have you not been listening? I've messed it all up.'

'Have you?' Amy gesticulated wildly, sloshing wine onto the couch. 'Okay, no more vino for me. Matt loves you, Molly. It's pretty obvious. All the stuff he's done, your friends saying he's changed. It's for all you, because of you and your baby. You need to sort this out. For God's sake, I am so happy.' She was beaming.

'What are you smiling about?'

Amy laughed. 'You tamed Matthew Loren and turned him into a lovesick puppy. There is hope for women out there, everywhere. Go get him, girl. Now.'

Molly thought of where Matt was right now, of how long it would take her to get to him. Well, it had already taken years and a confession or two already. Another few hours would be acceptable, if she could guarantee that she could keep him for ever after that. She didn't need the white picket fence. She didn't care about marriage. Hell, she would just rather keep dating her best friend. The father of her child. Or children. Living together, working together, raising their kids and just being them. Tangled in his sheets, and out. She just wanted him. She got up off the couch.

'I need a ride,' she said.

Amy punched the air. 'On it!'

Hours later, and a very anxious drive to the hotel still clinging to her clothing, she was at his door.

'Molly!' His smile was radiant, so bright it near blinded her, but then it was shuttered away. 'Is everything okay, with the baby?'

She touched her bump in reflex. 'The baby is great. I came to see you.'

'Well.' He looked to the floor, and her heart started to sink. 'I was on my way out.'

'Right.'

'To see you. I got your gift.'

'You did, huh?' Realisation spiked the end of her sentence. 'You were coming to see me?'

'Yes, I realised I didn't want to be anywhere without you.'

Molly felt her heart catch. 'So, you were just going to leave your mother's wedding?'

He rubbed the back of his neck with his palm, such an adorable, boyish move. Molly wanted to record it so she could replay it over and over. God, how could she ever have doubted that this man wasn't the one for her?

'Molly, I've...' He took her hand, pulling her into his room. He didn't stop pulling till she was flush against him, his arms coming around her. Caging her, like he always did. She felt so protected and safe in his arms, as if she could do anything. Be anyone, and he'd be right there, watching her. Rooting for her, looking out for her. Their baby was a lucky little one, having this kind of man in their corner. 'I've been trying not to be my father for so long that I ended up being like him anyway. Not telling you how I felt from the start. I'm so sorry.'

'I thought you might feel trapped. When I heard you on the phone...'

'I was talking to my mother and freaking out a little, that's all. I wanted the baby. God, I want him or her so bad.' His hand brushed against her stomach, a soft cradle of an embrace. The bump kicked his hand and they both laughed. 'Yes, see?' He was smiling through watery tears, and Molly couldn't take her eyes off his face. His beautiful baby blue eyes had never looked so lovely. Honest, and unfiltered. Just like him.

'I thought I'd trapped you. Any man would be lucky to have you, and here I was knocking you up after one night together, with no ring or promise of one. I felt like a cad, like I'd got you by default. I couldn't handle it, knowing that on the inside I'd be feeling so happy and you'd be looking at your friends, all loved up, and end up hating me.' His features wrestled with an unhappy thought. 'As much as it would have killed me, I'd rather have let you go than break your dreams apart and have you hating me. Listen, I think we could make this work. I—'

Molly put a finger on his lips to stop him talking.

'I don't need any of that. I never did. I don't need a fairy tale, Matt. Life isn't like that, and we both survived our childhoods by learning those lessons. The truth is, the happiest home I ever had was yours.'

Matt pulled her ever closer, trying to speak around her finger. She laughed, taking it away and silencing him with a kiss. He splayed his fingers across her hips, staking his claim on her with his hands, his mouth. When she finally pulled away, he didn't let her go far.

'You mean that? You came to the wedding to try again?' He looked down at her dress. 'You are the sexiest brides-maid I ever did see.'

She did a mini twirl in front of him. Well, with her current turning circle it was more like a large twirl, but when she saw Matt's appreciative gaze, she'd never felt sexier, more cherished, than she did right now. 'You like? Your mother has excellent taste.'

'Please don't mention my mother right now,' he groaned, reaching for her as he always did and spinning around slowly with her in his arms. 'Especially when I'm plotting approximately ten things I could do to you right now without even crumpling your dress.'

She laughed, watching as he lowered himself to his knees and put his hands around her bump. He looked up at her, and she half swooned. This man, her best friend. He was hers. Finally.

'I didn't write a letter to you, like your mummy did,' he said softly, speaking to the bump but looking straight up at Molly. 'So I thought I would set out my intentions right here. To you both.'

Molly held her breath. She didn't need him to promise

anything except to be by her side. That was all she needed. 'Matt, I don't…'

'Let Daddy talk,' he chided, and she pulled a face. He kissed her tummy in response.

'I promise you, right here, on the day of your grand-mother's wedding, that I am here. For you both. I love you.' This he said whilst locking eyes with hers, and she felt the pull of him. The delicious shivers his words sent flying around her body. 'I have loved you, always. I will love you, always. I will marry your mummy, commit to you both in every way you want me to. Hell, I will build you a darn white picket fence, and whistle while I work.'

Molly laughed, but realised she was sobbing too. 'No,' she said, after he'd stopped to draw breath. 'No, Matt, I don't need any of that. I don't need the big wedding—hell, I don't need a wedding at all. We did all of this the wrong way around. I mean, who has a baby with their best friend?' She was smiling, and he grinned right back. 'Only us. We have been ignoring what seemingly everyone else around us already knew.'

'True.' Matt muttered something about Liam. His mother had apparently had a few choice words for him too.

'My point is.' She took his hands in hers and tried to pull him to his feet. He came easily and ended up steady-ing her. 'I don't need—*we* don't need anything like that. We are not our parents, and we can just love each other and concentrate on that.'

'So, no marriage?'

Molly thought for a long moment about what her dreams had been, before all this. Before the stick had turned pink. She really did have what she wanted. Nothing else was needed.

'Nope.' She wrapped her arms around her love. 'Just this. Just us.'

'Always,' he murmured.

She caught him looking at the clock. 'What's up? Somewhere to be?'

He frowned comically. 'Well, I was supposed to pick up my date...'

She pretended to be offended, wriggling out of his grasp. He took her hands in his, and before she knew it, she was on her back on his bed.

'But...?' she breathed as he came to lie beside her.

'But...' His gaze fell on her lips, and he bent and kissed her as if he would die if he didn't.

She loved his hunger for her. She had a feeling that he would never lose it. Would always be this desperate to be close to her, as she would be to him.

'The love of my life is here, in my hotel room bed.' He waggled his eyebrows. 'And...' He skimmed his finger along the neckline of her dress, leaving a trail of her goose bumps in his wake. 'We have two hours to kill before we have to leave this room.'

Taking the time to run her fingers through his locks, Molly didn't say a thing. She was too busy enjoying the look on his face. Calm, at peace. Like all his worries had evaporated the second he touched her. She knew because she felt the same.

'Well, Mr Loren,' she said seductively. 'We'd better make them count.'

'Always,' he said, as he got to work on the fastener on her dress. 'I love you.'

And for the next one and a half hours, he showed her just how much he stood by that statement.

EPILOGUE

THE WEDDING DAY was perfect. Utterly, utterly perfect. Molly felt as if she and Matt had committed to each other too. Their vows that had been said in the hotel room, the naughty consummations afterwards, still left a blush on her cheeks and huge admiral butterflies in her stomach. Sarah and Duncan were thrilled to see her there. The pair of them together. When Molly had walked into the side room where the bride was waiting to take her second walk down the aisle, Sarah half screamed with delight.

Molly had walked down the aisle, and watched Sarah come to meet Duncan. Matt was holding his mother by the arm, looking every inch the devilish beast he was. Molly saw a couple of the waiting staff's jaws drop, but she didn't mind. They didn't matter to her and Matt. No woman would ever come between them.

Unless she had another baby, of course. It could be a girl the next time.

She hadn't meant to find out the sex, but when the scans had been done, she'd seen it with her own eyes on the screen. By accident. Their little boy was almost here, and she couldn't wait to see Matt love him too. Like he already did.

Much later that night, they were dancing together. Enjoying the smiles and waves from the other partygoers. She'd always felt like she was part of the Loren family, the good side, and she knew that was cemented now.

Matt had been amazing all day, and though he'd never let on, she'd seen him wipe a tear away when his mother said her vows to Duncan. Sarah had spoken about second chances, how a friendship had blossomed into a great love, quiet and loud in equal measure. About things being just how they were supposed to be in the universe. When Molly had looked across at Matt, she knew that he was thinking the same about them. They'd locked eyes, blue on to blue, and she saw him mouth 'I love you.' She whispered it right back.

She said it to him again now as they swayed together on the dance floor, and the second he heard it his lips were crashing down on hers.

'I love hearing you say that,' he murmured into her ear when he finally let them both come up for air.

'Come on. We always said it. Most days, if I remember rightly.'

His eyes darkened. 'Yeah, but now you know I really do.'

Molly shook her head at him. 'This new tell-all you is going to take some getting used to.'

He cocked an eyebrow. 'Well, we've got time. I take it you're moving back home?'

'That would be a yes, but only on a fifty-fifty basis.'

'Talking numbers isn't half as good as talking dirty,' he quipped. 'I know you're your own person, Molly. Whatever you want. I'll put your name on the mortgage tomorrow. It's ours. His.'

His eyes widened, and she realised what he'd said. He knew the baby was a boy!

'Shoot, Molly— I didn't mean to—'

'You saw it on the scan too! *J'accuse!*' She pulled away, pretending to be indignant with rage and sticking her finger right in his face. He laughed, flicked out his tongue and licked at her digit.

'Nurse Molly Moo, you just ratted yourself out. It's hardly either of our faults.' He grinned. 'Asher.'

'What?'

The music changed, a faster beat kicking in. Their slow sway never changed. Molly saw Sarah smile at her behind Matt and smiled back.

'Not what. Who.'

'The baby?'

'Asher Pritchard Loren. What do you think?' His nervous face was adorable.

God, I adore you.

The fact that he'd been thinking about a name at all should have surprised her, but it didn't. The name was perfect.

'I think it's settled.' She winced as her feet started barking at her. 'And I need to sit down.'

He must have felt her flinch because he rushed to comfort her.

'Chill out, it's only my feet. Stop doctoring me.'

He didn't relax. She could feel it in the muscles of his arm as he took her and led her to their seats at the head table. He said nothing though, silently observing her. She let him. She was fine. She felt great, just tired from the long last-minute drive and the even longer day. She was happy, only with swollen ankles and a heavy head. Putting her feet up on another chair, she tried to get comfortable.

Eventually Matt broke his silence. She ended up answering another twenty questions about her health and begging him not to ask the hotel to bring her a bowl of warm water for her feet in front of everyone. Finally Molly asked him to go and find her a bottle of water. Perhaps a sandwich or two. He looked torn at leaving her side, and it was almost comical. She really did feel fine, and he knew it. His protective streak was back in force, and she basked in it. She was still her, still independent, and this man accepted that. He pushed against it, sure. He turned her on and drove her mad in equal measure. She could go drinking with him, for a game of darts and it would be the best date night in the world. She knew that they'd do just that once the baby came.

Sarah and Duncan had offered to babysit earlier during a chat, and Molly had waited for some sign of discomfort from Matt. The air had changed at first, but then Matt had spoken, directing his words to Duncan, judging by his intent gaze. Those eyes were hard to ignore. Or forget.

'I think babysitting would be great. You will both be the baby's grandparents, after all.'

Duncan welled up, and his mother choked down what sounded like a little sob of relief. Joy, perhaps. Even Matt's face had flickered, and then instead of shutting down again, he'd grabbed her hand and squeezed. His features had taken on her favourite look, the one where he appeared so serene, happy, unhaunted—if that was even a word. It should be, because it described him perfectly.

'Overnight, weekends,' he was saying, his eyes so warm. 'You might get sick of us calling you. I can't wait to meet our little one, but I am also looking forward to whisking this one off once in a while too.' Molly couldn't wipe the smirk off her face.

'Try to stop us,' Duncan said, coming forward to hug Matt.

The whole day had been filled with moments like these, and the spectre of Matt's father didn't mar the event one bit. Molly had been worried, knowing that Sarah didn't deserve that. Didn't deserve any of it. The same as Matt didn't. She couldn't wait to prove to him over the years just how good he was. She'd fallen in love with her goofy, once-sullen best friend. Head over heels, in every sense of the word, but she was still her. He was still him. They were all in for each other, but their friendship meant that the people they were before were the people they were now, just better together. She had what she'd wanted all along, and what her mother had chased all her life and failed to find.

If Matt's father could see him now, he'd regret his actions. She hoped he would hear that Dr Loren was going places. They both were. Their careers were just as important to them, and their passion would only fuel them all the more. They were already talking about when she was going to return to work. How he could still be a good doctor without losing himself in work like he once did. Just a little snatch of conversation, but they both knew what today signified. Their new life started now. Together, like they'd always been.

When he took her into his arms that night, she knew. With her best friend by her side, she could do anything. She had the fairy tale ending, but in a perfect backwards

Matt-and-Molly way. She'd never had to kiss a frog to get her Prince Charming.

The happy ending to her story had been convincing the frog that he'd been a prince the whole time. Her Matt. Her everything. Matt Loren was *home*.

* * * * *

FLIGHT NURSE'S FLORIDA FAIRY TALE

DEANNE ANDERS

MILLS & BOON

For all the first responders in Florida, Cuba
and South Carolina, for their work
in the aftermath of Hurricane Ian.

CHAPTER ONE

"WHAT HAVE YOU DONE?"

Casey Johnson looked up from the crossword puzzle he had been working on for the last thirty minutes. He should have left work an hour ago, but he just didn't have the energy or the desire to face his empty house this morning. It was funny how watching someone fight for their life made you look at your own in a different light.

A pretty blonde stood above him, her face flushed red, with one baby on her hip and another in some type of sling across her chest. He searched his mind for what he could have done that would have set off Summer, his coworker and his boss's wife. The only thing he'd done in the last fourteen hours was work. Had he done something wrong on duty? Had someone complained about something he'd said or done?

The last call they'd responded to had been a rough one and the reason he had gotten himself engrossed in the daily crossword challenge. It was his way of escaping from all the horrific scenes that were sometimes part of the job. But this last call, a head-on collision, had been particularly hard to deal with. He pictured the small child they'd flown to the children's hospital in Miami. He had fought the urge to call and check on her condition ever since they had arrived back at headquarters. But sometimes not knowing was for the best. Otherwise this job could destroy you. You did everything possible for your patient, and then you had to walk away.

No, there was nothing that anyone could have been upset about on that call last night. He'd done everything in his power to keep their tiny patient alive. He just hoped it had been enough.

"Well, what did you do?" Summer's voice had lost some of its demand, but it still had a bite to it that he didn't understand.

"Maybe you could give me a hint?" Casey said as he laid down the daily paper, all interest in it gone now that he was remembering the last call of his shift. It was better to deal with Summer and whatever it was that had gotten her upset at him than to think about the patient he'd left clinging to life.

"Uh, Jo, of course." Summer juggled the baby from one hip to the other without taking her scorching glare from him.

"What about her? All I did was cover for her last night, just like she asked. It isn't like it was my fault that she got sick. It was probably that five-alarm salsa she ate at that new cantina we went to yesterday. I warned her that it would burn a hole in her stomach."

"She didn't tell you?" Summer asked, then turned away from him. "Of course she didn't. If she had, you would have talked her out of it." It was as if Summer deflated in front of him as she sunk into the chair beside him while repositioning the babies in her lap.

"Tell me what?" Whatever had Summer this upset

couldn't be good. But why did she think it was something he had done? It wasn't his fault Jo was so sick that she couldn't work her shift.

"Jo called this morning and turned in her resignation. She's leaving the island," a voice said from behind him.

He watched as his boss, Alex Leonelli, aka Prince Alexandros of Soura, stepped around him, bent down to kiss his wife and then each of his children. Casey was happy that his two coworkers had finally managed to patch things up, but there was something about that secret look that passed between them that sent a jolt of jealousy through him.

Not that he was truly jealous. He didn't need all the drama that came along with a serious relationship. He was happy with his life as it was. He had a job he loved and friends, like Jo Kemp, who he could always count on.

It hit him then what Alex had said. Jo had turned in her resignation? No. That was impossible. It hadn't been twenty-four hours since he'd last seen her. They were best friends. There was no way she would do something like that without talking to him about it first. Besides, she loved her job as flight nurse for the Key West office of Heli-Care. She'd never quit.

"Is this some kind of joke?" he asked them. "Are you two punking me?"

"Of course not," Summer said. And from the sag of her shoulders and the miserable look in her eyes, he had no choice but to believe her.

"There has to be a mistake." He'd been surprised when Jo had called to say she couldn't make her shift. She'd seemed fine earlier in the day, but there had been no missing the anxiety in her voice. He'd assumed she was worried about finding someone to cover her shift, though now that he thought about it, her voice had still seemed strained after he had reassured her that he could cover for her. So what had happened?

"She had to have given you a reason," Casey said as he stood, turning toward Alex.

"She said it was personal." Alex bent and took one of the twins from his wife.

"I tried to call her," Summer said as Casey pulled his phone from his pocket, "but she's not answering."

"Maybe she's still sleeping." Casey looked at the time on his phone, surprised when he saw that it was after eight in the morning already. "I'll just stop by on my way home and see if I can get to the bottom of this."

"I'm not sure that's a good idea," Summer said, grabbing hold of his arm as he went to pick up the duffel bag he'd dropped earlier. "Maybe you should wait until she tells you herself."

Casey patted her hand before pulling his arm away and taking his sunglasses out of his shirt pocket. "I don't think so. I know Jo. She loves her job. Something has to be wrong, and I'm going to find out what it is."

He'd heard it in her voice last night. She'd been breathless and very anxious to get off the phone. He'd assumed it was because she wasn't feeling well, but now he wasn't sure. Had she just been afraid to tell him that she was leaving?

He headed to the door. He and Jo had started at Heli-Care the same day over four years ago. He'd come to the company after flying search and rescue for the coast guard and then obtaining his nurse's license, while she had been an experienced nurse on her first flight assignment. They'd become the best of friends, and the Jo he knew wasn't afraid of anything. Especially not him.

"Casey, please tell her to call me," Summer called from behind him.

He waved back at her, acknowledging her request. By the time he finished talking with Jo and fixing whatever the problem she had, the only call she'd have to make was the one telling Alex that she had changed her mind. There was no way he was going to let Jo quit her job. And there was no way he was going to let her leave him behind. And if she didn't stay?

Choosing to ignore that thought, he blamed the sudden gnawing pain in his stomach on his last shift. He wasn't worried. Jo had been fine the day before. Whatever had happened since they'd had lunch together yesterday could be fixed. It was the fact that she hadn't told him about any of this that bothered him the most.

What could be so bad that she couldn't tell him? He'd thought they had a special friendship. One where she would be able to tell him anything. That she couldn't trust him to help her, that was the real problem. Because if she didn't trust him enough to talk to him before she did something as drastic as quitting her job and leaving town, how could he help her?

Jo sat on the floor and rubbed Moose's head. Her Great Dane had known something was wrong the moment she'd gotten off the phone, and he had spent the night trying to comfort her. Finally, unable to sleep, she'd gotten up and started the job of packing. Again.

For four years she'd stayed hidden. Four glorious years of feeling safe. She should have known it couldn't last. Nothing ever did.

"Well, Moose, we can sit here and bemoan our future, or we can start working. What will it be?" The dog's large tongue shot out and licked her from collarbone to cheek in one swipe. "Yeah, I don't want to do it either, but we don't really have a choice."

She'd spent the night going over all her options, and the only one that made sense was for her to get out of town as soon as possible. The last thing she wanted was to drag her friends into her problems. As her parents' had reminded her, she'd created the problem and it was her job to take care of it. Though as her sister had said, running away was not really taking care of anything. And then there was her brother offering to take care of the problem for her, something that would have had him spending time in jail instead of in college where he belonged. Thank goodness the courts had dealt with Jeffrey before her brother had gotten his chance.

The knock on the door startled her. Instinct had her hand going for Moose's collar while she looked around the apartment for a weapon of any sort.

The knock came again, but this time it was followed by a voice both she and Moose recognized. "Jo, open the door."

Moose pulled out of her hold, reminding her that she only remained in control of the big dog because he chose to let her. Standing, she looked down at the corner where she had been huddled then raised her hand, which held a spatula. How had that gotten there? She laid it on the kitchen counter and followed her dog to the door. A part of her, the scared part, wanted nothing more than to throw herself into Casey's big arms where she knew she would be safe from whatever it was her ex had planned for her.

Another part, the sane part, knew that would be a mistake. The last thing she needed was to let Casey know that something, or someone, had scared her. If she was lucky, he had just stopped by to check and see if she was getting over being "sick" the night before. She'd hated having to lie to him, but the alternative wasn't something that she could share. Eventually she'd have to tell him her plans, not that she had formed any, but for now Casey didn't know that she had turned in her resignation.

"Hold on a moment," she called as she tried to pull Moose away from the door so she could open it. Once the door was opened and all six feet five inches of the man she considered her best friend stood in front of her, she truly realized just how hard leaving her home and her friends was going to be. How was she supposed to walk away from here? How could she leave someone like Casey who had become so important in her life?

Her hands shook as she let go of Moose and he launched himself into Casey's arms. The dog had a special friendship with the man, just like she did. There had been a time when she'd hoped that she and Casey could be more than friends, but she'd accepted long ago that that was all Casey wanted from her. And it worked. They worked. If she occasionally suffered from a stray dream that had them participating in more romantic activities, what did it hurt? They were her secret, and something that she would never have to share with him.

And just because she still felt that little zing of pleasure that was far from friendly whenever he threw his arm around her or that painful sting of envy whenever he brought his latest girlfriend around, that wasn't a good enough reason to risk losing him and their friendship.

Though now it looked like she would be losing it anyway. Maybe she should have taken a chance for more when her friend Summer had suggested it a few months ago after Casey had broken up with his fifth girlfriend in as many months.

But none of that mattered anymore. Right now, all that mattered was that she keep him from seeing the fear that had her heart pounding with a tachycardic rhythm that it couldn't maintain if she wanted to keep standing.

"What are you doing here?" she asked as she held on to the door, hoping to stabilize her trembling hands as well as use it to help hold her up.

The look in his green eyes and the arch of one blond eyebrow told her all she needed to know. Had it been too much to hope Alex would keep the news of her resignation for at least a few hours?

She started to tell him that she was still feeling ill and he shouldn't be around her. It wasn't really a lie. She'd definitely felt better. But one look at Casey's stubborn squared-off jaw told her he wasn't going to leave until they talked.

"Come on in," she said as she opened the door. Now that her body was getting over its fight or flight instinct, she knew it was for the best to get this over with. Better to deal with him now than let the anticipation of telling him goodbye keep her tied up in knots.

Her apartment was small, a little living room, dining room and kitchen combination, with one small bedroom and bathroom in the back. When Casey walked in, it seemed to shrink even more. His head was just inches from touching the ceiling, and his shoulders barely fit through the small opening between the dining room and kitchen.

The size of him had intimidated her when she'd first met him, but within days she knew that she could trust this man to never hurt her. He didn't have a violent bone in his body.

"So it's true. You're leaving," he said as he stared down at the pile of pots and pans she had pulled out of the cabinets to pack.

"You spoke to Alex," she said. Not an answer really, but it was all she had. Admitting that she was leaving was too hard.

"You know I spoke to Alex. And when he told me that you had resigned, I told him he had to be mistaken. You'd never leave a job that you loved or a crew that is as much family as coworkers. And to do it without giving any notice? I knew he had to be mistaken." His eyes, those sweet, light green eyes that were usually filled with warmth and humor had gone hard now. "Do you know why I told him he had to be mistaken?"

She shook her head. His voice, usually booming, had gone quiet. He was angry. Very angry. At her.

And even though he was almost twice the size of Jeffrey, her ex-husband, his anger didn't scare her. She'd seen this man intubate the smallest of infants, his big hands gentle in their touch. She'd watched him carry a fragile elderly woman, who'd fallen and broken her hip, all the while reassuring her with his calming voice. She knew Casey. Knew him better than she had ever known her ex-husband. Even when he was as angry as he was at her right now, she knew she was safe.

And it wasn't just her heart that told her this. It was her body. It didn't tremble as Casey glared at her. Her eyes didn't dart around the room looking for a place to hide. She was safe with him. He was someone she could trust. Someone she could share her fear with and know that he wouldn't judge her because of the mistakes she'd made years ago.

So why hadn't she told him about her past before now? Pride? Embarrassment? Both? Her marriage had ended more than five years ago, and she still felt stupid for falling for her ex's lies.

And then there was the shame. While she knew she had been an innocent victim, she still felt shame when she thought of how she'd let her husband break her. She'd let her fear of him imprison her, freezing her in place, until she had lost the ability and the will to fight back.

Did she admit all this to Casey now? Would he still respect her when he discovered she wasn't the badass nurse he thought her to be? She guessed she'd soon find out.

"No, why?" she asked, knowing he needed to tell her, even though she already knew the answer.

"Because I knew that you would never have done something like that without talking to me, telling me first," Casey said. He'd begun to pace the six-foot path from the kitchen to her living room, making it necessary for him to turn every couple steps. She started to laugh at the sight, but she knew he wouldn't appreciate it.

"I can explain," she started, and then recognized the words as ones she used to use with Jeffrey. Why did she have to explain herself? She'd called Alex because her first responsibility was to her boss and the company she worked for. She was going to be leaving them short-staffed, and that was something she would never have done if she'd had a choice. But still, it had hurt Casey that she hadn't told him first and she couldn't help but feel bad about it.

She straightened her shoulders and began again. "I'm sorry I didn't notify you of my decision. I was going to call you later today after you'd gotten some sleep."

"What? On your way out of town?" he asked.

She didn't answer him. His words were too close to the truth.

"I just don't get it," Casey said. He stopped pacing and took a seat on the leather love seat she'd saved for months to buy. She'd decided sometime during the night that she could only take what she could load in her car. She'd have to leave it behind, just like the life she'd made here. She was leaving almost everything. Including a piece of her heart that she wasn't certain she could ever get back.

Casey ran his hands through his blond curls, which always seemed to be in the need of a trimming. "Just tell me why. Why have you suddenly decided that you need to leave? It can't be the job. You love your job."

"I do love my job," Jo said, taking a seat next to him.

"I know it's not the island, you love the Keys. Has someone made you a better offer?"

"No. Of course it's not another job. I wouldn't do that to Alex." There wasn't another job out there that would be good enough to make her leave the island and her friends.

"Is it me?" Casey asked. "Did I do something?"

"What?" His question startled her. "Why would you think it was something you had done?"

"Maybe because Summer thinks it's because of me," he said. He turned toward her, his eyes questioning her.

"Well, Summer is wrong. It has nothing to do with you," she said.

She'd known she should never have admitted her attraction to Casey to Summer. They'd been at a party. It had been late. She'd worked the night before, and they'd responded to a multicar pileup that had stayed with her long after they'd flown the last victim to a Miami trauma center. Both she and Casey had known that the young man wasn't going to survive. She'd been in a gloomy mood as she wrestled with the age-old question of why life wasn't fair. Then she'd seen Casey leave the party with another woman. Before she knew what she was doing, she'd spilled everything that she thought was wrong with the woman to Summer and why she, Jo, should have been the woman leaving with him.

It was the next morning, when she realized what she

had done, that she made the decision to put whatever feelings she had for Casey behind her. She wasn't going to be that bitter woman who wasted her time over a man who wasn't interested in her that way. Since then, no matter how much Summer had tried to get her to tell Casey how she felt, she'd refused. She had to accept their friendship for what it was. And she was glad that she had. No matter that sometimes she found herself shooting invisible arrows at the women he dated, she was happy with their relationship as it stood. She had to be.

"I'll never understand women," Casey said. His hand reached out and covered hers, but the intimacy of the act was lost on him. To him, she was just a best friend he was comfortable touching. To her, his touch reminded her of things she would never experience with him. Things that would have her blushing if he could read her mind.

"No, you never will," she said, shaking her head then laughing. "And that's probably a good thing."

"What?" he asked, before shaking his own head. "Never mind. Forget about Summer. Tell me what's wrong."

Pulling her hand from under his, she turned toward him. Did she tell him the truth? That the reason she'd moved to Key West in the first place had been because she was running away from her abusive ex-husband? Did she tell him that now she had to run again?

She didn't believe Casey had ever been afraid of anything. He'd told stories about his time in the coast guard that made her shiver with the knowledge of how close he had come to being killed each and every time they'd conducted a raid on a drug cartel's boat. How could she expect someone like him, someone who knew no fear, to understand the terror that filled her every time she thought of her ex finding her?

CHAPTER TWO

CASEY WAS TRYING his best to be patient. He'd seen how shaken Jo was when he'd arrived and had immediately known there was something very wrong. The fact that she hadn't denied that she was leaving the island made it even more evident that something had changed between the time they had left the cantina the day before and the time she had called him to cover her shift. But what?

"Is it a man?" He didn't know what made him ask the question. Maybe it was the memory of Anna leaving town all those years ago. She'd left a note stating she met someone that she truly loved. That it was the night before their wedding had just been one more turn of the knife in his heart. Could it be that Jo had met someone who'd talked her into leaving with him, too?

The silence that followed his question was all the answer he needed. He could put up a fight against Jo for leaving because of a new job or if someone had done something to upset her. He could fix that. But another man? Just the thought of Jo with another man threatened the control he had on his anger, though he knew he had no right to those feelings. They were best friends. He couldn't and wouldn't cross that line even if it left him frustrated at the moment. And besides these crazy proprietary feelings he was having, he had no weapons to use if she had fallen for some man, even if he knew right away that he couldn't be worthy of his Jo.

But she wasn't his. Not that way. There was no way to win this fight.

"So do you love him?" he asked.

"Love him?" Jo asked, her voice hoarse and her eyes wide as she looked up at him. "No, I don't think I ever did really. And that's on me. A lot of this is on me."

Her hands seemed to tremble as she ran them across her face, rubbing at her eyes that were red and swollen. Maybe she had been sick the night before. But still, her answer didn't make any sense. If she didn't love this man, why was she leaving with him? None of this made sense.

"Just tell me what's going on, Jo. Whatever it is, I can help."

He waited as she took a deep breath then looked him in the eyes. Was it possible that their chocolate brown color was even darker? Or was it just the haunted, desperate look she gave him?

"I don't know where to start. It all seems so ridiculous, so crazy. Like one of those made for TV movies that come on in the afternoon. But it's real. Do you know what I mean? It's like when we see some of those accidents our patients get themselves into and we say that we couldn't make this stuff up."

He just nodded. He had her talking now, and he didn't want to interrupt her. If she was in some type of trouble, they'd find a way to fix it.

"I met Jeffrey at a company party that was for my father's retirement. They were both partners in the same law firm, and my father thought a lot of him. My father said he went at a case like a dog after a bone. I didn't realize then that I would become the bone in that analogy." Jo looked around the room, and her lips turned down as they began to tremble. "I thought it was over. All of it. I thought I would be safe here."

"You are safe. I'll keep you safe. I promise," Casey said. If it was this ex she was afraid of, he would make it a point to have a talk with the man.

Jo suddenly stood. "How about I make us some lemonade? I have a bunch of lemons I can't take with me."

"That sounds good," Casey said, though his stomach had become a churning acid filled pit since he'd learned of Jo's leaving. And now? Now, he just wanted to punch something after seeing how scared she was.

He followed her into the small kitchen and found the pitcher sitting in a pile of dishes on the cabinet. It appeared that she had been sorting things to pack as there was another pile on the floor in a corner.

They worked together quietly, as they did when they worked flights together, neither one of them having to tell the other what they needed to do next. Once the lemons had been squeezed and the ice, sugar and cold water had been added, Jo poured them both tall glasses of the tart drink. Thinking a change in setting might be nice, he picked up the glasses and took them out to the patio off the back of her apartment, setting them on a small table.

"Tell me everything," Casey said, as they each took a seat facing the flower garden Jo had planted.

Her eyes met his and then dropped. "I was so dumb. There were flags, bright red flags waving in front of my face that I should have seen. I let myself be blinded by Jeffrey's charm. I was such a fool."

"I know you, Jo. You're not dumb nor are you naive. But that doesn't mean that there aren't people out there that are very good at fooling others, especially others that only look for the good in people."

"Thank you, but maybe you should wait until you hear the whole story before you decide," Jo said. She took a swallow of her drink and then sat it down. "Like I said, I met Jeffrey at a party. The next day there were flowers delivered to the critical care unit where I worked. I called to thank him, and the next thing I knew we were dating. I was wined and dined like a princess, and it was all like one big fairy tale. Just like our wedding. It was perfect. Everything was perfect, at least at first. That's how Jeffrey likes things to look. Perfect."

Casey straightened with this news. Jo had never mentioned being married. It seemed like there was a lot that she had never shared with him. Maybe she didn't trust him as much as he had thought.

"Tell me about these red flags," he said, trying to keep the hurt from his voice. This wasn't about him and his insecurities.

"Savannah's not really a large town, but it has its Who's Who crowd. My father and mother were always on the fringe of the upper society, which made my mother happy while leaving my father frustrated. Suddenly, I was surrounded by all these people who were beautiful and rich. Jeffrey wanted me to fit in. He said it was so I would be more comfortable around his friends. He made appointments for me at the best salons and the most elite boutiques. I tried to explain to him that I was a working woman who didn't have the time or money to keep up with his friend's wives, but it was as if I wasn't speaking. He just didn't get it. Finally, I had to put a stop to it. My credit card balances were rising faster than I could keep up. I tried to explain to him again, but he got mad and said I didn't appreciate everything he was doing for me. I didn't appreciate the fact that I was dating one of Savannah's most eligible bachelors." She stopped and took a sip of her drink.

From the little bit she had said, the man sounded like a real jerk. Couldn't he see that Jo didn't need any fancy salons or boutiques to make her beautiful? She was just as beautiful on the inside as she was on the outside, something that he found very rare in the women that he dated.

"I walked away then, but I couldn't help but think he might be right. I was twenty-four, and I had never had a serious relationship. Maybe I didn't know how. My parents loved him, and he was so charming most of the time. My mother had always told me that you have to pick your battles in a relationship, so when the flowers and the phone calls started again, I decided to give him another chance. I didn't really think he was a bad man, just a little full of himself. How things looked on the outside was very important to him. I thought I could change him. That I could show him that what was really important was what was on the inside. So I just ignored all the bad things and concentrated on the good I saw in him. The next thing I knew, we were married and living in an upscale subdivision. It was good at first."

"We'd only been married six months when he decided

I would quit my job. But this time I pushed back. I loved my job as a nurse. I didn't want to quit. I had a career plan with the goal to become a flight nurse, so I chose to ignore him every time he brought it up. That's when he got physical. He didn't like me not doing what I was told to do."

Casey had known this was coming. He'd seen the fear in her eyes grow as she had told the story, as if she was living through it again. She didn't have to say anything more for him to understand that she hadn't shared the worst of her story.

"So, you left him," Casey said. "Good for you. It takes a lot of courage to walk out of an abusive relationship."

"Don't try to make me a hero, I wasn't," Jo said.

Casey thought about disagreeing with her, but decided now wasn't the time. Right now, he needed to know if what he feared, that she was in danger from the jerk who'd hurt her, was the reason for her sudden need to leave.

"So, this man, Jeffrey—" just the name left a bad taste in his mouth "—I take it he's giving you trouble."

"Oh, yes," Jo said, sarcasm dripping on each word, "from the phone call I received yesterday, I know he's definitely determined to give me trouble. When I pressed charges, he lost his job. When he was sentenced to five years for domestic battery, he lost his license."

"When does he get out?" he asked. They would need to be ready.

"Apparently, he was released a few months early for good behavior. He said the first thing he saw was a pic-ture of me at Alex and Summer's wedding in Soura. Seeing me happy in my new life didn't sit well with him. Why should I be happy when his life has fallen apart? Now he's planning a trip to the Keys to 'see' me to talk about our marriage."

"You're still married?" This whole story was a lot to take in, but thinking of Jo still married to this jerk? That was too much.

"Of course not," she said. "But he fought against the divorce. Fortunately, I had a good lawyer, my dad, and the judge in the case granted me the divorce immediately."

"Did he threaten to hurt you?" Casey asked. He knew she had skimmed over the abuse. Jo was a strong woman. He'd seen her handle some of their most difficult patients while never losing her cool. She wouldn't want to remember the times when she had been the victim, and he would never ask her to relive them.

"No. He seems to think that he can talk me into going back to Savannah with him. It won't be until I tell him no that he'll begin with the threats. And if that doesn't work…" She didn't finish the sentence. She didn't have to. They both knew what she had been unable to say.

She stood and walked a few feet past him before turning around. "And now you know why I can't stay. Maybe I'm a coward, but I can't go through that again. I can't take the chance that he'll…" Her voice trailed off again.

She was afraid of the man because he had hurt her, both physically and emotionally, and she had good reasons to be. Who was he or anyone else to judge her as a coward? She'd survived the abusive relationship and found her way to Key West. To a new life where she had felt safe.

And he wasn't going to let her leave the life she had

made for herself because some bully of a man had it in his mind that he could come here and take her back. "I won't let him hurt you. You know that."

"I knew you'd say that. That's why I didn't want to tell you. I don't want to get you involved in this," Jo said, before turning her back to him. He watched as her arms came around her body as if to hold herself together.

Unable to stop himself, he went to her and put his arms around her, pulling her back against him. "I'm already involved. We're a team. You know that. Alex and Summer, they'll feel the same way once we tell them what's going on. Katie and Dylan, Roy, none of us are going to sit around and let this guy bully you."

She pulled away from him, and he had to let her go even though he wanted to keep her close to him where he knew she would be safe.

"Exactly. And if Alex and Summer get involved, the next thing you know they'll be in the press and Jeffrey will be turning everything around until he's the victim. That's what he did in the divorce. He was the poor heart-broken husband and I was the gold digger, even though I asked for nothing from our divorce. He'll drag them into this mess, and that's the last thing the two of them need when they're trying to stay out of the limelight and raise their babies." The more she talked, the angrier she was getting. The old Jo was back, and he couldn't be happier to see her. "And you. I won't have you getting hurt because of me either."

He came to stand next to her and looked down. "I can take care of myself. Besides, I doubt this Jeffrey would be willing to go up against me. He's a bully who wants to prey on someone smaller than himself. Once he sees me he'll back off. That's why you're moving in with me."

"What?" Jo asked, looking up at him.

"It's the easiest solution. You move in with me and when your ex-husband shows up, he'll have no choice but to run back home."

"It's also only a temporary solution. He might leave when he sees you, but he'll come back. As long as he knows he can get to me, he'll return. I can't live looking over my shoulder for him. I need to leave before he gets here. I need to go somewhere he won't look for me. Maybe Mexico."

"Mexico? Really?"

"His legal buddies couldn't help him there, and I don't think he'll take a chance of ending up in one of their prisons."

Casey shook his head at her. "Are you listening to yourself? The Jo I know would never let a man like this guy run her out of town."

"The Jo you know wouldn't have married him either. But I did. I'm the woman who married a man who had all the signs of being controlling and abusive, and now I have to live with it."

"For how long, Jo? And at what cost? You're the victim. You don't deserve to be punished. But he does. Stay here. Let me help you. We don't have to bring anyone else into it. Stay and fight. I've got your back. Together we make a good team."

Jo looked at the man who meant more to her than just about anyone. Only her brother and sister had fought for her, at least at first. Once their eyes had been opened to the danger their daughter was in, her parents stood by her. Part of her still resented the fact that it had taken an injury bad enough to send her to the emergency room to make them see how bad things were. Not that she could blame them. They too had been fooled by Jeffrey's charm and polite manners.

But Casey believed her and wanted to help her. It made her want to be the woman he believed her to be. A woman who would stay and fight for herself. She hadn't been that woman when she'd left Savannah. Then she'd been afraid to even trust her own judgment. She'd made a mistake, a big one. What was there to keep her from making another one? What if she was making a mistake running away now? How could she know the right thing to do?

"If I stay, what can I do to make Jeffrey not come back?" she asked as she walked over to the small table and sat. The sleepless hours the night before were catching up with her. She felt as if she had just finished a marathon only to find that she still had another mile to run before she could rest.

"First you pack a bag, and then we get out of here," Casey said, picking up the glasses off the table and heading inside.

"He just called last night. I don't think he'll be here this soon." Though hadn't she thought it was him at the door when Casey had shown up?

"If I go along with this, how are we going to explain to everyone that I've moved in with you without telling them about Jeffrey? They're bound to be curious. And what about Alex? He's going to have questions about why I've suddenly decided to stay," Jo said as she followed him inside.

And Summer? If her friend found out that it was a picture of Jo in her husband's family palace that had gotten Jeffrey's attention, she'd think it was all her fault. Summer and Alex were already concerned about how their private lives could spill over into their work lives and that of their coworkers.

"I've got an idea. How about we discuss it when we get to my place?" Casey asked.

"Okay," she said as she headed into her bedroom. She'd already packed most of her clothes into a large suitcase. She'd left only her flight clothes hanging in her closet, unable to throw them away. Unable to let go of what they stood for, the life she'd made and the job she loved. Grabbing those, she pushed her rolling case toward Casey, who picked it up with one hand while grabbing a mesh tote that held most of her shoes. She wouldn't need all of this for the short amount of time she was at Casey's, but she was too tired to go through it. She could just live out of her suitcase for a while. Besides, Casey's extra bedroom was only a small loft with an even smaller closet. But she'd make it work. She had to if she wanted to stay and face her ex-husband.

Because Casey was right, this was her best chance to make Jeffrey leave her alone once and for all. No, there were no guarantees, but at least with Casey's help she had a chance at finally feeling safe.

Safety. After her marriage, she had never taken it for granted again. It meant everything when you found yourself huddled in a corner afraid for your life.

While she packed up the things Moose would need, including the stuffed duck that he slept with every night, Casey helped her get everything into her car.

As she drove out of the parking lot, she looked back at her apartment. It wasn't the nicest place on the island. It wasn't even in the best part of the island. There were no scenic views or beach access, but it had been hers. Of course, she'd be back. Moving in with Casey was just a temporary answer to her problems. Once she had handled the situation with Jeffrey, she'd move back and be just as happy as she had been before.

Living with Casey might be the right answer for now, but she knew there would be drawbacks. Because no matter how much she told herself that Casey was only letting her stay to help out a friend, part of her, the dangerous part, the part that replayed every dream in which he had played the leading role, was looking forward to living with Casey a little too much.

CHAPTER THREE

ONCE SHE GAVE in to Casey and agreed to take his bed-room while he took the loft, the fact that Moose would have trouble fitting up the stairs being the deciding fac-tor, they brought in her bags and she unpacked what she would need for the next day. It wasn't until she found Casey asleep on the couch that she remembered that he had worked the night shift before he'd come over to check on her.

She should have felt uncomfortable watching him sleep. Hadn't she woken up with Jeffrey standing over her, watching her sleep? She shivered with the memory of feeling so helpless.

But this was different. Innocent. Just a friend admiring how sweet he looked with his feet hanging off the end of the couch and his arms wrapped around a pillow. His face was relaxed. His guard was down. Both were something that she saw very seldom. He slept like a babe without a care in the world. His blond curls, which always looked as if they needed cutting, had fallen over his eyes, and his mouth was curved with a secret smile.

He was such a beautiful man, though most people were more impressed with his size. More than once they'd been stopped by a tourist who had confused him with a national football player. They were always surprised when he told them that he was actually a local nurse. People just couldn't see such a big man taking care of their sick loved ones. They were so wrong. This man had a heart for caring for others as big as his six-foot-five frame and a commitment to do what was right as wide as his shoulders. What he was doing for her was just an example of how caring he could be.

And what was she doing? Oh, just standing there admiring the view while he slept. Nope, not creepy at all. When Moose moved to lie down beside him, Jo went into the kitchen and began to make a meal, something a lot more productive than staring at Casey. By the time she heard him shuffle into the room, she had a nice pico de gallo salsa made as well as all the toppings for fish tacos ready.

"I just have to panfry the fish," she said, turning to see him leaning against the counter while his heavy-lidded eyes studied her.

"Something wrong?" she asked, then realized what she had done. "I'm sorry. I didn't mean to take over your kitchen. I should have asked first."

"Why would you ask? We've cooked in this kitchen together before. And you don't need to ask. Haven't you always made yourself at home here? Why would that change now?"

She knew he was right, but somehow this felt different. Changing from welcomed friend to roommate was going to take a little getting used to. At least for her.

"Well, if it's not me taking over your kitchen, what is it? Something has you thinking very hard. Is it regrets?

You know I'd understand if you've changed your mind about all of this."

"I haven't changed my mind. Nor will I. You're stuck with me by your side until this is over. I'm just wondering if you are going to change your mind once I tell you what I think we should do." Crossing his arms, his eyes never left her. It seemed that whatever it was he planned, his mind was set.

She slid the red fish into the oven before turning back to him. "So tell me."

"You remember that girlie movie you made me watch a couple months ago?" he asked. "The one with the woman who's invited to her ex-boyfriend's wedding so she hires a coworker to pretend to be her fiancé?"

"First, I didn't make you watch it. It was my turn to pick the movie. You could have left if you didn't want to see it. Besides, I'd watched that ancient horror flick with you the week before. Second, that was a movie. No one does that in real life." She started to laugh then stopped. One look at his stubborn jaw told her he wasn't kidding. "You don't seriously think anyone would believe we were…are…"

She couldn't even say it let alone do it. Pretending to be more than friends with Casey would be very dangerous, and she already had enough danger in her life.

"It makes perfect sense. You can tell Alex that we had a fight, something like, 'Things between me and Casey changed, and I didn't know how to handle it.'" He spoke in a high-pitched voice as he tried to imitate her. She wasn't sure if he thought he was being funny, but she wasn't amused. Not by any of this.

"So I call Alex and tell him that I've come to my senses and see now that I belong with you. Oh, and also, we're engaged to be married?"

"Yes, exactly," Casey said. His face lit up with the smile of a man who had just won a great battle. How could such a smart man come up with such a plan?

"You don't really think he's going to believe me, do you?" Though her own heart beat a little faster at the thought of being engaged to Casey. Apparently, they both had a problem with separating reality from fantasy.

"What other explanation for your change of plans and moving in with me will they have? Unless you want to tell them the truth."

No. Telling her friends and coworkers would just put more people at risk. "I can't do that. Not now. Maybe later. Maybe if I manage to get Jeffrey out of my life for good, I'll tell them. But right now, especially for Alex and Summer, they are better off staying out of this."

"So, you agree?" he asked.

"I think getting people to believe that we are suddenly engaged would be a stretch. You've been too adamant about remaining the most eligible bachelor of the crew for too long. You have a different woman every season. It's who you are."

"I'm not that bad," he said, then grimaced. "Well, I haven't been lately."

A look came over Casey's face that she couldn't identify. He'd always taken pride in his bachelor status, something that she had teased him about for years. Why now did he look like he had lost his best friend? Was it because of her?

"I can't do it," she said. "It's not fair to you. I'll go back to the apartment. I'll be okay. If Jeffrey shows up, I'll call the police."

"We've already been through this. The best thing is to show Jeffrey that you are not alone. Let him see that you can take care of yourself, but also let him see that I have your back. What better way to show the man you're not scared of him than to show him you've moved on? You don't want Jeffrey to think that you've been waiting for him to show up and take you away. Show the jerk that you've moved on in every way. That you're involved with someone else now."

"He'll hate that," she admitted. And once he got a look at Casey he'd think twice about coming after her. "I can agree to everything except the fake engagement. I don't think it's necessary. We can pretend to have suddenly taken a romantic interest in each other and even stretch it a bit that we're trying out living together, but that's the most that I think anyone will believe. Also, that way when Jeffrey is taken care of, we can go back to our old relationship without any explanation. People will just think things didn't work out romantically, but that we are still friends. Agreed?"

Casey hesitated for a moment before offering her his hand. "Agreed."

Placing her hand in his, she felt that irritating hum of her body whenever she and Casey touched. She agreed with him that a united front would be the best defense from her ex-husband. She just hoped it was worth risking her friendship with Casey.

Because no matter what happened between her and

Jeffrey, she knew that her relationship with her best friend might never be the same. How could it be? He knew all her secrets now. Would he ever again see her as the strong woman she'd worked so hard to become? Or would he always see her as the victim she used to be? Even though doubt and shame still filled her when she thought of the way she'd let Jeffrey manipulate her, deep inside she knew she wasn't that person anymore. She'd changed. Now she just had to find some way to prove it to Casey. And she would, no matter what it took.

Jo walked out of Alex's office feeling like a terrible employee and an even worse friend. In a perfect world, you didn't have to hide parts of your life from the people you cared about. But her life hadn't been perfect in a long time. And right now, she couldn't let the guilt she felt talk her into turning around and walking back into the office and spilling the truth. She and Casey had a plan, and she would stick to it.

Her radio went off, drawing her mind back to where it needed to be. She wouldn't let the drama in her life overflow into her job. That would be dangerous for both her patients and her career.

As she listened to the report of a Jet Ski accident near Fort Zachary, she caught up with Casey and their pilot, James, as they were headed out the door. Once in the helicopter, Jo buckled herself into her harness and put on her helmet.

During liftoff, she listened as James got more information on the location of the accident. From the report, it sounded like it would be a "scoop and run" call due to the traumatic head injury the patient might have suffered—as long as they could get the patient stabilized. Time meant everything when you were dealing with a head injury, and without a neurosurgeon available on the island, they'd be flying straight to the nearest Miami hospital that would be able to accept them.

"Everything okay?" Casey asked.

"It's all good," Jo said. Looking over at him, she gave him a thumbs-up. She had known Casey was watching her and had to be anxious to know how things had gone with Alex. It wasn't that either of them thought Alex wouldn't let her rescind her resignation, but they also knew that he would want more of a reason than she was able to give.

Fortunately, Alex had taken her excuse of just needing to make some changes in her life without much questioning. His eyes had told her that he knew there was more to the story than she was saying, but he was too polite to ask. Not that he would be wondering for long. It would get out that she was "involved" with Casey eventually, and rumors would be flying about the change in their relationship. It was exactly what they wanted. By the time Jeffrey showed up, they needed everyone to believe that she and Casey were a couple so that they could fool him.

She hoped to have some warning before her ex showed up, but so far Jeffrey hadn't tried to contact her again. She couldn't help but think he was dragging the suspense out, thinking that she would be cowering somewhere, afraid to go out. It was the kind of mental game he liked to play with her.

But he was in for a surprise this time. A big one.

She looked over to where Casey was setting up an IV bag for infusion, and her lips curled up in an unexpected grin. She was almost looking forward to the look in Jeffrey's eyes when he saw all six feet five inches of her muscled friend standing beside her.

The dispatcher informed them of the receiving hospital that they would be transporting to, and Jo returned her attention to preparing the items they would need for their patient. They began their descent to a location that Fire and Rescue had cleared, and Jo could see a small crowd gathered around the EMTs.

Her body went on alert as soon as the skids touched the ground. Taking the lead, she grabbed their supply bag while Casey followed behind with the stretcher.

"Jo. Casey. Nice of you to join us," one of the EMTs said as the crowd moved back, giving her the first view of their patient. No more than twenty, the young woman was conscious though there was a lot of blood in the sand surrounding her head.

"Nice to see you, too. Who's our patient?"

"This is Zoe," the EMT said, and Jo listened as he began to give a full report on the accident and the patient's injuries. From the description of the collision, the woman was lucky that she hadn't been killed when she had crossed into the path of the other Jet Ski.

"The other person?" Jo asked as she kneeled beside the young woman's head.

"The patient's boyfriend, Daniel. He's shaken up—" the EMT looked over at the young man crouched near the woman "—but no injuries that we can see."

"Hi, Zoe, my name is Jo and this is Casey. Have you ever been in a helicopter before?"

"Yes," said the woman. The word came out slow, which was cause for concern that this was more than just a head laceration. There was a good chance it was a sign of a serious head injury. But when Jo checked Zoe's pupils, they were reactive.

"Can you tell me your name and where you are?" Jo asked as Casey began to apply the electro pads so that they could monitor their patient's vital signs.

The woman looked over to the young man beside her. He was as pale as the white sand under their feet, and his eyes were wide with shock. "Her name is Zoe. We're just here in Key West for the week. We're getting married next year when I get out of college, and we wanted to check out the wedding venues. Can you tell me if she's going to be okay? Do I need to call her parents?"

"Well, that's what we are here for. To make sure she's okay. And, yes, I would call her parents. But what we need now is for her to answer our questions. It will help us and the doctor know how serious her injury is."

"Sorry," the young man said, before looking back at Zoe.

"No problem," Casey said from beside him. "We understand you're trying to help."

"Zoe, can you tell me where you are right now and what month it is?" Jo asked again.

"Key West, and it's August," the woman answered.

"That's good. Real good. Now, can you tell me if you hurt anywhere?" Jo asked, pulling back a dressing that had been applied to Zoe's head. There was a laceration across her forehead that was still oozing blood. She didn't see any deformity of the skull, but without a CT scan there wasn't any way of knowing what other damage could be present.

"My head hurts. Bad. Like the worst headache ever. And my stomach feels sick," Zoe answered.

"Vital signs are stable," Casey told Jo as he watched the monitor screen. "Normal sinus rhythm in the nineties."

A little fast but it that was to be expected.

"O2 saturation?" she asked.

"Good. Ninety-eight percent."

"We'll give you something for the nausea as soon as we get you loaded in the helicopter," Casey told her.

"Can you give her something for the pain?" Daniel asked. Some color had returned to his face, but he was still in shock. He was so young. The both of them were. Too young to be graduating from college let alone getting married. Not that she had been much older when she'd married Jeffrey.

But she couldn't judge every marriage by her own. She knew that, though sometimes she found it difficult. It was just instinctual to want to protect others from her mistake.

"Nothing for pain yet," Casey answered for her. "We have to be able to do the neuro assessments that are necessary right now. Even a slight change can make a difference."

While Jo and one of the EMTs placed a C-collar to stabilize Zoe's neck, Casey gave the fiancé the information on the hospital where they would be taking her. But when Daniel began to follow them to the helicopter, Jo called one of the EMTs to the side.

"Can you check over this young man before he leaves? I don't like the idea of him driving without being sure he's okay," she said.

When the EMT nodded and headed toward Daniel, she and Casey rushed their patient into the helicopter and prepared for flight. In minutes they were airborne and headed to a Miami trauma center where she hoped the neurosurgeon would have good news for the young couple. By the time they landed, Jo was feeling even more hopeful. Zoe's vital signs had remained stable and her neuro assessments were unchanged. Maybe she'd be one of the lucky ones.

They rolled into the trauma room with the trauma doctor waiting for them, and while Casey began to report off to the hospital team, Jo finished their charting and went to drop it off with the unit coordinator. When she returned, she found the trauma room empty except for Casey and one of the emergency room nurses—Sarah? Or was her name Susan?

"They've taken Zoe to CT," Casey said, before clearing his throat. Why did his voice sound so strained? Then she noticed he was staring at the doorway, as if he was about to make a run for it at any moment.

"Did something happen?" Jo asked, afraid Zoe had deteriorated in the few minutes she'd been gone.

"No, she's fine," said the nurse, whose name tag read Sarah. Her gaze never left Casey. "I was just telling Casey that I'm going to be in Key West for a vacation in a few days."

It had taken a few minutes for Jo to recognize the woman, but now that she did the tense atmosphere in the empty trauma room made sense. Sarah and Casey had dated briefly a few months earlier, and she had not been happy when Casey had told her he had no plans for anything serious.

It had been just one of many such conversations that Casey had relayed to her over a drink at their favorite tiki bar. Jo had tried to support him and see his side. She knew that he never meant to hurt anyone he dated, and most of the women he chose to go out with were just looking to have fun like he was. It was the other women, the ones who thought they could end Casey's self-declared eternal bachelorhood that bothered him the most. He just couldn't understand why they thought he was looking for anything more.

Because of her history, Jo had understood the dangers of someone becoming obsessed with you, and on more than one occasion she had advised him to cut all contact with the woman before things could get ugly.

"That's nice," Jo said. She ignored the little jealous devil that seemed to sit on one of her shoulders every time she had to talk to one of Casey's girlfriends. For the first time, she wondered if Casey had ever thought it strange that she had never been overly friendly with any of them. "I sent the paperwork and radioed James that we were headed up to the roof."

"Great, we better get going then," Casey said, all but running out of the room, not bothering to tell the other woman goodbye.

"Hold on," Jo said as she caught up with him at the elevator. "What was that about?"

"Nothing. It was nothing," Casey said, though Jo noticed that he was watching the hallway as if he thought someone might be following behind her.

"I didn't mean to interrupt," she said, not sure if Casey was upset at her or at Sarah.

"There was nothing for you to interrupt," Casey said, his tone defensive.

"Okay. I get it. It's none of my business," Jo said as she got into the elevator that would take them to the roof, leaving Casey to follow her. Was he upset because he wasn't free to see Sarah now?

"I'm sorry. Sarah cornered me in the room and started telling me how much she's missed me. She wanted to see me when she comes down to the Keys on some girls' weekend trip she has planned. I didn't know what to say. I mean we were at work. I couldn't be rude."

"What did you want to say?" Jo asked, trying to keep all emotion out of her voice. It wasn't fair to Casey that he'd become saddled with Jo's problems if it came between him and Sarah making up, though Jo found it hard to believe that was in Casey's plans at all. Once he ended a relationship, he moved on. He never seemed to look back at anything in his life. He lived his life with no regrets while she lived with her regrets on a daily basis.

"You know I'm not any good dealing with women when they get all emotional. I don't know what to say."

But he sure knew how to run away whenever a woman declared she wanted more than a good time from him.

"If you didn't want to see her again, you could have

just told her you were involved with someone else." It shouldn't bother her that he hadn't spoken up and told Sarah about her and Casey's new "relationship." It wasn't like they were a real couple. Instead of being resentful that he hadn't been willing to claim that he was involved with her, she should feel bad that she was putting him in this position.

"I was just trying to get out of there before things became any more uncomfortable," he said, walking out onto the roof as soon as the elevator doors opened, leaving her behind to regret that she'd even mentioned their pretend relationship.

Casey was quiet on the trip back to headquarters, which started to worry Jo. Was he mad at her because of what she'd said? She had caught a glimpse of the look Sarah had given him as he walked away. It was plain to see that she was not giving up on Casey.

She should feel bad, if not for Sarah at least for Casey. But seeing the way the woman had looked at him had made Jo want to yell "stay away, he's mine" at the top of her lungs.

Guilt began to eat at her. She didn't have any right to feel possessive of Casey. She needed to remember that this pretense would be over soon. What if she was reading the whole situation wrong? Maybe Casey had been happy to find out Sarah was going to be on the island and then had remembered that with the complication Jo had brought into his life he wasn't free to spend his time with her.

But what could she do about it? It was too late to change their minds now. She'd reassured Alex that she would not be leaving the island. She couldn't turn back. He wouldn't agree to it if she asked him to. They'd started on a path that would hopefully set her free from her ex-husband, and until that was done they'd both be living a necessary lie.

She just had to keep reminding herself that this was all make-believe. She'd let Casey ride in like a knight in shining armor to rescue her because he was her friend. She had to protect that friendship, even if it meant she had to protect it from herself.

CHAPTER FOUR

THERE WAS SOMEONE knocking on the door. Only the sound didn't seem to be coming from the right location.

Jo opened her eyes at the same time that Moose chose to send out an alarming bark that would have woken her whole apartment building. But she wasn't at her apartment, which explained why the sound was coming from somewhere unfamiliar.

"Wait a moment," Jo told Moose as he began scratching at the bedroom door. Except for her hair, which felt like a nest on top of her head, she was decent enough in an oversize T-shirt and bike shorts.

Opening the bedroom door, she headed to the front door, only to stop when she recognized the voice on the other side.

"Open up, Casey," Summer called from the other side. "We need to talk."

Jo turned toward the staircase leading up to the loft and wasn't surprised to see Casey standing at the top of the stairs. He was shirtless, with a pair of pajama pants riding low on his hips. Jo wanted to forget her friend at the door and just spend an hour, or maybe two, enjoying the view.

She blinked and tried to clear her head. Sharing a place with Casey should have come with a warning label.

She made her eyes move up to Casey's face, and was relieved to see that he hadn't noticed her moment of weakness. "It's Summer. What do we do?"

Casey's eyes brightened a moment before he turned before disappearing back into the loft. "Answer the door, Jo. I'm pretty sure it's you she's looking for."

"Jo, is that you?" Summer called from the other side of the door. The woman had to have supersonic hearing.

"Casey, where are you going?" Jo called up the stairs. "What am I supposed to tell her?"

He didn't answer her, making it clear that he was leaving her on her own to handle their friend. With everything he had done for her, she couldn't be mad. She was closer to Summer than Casey, so it would seem right for her to handle all the questions she was bound to have about finding Jo there. Of course, Jo could pretend that she had just stopped over to visit. But that would just be putting off the inevitable.

With that thought, Jo opened the door. Summer stood on the other side, alone.

"Where are the babies?" Jo asked.

"Alex's mom is in town. She was thrilled for a chance to watch them," Summer said as she looked inside the door. "Where's Casey?"

"He's asleep. In case you don't know, we worked last night."

"I know that," Summer said as Jo stepped back to let her in. "Hey, Moose."

"Then why are you here? I can't believe you asked

your mother-in-law to keep the babies so you could visit with Casey," Jo said as Summer gave Moose a head rub.

"Maybe the better question is, what are you doing here?" Summer asked, her face coming alive with a mischievous grin. "Are the two of you having a sleepover?"

Jo started to deny Summer's suggestion then thought of Casey up in the loft listening to them. He wanted her to take the lead on this, so she would. And if she had a bit of fun with it, it was his own fault.

"Shh, don't wake him up," Jo said, looking to where she had shut the bedroom door. "We were both exhausted when we finally went to sleep."

Jo watched as Summer took in the innuendo she had planted. Summer's naughty smile let her know right when her friend had fallen for it.

"I knew it. When your neighbor said he saw a blond giant helping you load a suitcase in your car, I knew it had to be Casey. What happened? Did you finally tell him how you feel?" Summer said as she took a seat on the couch. Jo's stomach dropped to her feet. Had Casey heard that?

"What are you talking about?" Jo said as she kicked Summer's shin with her bare foot then took a seat beside her, grabbing her toes. "Ouch."

"What is wrong…oh…" Summer said, finally understanding. "So, what happened? I mean you must have decided that you feel something for him. You are *sleeping* here, right?"

"It's complicated," Jo said. Now that Summer had covered her slip, Jo was left not knowing how to proceed.

"It has to be if you were about to leave the island. I

couldn't believe it when Alex told me. You leave Key West? It didn't make sense. I thought you were happy here." Summer said as she moved over and made room for Moose beside her.

"I am happy. I don't really know what I was thinking. It just seemed the only thing I could do at the time." At least that was the truth, even if it did lead Summer in a different direction. "But everything is settled. I understand what I need now."

"To make you happy?" Summer asked.

"Yes, to make me happy," Jo said. Getting rid of her fear of her ex-husband would make her very happy.

"I'm glad. For you and Casey. He's not been himself lately," Summer said, and then smiled. "And now I know why."

"You do?" Was there something going on with Casey that she didn't know about? Had his mood been a little more serious lately? A little less carefree?

"Sure. You don't think this thing between you two just happened, do you?"

If Summer only knew. Someday she'd tell her the truth. When everything was done and Jeffrey was out of her life for good, Jo would take Summer out to lunch and explain everything. Her friend wouldn't be happy, but of all the people she knew, Summer would understand. Her whole life had been opened up to the public when she became pregnant with Alex's babies. Now, as the princess of Soura, she fought to keep her life as private as possible.

"I've got to get back to the babies, and I know you need some more sleep," Summer said as she moved Moose's big head from her lap and stood. "Oh, and your neighbor wanted me to tell you he has a package that was left for you. He didn't want to leave it out when you didn't come home the other night."

Jo didn't mention the fact that she moved in with Casey. Now that Summer believed that they were an item, she didn't seem surprised that Jo was staying with Casey. And though she hated to think about what would happen when Jeffrey did show up, she wished he would just get it over with. Waiting for him while having to constantly lie to her friends wasn't the way she wanted to live her life. Even worse was asking Casey to continue this farce with her. But what else could she do? If she was ever going to get Jeffrey to understand that she had moved on and would never let him into her life again, they needed to look like the happy couple. Jeffrey needed to believe that Casey was in her life for good and would be there to protect her if he tried to hurt or threaten her again.

If she knew her ex-husband, he was busy making plans on how he would intimidate her into doing whatever he wanted from her. The plan she and Casey had was her only defense, and she had no choice. They'd play the loving couple for everyone, and she'd do it with a smile on her face. She wouldn't give Jeffrey one reason to doubt them. Her ability to remain here with her friends demanded it.

"Sarah, again?" Jo asked, her voice sharp with aggravation.

In the three days since he'd seen Sarah at the hospital in Miami, she'd called him four times, each with a different excuse. And while he couldn't understand why Sarah insisted on calling when he'd made it plain to her that there was nothing left between them, Jo's reaction seemed off. Was there something between the two women that he wasn't aware of? Or was this just another sign that he didn't understand women. He'd known enough of them that you'd think he'd have them all figured out by now. When he'd been younger, he'd been sure that he understood everything about them. Then Anna had run off and he'd been stunned. He'd never even known she was unhappy, though he would have sworn he knew everything about her. That was when he realized he knew absolutely nothing about women. And now, over ten years later, he still couldn't wrap his mind around what a confusing bunch they were.

But he'd always thought Jo was different. She'd always been so levelheaded. She didn't lose her temper and yell at him when he climbed into her car covered in sand from a volleyball match. She didn't pout when he was late for lunch because he stopped to help Ms. Terrie next door with her garden. She was different from all the women he dated. Except right now she wasn't acting very Jo-like at all.

"Sarah just wanted to update me on Zoe's condition. She got permission from her first," Casey said. And why he was defending Sarah? Maybe it was because he still felt bad about the way she'd taken it when he'd had to end things between them. Their relationship had no future. He still didn't understand how Sarah could have read anything more into it. But then, he didn't understand women.

"If that was all she wanted to do, she could have texted you," Jo said, before taking a sip of the wine he'd opened to go with the lasagna he had baked for their supper. "She's trying to start things back up again."

"Maybe," Casey said. Sarah had been very insistent that he know the hotel she would be staying at while in Key West. "But it's not going to happen. I was very open about the fact that I don't plan on getting seriously involved with anyone. Besides, now that—"

"Now that you're stuck with me as your pretend girlfriend?" Jo asked with sarcasm in her voice, which he had never heard before.

He stopped eating and studied her. Her face had been scrubbed to a healthy glow, and her hair, damp from a shower, had been pulled into a bun on the top of her head. She still looked tired, her eyes puffy from lack of sleep, but with them both coming off their second shift in three days it was to be expected. It was the stubborn look on her face that was a surprise. She had moved in with him three days ago, and she wasn't any happier about their arrangement now than she had been when he'd first suggested it. Was it because of this thing with Sarah? Or maybe it wasn't Sarah at all.

"Is that embarrassing for you?" he asked. Maybe dating him—pretend dating him—wasn't up to her normal standards. She'd married a lawyer. He was a small island nurse with no future of anything more.

"Are you kidding?" Her tired eyes sparkled with humor, and he relaxed. There was the Jo he knew and loved. "I'm the first woman you've let inside this place. I'll be envied by half the single women in the Keys."

"Just half?" he asked, getting the laugh he had intended from her.

"Okay, maybe two-thirds. There's probably already a betting pool going at work on how long this will last," Jo said. When the light went out of her eyes, he knew that she was once again thinking about Jeffrey and when he would appear.

"Is there a bet on who calls it off? You or me?" Casey said, hoping to lighten things up again. When all he got from Jo was a quirk of her lips, he knew he had failed. "Quit worrying about it. Even if Jeffrey shows up, he'll go to your apartment first."

He could see that his words were not helping. "Let's stick the dishes in the dishwasher and go out."

"Now? Aren't you tired?" Jo asked.

"I got a good nap, and I think both of us would sleep better tonight if we got some fresh air. Don't you?"

In minutes they finished their meals and had the dishes taken care of and Moose loaded into Casey's truck. Not sure if Jo would be up to their usual crowd and the questions they were sure to ask now that it was out that the two of them were "dating," he headed to Key West Dog Beach.

While Moose had gotten his two walks a day while they were working, the big guy loved to run on the beach and he headed straight for the water the moment Jo let him out of the truck.

"We could be here for hours," Jo said as she watched Moose run through the waves.

"The only thing I have to do tomorrow is work a dog food donation drive at the shelter," Casey said as he pulled a blanket from the oversize toolbox in his truck.

He took her hand as they waded through the deep

sand. It was something he had done a hundred times, helping a woman this way, but it somehow felt different tonight. He knew that Jo was vulnerable. He'd noticed that she had mostly just moved her food around on her plate. Waiting for Jeffrey to make a move was getting to her, and Casey didn't like it.

"I don't understand why you're always working to help the shelter, but you refuse to get a dog of your own," Jo said.

"I got you Moose," he said. It was a long argument between the two of them. Jo didn't understand that the responsibility of a dog was something he wasn't prepared for. Having someone—or a dog—depend on you tied you down, and that wasn't for him.

"And I will always be grateful," Jo said, then groaned when the big dog rushed them, almost knocking her to the ground.

Casey easily caught her, pressing her to him as Moose ran circles around them, pouncing against them and almost taking them both down.

"Maybe he needs to go back to obedience classes," Jo said, then threw her arms around Casey as the dog made a jump into the air before running back to the surf.

Casey rested his chin against the top of her head and breathed in the floral scent of her hair along with the salty ocean water that Moose had splattered them with. "He's just enjoying himself. He's been cooped up in the house for the past couple of days. He'll calm down."

Jo pulled away, looking up at him with a smile that did something funny to his insides. What was this? It wasn't like this was the first time he'd given Jo a hug. But this? Again, this felt different. Scary. And totally inappropriate.

He stepped away from her and began searching for a flat piece of beach. With the help of the moon and stars shining over them, he found the perfect spot and spread out the blanket. If he sat a little closer to the edge, Jo didn't seem to notice.

"I can't believe I was going to leave this place," Jo said as she stretched out beside him and stared up at the moon. "I'm glad you talked me into staying. Into fighting to keep the life I have here. You're a good man, Casey Johnson."

"I'm glad you came to your senses." Casey couldn't admit that it had been for his own selfish reasons that he had worked so hard to keep her on the island. When he'd heard Jo was leaving, it had been like a punch in his gut. He'd been left behind by his high school sweetheart. His grandmother had passed away. Even his own parents had left the island for one of those adult only communities that Miami was famous for. All of those things had hurt him, though he'd never tell his parents. They were happy where they were, and it was a lot easier for them to live out their retirement on the mainland than it would have been for them to stay in the Keys.

But Jo leaving? He didn't know what he would have done if she had left him behind. She was an important part of his life. His constant support and companion. It was something that his girlfriends had never liked. And he'd never shared with Jo that she was one of the reasons that a lot of his relationships ended. It seemed asking a woman to accept his best friend was a woman was too much. Pointing out to them that it was a sexist attitude hadn't helped either. Nope, he'd never understand them.

"I never dreamed I would be living here, in Florida, let alone the Keys. I did dream of being a flight nurse. But that was before I met Jeffrey. He always thought it was a stupid goal."

"And you were going to just give up your dream for him?" Casey had a hard time imagining the woman Jo had been back then. It was as if the woman she had been had risen from the ashes of her marriage and taken on another life. Life did change people. He'd seen that and experienced it himself. Once he'd been a young man wanting nothing more than to settle down and raise a family. He couldn't imagine being that person again.

"Did you always want to be a flight nurse? Is that why you got out of the coast guard?"

"I always wanted to live here on the island. I was lucky to get stationed here for the first two years, and then I was stationed in Ketchikan, Alaska, for the last three years. It's beautiful country. I saw sights that I never dreamed I'd see. But it wasn't home."

He leaned back and relaxed beside her. This felt right. This was easy. Talking to Jo had always been easy. He thought of the way she'd been when Sarah had called. He knew she was just being protective and now, knowing what she had went through with her ex-husband, he understood why she'd always warned him when a woman's interest began to cross the line into stalking. He was lucky to have her in his life.

"Promise me that you won't ever leave without talking

to me first," he said, not sure why he needed to have the promise. She'd already agreed to stay and face Jeffrey.

"I told you I was sorry. I wouldn't have left without talking to you. It was wrong, and I was being a coward not telling you first," she said. "But I promise. If I feel I don't have any other choice but to leave, I'll talk to you first."

"Now, you have to promise me that we won't let all this drama with Jeffrey destroy our friendship. If you change your mind about faking this romance with me, you have to tell me." Jo turned her head to his and the moonlight washed over her face. Her dark eyes searched his, for what he wasn't sure. Why was she so afraid that something would come between the two of them?

"I promise, but I won't change my mind. This will work, Jo. Once Jeffrey comes and sees that you've made this new life he'll have no choice but to leave. Having me standing beside you will show him that you're not alone. He'll leave as fast as he can get a plane out of here, I guarantee."

"I hope you're right. I wish he'd come tomorrow so we can get this over with. Lying to our friends, pretending to be something we're not, it's all wrong."

He covered her hand with his and squeezed it. He knew she was nervous. He couldn't imagine facing someone who had threatened and abused you.

When her fingers locked with his and she laid her head on his shoulder, his body hardened and his stomach shuddered. He froze, unable to move, while his brain tried to talk some sense into the rest of his body. It was an old fight between the two of them. His body insisting on its attraction to Jo while his brain accepted that their friendship meant there was no place for anything else. Years ago, when Jo had first arrived in Key West, before they'd built the friendship they had now, he'd asked her out. Her sharp "no," before she'd gone on to explain that she needed a friend more than anything else had been enough to stop any ideas he'd had about anything romantic happening between them.

And she'd been right. He found the relationship they had was much more rewarding than he'd ever had with one of his girlfriends. That took her off his list of available women. So why was he having this primal reaction to her now? Was his body getting confused by all this pretending they were doing?

He removed his hand from hers and sat up, casually putting some room between them. Maybe Jo was right. This pretending to be romantically and physically involved could be dangerous. The best thing for both of them was for Jeffrey to come so their lives could go back to normal before he did something that they both might regret.

CHAPTER FIVE

"WHAT ARE THE two of you doing?" Alex asked from the kitchen that opened out into the multiuse room.

Jo stomped down on where Casey's instep had been just seconds before then turned and pushed the palm of her right hand at his nose, stopping only inches from making contact.

"I'm just teaching Jo a few self-defense moves," Casey said as he stepped back from Jo's outstretched hand.

She hadn't been sure what Casey had in mind when he started moving the furniture to the side of the room. Dancing? Aerobics? Yoga? With Casey, you never knew.

But no, the man was on a mission to keep her safe, and teaching her to protect herself was his goal. She didn't want to break it to him that she had taken a defense class before coming to the island. Then it had been her brother who had insisted she learn some moves to protect herself. It wasn't that she didn't know the moves. It was that she panicked where Jeffrey was concerned. The memories of what he'd done to her in the past seemed to surround her. They had kept her frozen in place with fear until it was too late to fight back.

But it wouldn't be that way this time. Not with Casey backing her up.

"Nice," Alex said. "Maybe I should get Summer a class on defense for her birthday."

"I don't think that would be a good idea." While she might enjoy the class, Jo was sure that Summer was expecting something a little more romantic.

"Jewelry. Women love jewelry," Casey said as he began to move the furniture back into place.

"She has lots of jewelry and she barely wears any of it," Alex said. "She says she never has anyplace to wear it to that wouldn't make her look ridiculous."

"So take her out somewhere she can wear it. There's a new French restaurant downtown that would be perfect." And Jo knew Summer would love it. Alex's wife had become a total foodie since spending time in his father's palace where the chefs had gone out of their way to spoil their princess.

"We both agreed after the last time we took the twins out that we wouldn't do it again until they were in college," Alex said.

Jo had heard about that experience and knew that Alex was only partly kidding. "We can keep the babies for you. Just schedule it during a time the two of us are both off."

"We?" Casey asked. "I don't do babies."

"*We* do babies every day," Jo said as the radio clipped to her flight pants went off.

Pulling her arms into the top of the suit she'd unzipped and left hanging around her waist when they'd come in from their last flight, she grabbed the bottle of water she'd left on the floor and rushed for the door while the dispatcher was still giving the location of the fire they were to respond to.

"I hate fires," Casey said as they buckled up and began to ready their equipment.

Jo understood. The smell of burned flesh made her stomach sick, and more than once she'd resorted to a mask lined with menthol salve. "Hopefully everyone got out."

But Jo's heart sank when she saw the tall, bright orange flames towering into the sky above the building. It would have been full of people as it was still early in the afternoon as their helicopter flew over the island.

"The police have cordoned off a place at a strip mall just north of the fire's location," the dispatcher said.

"Visibility is good from up here, though the smoke seems to be spreading," Roy, their pilot, said. "ETA two minutes. I'll be waiting for them to let me know it's all clear."

"Have they radioed in what we'll be transporting?" Casey asked the dispatcher.

"From what I've been told, you will be emergency backup at this time. No victims or fatalities identified as of now," the dispatcher said.

"I say we take the stretcher just in case," Jo said as she stuffed extra dressings into the big duffel bag that held all their equipment.

"I'll take one of the oxygen tanks too. There could be some inhalation problems for the responders," Casey said.

The moment the skids hit the ground Jo unloaded with Casey right behind her.

"I'm to take you to the EMTs," a young police officer said as she joined them.

They followed closely behind her, weaving through the

crowd of onlookers that had formed around the engulfed building. Jo recognized the place as Lucy's, a place where their whole crew often met. "This will break Lucy's and Darren's heart."

"Let's just pray they both got out," Casey said.

"That's where they want you," the officer said, pointing to where two crews of EMTs were treating people. "I'm going to get some help to get the crowd back so you'll have more room."

"Thank you," Casey said. "We appreciate the help."

They split up as Casey headed toward the EMT crews and Jo started toward the local fire chief, a man she had met, unfortunately, on too many flights.

"How many men do you still have in the building?" she asked, stepping over a long thick hose that ran from the fire truck where they stood toward the pub. There was no way they could save Lucy's place, so if anyone was inside the building it had to be in the hope of rescuing someone.

"Only two left inside. The wait staff claim that one of the owners went toward the kitchen where the fire started instead of out the front. They've got two minutes left before I call them back."

So either Lucy or Darren was still in the building? Knowing the two of them, it would be Lucy. She loved their pub. She'd told Jo once that having the pub had been what had saved her when her first husband died. She'd bought the building with the insurance money she'd received after his death and moved to Key West to open a pub. It had been their dream for years, and she had been determined to live the life she knew he wanted for her.

It was here she had met the second love of her life, Darren. Jo had loved to hear that story with its happily-ever-after ending. It had to be wonderful to be loved like that.

The smoke coming off the building was intensifying, and as the firemen worked to keep the flames down as best they could, she was forced to move back. There would be no happily-ever-after today.

Two large men exited the building carrying a body. When the person in their arms coughed, Jo took a much-needed breath, coughing as the smoke entered her own lungs, then followed the firemen to where the EMTs waited.

Casey and one of the EMTs made it to the firemen first, and Casey helped them lower the patient onto their flight stretcher. Though everything on the person was covered in black soot and a towel was wrapped around the face, Jo could see a mop of wet gray hair and knew it was Lucy.

As the other EMTs rushed to care for the firemen that had over heated, Jo and Casey started their assessment. Neither of them had any doubt that Lucy was in critical condition from the smoke she'd inhaled. That would make her their patient to get to Miami as soon as possible.

"Lucy," Jo said as she unwrapped the towel the rest of the way from her head, "it's Jo and Casey. Do you know where you are?"

"Jo?" the woman asked, then started coughing. "Heli-Care Jo?"

"Yes, ma'am. Casey is here too." Jo examined the woman, peeling back a partially burned apron carefully.

Under the apron, there was a golf-ball-sized hole where a deep burn was visible on Lucy's chest.

"I'm going to put a mask over your face now to give you some oxygen to help you breathe," Casey said, from beside her.

"Casey? My boy, Casey?" the woman asked.

As he had grown up on the island, Jo knew that Casey had known Lucy a lot longer than she had. Like most women, Lucy had a soft spot for him.

"I must be really bad if you two are here. I guess you're finally going to get me up in one of those helicopters," Lucy said. Her hands came up to touch her face, but Casey took the woman's small wrists and eased them back down. Lucy's hands had been burned badly, and Jo suspected the woman had gone into the kitchen to try to stop the fire herself and had received the burns in her efforts. "My face?"

"Still as pretty as ever," Casey said as he applied the electro pads for their monitors. The monitor began to alarm with an oxygen saturation reading in the eighties; he turned up the O2. "You're a smart lady. Putting the wet towel over your face was the best thing you could have done."

Lucy gave a muffled laugh against the oxygen mask, and then followed it up with a bout of coughing that wracked the woman's small frame.

Jo wanted to tell her that running from the fire instead of to the fire would have been the smart thing, but she'd wait until the woman was recovered to scold her.

"Call Dispatch and have them get us a receiving trauma hospital with a burn unit to transport to," Jo said to Roy via the radio hooked to her flight suit. Lucy was going to need some long-term care for the burns on her hands. Lucy loved to cook, and Jo hoped Lucy wouldn't lose the functionality she needed to run their busy pub.

Jo saw Casey motion to one of the EMTs as they began to strap Lucy onto the stretcher and she tried to speak, only the word *Darren* recognizable as she was overcome with another coughing spell.

"I'll call Darren as soon as we get you loaded up and headed to Miami," Casey said as they headed through the crowd with the people surrounding the scene moving quickly out of their way.

Jo saw that some of the onlookers began crying when they saw who was on their stretcher. Lucy was loved by so many people on the island.

"Wait," a man called from behind them as they exited the crowd and entered the area that the officers had cleared for their landing. "Casey. Jo."

Jo turned to see a man running up behind them, his long gray ponytail flapping against his back as he ran.

Recognizing the voice, Lucy tried to sit up, but the straps secured her in place.

"I'll talk to him," Casey told Lucy, walking back to where the man was being held back by officers. "Go ahead and load her up. I'll be right there."

By the time Roy had the all clear from the officers to start up, Casey had returned and they had Lucy hooked up to the monitors. As Jo began to radio the receiving hospital report, Casey got an IV started. Lucy needed the fluids as well as some pain medication.

"I gave Darren my cell phone number, and I'll call him as soon as we get you to the hospital," he told Lucy.

Jo watched as Lucy nodded. The fact that the woman wasn't trying to talk told Jo that Lucy's adrenaline rush was wearing off and now the extent of the situation was hitting her. A single tear slid down the woman's sooty cheek, clearing a path for what was sure to be more to come.

"It's going to be okay, Miss Lucy," Casey said. "Darren's headed to Miami right behind us."

"But my pub," Lucy said, the words so low that Jo read her lips more than heard them.

"You'll build it back. We'll help. Everyone will. Just rest right now," Jo said as Casey injected the IV port with some morphine.

Lucy's eyes closed and Jo watched as the tension eased from the woman's body, then another spell of coughing hit her.

The rest of the flight was silent, except for Lucy's coughing and the occasional beep of a monitor, until Roy gave them an ETA of five minutes.

Jo always thought of her job as a crazy mix of heartache and triumph. She had seen and experienced things that she never would have in any other profession. Some of it was good and some of it was not so good. Add to this the fact that the islands were small, it wasn't unusual for her to know one of their patients, which made it even harder for her and her coworkers when things ended badly. She'd had nightmares from some of the scenes she'd responded to and shed tears with coworkers over their losses and their wins. Today, she was going to count this one as a win. Lucy would have a lot of work ahead of her, but Casey had been right. They would all be there to help her.

That was just one of the things she loved about their island. One of the many reasons she was thankful that Casey had talked her into staying, even though their situation was awkward at times. They'd get through this and after Jeffrey left, things would get back to normal. She'd have her friends and her community and the job she loved.

She just wished she didn't have to keep reminding herself that things with Casey were just temporary. She told herself that soon they'd be back to their old friendship. But she was telling so many lies right now, letting people think she and Casey were romantically involved, that she wasn't sure if she could even believe herself.

CHAPTER SIX

"IF SUMMER CALLS one more time, I am not answering the phone. She acts like we aren't capable of watching two babies," Jo said as she walked into the nursery where Casey sat in the middle of what looked like the aftermath of a hurricane.

"What happened?" she asked, unable to believe the tidy room she had left just minutes before could have been destroyed so fast.

"They ganged up on me," Casey said, from the floor where two eight-month-olds sat staring up at him, both faces angelic with their blond curls and big brown eyes.

"Sure they did," Jo said as she started picking up toys and putting them into the large toy box that had been emptied in record time.

"I was trying to figure out what they wanted to play with, but they don't seem to like any of their toys," Casey said as he wound up a toy car and sent it across the nursery floor while both the babies ignored it. "See."

"It seems they find you more fascinating," Jo said. Not that she could blame them. Dressed in jeans and a fitted black T-shirt, the man looked more like he was ready to hit the downtown clubs than babysit. She looked down at her own khaki shorts and the baggy novelty T-shirt she'd bought at a tourist stop in Miami, which was much more practical for the night ahead of them.

"Summer said they'd be getting hungry soon. Maybe we should change and feed them." Though the two babies didn't look hungry, they looked more puzzled by Casey's presence in their room. "I thought you had spent some time with the twins."

"I see them at work sometimes when Summer brings them in to see Alex," Casey said.

"But you like kids," Jo said as she bent over to pick up the little princess, Maggie, leaving the little prince, Jacob, for Casey.

"I like kids. These are not kids. Kids walk and talk. I don't know what to do with babies," Casey said, though Jo noticed he seemed very comfortable picking up the little boy.

"Don't you want kids someday?" Jo asked as they made their way to the kitchen.

Casey stopped and held the boy out at arm's length, studying him. "I don't know. I haven't given it much thought."

"It might be time for you to start thinking about it. You're not getting any younger, and you don't want to be one of those fathers that get mistaken for the child's grandfather." Though the thought of Casey becoming a father was hard to imagine. He'd have to find a woman to stick with longer than three months, something he hadn't done in all the time she had known him.

"I've got plenty of time. I'm not the one with the biological clock ticking. You should be worried about yourself," Casey said as he studied the buckle of the high chair that matched the one Jo was buckling Maggie into.

"My clock is doing just fine," Jo said, hearing the edge of anger in her voice. Her fertility had been discussed too many times when she'd been married to Jeffrey. He'd wanted to discuss the when, the where, even the how. It had just been one more thing he wanted control over.

Now she had come to terms with the fact that she might not ever have children, but there was still a tender spot in her heart that throbbed at night when she was alone in bed. A part that ached for the happily-ever-after she'd been promised. The fact that it had turned into a nightmare instead should have taught her that the fairy tale of undying love was just that, a big fat lying tale. But still she dreamed of finding that love with someone, someday. That it was Casey who always played the part of the prince in those dreams was something she refused to acknowledge.

Casey gave her a questioning look, but she chose to ignore him as she prepared the food Summer had left for the babies. When Jacob began to fuss, she handed Casey a bowl with mashed sweet potatoes and a small spoon.

He studied the spoon and then began to feed the little boy. Maggie, seeing her brother getting fed before her, began to cry.

"See, this is what I mean," Casey said as he stopped and stared at the red-faced, crying little girl who had been an angel until then. "Kids don't do this. If one kid was eating and the other got tired of waiting for their turn, they'd just grab the other one's food."

"I'm sure that will happen in the future between these

two, but right now crying is the only way they can tell you that they're not happy." Jo placed a spoonful of sweet potatoes in the crying girl's mouth. The silence that followed was priceless.

Her phone rang and she pulled it from her pocket. Maybe once Summer knew her children were being fed properly she'd relax and enjoy her night out. "They're eating their sweet potatoes and I've already cut up their bananas, so you can quit worrying. Me and Casey have this under control."

"Joanne? What are you talking about? And who is Casey?" Jeffrey asked, his voice so clear she looked around the room to make sure he wasn't standing in there with her.

Startled and cursing herself for not checking her caller ID before answering her phone, she couldn't answer him. When Casey took the phone from her hands, she didn't object. She knew that Alex and Summer had the best security that money could buy, but at that moment it did nothing to make her feel safe. All she could think was that Jeffrey could be here, in Key West or even on Alex's property.

She looked over at the babies. No matter what, she wouldn't let him bring her friends and their children into this.

"Who is this?" Casey asked, though she was sure he knew exactly who it was just by her reaction.

With the roaring of the adrenaline rush in her ears, she couldn't hear whatever it was that Jeffrey said to Casey, but she didn't need to. There would be threats and bullying. It was how he handled everyone who did something he didn't like.

"I'm a friend," Casey said as he turned toward her and she met his eyes, "and her lover. And who are you?"

They both stood there a moment, then Casey held the phone out to her. Jeffrey had hung up.

"Well, that was short and sweet. I thought he'd have more questions for me. I guess he decided we couldn't be friends. And I was so looking forward to getting to know him better after the nice threats he issued if I didn't put you back on the phone."

"It's not funny," Jo said. "I don't even know where he is. What if he's on the island? What if he tries to get in here?"

Casey handed her the phone before wrapping his arms around her. "I'm sorry. I know there is nothing funny about this situation. I should have thought to ask him where he was calling from, but I don't think he would have told me."

She sank into the warmth of him. His arms felt so good around her. She felt safe and treasured there. She let her own arms wrap around his waist, needing to feel closer to him. It was something she'd never felt free to do before. It was funny how fear could give you the strength to do things you normally wouldn't be brave enough to do. Resting her head against his chest, the soft cotton shirt against her cheek, she could hear the drum of his heart. So steady. Just like him. Never sputtering. Always constant. He was her rock right now.

And she couldn't take advantage of that by pretending what he felt for her was anything more than friendship, even though she wanted nothing more than to stand there in his arms, his body warm and hard against her own, forever. But she had to step away before her body did something that her brain knew would be a mistake.

"What the…" Casey said.

She tensed, afraid that he had somehow realized that it was desire that kept her in his arms instead of the need for comfort. Looking up, she saw that he was focused on where the twins sat quietly in their high chairs. It was the realization that they'd been a little too quiet that had her spinning out of his arms.

But the royal twins sat perfectly content. It didn't seem to bother them a bit that they were covered in the orange sweet potato that was supposed to have been their dinner.

"What do we do now?" Casey asked.

"We clean them up and start again," Jo said as she reached for a cloth, glad that there was something to do to keep her mind off Jeffrey's phone call. She had to find the strength to fight down the fear his voice automatically produced. She'd looked forward to tonight all week and now he'd ruined it. Hadn't he ruined enough of her life already? Why couldn't he just leave her alone?

Casey carefully laid the little boy down in his bed. The only babies he had ever cared for had been ones that were sick and, most of the time, fighting for their lives. He'd seen the faces of their parents and wondered how they endured the fear and the heartache of having a child who was suffering, or worse, one they were in danger of losing. But this little guy, dressed in the superhero sleeper Jo had let Casey pick out, was healthy and content. Babies had always seemed so fragile to him. But wasn't everyone at some point in their life, even after they grew up?

He looked over to where Jo sat in a rocking chair, holding the little princess. He'd seen the baby's eyes shut even before Jacob had fallen asleep in his own arms, but still Jo held her, the chair slowly moving backward and forward. They both knew that Jo was continuing to hold her more for her own comfort now than the baby's.

She'd been nervous throughout the night, jumping every time the air conditioner unit turned on or the wind rustled something outside. He'd reminded her that Alex's security system was state-of-the-art and monitored live by a company in California that would notify both Alex, the local police and whoever was in the house if there was a breach in their security. It didn't help. She was determined that she was putting everyone in danger by being there. What did she think her friends were going to do? Just stand by and let her ex-husband hurt her? They'd all stand up for her if they needed to.

He'd felt her body tremble against his, and it had scared him. He would have destroyed the man who had done that to her if he could have. But it seemed no matter how much he told her that he would keep her safe, she didn't believe him. She didn't trust him to protect her, and he needed to fix that or she was going to run.

Finally, she stood and placed the baby in her crib, though she stood there beside her for a few minutes before joining him at the door.

"I saw some pizza in the fridge we can heat up," Casey said as Jo followed him silently down the hall.

"I'm starved. I didn't know babysitting could be such hard work."

"It's one of the parenting rules that you make sure you feed your babysitter. Summer was just so excited about a night out that she didn't think about it. I bet if I break into her secret stash of lobster bisque in the freezer she'll feed us better next time," Jo said.

"I'm okay with the pizza, but feel free to eat the bisque and give Summer a hard time. Not that I'm volunteering to do this on a regular basis." It had actually been a fun evening once the babies had warmed up to him. While Jo had taken on bath duty, he'd been assigned the duty of getting them dressed. It had reminded him of a wrestling match. One which he had won, as witnessed by the fully clothed babies asleep in their cribs.

As he heated up the pizza, Jo turned on the sound system, setting it to some mellow jazz, his favorite. They ate on the couch, him with his pizza and her with her soup, and talked about everything except what was on both of their minds. He could ignore this thing that hung between them, but that wasn't his way.

He believed in facing a problem head-on as he had done when he'd taken the phone and tried to get Jo's ex to talk to him. Had it agitated the man more? Oh, yeah. He'd hit home with his lie about being Jo's lover. Jeffrey was full of jealousy and rage right now. But it was at him, not Jo, which had been his intention. If Jo realized that had been his plan, Casey would be in trouble. Right now, though, he didn't have to worry about it. If or when Jeffrey showed up, Casey would deal with him man-to-man while assuring that Jo went unharmed. Until then,

Casey's job was making sure Jo stayed put in Key West where he could keep her safe.

"Feeling better?" he asked. He needed to get Jo to talk to him. He wanted to find out where her head was.

"Some," she said. "I might have overreacted. And I know that you're right. Jeffrey isn't going to break in here tonight. Besides having great security, it isn't his way. He prefers to appear as the good guy. But what you did, telling him that we're lovers, I wish you hadn't. He'll see it as a challenge."

"Wasn't that the plan all along? That we let people think that we're lovers so that when he showed up he'd see that you've moved on and that I'm here with you. That I'm going to be there to protect you. That he can't have you back. Can't threaten you or hurt you anymore."

Casey's throat got tighter with each word. He felt like he'd been sitting on a keg of dynamite ready to explode ever since he'd gotten on the phone with Jo's ex. He'd known the man was worthless and a bully, but hearing his rants on the phone and the threats he'd made to him and Jo had given him a taste of what she had gone through in her marriage. No one should treat someone that way. Not man or woman.

"I know that's the plan. I agreed to it. But I have some second thoughts now. Besides, I'm not sure anyone is buying our act," Jo said.

"Why do you think that?" he asked.

"I don't know. It just seems that people would have their doubts. You have to admit that I'm not like the women you usually date."

"What? I have a type now?" he asked. With Key West

being a popular international tourist spot, he'd dated a diverse group of women from all over the world. "I don't know why you would think that."

"Maybe because all your women are gorgeous. When's the last time you dated a plain Jane like me?"

Her question startled him and then made him mad. "Plain Jane? What does that even mean? There's nothing plain about you. Besides being smart and beautiful, both inside and out, you're too complicated for anyone to call you 'plain.'"

He put his pizza down and turned toward her, taking her face in his hands. "When I see you, I see a caring woman who works hard every day to help others. A woman who would take time from her life to babysit for a friend. And a woman who has always been there when I needed her."

"That's not what I meant. I meant I don't look like the women you date."

"So you're saying that I think you're good enough to be my friend, but not good enough for me to date? Is that what you're saying?"

"No. Yes. I don't know," Jo said. She tried to turn away from him, but when he rested his forehead on hers, she stilled.

"I don't know who told you you're plain—" though he had a good idea "—but they were lying to you. You're beautiful, Jo. Men look at you all the time. I've told you that."

"And you growl at them," Jo said, her lips forming a saucy pout that had him forgetting what he had been saying.

"If that's all it takes to run them off, they don't deserve

you. Any man would be proud to be seen with you. If it wasn't for you being my best friend, I'd ask you out and no man would scare me off." He stilled, realizing what he had just admitted.

Jo stared at him, her eyes wide as the tip of her tongue swept across her bottom lip.

He'd never noticed just how plump or how sexy her wide lips were until now. As if in a trance, he couldn't take his eyes off them. Before he knew what he was doing, he was moving in to taste them, a part of his brain going haywire as his lips were about to touch hers. A part he had tried to ignore for years had always wondered what it would be like to kiss Jo. Now he would know.

The front door suddenly opened, and they looked up to see Alex and Summer standing in the doorway staring at them.

"So, we leave you to babysit my angels and you end up making out. I am so disappointed in you two," Alex said, though there was a big smile plastered on his face.

For a moment he felt as if he had gotten caught making out on his parents' couch, something that might have happened a couple times in his high school days. Then, remembering that he and Jo needed everyone to believe they were a couple so that when Jeffrey showed up their story would be supported, he put his arm around Jo's shoulders and pulled her against him.

"I'm not disappointed," Summer said as she ducked under her husband's arm and came toward them. "I think it's wonderful. I just wish I'd taken a picture so I could post it around town. It's time everyone knows that the great Casanova of Key West is off the market."

Casey groaned loudly, getting the laugh from his friends that he had wanted. He wasn't sure what had just happened between him and Jo, but he knew that if they hadn't been interrupted they'd be doing exactly what his friends were accusing them of. He could still feel desire racing through his body with just the thought of his lips touching Jo's. Unable to help himself, he looked down at her. Oh, yes, those lips still looked way too kissable.

Her eyes met his, and he saw a hunger that matched his own. Where was this coming from? There had never been anything physical between them before. He'd always made sure of that. Friendship and romance didn't mix. He knew it, and he was sure Jo would agree with him.

Maybe they were just confused by this act they were playing. He knew his body sure seemed to be. Or maybe this was just a temporary thing that would pass by morning, leaving them laughing at what fools they'd been. But what if it didn't? What if he'd ruined everything by giving in to that one moment of desire?

The fact that he was still thinking about that almost-kiss, even now, after Summer and Alex had saved them from that danger, was not a good sign.

CHAPTER SEVEN

JO LIFTED THE bucket of smoked-damaged sheetrock and began the walk to the dumpster that had been delivered to Lucy's to help with the cleanup. While the block exterior walls were still standing, the old interior had to be cleared out so that a contractor could begin rebuilding it. It was hard work, but she was glad to do her part for her friend.

Besides, it gave her a good reason to get out of the house where Casey had been tiptoeing around her. What did he think she was going to do? Hold him down and kiss him so that she could finally find out what it felt like to have his lips on hers?

Okay, maybe she had given that a thought or two, but not seriously. Maybe she should just come out and tell him that he was safe around her. She'd made it this many years without attacking him. That should count for something.

"You okay, Jo?" Darren called out from the door.

She looked around and realized that she had been headed in the wrong direction. "Sorry, I wasn't paying attention."

While Lucy was still recovering from her burns and the smoke inhalation, Darren had arrived to be on hand to supervise for her. He was quick to answer everyone's questions on Lucy's recovery and pass on how grateful the woman was for all their help. By the time they had the dumpster half-full, he had set up a couple barbecue grills and the smell of steak and burgers cooking began to overtake the stench of the burned building.

She had just emptied the bucket and started back when a familiar Jeep pulled up. Moose jumped out and headed toward her as if he hadn't seen her in days.

"Whoa, Moose. Be careful or you'll end up with soot on you and you'll have to get a bath." Moose's ears went on alert, and his tail began to wag. Her dog loved being in water more than anything else.

"It looks like you've got a lot done," Casey said as he joined them, his eyes going everywhere but to her.

She wasn't surprised to see him. He'd offered to come by after his work at the dog shelter was done. Jo knew it was mean and petty that she had hoped he would stay away. They could use his help. If only she could get over this awkward feeling around him. This feeling that he knew she was looking at him while at the same time, she somehow knew he was looking back at her. They had danced around each other like this for two days now, and it was getting old. The tension between them was becoming unbearable. Was it so terrible that he had almost kissed her?

"We need to talk," she said, unable to go another minute without dealing with this invisible wall that had come up between them. They'd never had this awkwardness between them, and she didn't know how to handle it.

"About what?" Casey asked, finally looking at her before glancing away. He looked down at his feet then shuffled them around. She'd seen this before. It was the telltale sign that he wanted to be anywhere but where he was right now, which shouldn't have been the case. What did he see when he looked at her that was making him avoid her like this? She was the same old Jo she had always been. Was it so strange, so out of nowhere, that he recognized her as a woman? A woman that he'd almost kissed?

She thought about doing it. Just kissing him, right then and there, beside an old rusted dumpster so that she could get it over with. Maybe neither of them would like it. Maybe Casey would laugh and forget about it and life would go back to normal. At least for him.

Only she wasn't sure she wanted it to go back the way it was. She was tired of ignoring how she felt. She was tired of denying the attraction she had for him. An attraction that would be more than apparent if she did ever kiss the man, something that she didn't want to get into right then. Not the time. Not the place.

She turned to walk away. She'd just leave him there to stare off into space like he was doing right then. How long would it take him to notice that she was gone? A minute? Five?

"Food's ready," Darren called over the noise of the hammering and scraping going on in the pub.

"Just forget it," she said as she started toward where the rest of the crowd was headed. When a hand touched her shoulder, stopping her, she turned back to Casey, shocked to see the look of desire in his eyes.

"We promised not to mess things up between us," he

said, reminding her of the vow she had insisted he make that night on the beach.

"I know," she said. "I just didn't know it was going to be this hard."

"Me either. You're important to me, Jo. Our friendship is important to me."

She didn't know what to say. Was it possible that she was reading Casey all wrong? Maybe it had just been her imagination. Maybe he had never even thought of kissing her.

Which would mean what? That she was the one causing all the tension in the relationship? If so, this would be even more awkward for her. How could she fix this?

"Our friendship is important to me too. I would never do anything to risk it. You know that." She spoke the truth; she just needed to remember it herself.

"I don't want things to change between us," Casey said as he bent down and picked up a piece of wood that had fallen from someone's pile of debris on its way to the dumpster.

The finality of his voice told her everything she needed to know. Maybe Casey had started to kiss her, but he wasn't happy about it. And he wasn't planning on repeating it. Which left her only one choice. She had to accept what he was saying now and his reasons for it so that this awkwardness between them could go away.

"Hey, you two," one of the EMTs said as he walked past them with a bucket of soggy Sheetrock, "you need to see this. It looks like we're about to get busy."

"We're both off today," Casey said as they followed the man to where Darren was serving food.

"Me too," the man said. "We better enjoy it while we can."

They grabbed some burgers and drinks then joined the crowd that surrounded the small television Darren had set up to watch the college football games. Only it wasn't football they were all watching. Instead, on the screen a picture of deep blue water showed a red swirl moving through the Atlantic. When the weather forecaster drew lines from the tropical system, which had just been named Ileen, up to Florida with more than one line crossing close to the Keys, they all groaned. She was using words like sheering and fronts, but all Jo saw were the spaghetti models that showed the storm headed straight for them.

"It's only a tropical depression," Jo said, trying to find some hope for the group, which was made up mostly of first responders. "Maybe it will only bring us some rain."

"It's rained all summer. We don't need anymore," one of them said while another groaned in the background. "I'm tired of rain."

"But the winds are already at forty-five miles per hour," another one said.

"I hope Lucy isn't watching this," Darren said from behind them. "She'll worry even more about this place."

"Then we better get back to work and get the pub boarded up before she breaks out of the hospital and heads down here," Casey said, getting another groan from the group as the television returned to the football game that was in progress.

"Do we need to be worried?" Jo asked Casey, watching as the others filed past them back into the burned-out interior of the building.

"No. We've weathered storms before. We'll make it through this one too," he said, giving her a smile that she hadn't seen since the night they'd babysat the twins.

Jo stopped and stared at him as he followed the others into the soot-covered entrance, a big shovel slung over his shoulder. Was he talking about the weather or their turbulent relationship? Either way, she knew a storm was coming, and she didn't share his optimism. All storms were dangerous. They could hurt and destroy. The only thing she could do now was to hope that the two of them and their friendship were strong enough to get through it.

When Casey's phone went off the next morning, he wasn't surprised. He'd closed down the bar with some of the other EMTs, and they'd all made a point to keep up with the weather updates during the evening. The higher the winds got, the more somber the crowd became. By the time he'd headed home, the winds had reached seventy-five miles an hour and Tropical Storm Ileen had gotten an upgrade to Hurrican Ileen. Only the timing of a low front would decide whether the islands would be impacted.

"We've got an hour to report to headquarters," Jo called from below the stairs.

He grunted something he hoped sounded like "okay" then rolled onto his back and stared at the ceiling. He should have headed home when Jo had. He wasn't one for staying out all night. He spent so many nights working that he had learned to appreciate a night of good sleep. But last night, when Jo had left, he found himself holding back. He wasn't even sure why. All he knew was once Jo had checked in and let him know she'd made it home safely, the tension he'd felt for the last few days finally subsided.

What he didn't want to admit, even to himself, was that without Jo around he could finally relax. He didn't need to be on constant alert. He didn't need to look away whenever he caught a glimpse of those tempting lips that had almost got them in trouble. He didn't need to leave the room when the atmosphere began to hum with a sexual tension that he had never experienced before. There at the bar, he could nurse a beer and think of nothing more dangerous than the threatening storm that seemed intent to visit the Keys.

"I'm putting on some coffee and making some eggs and toast. Do you want some?" Jo called, her voice nearer now.

He looked over from his loft bed to see her standing on the ladder. Her hair was wet from her shower, but she had already dressed for the day in a pair of fitted jeans and a pink-striped shirt. His body reacted like it was a force of nature, becoming hard and demanding. He fought against a groan that was instinctive. All he wanted right then was to pull the sheets back over his head and go back to sleep. Not that he wanted to return to his dreams. The erotic picture of Jo spread out on his bed, this bed, was part of the reason he was in trouble right then. The only safe thing he could do was remain where he was and find a way to get rid of her.

"Coffee sounds amazing, but I'd really love some bacon with those eggs and toast. And maybe instead of eggs you could make it a cheese omelet? And there's some onion and tomatoes you can add too." He felt bad for asking her to do more work, but it would keep her busy. And it would give him and his traitorous body time to recover.

"Okay, but you better hurry. We don't have a lot of time," she said as her head disappeared from the landing and she headed back down the stairs.

Once in the shower, he didn't want to leave. His world was complicated with problems he had never imagined, and he'd rather cower in the shower than face what was waiting in the kitchen. But that wasn't possible. He only had a few minutes to eat and get to work. After the water was turned off, the smell of frying bacon drifted over the steamy bathroom. Unable to help himself, he quickly dressed and followed the smell into the kitchen, only to find it empty with the plate of food waiting on the stove for him.

There was no Jo waiting there to ask a million questions about what he thought of their bosses' request for all staff to report for a mandatory meeting. No Jo to drill him on the possible damage Hurricane Ileen could do if she hit the islands. No Jo to tell him all about what was trending on her news feed.

No Jo to smile at him from across the table. And instead of feeling free, he felt disappointed. Which didn't make any sense at all. He'd been the one to tell Jo that he didn't want their relationship to change, that he wanted their lives to go back to the way they were before they had started all of this pretending. He'd always liked his quiet mornings in his home before Jo had moved in. What was wrong with him?

Unable to sit there, alone, any longer, he poured his

coffee in a mug and made a sandwich from the toast, eggs and bacon. He told himself it was because he didn't have the time to eat. He tried to believe it.

When he arrived at work, he was surprised to see so many people. Every chair in the building had been rounded up and there were still people standing. There were the nurses and paramedics that he worked with, and the three pilots who rotated in and out of duty. But there were a couple others he didn't recognize.

"Who are the suits?" he asked as he took a place next to Dylan, Alex's assistant and one of the best flight paramedics Casey had ever known.

"They're from the county emergency services and the tourist council. They just finished a meeting with Alex. He must have invited them to stay, probably so we can ask any questions." They both moved over as Katie, Dylan's wife, joined them.

Casey looked through the crowd and saw that Jo was sitting up front. As he looked, she turned and waved. He started to wave back then realized it was Katie she was motioning to.

"Jo and Summer saved me a seat in the front. Do you mind?" Katie asked Dylan.

"Of course not. I'll see you after the meeting," Dylan said, before dropping a kiss on his wife's upturned face.

"Lunch at Marco's?" she asked.

"That sounds perfect," Dylan said.

Casey watched as Katie made her way to the front, where she was quickly surrounded by her friends. When he looked over at Dylan, he saw that he was also watching his wife.

"Don't the two of you ever get tired of spending so much time together?" Casey asked, only realizing too late that his mouth had voiced what his brain had been wondering.

"Me and Katie?" Dylan asked. "Of course not. Why? Are you already getting tired of having Jo around all the time?"

"I guess everyone knows she's staying with me?" Casey asked. Not that he was surprised. Though there were easily fifteen people at the meeting, they were still a tight crew.

"Staying with you?" Dylan asked. "Don't you mean she's moved in with you?"

Casey didn't see the difference, but he nodded. "It's all kind of new. I'm just trying to figure it out as I go."

"Says the man who swore he'd always remain a bachelor," Dylan said.

"It wasn't so long ago that you were saying the same thing," Casey said. But Katie had barely arrived on the island when Dylan had fallen for her. "And I'm still a bachelor. We haven't made any long-term plans."

"The two of you have been headed this way for years. You just didn't know it," Dylan said.

Casey started to ask what he meant, but Alex had made his way to the front of the room. Everyone paused their conversations, as all of them were anxious to hear why they had been called in.

"Thanks everyone for coming," Alex said. "I'm sure by now you are all aware that there is a storm out in the Atlantic. The National Hurricane Service is watching this one closely as it has become more organized overnight.

Mr. Dean is here from Monroe County Emergency Services and had asked that I hold this meeting on the chance that the Keys are impacted. As we all know, these storms can be unpredictable, but we need to be prepared."

As Alex stepped back, one of the men in a dark suit came forward. "As your boss was saying, these storms can change quickly and here on the Keys we want to be ready. If it's determined that Hurricane Ileen will threaten the Keys, a mandatory evacuation order will be issued asking all visitors to leave. If this happens, the county tourist development council will advise those visitors on the evacuation. That decision would be made by emergency services, hopefully twenty-four hours before impact."

As Casey listened, the man went into the necessary bridge closings due to winds, evacuation of locals, and finally, why they had all been called in—the possibility of needing to evacuate patients from the local hospital.

"We've been here before. We prepare for the worst and hope for the best. But Hurricane Irma taught us that though we don't get hit often, the Keys are as vulnerable as the rest of the state of Florida. We want to have a plan in place in case the worst happens."

The man stepped back and Alex stepped forward. "I'll be sending out emails to each one of you with a plan and schedule for evacuations if it becomes necessary. If Hurricane Ileen does decide to make a visit here, we will be prepared. I ask that you stay in touch and prepare your families and stay safe."

As soon as Alex stepped back, everyone seemed to talk at once. If the local emergency services issued an evacuation order, it would be all hands on deck. There wouldn't be time for the first responders to get their own homes ready for the storm, and they all knew it.

The small cottage that was his home had been entrusted to him by his grandmother, and he took the responsibility to protect it seriously. He checked the weather app on his phone and saw that the winds had increased. Eighty miles an hour. Still a Category 1.

"What's up?" Jo said, from beside him.

Startled, he looked down to see that most of the room had cleared out. It looked like everyone had the same thought that he did. Time to prepare. "How do you feel about helping me hang some hurricane shutters?"

"I can't think of anything I'd rather do," Jo said.

And just like that everything seemed right between them.

CHAPTER EIGHT

"ONLY ONE MORE to go," Jo said as she climbed down from the ladder. Her back was killing her and her arms had begun to shake with the weight of the metal hurricane shutters, but it was good, hard work and it was just what she needed right then. There was no worrying about Jeffrey, Casey or the hurricane while you were up on an eight-foot ladder stretching for every inch while supporting your side of a heavy metal shutter.

Her phone went off with an update from her weather app as she reached the last step. It looked like Hurricane Ileen was not in a hurry to share her destination as she spun around the Atlantic at a crawl.

"Any change?" Casey asked as he came off his own ladder.

His T-shirt was plastered against his chest with sweat, but somehow he still looked good. Meanwhile, she was sporting a pair of underarm sweat rings, and the hair she'd knotted on the top of her head had come loose and hung limp from the smothering humidity. It was so unfair.

"The winds have increased to eighty-five miles an hour but no change in direction. Cuba's talking about evacuation orders now."

"If it doesn't change in the next few hours, we'll be

sending out our own evacuation orders. Then the real work will begin. People will panic trying to leave the Keys, and we'll be flooded with wrecks on Highway 1 and boating accidents in the Gulf," Casey said. "Thanks for the help here."

They both looked back at the house. Jo knew how much it had meant to Casey when his grandmother had willed it to him. It had stood up to many storms throughout its lifetime, but somehow they both knew this was different.

"It'll be okay," she said, though she still worried.

"I hope so. And now that we've done all we can here, what about your place?" Casey said.

Her place? She hadn't even thought of her apartment. It had only been a few days since she'd moved into Casey's place, and she had almost forgotten the little apartment she had called home.

"My landlord will take care of boarding up the windows, if it comes to that. I should probably go over and check things out though." She'd packed up her books, personal papers and pictures to take with her when she had planned to leave the island, but she hadn't brought them with her to Casey's. She needed to make sure they would be safe. "It won't take but a moment though. I don't have that much there to worry about."

Casey's phone dinged with a message, and he pulled it out. "Roy says a bunch of the EMTs are getting together tonight at the tiki bar. Want to go?"

"Sure. I'll drive my car and stop by my place on the way." It could be a long time before any of them got a chance to get together if Hurricane Ileen didn't decide to take a detour.

"Maybe I should go with you," Casey said as they headed indoors to clean up.

"I'll be fine. It'll only take a moment, and even Jeffrey is smart enough to not visit an island that has a hurricane headed its way. I'll have my phone with me in case there's a problem."

"Okay, but call me if anything doesn't feel right. I'll only be a few minutes away," Casey said.

"Come on, Moose, let's go get cleaned up and put on our party clothes," she called to the dog who'd been giving them moral support by barking at each and every car that had passed the house as they'd worked.

By the time Jo and Moose headed to her apartment, the sun was starting to set. She was relieved to see that the landlord had begun the process of nailing the large sheets of plywood across the windows of the apartments. There were still some windows where supplies had been stacked for work to resume the next day, but all of the windows of her own apartment that she could see from the parking lot had been covered.

But as she opened the door to her apartment, she hesitated. With no light from the windows, the room was darker than a moonless night sky. There was none of the warmth of the home she had known for the last four years. Instead, it seemed abandoned and lonely. Moose whined from beside her and her hand went down to pat his head.

"It's okay. We just need to turn the lights on," she told him, then flipped the switch that flooded the room with a stark white illumination. "See, Moose. Everything is okay."

Still chilled from the eerie atmosphere, Jo went

through each room turning on the lights. When the last room had been explored by both her and Moose, her nerves finally settled. "This is ridiculous," she told him. "We have a party to get to."

Not sure where the safest place for her treasured belongings would be, Casey had offered to keep them at his place inside an interior storage room and she'd agreed. His home had withstood hurricanes for generations. It was out of the usual flood zones and about as safe as she could ask for.

She'd just finished loading her last box when George, her neighbor, drove up.

"Are you coming or going?" he asked as he got out of his car.

"I just stopped by for a few things," Jo said. They'd been neighbors for as long as she'd lived there, exchanging pleasantries and gossip about other renters as they came and went. He'd always been nice, and she'd felt safe knowing he was living beside her. More than once he'd helped with small projects around her place, and she'd always returned the favor by taking care of his cat, Flo, when he'd headed to Miami to visit his parents.

"I'm glad to see they've got most of the windows boarded up," she said.

"Yeah, they started late, but maintenance says they'll have it finished by noon tomorrow. I'm packing up me and Flo tonight and going to stay with my parents. Hopefully I'm just being cautious, but it will make my parents feel better. My dad even agreed to let Flo stay."

She knew George's dad had terrible allergy issues, so his agreeing to host Flo as well as George was a sign that people were beginning to take this storm seriously. "I think that sounds like a good idea."

"Oh, yeah. I've got a package that was delivered a few days ago. I had told one of your friends, the one that's some kind of royalty. I recognized her from the TV. She seemed real nice too. I'll go get it for you."

Jo remembered that Summer had said something about a package, but as Jo hadn't ordered anything online recently, she hadn't given it another thought. It was probably something from her parents.

She waited while George opened his door then returned with a long rectangle package.

"Here it is," he said, handing it to her.

It was wrapped in brown paper and didn't weigh much. She tried again to recall anything she might have ordered, but there was nothing. Then she saw the address from the sender. Written in a thin cursive that she would recognize anywhere, Jeffrey had scrolled his name and address.

Something skittered up her spine, a foreboding or a premonition, she wasn't sure what it was, but it wasn't good. It sent her on alert and her eyes scanned the parking lot, looking for any sign of her ex-husband. But there was nothing. She recognized the few cars in the lot as belonging to other renters. Besides, this package had been delivered days before.

She remembered the call she'd received from her ex-husband while she and Casey had been babysitting. Was that why he had called? To see if she had received this package?

"Thanks, for keeping this for me," she said, though every inch of her body wanted to recoil from the box.

"No problem. I've got to get packed, but you stay safe up there in the skies while I'm gone," George said, before heading back into his apartment.

Jo tightened her hand on Moose's leash as she made her way back to her car. She loaded Moose then laid the box on the seat beside her before shutting the car door. She didn't want to open it. Not now. She'd been looking forward to sharing the next few hours with Casey and the rest of their friends. She'd dressed in a short, fitted, pale blue dress that screamed to be let out onto the dance floor. And now all her excitement for the night had vanished.

Knowing that waiting to open the package would only make this worse, she picked the box up and read Jeffrey's address again. It was the same one they had shared once upon a time. It was supposed to have been their forever home. The one they would raise a family in someday. It had been none of those things, at least not for her. She hadn't even blinked when he insisted on keeping the house in their divorce settlement. She'd wanted nothing that she had shared with him.

Pulling the brown paper from the package, she found a white floral box underneath. The cloying smell of wilted red roses seeped from the box before she lifted the lid. Inside there was a note, one of those small rectangle cards that were provided by the florist. As she read the words, her hands began to shake.

She shut the box carefully then set it to the side. Cranking her car, she rolled down her window as she started down the road. The warm air, heavy with late summer humidity, did nothing to cool the anger that was beginning to boil through her veins.

Yes, she'd made mistakes. She should have been stronger. She should have seen Jeffrey for who he really was instead of the charming prince he had made himself out to be, but how long would she have to pay for her mistakes? What was it about her that had screamed victim to him? She'd been an independent woman before he had come into her life. Why couldn't he just accept that she had moved on with her life and leave her to it?

He'd made her leave her home. He'd taken away the safety she'd always felt in her new life. Now, when she'd made friends that were more like family, he was trying to take all that away from her by scaring her into running. Why did he have to spoil all of that?

Casey had been right when he'd told her she couldn't run away again. She'd left her hometown and Jeffrey still hadn't forgotten about her. She hadn't even been home to see her parents since the day she'd packed her little car and headed as far south as it was possible to go.

She pulled into the small parking lot and her eyes immediately went to where Casey's truck sat. She needed him. She needed to know he was near. Know he would keep her safe. Know that someone cared about her even though she was bringing them into a situation that was all her fault. She just needed Casey to put his warm arms around her and make the awful coldness that had seeped into her bones go away.

Jo saw him the moment she walked up to the open-air bar, and she froze. Standing by Casey, her hand resting against his chest as she spoke, stood Sarah. Something broke inside of Jo. It wasn't her heart. She'd built too many barriers around it where Casey was concerned. Instead, it was this buildup of anger, this boiling cauldron of every pain and fear and the resulting fury that she'd repressed over the last five years that had finally broken free. Anger at Jeffrey for destroying the safe life she had made for herself on the islands. Anger at herself for putting up with the way he had treated her when they were married. And a new anger, one directed at Casey for letting this woman touch him when, at least to the rest of the world, he was supposed to be loyal to her.

Before she knew it, she found herself across the room and pushing between the two of them. As Sarah protested with a shriek that could be heard from across the crowd, Jo turned to Casey.

Driven by the anger, the hurt and a stupid feeling of betrayal that she had no right to feel, Jo turned away from Sarah and grabbed the collar of Casey's shirt, pulling his head down till his face was even with hers. Laughing blue eyes met hers, and it only made her madder.

"You think this is funny?" she asked. His lips parted in a grin that answered her question. Was he laughing at her? Really? She'd just saved the man from his troubled ex and he just thought it was a game. But wasn't his whole life a game? He played women like they were instruments then moved on when one of them wanted more than to be a playmate. Well, if he liked games, she would be happy to play one with him. Let him see how he liked it.

She pulled his face closer and before he could realize what she was going to do, she crushed his lips against hers. It wasn't a fun kiss or a friendly kiss. No. This was a kiss meant to conquer, and she poured into it every bit of frustration she'd ever had while watching this man kiss another woman.

When he didn't pull back, she let go of his collar and wrapped her arms around his neck as she pressed her body even closer to his. Her breasts rubbed against his chest, and her nipples tightened to painful peaks. A heat she'd forgotten existed lit down in the pit of her core and exploded outward until her whole body seemed on fire. Her lips parted against his, and it was only when his tongue swept inside, tangling with hers, that she discovered she wasn't the only one being drawn into this dance of need and want.

His hands clasp her bottom and lifted her, turning her until she found herself pressed against something hard and rough against her back. Her hands tangled in Casey's blond curls and his hands pressed her even closer, the hard length of him imprinted against her body.

It was only when someone yelled, "Get a room!" from across the noisy bar that Jo's overheated brain began to surface and take control from a body that wanted nothing more than to finish what Jo had so stupidly started in a room filled with people she'd have to face later.

The thought of the smiles and winks she would receive from more than one nameless EMT after this stunt sobered her instantly. She'd made a fool of herself in front of everyone. And Casey? He probably thought she was putting on a show for Sarah and the crowd just to convince them that he and Jo were involved.

For a second she buried her face in Casey's shoulder. She couldn't face him. Couldn't face anyone. She didn't even want to face herself. She pushed away and started for the restroom, then turned at the last minute to the steps that led down to the beach. Jo could still hear Sarah's voice, raised in anger at Casey, when she made it down to the bottom step. Kicking off her shoes, she began to run down the beach, only discovering that Moose ran beside her when she heard his panting.

She ran until the only sound she could hear was the waves crashing against the shoreline. Now panting herself, she stumbled then tripped on her feet and tumbled into the sand.

She lay there doing nothing, feeling nothing. The fear, the anger, the need; they were gone now, washed away as the rhythmic waves rushed in and out. She was only numb. Just numb. She couldn't even cry, though she wanted to. A good, cleansing cry, as her mother had always called it, helped set things right sometimes. But she didn't have it in her.

It was shock. That had to be it. She'd gone from one emotion to another too close together, and her body couldn't handle it. She rested her overheated cheek against the cool sand and closed her eyes. She was tired and wrung out. She'd just rest a few minutes, then she'd get herself up and march back to that bar and face whatever she had to face. But not now. Not yet. Now she just wanted to be alone and to rest.

Casey looked up and down the beach. Though not yet full, the moon was on the increase, brightly reflecting against the water. Where had Jo gone? By the time he'd managed to get rid of Sarah and her accusations that he had lied to her about his feelings for Jo, there had been no sign of her. He didn't like the thought of her out alone on the beach at night, though he knew Moose would be able to protect her from most dangers.

As if on cue, Casey spotted the Great Dane to his right, loping down the beach toward him. He waited a moment, expecting Jo to be lagging behind the long-legged dog, but there was no sign of her.

"Where's Jo, Moose?"

The dog sprinted around him circling once, then twice, spraying sand as his paws dug into the ground. Then just as suddenly as he had come, he headed back down the beach.

"I guess that means I'm supposed to follow him," Casey said to himself as he took off at a jog.

He'd almost given up on reaching Moose when he spotted him at the top of the beach. Beside him sat Jo, one arm around the big dog. His breath came a little easier now that he could see that she was safe.

But now that he had found her, he didn't really know what he would say to her. It seemed like they had said everything there was to say with that kiss they had just shared. Where did they go from here? It was all good for them to play at being more than friends, but that kiss hadn't been an act. It had been hot and fresh and more than a little decadent. And now they had to face the reality that there was more, at least physically, between them besides friendship.

But it was the last thing he wanted. He didn't want to mess things up with Jo; he treasured their friendship too much. And while there were a few women he'd been able to remain friends with after their relationship had run its course, Jo was different. She'd been hurt by that rotten ex-husband of hers, and she deserved better than that. She deserved a man who understood how to treat her. He wasn't that man. He'd never been that man for anyone. He knew that.

He took life one day at a time with no worries about a future. Free and simple, that was the life he'd lived for years, and he didn't know if he could change. He didn't know if he wanted to. It was safe to live the way he did with no chance of being hurt by someone you trusted. He'd once planned a future with a woman, and then she'd walked away with someone else stating that what they'd had wasn't really love. It was just a friendship they'd mistaken for love.

If it hadn't been love he'd felt for Anna, what had it been?

He'd thought then that he'd never get over her. He'd been stupid and done things that had almost got him kicked out of the coast guard because the military didn't care how bad your heart was broken when you didn't show up for duty. He'd also learned that trying to drink your troubles away never worked. You just ended up with more trouble. Then his captain had called him into his office and given him some advice. Instead of worrying about falling in love with a woman, he just needed to concentrate on his job and if a woman got in the way of that job, he needed to stay away from them. Sure, it was okay to date women for fun, but he had to put the coast guard first. With that advice, he'd changed his lifestyle and priorities.

And when he'd left the coast guard, he carried that advice with him. Getting over his fiancée leaving him had taught him what was really important in life. Someone you thought cared for you could let you down, but your job and coworkers were always there for you. He liked to think he'd become a better man because of the experience, but that didn't mean he ever wanted to live through it again. And none of that was going to help him with the situation he was in with Jo.

Because there had never been another Jo for you.

And that scared him more than the kiss the two had shared.

Climbing up on the sandy hill, he took a seat, leaving Moose between them. They sat there with only the sound of the waves and an occasional car off in the distance. Silence had always been something that they were comfortable with, neither of them feeling the need to fill it with unnecessary chatter when they were together.

"I'm so sorry," Jo said, the words just above a whisper. "I don't know what happened."

Casey could describe in detail everything that had happened from the moment her soft, but demanding lips had had touched his to the moment she'd pulled away, leaving him hard and desperate and unable to focus on anything but the fact that she'd walked away from him without even a backward glance.

It had taken him a few minutes to understand that it had been the cheering crowd that had startled her into breaking whatever had taken hold of them. Only once he'd understood that she'd probably been embarrassed by the attention and had wanted to get away from the crowd, not running away from him, had he been able to clear his mind and deal with the nonsense Sarah had been saying about him not being honest with her about his feelings for Jo.

"There's nothing to apologize for," he said. At least not on her part. He had been the one who had lost control, pushing her back against the hard wooden railing that encircled the bar's deck and plastering his body against hers. Just the memory of her body, so soft and responsive as it moved against him, had him rock hard in an instant.

"I embarrassed you," she said, her voice a little stronger now, though her eyes never strayed from the ocean waters that seemed to go on forever.

"Are you kidding me? I got more backslaps from the guys than I got the day I delivered that baby in the back of the tour bus." It had been the highlight of his career for many years now.

"They must think I'm demented, jumping you like that," she said, then laughed. "Did you see Sarah's face? I was afraid she was having some sort of seizure."

"And you left me to deal with her alone," he said. He took a breath and let himself relax just a bit. Jo laughing he could deal with. "And no one thinks you're demented. We're supposed to be together. A couple. Couples kiss. Do you have any idea how many of those guys would like to have been in my place?"

"Why would you say that?" she asked.

The woman really had no idea how many heads turned when she entered a room.

"I said it, because it's true. Men look at you all the time."

And he'd never liked it. "Some have even tried to ask you out, but you always seem to be able to dodge them."

"Maybe I'm waiting for Prince Charming so I can be a princess like Summer and..." She stopped. "No, I take that back. I married someone I thought was Prince Charming, and he turned out to be a frog in disguise. I have no desire to kiss another frog in my lifetime."

And just like that they were back to the subject of kissing.

Jo took a deep breath and finally looked at him. "I guess we need to talk about it."

"I guess we do." He knew she was right, though he had no idea what to say.

"Your place or mine?" she asked, before winking at him.

Was she serious? Or was she just joking with him as she tried to lighten the mood? A certain part of him hoped she wasn't joking. His brain, on the other hand, wasn't sure what to think. "Are you serious?"

"I don't know," she said. "What do you think we should do? Pretend it never happened?"

"That would be the easiest thing to do, wouldn't it?" he asked, though he didn't believe for one moment that it would work. A peck on the lips they could have ignored. What they'd shared had been much more than a kiss. It had been a whole-body experience, from lips to hips. If he'd found it hard to be around Jo after their almost-kiss at Alex and Summer's place, how was he supposed to ignore what they'd shared tonight? Things were just going to get worse between them if they didn't deal with this now.

"Maybe it was just a fluke," Jo said. Her eyes met his and held this time. "Maybe it was just the timing or something."

Did she really believe that? Something in her eyes told him that she didn't mean a word she was saying. So what was she after? "How do you suggest we find out?"

"I guess we could repeat it. Like an experiment. If nothing happens, we can laugh about it and move on, right?" Jo said as her hand came up and stroked Moose's neck.

It would be crazy to go along with this. His body was still recovering from just thinking about that kiss. But what if she was right? What if it had just been a one-time thing? Jo had always been off his sexual radar due to their friendship. Maybe all it had been was the temptation of forbidden fruit that had caused him to react so strongly.

"Okay. I'm game. When and where?" he asked, suddenly nervous and excited all at the same time. He didn't have to check his pulse to know that his heart was beating too fast; he could feel it trying to come out of his chest.

"How about now? Right here?" Jo said with a voice that showed none of the nervousness he was feeling, though he noticed she held Moose's collar in a death grip.

"Okay. Let's do it," he said with a fearlessness he didn't feel. "Are we going to try this with Moose between us?"

"Down, Moose," she ordered.

They both watched the big dog as he jumped down

the hill in one big leap. The empty space Moose left between them was like a large gully that one of them had to cross. Neither made a move.

CHAPTER NINE

Jo STARED AT the space between them. What had she been thinking to suggest this? That this was their one chance to find out if there was something more between them? And if there was? Casey had made no secret of the fact that he didn't want anything but her friendship. He was like an old man so set in his ways that no one was going to change him. He didn't want a permanent lover. He didn't want to be anything but a friend to her. He didn't want to accept that the passion in the kiss they'd shared had been real. But what about what she wanted?

She slid into the space between them and stopped. She had made the first move and now it was up to him. Jo needed to know that he wanted to see this through. If the kiss fizzled, she'd accept that it had been only her imagination that had dreamed up Casey's response to her. And if the two of them went up in flames like they had at the bar?

"It's your move," she said. "If you don't want to take it, I'll understand."

"And if I do?" he asked, his voice so deep and rough that it sent goose bumps over her bare skin.

She looked up from where she had been studying the empty beach to find him bending over her. She clenched her hands, willing them to remain by her side when all she wanted to do was wrap them around his neck and pull him closer. His firm lips softly stroked hers, and for a moment she thought that was all he intended. Then his tongue was licking its way inside her mouth and everything inside of her gave way to her body's instinctual need for him as she arched her body up toward his. She'd always known it would be like this between them.

Her hands found their way up his chest until they encircled his neck while she tried to remind herself that they were only sharing a kiss. Nothing more. Just one kiss.

One kiss that seemed to go on and on in a never-ending pleasure that she had never experienced before as he kissed her with a wickedly, wild tongue that stroked a fire deep inside of her. That flame spread up her chest and across her breasts, causing her nipples to harden.

Just a kiss? There was no such thing when she was in Casey's arms.

And it made her desperate for more. She wanted him closer. She wanted the clothes between them gone. She wanted him inside her with a need she'd never known for another man.

As if he could read her mind, Casey pulled his lips from hers and quickly moved away, leaving her head spinning and her body disoriented. It was as if she'd been climbing some tall mountain and suddenly everything that had kept her safe was gone. Slowly, she returned to the reality the two of them shared. One that she couldn't help but question now. Just why was it so wrong that they enjoyed each other like this? People did it all the time.

But Casey wasn't like other people. He didn't want to

blur that line between friends and lovers. She looked up to see him staring at her like he'd been struck by lightning. The fact that she could hear him breathing in quick ragged breaths gave her some hope. She wasn't the only one who had felt the force of that kiss. He had to see there was something more than friendship between them now.

"So do we call this experiment a failure or a success?" she asked. It wasn't the question she wanted to ask. She wanted to ask why they had waited so long before doing this and how was she supposed to forget it now that they had?

"I don't know," Casey said, still staring at her like he'd never seen her before.

"Does that mean we need to do it again? Two out of three or something?" she asked, though as far as she was concerned the first two had been very successful.

Casey cleared his voice then looked away from her. "No, I think we can both agree that it wouldn't be a good idea to try that again."

Not knowing what else to say, she leaned back against the bank of sand and stared up at the stars. There were so many questions she wanted to ask, but every one of them seemed to lead back to what it was that prevented Casey from letting a woman inside those walls he'd built around his heart. He didn't talk about it much, but she knew it had to have something to do with the fiancée who, according to rumors, had left him at the altar.

"Do you ever wonder what would have happened if your fiancée had gone through with the wedding?" she asked. She was letting her subconscious take over her mouth tonight, and it didn't seem to care what came out. "I'm sorry. That was rude."

"It's okay. I was angry with you about not telling me about Jeffrey. It's only right that you get to ask me about Anna." He leaned back beside her, though she noticed he left plenty of room between them.

Would it always be like this between them now? Him, afraid to get too close to her, while she yearned for the feel of him next to her?

"I can't say I've considered what it would be like if we had married. When she left town with someone else, it was the end of things. What I thought we had together hadn't really existed according to her."

"But don't you ever wonder what marriage to her, or to someone you loved would be like? I know my marriage was a nightmare, but that doesn't mean I think they all are."

"No. I don't. She decided that we had mistaken our friendship for love. End of story."

But it wasn't the end. Jo knew that. He'd carried that dismissal of his feelings around for years now. It was time for him to let it go and move forward with his life, whether it was with her or with someone else.

And the fact that this woman had insinuated that you couldn't have a friend and also be in love? That didn't make sense. A love without friendship would be very sad. She knew they could have both.

But if the kiss they'd just shared hadn't shown him that, what could? It had definitely taken them out of the friend zone as far as she was concerned.

"It's getting late. We better get back to the party," he said as he stood, reaching a hand down to her.

Placing her hand in his, she stood. It seemed as far as he was concerned things would just go back to normal. If only she could ignore the way their kiss had made her feel as easily as he was.

"So we just forget this ever happened? Maybe you can, but I don't know that I can do that."

He let go of her hand instantly. Without waiting for her, he started back up the beach, only speaking when she caught up with him. "Don't you see, Jo? What I feel for you is too much to risk for some temporary fling. It would just end with hurt feelings because there are too many emotions involved already. Do you really want that? The two of us angry or hurt?"

She wanted to tell him that it didn't have to be that way. People had relationships that lasted forever. She'd been through hell in her marriage, but she still believed there was everlasting love. But even believing that, she couldn't promise him that what they had would last forever. He wouldn't believe her if she did. He had compartmentalized relationships into friendship or romantic flings, something that she knew now she could blame on his ex-fiancée.

He moved away from her, putting a couple feet between them as they headed back to the bar.

The rest of the walk was silent, except for when Moose decided to splash through the waves at the edge of the shore. What more was there to say? One look at that stubborn jaw of Casey's had told her he'd decided to put tonight behind them.

She hadn't realized just how far she'd gone when she'd left the bar. She'd only wanted to escape the humiliation of what she had done. Finally, the strings of lights that crisscrossed over the tiki bar's ceiling came into view. As they got closer, she was surprised that she couldn't hear the reggae music that usually blared across the outside speakers.

"Something must have happened," she said as they climbed the stairs to the bar that had been overflowing with people when she had left. Where had everyone gone?

"Hey, you guys." Jerry, the bartender for the night, came out of a small storage room that was the only enclosed part of the bar.

Unable to walk any farther, she took a stool at the bar. Her eyes went to the large television screen that was usually tuned to some sporting event for the crowd's entertainment. Tonight there was no rerun of a soccer or football game playing. Instead, it had been turned to a local news channel that was broadcasting a weather map showing the distinct outline of a hurricane.

"Where did everybody go?" Casey asked, taking a seat beside her at the bar.

"They all scattered about thirty minutes ago when the weather update came on. It seems Ileen has finally decided to make her move. Unfortunately, she's headed straight for us," Jerry said, before he went back into the storage area pulling a cart behind him.

Casey reached behind the bar and peeled the remote from its Velcro holder before turning up the volume so that they could hear what the local meteorologist was saying.

"Cuba is asking that its citizens evacuate inland as

soon as possible as Hurricane Ileen, now a Category 3 hurricane, is expected to make landfall there before crossing back into the Atlantic, where we're now being told there is a strong probability that it will strengthen once again into a Category 3 hurricane as it heads toward the Gulf of Mexico. Monroe County Emergency Services has issued a mandatory evacuation of all nonresidents beginning at dawn this morning."

Jerry walked out of the storage room pulling a cart full of glass bottles behind him. It all made sense now. He was clearing out the bar's stockroom as fast as he could.

"Let me help," Casey said, taking the handle of the cart and following the man to where he had stacked up crates of alcoholic bottles and the clear glasses the bar used for serving.

"What do we do now?" Jo asked, after they had helped load the crates into Jerry's truck.

"I checked my phone. Alex hasn't called us in yet. We're both working tomorrow night so we'd better get some sleep while we can" Casey said as he dug his keys from his pockets.

Jo pulled her own keys out of her dress pocket and headed for her car with Moose beside her, glad that they had come in separate vehicles. She needed a few moments alone. Things between her and Casey had changed tonight and no matter if he wanted to or not, there was no going back. They both needed some time to figure things out.

As she loaded Moose into the car, she saw the box of dead roses Jeffrey had sent with his cryptic message. He might be planning to come after her, but she couldn't worry about her ex-husband now. Nor could she get sucked into the what-ifs that kept circling around in her head concerning her and Casey.

Because Casey was right. With Hurricane Ileen threatening the islands, this could be the last chance she got to sleep for a very long time.

CHAPTER TEN

THEY'D JUST FINISHED their third flight going back and forth to the mainland transporting patients from the small Key West hospital that were too sick to go by ground, when a call came in for assistance at the request of the coast guard medevac unit.

"Any idea what we're looking at?" Casey asked the dispatcher as soon as they were in the air. Familiar with the guys who were stationed at the local coast guard base, he was more than a little surprised that they'd be asking for help from civilians.

"From the info we were given, it sounds like a catamaran got caught in the waves and turned over on its way back to land. It was carrying twenty passengers. There are two patients that need transport to Miami, which is why they've called for help. They're backed up with calls coming in from boats from here to the Dry Tortugas. They're going to meet you on the beach and transfer the patients. That's all the information we have at this time. James has the coordinates for the pickup. If we hear anything else, we'll radio it to you. Be careful out there. The winds are starting to pick up off the coast. I wouldn't be surprised if you're not grounded in the next few hours."

"Thanks, for the info. Roger out," Casey said. The

radio went off again, and he listened as James took instructions from the local Fire and Rescue for their landing spot.

"We're getting low on IV fluid supplies. We'll need to restock when we get back to headquarters," Jo said, stringing up a bag then setting it aside and starting on another one.

"Most of the patients from the hospital have been evacuated. Unless something else comes in, this might be our last flight," Casey said. As he went through the second bag of supplies, he could see that Jo was right. They were low on fluid and some of the meds used for sedation. Their last flight had been a motorcycle victim with a head injury who they'd been forced to intubate while in midflight. He'd been a big guy, and it had taken a lot of meds to keep him under so that they could get him safely to a neurosurgeon at the nearest hospital. They had tried not to sedate him, but he'd become too combative to handle while ten thousand feet in the air.

"I hope so. I'm starting to drag," Jo said, the circles around her eyes telling him that she hadn't slept any better than he had.

"ETA five minutes," James called out to them.

Casey looked down at the road below him, still full of cars headed north out of town. They'd flown over Highway 1 several times that day, and the traffic remained bumper to bumper.

Two fire trucks came into view and Casey recognized the empty parking lot they would be landing in as part of Fort Zachary, but there was no sign of the coast guard medevac.

"I've got a visual," James relayed to the dispatch.

When the dispatch radioed back an all clear from the first responders on the ground, James began their landing.

"But where's our patients?" Jo asked as she studied the empty parking lot.

The skids hit the ground, and they each grabbed a bag and unloaded.

"Where's our patients?" Jo asked again, this time speaking to one of the firemen.

Before he could speak, Cascy heard the slap of rotor blades overhead and the orange Dolphin came into view. Much bigger than the copter that Heli-Care used to transport patients, it was a multi-purpose, short-range recovery machine that could fly in all weather on its search and rescue missions.

"What you got for us?" Casey asked the two coast guardsmen as they began to unload the first patient.

"Two head injuries. This one is responsive. The other one isn't. Both were hypothermic, but we got them warmed up on the way in," one of the men yelled over the noise of the rotors.

"They've been married over forty years. They're here celebrating their anniversary," the other man said, joining them with the second patient and handing two ID cards to Jo.

"Why was there a tourist boat going out today?" she asked.

'Not today, last night. The owner thought he could get one more cruise in before the weather got bad," one of the guardsmen replied.

"You mean they were out there all night?" Jo asked,

her voice reflecting her horror at the thought. "What about the rest of the passengers? And the crew?"

"We're bringing them in now. These two were the most critical. The rest are suffering from hypothermia and are banged up some, but they'll be okay. They managed to get back on the boat, but the mast was damaged. We'll be triaging them as we bring them in, but it looks like these are the only two that will need to be evacuated right now."

At that moment a strong wind picked up the sand and sent it flying in the air. Casey steadied the stretcher he helped push as the wind rocked it back and forth. Casey hoped the young man was right. The winds were picking up now, and before long it would be too late for anyone to fly. Even the coast guard had begun to evacuate its aircraft to other stations for safety. Only their all-weather Dolphin helicopters were staying behind to help with the evacuations and any rescue calls they received.

A voice came from the stretcher, and Casey had to bend over to hear what his patient was saying.

"It was supposed to be romantic." The man's voice was weak, but Casey heard every word.

They loaded his patient first, and then Jo followed with her patient. They had the stretchers secured, and then they left the ground in record-breaking time.

The high winds were left behind the farther they got from the coastline. Heading north, away from the storm, Casey relaxed and got into the rhythm he and Jo always found when they worked together.

"Mr. Dugger." Casey read the name on the patient's

ID, then stuck it in the top pocket of his flight suit. "How are you feeling? Any pain, nausea?"

"I'm okay. Just take care of Sandy. She went under. I couldn't find her." The man began to fight against the straps that restrained him.

"It's okay, Mr. Dugger. Sandy is right here beside you," Jo said. "We're going to get you both to the hospital."

Jo gave him a look then glanced pointedly at Casey's patient. Something was wrong with her patient, but she couldn't say anything in front of the woman's husband.

Casey looked over at Jo's monitor. The woman clearly had a change from the quick report they'd been given from the other crew, which had stated that both patients' vital signs were stable. Hypotensive, with tachycardia and a blood oxygen saturation in the eighties, the woman was about to crash if they didn't do something fast.

Without Jo asking, Casey pulled out a bag of norepinephrine and put it in her waiting hand. As Jo spiked the bag of IV medication, Casey checked his own patient's vital signs. Still stable. Good. It was going to take both of them to stabilize this man's wife.

"What's our ETA?" he asked James.

"Forty-five minutes," James said. "I got a call from Alex while you were loading up. We've been ordered back to the office after this flight."

"Got it," Casey said, not surprised that they were being called in. While he and Jo could go on working for hours, James had exceeded the flying time he was allowed per day. Besides, this was probably their last flight before the weather shut them down.

Casey looked back to Jo's monitor and was relieved to

see that her patient's blood pressure had begun to turn around. The vasopressor was working, but her oxygen saturation was still low.

"King airway?" Casey asked as Jo opened their respiratory equipment box. She held up the laryngeal tube for him to see.

"What's going on? Is there something wrong with Sandy? Why hasn't she woken up yet?" Mr. Dugger asked, his voice getting weaker with every word until it became just a whisper. "I should have insisted we canceled the trip. But she was so excited. It was supposed to be romantic."

"I just need to ask you a few questions," Casey said, trying to get the man's attention from what was happening to his wife beside him, while he watched Jo carefully place the laryngeal tube. "Can you tell me the date?"

"I've got it," Jo said, attaching the tube to an Ambu bag, she began to squeeze the bag. When the woman's chest began to rise and fall in time with her ventilations, Casey bent over the woman and placed his stethoscope against her chest, listening for lung sounds.

"I've already told you. It's our anniversary," Casey's patient answered as Casey gave Jo a thumbs-up.

The woman's vital signs began to stabilize, and Casey continued to keep her husband occupied with his neuro assessment. The man had a laceration across his forehead, but appeared neurologically intact.

"ETA five minutes," James called over their headphones.

"Go ahead and call report," Casey said to Jo, then

began another round of questions to his patient, hoping to keep the man from listening to Jo's report on his wife.

"Well, I don't want to do that again anytime soon," Jo said, twenty minutes later as they climbed back into the helicopter to head back to the island. "Can you imagine if we'd had to code the poor woman in front of her husband?"

"You both did great. That took real teamwork to do what you did and keep that man calm. I thought he was going to be a problem there for a minute," James said. "Not that I blame him. He had to feel helpless laying there beside her."

"Hopefully, his wife will recover and they can come back someday for another anniversary," Casey said. He'd seen patients in worse condition survive.

"At least we gave her a chance by getting her here. With Highway 1 backed up with everyone evacuating, it would have taken hours to get them to the hospital," James said. "By the way, I don't understand why everyone was so surprised by you two getting involved, you know, romantically. Anyone can see you were meant to be together. My Mona told me months ago that she thought something was going on between you."

Casey knew that James's wife, Mona, considered herself a bit of a matchmaker, and she looked at him as a challenge. But James was right; he and Jo had always made a great team. She'd always been able to anticipate what he needed from her, and he'd been the same with her.

Memories of the night before filled his mind. Somehow their intuitiveness had led to the most passionate kiss of his life. It should have felt awkward, like kissing his sister. But there had been no awkwardness, no embarrassment. There'd only been a hunger for more. A hunger he'd gone to sleep with.

And a hunger that still ate at him. One he didn't know how to deal with. No matter how much he wanted her, she was still Jo. They'd promised to remain friends after this fake romance was over, and then they'd gone and complicated everything.

"What's the latest on the storm?" Jo asked. "Any changes?"

"It's almost stalled again, but it's track hasn't changed. They've officially put out tropical storm warnings for the Keys now. We're expecting hurricane warnings to come out soon," James said.

"Sounds like we better get home then and see what Alex has planned for us. There's still a lot of people on the island who are going to need help," Casey said as James took them up. It was better to concentrate now on the storm ahead instead of on what had changed between him and Jo. They'd have to talk about it eventually, but right then he'd rather ride out a hurricane than try to figure out what he was going to do about Jo.

CHAPTER ELEVEN

"IT'S LIKE WATCHING your baby leave the nest," James said as the three of them watched the helicopter fly out of sight on its way to make one last transfer from the hospital to the mainland.

"Why didn't you fly out with them? I hear Heli-Care has rented rooms at one of the hotels to put up the staff that is evacuating," Jo said.

"Mona wouldn't leave without me. She's packed and waiting for me now. They say the bridges will be shut down by tonight. What about you two?" James asked.

It seemed Hurricane Ileen had finally decided that it was time to move, and Cuba was getting battered by the wind and rain the storm carried.

Jo looked over to where Casey stood. They'd been so busy that she hadn't really thought to make a plan. She had assumed that they would pack what they could and leave the island together. It's what they normally would have done. At least, it would have been before last night. It seemed the kiss on the beach that they'd shared had changed everything, though no one would know it by the way they had worked together for the last ten hours. They'd flown patient after patient out of the Keys as if that kiss had never happened. But it had. Eventually, when this storm had passed and things with Jeffrey were finished, they'd have to deal with it.

Her phone rang, and she pulled it from her pocket and saw that it was Casey's neighbor. They'd seen the woman that morning when they had left for work. Her son had been working at boarding up her windows before he and his mom evacuated, but that had been hours ago. "Hey, Ms. Terrie, what's up?"

"I'm so sorry, Jo. I just meant to leave that hammer we borrowed in case Casey needed it. I only left the door open for a moment, and then he was gone."

"Who was gone?" Jo asked, sure that her son would never have left his mother behind.

"It's Moose. He was there, and then he wasn't. I didn't think he'd run off like that. But now my son says we have to leave and I can't find him anywhere," the woman said, her voice shaking with each word.

"Moose ran off?" Jo said. It didn't make sense. They'd left him safe inside the house, knowing they'd only be gone a few hours before flights got suspended.

There was a rustling on the phone and a man's voice came on. "Hey, Jo. Sorry about this. It's my fault, not Mom's. I went in to hurry her along and left the door open."

And Moose had seen a chance to make his escape. It wasn't the first time he'd set off on his own, but she'd always been there to catch him before he'd gone too far. And it'd always been around her apartment where everyone knew him.

"How long ago?" she asked as she tried to fight the panic that filled her. Moose was a big dog. Surely someone would have seen him and taken him in. His name and her phone number were on his collar.

"We've been looking all afternoon, and I'm afraid if we don't get on the road we'll never make it out of town."

She'd seen the bumper-to-bumper traffic headed out of the Keys get longer and longer with each flight they'd flown. The man was right. "It's okay. Go ahead and leave. I'll head over there now."

Jo waited as the man apologized again and again before ending the call, then she headed for her car. She knew Casey would be right behind her. "Moose is missing. I'm going to start at the house and work outward. Can you call the shelter?"

The driver's side door opened as she unlocked the car and Casey got inside. "If he got picked up they should have called you, but I'll check with them. I'll check with the neighbors, too."

As he started on a string of phone calls, Jo searched her mind on where Moose could have gone. Her apartment was too far away, and she couldn't think of a reason he'd head back there. He'd settled in at Casey's house just fine. It was more likely he was just having a walk around town.

"Most everyone has already left town and the shelter isn't answering. I assume they're busy evacuating the animals," Casey said.

"I don't understand. He hasn't run off in months, and then he stayed around the apartment complex," Jo said.

"He's probably right around the house somewhere. We'll find him, Jo."

Casey laid his hand across her thigh, and she had

to stop herself from jumping. It was the first time he'd touched her since the night on the beach, and her body responded with a spark of delight that she immediately squashed. There would be no repeat of that night. Not until they had a chance to talk about what had happened. If they were going to make it out of this with their friendship intact, they'd have to face the fact that they were very much in lust with each other.

It only took fifteen minutes after they made it to Casey's house to rule out Moose being in the neighborhood. While Casey walked through the neighbor's backyards and called out for him, Jo drove slowly down the block, looking for anyone that she could ask if he'd been there. It wasn't like he was a poodle. Moose's size alone would make him stick out wherever he went.

"What if someone took him?" she said, when she stopped to pick Casey up at the end of the road. "You know how friendly he is. He could have just jumped inside someone's car and stuck his head out the window like he knew where he was going."

"No one picked him up," Casey said. "He has to be somewhere where there aren't a lot of people, otherwise someone would have checked his collar and called you. Where does he like to go?"

"They've closed all the shops downtown that give him treats. Besides that's too far away. There's the dog park, but that's probably locked up too. The only other place is the beach." That would make sense; it was one of Moose's favorite places in the world, but it was over three miles down the road.

"The closest one is Smather's Beach. Take a right on Flagler."

"Got it," Jo said as she pulled back onto the road. They'd only passed a handful of cars when they drove up to the beach parking lot. A few people dotted the sand, and there were some die-hard surfers who were enjoying the rough surf Hurricane Ileen was bringing in. "Should the surf be this rough already?"

"I don't know," Casey said as they walked up to the surf. "We've been so busy I didn't check to see if there have been any changes to the forecast."

"He could be anywhere," Jo said, looking up and down the beach and seeing no sign of her great, big, lovable dog. She'd had her doubts when Casey had talked her into taking Moose. It had been a challenge to keep him out of trouble in her small apartment, but they'd made it work. He was her best friend, besides Casey.

She had made lots of other friends on the island, but none of them could replace the big dog that had loved her the moment they met. She'd been beaten and broken by Jeffrey and had believed him when he'd said she was unlovable. She knew now that he was wrong. It had just been another way for him to abuse her. But she would never forget the love Moose had given her from the moment he'd come to live with her.

"We need to split up," she said to Casey.

"Let's see if anyone here has seen him first," Casey said.

They went from person to person with no one having seen a dog on the beach. She had finally convinced Casey that they would have to split up, when a surfer came out of the water and hurried toward them.

"Hey, are you the guys asking about the dog?" the young man, who couldn't have been more than nineteen, asked.

"Yes, have you seen him? He's a Great Dane, a really big Great Dane. He's black with white paws and he likes the water. He's usually splashing around in it." She knew she was rambling, but she couldn't seem to stop. "He ran away a few hours ago."

Casey put his arm around her, and she stopped talking. The guy was looking at her like she'd lost her mind, and she wasn't sure she hadn't. The last twenty-four hours had been draining, and she didn't think she could take much more.

"It sounds like the dog I saw. He was headed that way. I hope you find him," the teenager said before heading back into the surf.

"Thanks. Be careful out there. The surf is starting to look dangerous," Casey said.

She waved her thanks to all the young men and women sitting out on their boards, waiting for that next big wave. She had no way of knowing which of them had mentioned to the teenager that they were searching for her dog.

When Casey took her hand as she made her way through the deep sand, she knew it was only to help her keep up with him. It was something he had done before without either of them ever thinking about it. She shouldn't be thinking about it either. Not that way at least. Except it seemed her skin had become hypersensitive to even his lightest touch now. She couldn't ignore it. And it felt right. As if all the other times he'd touched her had only been a build up to what she felt now. A build up to last night and the kiss they'd shared. And if Casey knew she was thinking this way, he'd drop her hand like it was a hot poker.

She wasn't sure who saw whom first, her or Moose. He came at her like a bullet, knocking her down into the sand and licking her face like he hadn't seen her in months.

"He must have been scared he'd lost me," Jo said as Casey held the dog back while offering her a hand up. "It's okay, Moose."

"Are you okay?" Casey asked. "He doesn't usually jump people like that."

"But I'm not people. I'm his mom," Jo said. "And I should be grounding him for the rest of his canine life."

As if knowing he was in trouble, Moose hung his head.

"It's okay, boy. We'll let it go this time," Casey said, patting the dog and hugging him. She'd known Casey was as worried as she was. He just wasn't going to let her know it.

"Let's just get home before this wind gets any worse," she said. The sun had already begun to set, and the wind had picked up since they'd arrived. The sand stung as the wind sent it splattering against her arms. She was glad she'd changed into jeans when she'd got off work instead of the shorts she usually wore.

When they made it back to the parking lot, they found it empty except for Jo's car. A note had been left under her windshield wiper advising her that Key West was under a mandatory evacuation order and they needed to leave the beach.

As they drove through town, the streets were abandoned, and almost all of the businesses and homes had been boarded up. "It's kind of creepy."

"Hopefully, it won't be like this for long," Casey said, though Jo could tell the deserted town bothered him too. The fewer cars they saw, the more worried she became. Something had changed in the last two hours while they had been hunting for Moose. The gusts of winds were getting stronger, and dark clouds had begun to roll in from the south.

"We might be in trouble. It looks like the timeline for Ileen's landfall has been moved up. They're predicting landfall in the early morning hours. The only good news is that it's moving now and hasn't had the chance to build its strength back up after landfall in Cuba. Still, they're predicting it to be a Category 2 before it reaches us. The hurricane hunters are set to fly out in the next two hours, but right now winds are measuring in the nineties. It's going to cause a lot of damage." Casey looked up from the app he was reading on his phone. "We've got eight hours before it hits."

Parking the car in the driveway, they both stared at Casey's little house. It had been built over seventy years ago and had been in Casey's family ever since. It wasn't a large house and the land, being in midtown, was more valuable than the house itself. But Jo knew it was the memories of Casey's grandmother that made him cherish the home.

"What do you want to do now?" she asked. If Casey wanted to stay in his home, she'd stay with him. But both of them knew that would not be safe. They could try to make it off the island, but the roads would still be packed and the bridges would be closed soon due to wind and flooding.

Her phone dinged, and she found she had missed four calls from Summer and had two text messages from Alex. "Alex says everyone has reported in except for the two of us. From the language he's using, he isn't very happy about that."

Casey's phone dinged and he read the message. "I got the same message. I'll text him back, though I don't know what to tell him. Staying here is an option, but not a good one. There are no shelters open on the island. All we can do is try to make it off."

He received another incoming message only seconds after he'd answered Alex. "He wants us at the hospital. He's volunteered to stay, and he says he's got a place for us."

"What about Moose? We can't take him into the hospital. Their administration will have a fit." She reached back and rubbed her big fur baby's head. "And I'm not going to leave him here."

"We'll sneak him in. I can guarantee the last thing administration will be worried about is having a dog in the building."

Casey looked around the small bare room. There were no pictures on the walls. No rugs on the vinyl floor. There wasn't even a chair to sit in. But tucked away inside a group of offices shared by the hospital's medical staff, the doctors' sleep room was the perfect place to hide Moose. With only one other physician remaining in the hospital besides Alex, and the two of them holding down the ER where a few patients had straggled in at the last moment, there wasn't any chance of the three of them being disturbed. There was just one problem with the setup. There was only one bed, and it was a small one at that. The only way they could share the bed would be with one of them almost piled atop the other one.

And that was either the worst idea or the best idea he'd had all day.

"We can take turns sleeping," he said. He didn't want to make Jo uncomfortable.

"What? You don't want to share this lovely bed with me? Don't worry, you're safe from me, tonight. I'm too tired right now to think about anything but sleep," Jo said, falling into the bed face-first. "Come on. You have to be as tired as I am."

He was tired. The last couple of days had been hard on them both. He should catch a few hours of sleep while he could. There would be a lot to do in the morning after the storm was gone. Only now, waiting for whatever Hurricane Ileen had planned for them, he was too wound up to rest. Then there was Jo. Climbing into bed with her was the worst thing he could do right now. Just the thought of lying beside her had him wanting more than just the kiss they'd shared the night before.

"I'm just going to check on Alex and see if there have been any updates on the weather station."

"Okay," Jo said, her voice muffled against the sheets, "chicken."

Chicken? Had she just called him a chicken?

He started to turn around. He'd show her he wasn't

afraid of her or of climbing into that bed beside her. But the truth was, he was afraid. She should have been able to see how dangerous it would be to have the two of them piled into bed together. Instead, she was making a joke about it.

Being with Jo had always been relaxing; they could talk about anything. They could disagree on a subject without becoming angry with each other. His relationship with Jo was probably the least stressful one he'd ever had, which was especially surprising since she was female. It was one of the things that he liked most about being around her. And now all of that had changed because of one kiss on the beach. Wasn't that proof that mixing friendship with romance was a mistake?

When he shut the door behind him with a little too much force, he heard Jo laughing. At least one of them seemed to be having a good time.

Making his way down to the emergency room, he saw an ambulance bringing in a man on a stretcher.

"I can't believe you're still running calls," he said to one of the EMTs.

"It's our last. We've been told to stay here until the county emergency services clears us to go back out after the storm passes."

"I thought we were the only ones not smart enough to get off the island," Casey said, following them into a trauma room. By the way their patient's leg was twisted they didn't need an X-ray to know it was broken. "What did this guy do?"

"He was trying to board some windows in the dark

when the wind blew his ladder over. He's lucky that he only broke a leg. It could have been his neck."

Casey moved on to the next room where he found Alex stitching up a man's hand that had been cut open by a homemade metal shutter. After all his offers of help were turned down, he made his way out to the ambulance bay. Sheets of rain were now slamming against the building, and in a few minutes he was soaked. This storm was coming in strong. No one else would be able to get to the hospital in this weather.

With nothing left to do, he went back up to where he had left Jo. Moose lifted his head and began to growl until he saw that it was Casey. Thankfully, Jo was sleeping soundly, so he grabbed the bag he'd packed and headed into the bathroom. His experience with storms throughout his childhood told him he better get a hot shower while he could. There was no telling when the county would be able to get the island's utilities back up. He'd spent two weeks without electricity once when a tropical storm had taken down the electrical lines on the island.

When he made it back to the bedroom, Jo had turned over on her side, leaving half the bed open. If he climbed in then and didn't move, it would be safe. He stretched out on the bed, careful not to wake her, and turned onto his side so he faced the opposite wall. It wasn't as nice as having his king-size bed to himself, but he'd slept in worse. All he had to do was stay on his side of the bed.

A hand on his leg woke him from the deepest sleep he'd had in weeks. "Casey, wake up. It's here."

What was here? "I don't know..." he started, then

heard a crash outside that had him jumping up and covering Jo with his body.

He could hear the howling of the wind that seemed to circle the building. Alex had told him the hospital had been built to withstand even a Category 5 hurricane and they were in an interior room, so he knew they should be safe. Still, the sounds from outside left no doubt that this storm was destructive.

He felt Jo shiver against him. "It's okay, Jo. We're safe in here."

"I know that," she said, though her shivering didn't stop.

"This building is fairly new, and it's rated per the building code safe for the strongest hurricane possible. We're as safe as we could be anywhere on the island," he said, wrapping his arms around her. "I won't let anything happen to you."

"I know that," she said again. "I'm not scared of the storm."

He eased back and tried to make out her features in the dark. "Then what's wrong? Are you cold?"

"Cold is the last thing I am right now," she said as one of her hands slid up his bare abdomen to his chest.

His breath caught and his heart did a skip and then a jump. "We probably should see if Alex needs any help downstairs."

"I'm not getting on the elevators. If the generators go out we could get stuck there. And the stairs have all those windows. I'm afraid you're stuck here with me right now. Just listen to that wind. Isn't it amazing?"

He took a breath and relaxed as best he could while

still keeping Jo protected. The wind continued to blow outside, its loud moan seeming to travel around the top of the building. The power of it was humbling. There was nothing fiercer than Mother Nature. Never had he been reminded of that as much as he was at that moment.

"How long do you think this will go on?" Jo asked, snuggling deeper into his arms.

She knew what she was doing to him. There was no way she could miss the evidence that holding her like this had aroused him. He was hard, and his body was anticipating something that he knew should not happen. "I don't know. It's a good size storm. If we're directly in its path, it will all stop when the eye passes over. But it won't be for long. Then it will all start again."

"Is it terrible that even though I know it's plowing through the island damaging homes and businesses and possibly causing deaths, that I still find the force of it thrilling? The power of it reminds me of just how small and insignificant we all are. Up here, tonight, it's as if we are all alone in the world."

He knew that feeling of aloneness. He'd been filled with it a lot lately, that was until Jo had moved in. He'd forgotten how much he'd dreaded going home after a long shift to his empty home.

Her bare legs rubbed against his, and he realized as her damp hair tickled his nose that he hadn't been the only one to take advantage of the shower. Now only his shorts and her oversize T-shirt seemed to separate them. When her hand slipped down his chest to his abdomen, then further, he gasped.

"What if we never get a chance to be together like

this again? All alone in this room, no one to interrupt us. Just you and me and this one night together. Would it be so bad if for just one night you let down those walls and see where whatever this thing is between the two of us takes us?" Jo asked, her hand stilling on the button of his shorts. "Aren't you tempted to find out?"

"We're going to be okay, Jo. This won't be our last night," Casey said as he shook his head, trying to shake away the fog of desire that had spiraled around him with her words. Was he tempted? Oh, yes. But still, he knew the morning would come, and with it reality.

"Are we?" she asked, one hand coming up to his cheek, soft and cool against his overheated skin.

The darkness of the room kept him from seeing her expression, but he understood what she meant. It wasn't the hurricane she was afraid of. With that kiss they'd shared, they'd broken their own rule, shattered it with the passion that burned between them that night on the beach. He'd tried to convince her to put it behind them. It would be easier for them to go back to their normal lives that way.

It might be too late to fix what they'd broken. How could they when his body continued to respond to hers this way? Could they go back to being only friends now? He didn't know.

But would one night together change that? The line had already been crossed. Maybe this was the only way to put it behind them. Maybe they could end this overwhelming need to finish what they had started on the beach by letting it burn its way out.

Something outside crashed against the building and he held her closer. Her mouth was so close, her breath warm against his lips, he had no strength against this. His lips moved over hers, for comfort or pleasure, he didn't know. Then her mouth opened under his and the heat of it made him forgot every reason he'd ever had that this wasn't a good idea.

He took his time, stretching the kiss out until they both needed to come up for air. His lips traveled down her neck, and her moan echoed the sounds of the wind. Her tongue, warm and soft against his ear, had pleasure shooting down through the length of his shaft.

Clothes were peeled off, one by one, each revealing a treasure for him to explore. Inside he knew that this was his friend, Jo, but here, lying with her naked in his arms, she was his lover tonight.

As the wind raged outside, he buried himself inside of her. Her heat surrounded him, drawing him deeper until there was no him or her. They were one.

Her legs wrapped around him and they rode out the storm together. He lost track of time. He forgot about all the ways this could complicate his life. Jo. The taste of her, the smoothness of her skin, the way her hands and mouth moved against him; she was his whole world tonight. Something broke inside of him as her body shuddered in his arms, flooding him with an emotion he couldn't name. Happiness? Pleasure? No. This was something more. And it scared him.

"I love you Casey Johnson," Jo whispered in his ear.

His eyes shut tight, even as his body trembled with pleasure. So many women had said those words after they'd shared their bodies with him. They meant nothing. Not to him. Anna had whispered the same words the first time they'd made love. He'd believed her then.

And this was Jo. His best friend Jo. After what she'd been through with her ex, she was vulnerable. It was understandable that she could be emotional right now. That was all it was. Tomorrow, when the storm had passed and the sun came out, she'd want to take back those words.

As the storm still raged, he held Jo until her breathing became slow and deep. He was so confused by emotions that didn't make sense to him. But the night would be over soon and they'd have to face the damage that had been done. They'd rebuild what was needed, and the island would come back even stronger. He just hoped he and Jo could do the same.

CHAPTER TWELVE

Jo woke up in a tangle of legs and arms. She lay still, enjoying the weight of Casey's body on hers, and she listened to…nothing. There was no howling wind or slashing rain. There were no noises coming from the rooms around them. No people. No storm. Everything was quiet. It was like she and Casey were the only two people left in the world. It had been the same last night when they'd made love. With the storm outside, she'd felt totally alone, except for Casey. She'd felt safe and cared for in his arms. She'd felt…loved.

So she'd opened her mouth and let her sex-boggled brain convince her to say the last words Casey wanted to hear from her. She'd managed to keep them bottled up inside of her for so long, why now? Maybe that was the reason. Because she'd known if she didn't say them then, while Casey held her, that she might never get the chance?

And what was so wrong with telling someone you loved them? Wasn't that what everyone wanted? To be loved. Well, everyone but Casey if he was to be believed. The man had let an old heartbreak destroy his ability to understand that feeling love wasn't a weakness, it was a gift. Until he figured that out there would be no hope for anything more than friendship with him, and she knew now that would never be enough for her.

And now she had to look at him and hope she hadn't made a complete fool of herself. The eerie quietness of the room penetrated through her thoughts. It really did seem that they were the only people in this building. That thought sent a shiver down her. She'd seen too many apocalyptic movies that had ended this way.

"Casey, wake up. We've got to get downstairs," Jo said, untangling her legs with his until she could stand, then almost tripping on Moose where he lay beside the bed.

"What's wrong?" Casey asked, raising his head.

"We need to check on the others." She reached for the light switch, and some of her panic eased when light flooded the room. "We have power. Maybe the storm wasn't that bad."

"It might be the backup generators. They kick in when the power goes off. Alex said the hospital can run on those for three days. The power company should have power back to the hospital by then." The messy, flop of his blond curls hanging over his green eyes and the sight of his bare, sculpted chest made her want to climb back into the bed beside him. If only she could. But from the hooded look he was giving her, she knew he was already working to bring up those walls between them.

Grabbing her bag from the floor, she went into the bathroom and dressed. When she returned, she found Casey dressed and waiting for her. When he didn't make eye contact, she knew things between them were still on shaky ground.

Why had she opened her mouth? She'd ruined everything. They'd had sex. Couldn't she just accept that was all it had been?

She looked away from him. Right now wasn't the time to talk about it. The storm was gone and now they needed to make sure everyone downstairs was safe.

"Moose, stay," she said as she filled one of his bowls with the water from the water bottle she'd packed, then filled the other bowl with his dog food.

"We'll be right back," Casey said, patting the dog. "You were a very brave boy last night, and I'll take you outside as soon as I know it's safe."

Moose looked at him with trusting eyes and then started on his food.

"Thank goodness he isn't afraid of storms. There's no way the staff wouldn't have heard him even with the floors between us if he'd started howling, though they probably would have thought it was just the storm," she said, waiting for Casey to say something, anything, to break the tension in the room.

When he only nodded, she gave up. Knowing Casey, it was possible he'd never say anything about last night again. He was good at ignoring anything that made him uncomfortable.

Part of her hoped he would pretend nothing had happened while part of her wanted to have it out in the open. Just get it over with and see what happened.

Why? Because she thought last night had meant as much to him as it had to her? If it had, there was no sign of it this morning. He was making it plain that he was uncomfortable with her now. That wasn't something a man who had spent the night discovering that they had more than just a friend relationship would do.

They took the stairs, stopping at every floor to look out the windows that opened to the back of the building. There were trees down and a dumpster mysteriously in the middle of the parking lot, but that was all the damage she could see. She looked for her car and was relieved to see that it had escaped being squashed by the fallen trees. Not all of the staff had been so lucky. She knew Casey had to be anxious to check on his home too, but first they needed to check in with Alex.

Stepping into the ER, she found it almost deserted. The unit coordinator sat at her desk and there were a couple rooms occupied by patients, but the rest of the staff was missing.

"Where is everyone?" Casey asked when they passed one of the nurses.

"They've just stepped outside to look around," he said, before continuing to one of the patients' rooms.

They stepped out into the ambulance bay to find Alex along with some of the nurses looking up at the sky. Jo had been so busy looking at the ground on the way down the back stairs that she had never looked up.

The sky was blue and cloudless, and the sun seemed to shine brighter than she had ever seen it. It was hard to believe that there had been a storm just a few hours ago. It was as if the hurricane had washed the sky clean and left it vibrant and sparkling when it had moved on.

They heard the wail of a siren and turned as an ambulance pulled into the bay. "It looks like it's time to get back to work," Alex said.

"If you don't need us here, we can head over and check out HQ," Casey offered.

"My relief should be here in a few hours, and I'm headed home to see what damage I've got at the house. I want to get Summer and the babies home as soon as it's safe," Alex said. "Check out your own place on the way to Heli-Care. We can station here at the hospital if we need to if we get the helipad cleared. I know I'll be getting calls from the corporate office soon."

"I'll text you some pictures as soon as we get there," Jo said, already following Casey inside.

"Don't do anything stupid. There will be power lines down all across the island, and a lot of the roads will still be flooded. Take the interior roads," Alex said, before heading into a trauma room where the EMTs were unpacking their patient.

"Those guys are going to be busy today," Casey said as they left the ER and headed back upstairs for Moose.

The trip to Casey's place should have only taken fifteen minutes. Instead, they spent over an hour weaving their way through street after street that had been blocked with fallen trees or flooding. They ran into an officer who advised them on areas to avoid after he checked their IDs to make sure they were residents who belonged on the island.

When they finally made it, they were relieved to see that except for some shingles that had been stripped from the roof, Casey's house remained undamaged. Ms. Terrie's house hadn't been so lucky.

"She's going to be so upset when she sees this," Jo said

as they looked at the tree that had crashed through the top of the woman's home.

"I'll come back and put a tarp over it for now," Casey said, shaking his head. "It's not much though. She'll need a new roof, and there will be water damage from the rain that she'll have to deal with."

"We'll help her, just like we helped Lucy," she said. It would take months to repair the damage to the island, but everyone would pitch in to help. That's what people did here.

They left Moose safe inside the house and changed Jo's car for Casey's truck, which would be safer on the flooded roads.

"I wonder how long it will take till things get back to normal," Jo asked. "That officer said that they were already sending engineers out from the county to check the bridges."

"If the bridges are okay, they'll start letting residents in today," Casey said.

"Good. It's weird being here without everyone. I don't like it."

"You don't like being alone with me?" he asked. Jo searched his face, looking for any sign that he was serious. Any sign that he wanted to talk about the night they'd just shared. The smile disappeared from his face. Yeah, he was thinking about the night they had just spent alone.

They had to face it. They couldn't keep pretending like nothing had happened between them. Even if he considered it just a one-night fling, she knew it was more.

Those three little words she'd spoken had changed everything. She could make an excuse for it. She was overwhelmed by the storm, by the passion. Casey would accept any excuse she gave just to get out of having to face it. Wouldn't that be the best thing to do? Just let him think she was just being "emotional" as he called it?

They'd crossed several lines, broken all the rules, and now she had to accept more than half the responsibility.

She'd been the one who'd reached out for him last night. Yes, part of it had been the storm. Lying in the bed all alone, not knowing what was happening outside of that little hospital room had been scary. She'd wanted him to hold her.

Telling Casey that was the reason she had declared her love for him would only be partly lying. A part of her had been affected by the storm and by their lovemaking. Would it really be that bad to take the cowardly way out and pretend that was all it had been?

If only she hadn't felt the truth in those words. She loved Casey. She couldn't deny it any longer. Why should she? Because she was scared? Maybe once that would have been true, but not now. She'd been through too much to let something like fear keep her from admitting her feelings for someone. She wasn't the woman she'd been when she'd married Jeffrey. She stood up for herself now, and she went after what she wanted.

And if Casey can't give you what you want? What will you do then?

"I don't know what to say," she said, refusing to let fear keep her from doing what she knew she needed to do. But how did you tell someone that you loved them when you knew it was the last thing they wanted to hear?

"What do you mean?" Casey said, his eyes never leaving the road ahead of them.

"We need to talk about it, Casey. You know that."

"Why?" he asked. "What's there to say? It happened. It's over."

"What's over? Us?" Her voice was not much more than a whisper. How could he be so cold? How could he dismiss what they had shared? Or was that fear she heard in his voice? She should know. She'd let fear of rejection keep her from admitting her feelings for Casey for years.

He stopped the truck in the middle of the road and turned toward her. "Look, we got caught up pretending to be involved. I should have known this could happen. We let down our guard for a few minutes. We won't do it again."

"What do you mean 'we'?" she asked, her voice rising.

"We're a team. That's what we do," he said, his own voice rising now.

"A team? So what, last night was just teamwork?" How could he be so smart yet so dense? How could he not see what they could have together?

"It was a mistake. The storm and the situation was overwhelming. We got caught up in everything around us. It happens," he said.

"It doesn't happen to me," she said, refusing to take the easy way out of this. Didn't he know she could be as stubborn as he was?

He started the truck and headed back down the road as if the subject was closed. Well, it wasn't closed as far as she was concerned. "We can't pretend it never happened just because it makes you uncomfortable. It did happen. We made love and I told you that I love you."

She watched, waiting for his next move. His hands tightened on the wheel until his fingers went white, but he didn't respond to her words. Had she pushed too hard?

Her phone rang, startling her. For a few minutes she'd forgotten the world outside of the two of them. "Hey, Alex. We're almost at headquarters."

She listened as her boss relayed a call for help from the local emergency services. While a part of her asked the appropriate questions, another part of her withdrew inside of herself. She'd been here before when she'd realized that Jeffrey didn't really love her. He'd only wanted her as a submissive wife who would represent him in the perfect world he thought he could create. Casey didn't want her love either. He only wanted her friendship. He wanted his life free of all the messy emotions that made up a real life.

"Emergency services received a call for help off of North Roosevelt, but they only have the one crew up and running and they're tied up. Apparently the caller was frantic. Alex asked if we could respond."

"Address?" Casey asked as he made a U-turn in the middle of the road, the action fast and sharp, sending her into the passenger door. She grabbed the handle above the door as the truck swerved back onto the road.

"They didn't have an address. The caller said he'd be on the road to meet us." Jo braced herself as Casey hit the gas pedal. What was wrong with him? Casey never drove this way. He was always in control when he was behind the wheel. "Slow down. If you wreck us, there'll be no one to help these people."

She relaxed her hold on the door handle as their speed slowed, but she didn't let go. She was headed into uncharted territory. She didn't know what to expect when they reached the person who had called for help. She didn't know what to expect from Casey now that she had been honest about her feelings. All she could do was hold on for the ride.

CHAPTER THIRTEEN

CASEY TRIED TO loosen his hold on the steering wheel. Jo's insistence that they discuss the night before while he was still trying to come to terms with it was too much right now. Hearing her declaration of love had rocked something inside of him. He was suddenly filled with emotions that he didn't know how to handle. Fear, for what he and Jo could lose, along with a surprising hope that maybe there was something more between them. What if what he felt for Jo was more than friendship? Or were the two of them just confused by this unexpected passion between them? And what if it was love? That brought about a whole new level of fear. He'd almost destroyed his life after his and Anna's breakup. How much worse would it be if things between him and Jo went wrong?

His whole life felt out of control, and losing control was not something he did. If you lost control, you made mistakes. He couldn't afford to make mistakes. Not when someone's life might be depending on him.

"All I have in the truck is a first-aid kit," he said, trying to get their attention on the job ahead of them. "You would think they would have gotten more information from the caller."

"Alex said they lost their connection to the caller, and he didn't answer when they called back. Fire and Rescue said they would be there as soon as possible," Jo said.

They backtracked to First Street then took it to North Roosevelt. He had grown up on this island and knew every road and pothole. If you gave him an address, he could find it. Without an address all they could do was keep their eyes open and hope they found the 911 caller before it was too late.

"Where do we go from here?" Jo asked.

Wasn't that the question of the day? He had no idea where they were going. And to think a couple weeks ago he had total control of his life.

"You decide. Left or right?" he asked her. Their argument had left him drained and feeling that whatever he said would be wrong.

"Go right and you never go wrong, right?" she said.

"Sure," he replied, unable to put any enthusiasm into his voice. They'd only made it a couple blocks before they came to a spot where the road had been washed away, leaving an opening that even his truck couldn't drive over.

"What do we do now?" Jo asked.

"I guess we walk," he said, opening the door and climbing out. "I'll get the first-aid kit."

"We don't even know if we are going the right way," Jo said as they made their way down and over the sand and water that was left where there used to be a road.

"There's something big there on the right side of the road. Let's check that out. If we can't see anything from there, we'll turn around." Casey wasn't sure what he was seeing. A bus? Someone's shed? It could be anything that the storm had picked up and dumped on the side of the road.

As they got closer, he started to make out the squared off sides of a large vehicle. "It's an RV that's been flipped."

They were only twenty yards away when he saw the man sitting on the side of the road, a small dog at his side. "Hey, did you call for help?" Jo called as she hurried over to him.

"Oh, thank God you're here," the man said as he tried to stand.

"Don't move," Casey said, getting to the man's side and easing him back down onto the road. "Where are you hurt?"

"Me? I'm okay. It's my wife. She's in there. I can't get her out," the man said, his breathing fast and ragged. "She's pinned down. I just managed to get out myself a few minutes ago. I had to leave her."

Casey looked at the RV lying on its side. The thing was as big as a bus. "What happened?" he asked the man.

"We left too late. We thought we had time. We didn't want to leave the RV behind, so we packed it up for the trip," the man said. His color was good, but he was still out of breath.

"Casey, I think I can get in," Jo said, calling from the other side of the vehicle.

"I'll be right back," Casey said to the man then rushed to where Jo was climbing up on what would have been the RV's top. "What are you doing?"

"If I can get to the top, there should be a window I can get in through," she said as she climbed higher.

"Get down and I'll do it," he said as she reached the top. His heart pounded and he started up behind her. "We're not Fire and Rescue. We're not trained for this."

"I'm just going to look inside. If I can't get in, I'll climb down."

He glanced around them for something he could use to describe their location and situation then texted the information, knowing his boss would find a way to get them some help. He waited till he got a thumbs-up from Alex, then he headed up after Jo.

He caught up to her as she pulled herself onto the top of the vehicle. "Be careful up there."

"I'm okay. This thing is huge. It's not going anywhere," Jo said as she knelt and looked over the side at him.

"That's what they thought last night." All the blood in his body rushed to his feet when she let go of the side and stood up. "What are you doing? Just wait a moment till I get up there."

"I'm just going to look into the window. I'll be right back."

He looked for something he could use to pull himself over the side of the vehicle. How had she gotten up there?

"I can see her," Jo called from where she had disappeared on the top.

"Ma'am, can you hear me?" she called as she knocked against what he assumed was a window. "Casey, she's not responding. There's a cabinet on top of her. I think it's a pantry because there's cans of food everywhere. If I had a way to get this window open, I could drop down beside her."

"The windows are probably locked. Is there a door?"

Casey asked as he finally made his way over the top. He knelt, making sure he could keep his balance, before standing and making his way over to her.

Looking in the window Jo was leaning over, he could see the woman where she lay flat on her back. "Something has to be on top of that cabinet or they would have been able to push it off. The whole inside of this thing is destroyed. It's amazing that it didn't break in two."

He stood and headed to the front of the vehicle. "This has to be how her husband got out."

Casey tried to pull the door open but it was stuck. He looked around for something to pry it open. Where was Fire and Rescue? "If he got out this way, it must have locked when it shut."

"There's a window open here," Jo called from behind him.

Giving up on the door, he joined her where one of the small windows had been slid open. There was no way he was fitting through that. "We should have help here soon. They'll have the equipment to get the door open."

"I think I can get through," Jo said as she moved over the window and placed her feet into the opening.

"And do what? You can't get her out of there. We should wait until Fire and Rescue arrive. I texted Alex our location before I climbed up here. He'll get us some help."

"She's been down there for hours. I can at least assess the situation and let you know what we're going to need so you can forward the information to Alex."

"It's too dangerous. You could fall on something getting down there. We should wait here for help." Couldn't she see the danger? If she fell and broke something, he'd have two patients.

"Let me do this. It's not that far down. You can lower me most of the way."

She climbed into the small opening and he grabbed her hand, lowering her inside as far as he could, stretching his arm down inside the RV.

"Let me go. There's an overturned chair here. I can make it from this point," Jo said as she let go of his hand.

He hesitated then pried his fingers from her hand. He saw the top of her head as she dropped to the bottom with a thud. "Are you okay?"

"I'm fine. I'm going to head to the back," Jo said before disappearing from his view.

As he headed to the back, he heard a siren in the distance. It sounded like they were coming in from the north so they would be able to avoid the washed-out road.

He needed to go check on the woman's husband, but he couldn't leave Jo even though there was nothing he could do to help her from where he was.

"I think she has a fractured hip. We'll need to stabilize it when we take her out of here. Her pulse is fast and weak. She's awake but not oriented. There's a laceration to the back of her head. She'll need a CT when she gets to the ER. There also appears to be an open fracture of the femur. It's hard to see because of the cabinet on top of her. She's going to need an ortho surgeon. Do you to have a C-collar in your first-aid kit? I need to stabilize her neck. I wouldn't rule out a cervical fracture from the way she's laying. I don't know how her husband got out of here. The whole place is a danger zone."

"I've got one. I'll go down and get it and some bandages for her head too. Don't move while I'm gone."

He made the trip down the side of the RV to where he'd left his first-aid kit and back up as quickly as possible. The siren he'd heard earlier didn't sound any closer. They must have run into some debris on the road or another place where the road had been washed out.

"What are you doing?" he hollered after sticking his head through the open window and seeing Jo trying to lift the cabinet from the woman.

"I wanted to try to prop this cabinet up so I could get to her leg, but it won't budge."

"I'm going to try to get the collar as close to you as possible," he said, easing his head out of the window so that he could place his hand holding the collar inside. He threw the plastic-wrapped foam collar as far as it would go, then pulled his arm out and stuck his head in to see where it had gone.

"I've got it," Jo called as she scrambled up the side of an overturned couch to retrieve it.

He watched as she made it back to the woman and carefully placed the collar while explaining to her injured patient what she was doing. It wasn't much, but maybe it would protect the woman if she began to move around.

"Okay. Throw me the bandages," Jo said as she headed back toward the open window.

He saw the look of surprise on her face before he realized she had slipped on something on the floor. As if in slow motion, he watched as her body was pitched forward and came down, her head slamming onto what looked like the edge of a cabinet.

"Jo?" he called through the window, expecting her to lift her head and reassure him that she was fine. But instead she lay as still as death. Death? No. Not Jo.

"Jo, answer me. Are you okay?" His voice carried through the RV, loud and booming. But she didn't answer.

He rushed over to the door he'd tried earlier and tried again to pull it open. It didn't budge. The door seemed to be the only thing on the vehicle that hadn't been broken. He looked inside its glass opening and saw that the handle appeared to be locked as they had assumed earlier. Taking his T-shirt off, he wrapped it around his fist and began punching through the glass. After a few good punches, the glass began to shatter. Another punch, and he had a hole big enough to get his hand in so that he could remove the rest of the glass. In seconds, he had the glass removed and he reached in and over to the handle, lifting it carefully while holding the outside door handle.

Swinging the door open, he lowered himself onto the edge of the driver's seat then made his way back to where Jo lay. She moaned when he reached her, and he took a deep breath. Okay. She was injured, but alive.

"Stay still," he told her. He moved a pillow and basket that lay between them and carefully examined the laceration across her forehead. "Jo, can you open your eyes for me?"

"Fire and Rescue," a voice announced as a tall man came through the door, which had been left open. He was followed by a young woman Casey recognized. "You're Casey from Heli-Care, right? They said we were to meet you. Is this our patient?"

"I thought you'd never get here. No. Your patient is

over there. She has an open femur fracture and a laceration to the back of her head. Possible hip fracture too. Jo
put a C-collar on her neck," Casey said.

"Is that Jo?" The young woman moved down beside
him as her partner made his way to the other woman.
"What happened?"

"She fell. Hit her head on this counter—" Casey
pointed to the stone counter behind him "—and lost con-
sciousness. It just happened, but she's not coming around
like she should."

"We had to stop and move some downed trees on the
way in. The roads are a nightmare right now, but there's
an ambulance behind us that can transport both of them."

Jo moaned again, but her eyes still didn't open. The
relief he'd felt when he'd realized she was alive was starting to drain away. If it was just a concussion, she should
be waking up by now. If it was something more serious,
like a brain bleed, she needed to get to the hospital as
soon as possible.

An EMT dropped down into the RV and looked around
the scene. "This is a mess. Where's the patient? Wait, is
that Jo?"

As Casey explained once more how Jo had been injured without taking his eyes off her, dread began to fill
him. Why wasn't she waking up?

"Okay," the EMT said, "we need to get both of these
women out of here fast. Jo's going to be the easiest to get
out, so we take her first. My partner and one of the Fire
and Rescue guys is bringing up a basket so we can strap
them in and lower them down the side. Casey, once we

get Jo out, we're going to need you to help us lift that cabinet off our other patient."

He started to protest, but stopped. The faster they got the other woman out, the faster they could get both of them to the hospital.

The EMT was right. They'd managed to get Jo out of the RV quickly and down in the metal basket to a second EMT waiting below, but getting the other woman out from under the debris while stabilizing her hip and fractured leg had proven to be a challenge. As soon as they had her lowered safely down, Casey climbed off the RV to check on Jo. When he saw that she was still unconscious, he almost panicked.

As they started to close the ambulance doors, she moaned again, but her eyes fluttered open this time. A confused look crossed her face, and then her eyes shut again. "Casey?"

"I'm here," he said as he grabbed one of the doors.

"We've got to go. He'll see you at the hospital," the EMT said as he shut the door in Casey's face.

As the ambulance pulled away, Casey looked over to where the Fire and Rescue crew was talking to the older man. He'd forgotten about the woman's husband. He had to be as worried about his wife as Casey was about Jo.

"How about I give you a ride to the hospital?" Casey asked. "They can get you checked out while you're waiting to see your wife."

"This is all my fault. She wanted us to leave yesterday, but I wouldn't listen," the man said. "I thought we had time. Last night, when the storm came in and everything was rocking back and forth in the RV, I didn't know if we would survive the night. I sat there helpless beside her, unable to get her free. All I could think about was what my life would be like if I lost her. I have nothing without her. I am nothing without her. We're two halves that make up this one whole."

Casey couldn't imagine what this man had gone through during the night. While he'd held Jo in his arms as the storm had passed, this man had lived through a nightmare.

"The doctors at the hospital will take good care of her."

"They won't let me bring Sugar with me, and I can't leave her here alone. Paula would have my head." The man petted the small, wiry-haired dog of undeterminable breed. The dog hadn't made a sound since they'd arrived, and Casey wondered if it was in some kind of shock too. "My name's Jack."

"I'm Casey and I think they'll make an exception. If not, I'll find someone to watch her." Casey helped the man up. He watched as Jack settled on his feet then headed toward Casey's truck.

"They said your girlfriend was hurt helping to care for Paula. I'm sorry for that," Jack said as soon as he climbed in the truck.

"Her name is Jo. She's my friend. My best friend," Casey said, though why he felt the need to correct the man he didn't know.

"That's the best kind of girlfriend, don't you think?" Jack said as he petted the dog in his lap. "Of course it doesn't always work out that way. Sometimes there's a spark of chemistry that sets things going between two people. Then they have to learn to be friends or it doesn't work out."

"Is that what happened with you and your wife?" Casey asked. He wanted to hit the gas and race to the hospital, but he knew he couldn't do that with Jack in the truck.

"We've known each other most of our lives. We didn't always like each other, but that changed when we made it to high school. I enlisted in the navy as soon as I graduated, and we were married after I graduated from boot camp. Moved all over the country while in the service. We raised four kids, and now have seven grandkids. There's another on the way. Paula always said she wanted ten grandkids, and she might get them."

Cascy thought of the condition the woman had been in when she'd been loaded onto the ambulance. He hoped she would be around to see those ten grandkids.

They pulled into the hospital parking lot, and Casey stopped to let Jack and his dog out at the front door. After promising to come back to take the man to the emergency room, he parked the truck.

When they entered the emergency room, one of the nurses spotted the dog and opened her mouth to object, then saw Casey shake his head and she quickly looked away. He led Jack over to a trauma room where he could see the doctor examining his wife before he went in search of Jo.

"She's in CT, Casey," the unit coordinator said when he approached her desk. "They'll bring her back to trauma room two when they're finished."

"Can you let me know when the CT results come

back?" he asked. He'd imagined all kinds of complications Jo could have from the trauma to her head.

"We don't have an in-house radiologist due to the storm, but we're sending them off to a radiologist in Miami to be read. It will take a little longer. I'll let Dr. Patel know you're here, though. He's busy working on the other patient the EMTs brought in. I sure wish we could get Heli-Care in here."

"I thought Alex was working on that," he said, at the same time remembering that he and Jo had never made it to check out what damage had been done to their headquarters. "He'd said we might be able to fly in here."

"Our maintenance man has been trying to clear the helipad all morning. It's just too much for one person, and we're short-staffed. There's no one to send to help him."

"Let me make some phone calls," Casey said. He walked by the trauma room where he'd left Jack and saw the man clutching his wife's hand as he held the little dog in his other arm. From the look on Jack's face, the news he had received from the doctor wasn't good. The woman needed care that couldn't be provided here. And Jo? If she had a serious head injury and needed surgery, there was no one here who could do it.

He hit the callback button on his phone as he made his way out of the ambulance bay. If Alex could get a helicopter here, he would find a place for it to land.

CHAPTER FOURTEEN

BY THE TIME Casey and the maintenance man had cleared the helipad, the sound of rotor blades could be heard in the sky. The local ER doctor had made arrangements for both Jack's wife and Jo to be transferred to a receiving hospital in Miami while Casey had got ahold of Roy and Alex to get a flight arranged. Roy had been the first pilot they could contact, and Dylan had volunteered to help Casey with the two patients.

"I don't think this is necessary," Jo protested as she was loaded on the helicopter. "I just have a headache. You need to concentrate on taking care of the woman from the RV. She's the critical one."

"You have a subdural hematoma from hitting your head. The neurosurgeon Dr. Patel spoke with wanted you flown into Miami so you can be watched closely in ICU in case it expands and you need surgery." Casey reminded her of what the doctor had explained just minutes before the helicopter had arrived.

"I heard the doctor," Jo grumbled.

"Nurses do make the worst patients," Dylan said from beside him. "I'll take care of Jo, and we can still tag team the trauma patient."

Casey had spoken to Jack before loading his wife and

assured him he'd call as soon as possible. Jack planned to take the first flight to Miami as soon as the airport was opened back up.

Once Paula had been loaded and secured, Casey was busy handling the number of IV drips that were required to keep the woman sedated and comfortable. Since Paula would be taken directly to surgery from the ER—after the flight—Dr. Patel had chosen to intubate her before their flight.

It only seemed like minutes before the shoreline of Miami came into view. Looking over at Jo, he was glad to see that her color was good and her respiration even. Her vital signs registering on the monitor were stable too. "No neuro changes?"

"No changes. She's stable right now," Dylan said. They both knew that with a head-bleed things could change quickly. "She had to have taken a pretty hard knock to her head to get that bleed."

Just thinking about the moment when Jo had fallen made his stomach churn. He was a seasoned nurse in a job where he saw the worst of the worst injuries, but seeing Jo lying there, not moving. Nothing had ever affected him that way before. It was like his own life had stopped in that instant.

Looking at her now, her eyes closed and her chest moving in rhythmic motions, gave him a peace of mind that he hadn't had since that moment. She was going to be okay. She had to be.

He looked back over at his own patient and thought about Jack. He'd felt so bad leaving the man behind. He knew he wouldn't want to be the one watching that helicopter fly away with Jo while he was left on the ground.

"ETA five minutes," Roy called over their headphones.

"I'll call report on both of them, if that's okay with you," Casey volunteered, then radioed into the hospital frequency when Dylan nodded.

An emergency room crew met them on the helipad and helped Casey take Jack's wife straight to the operating room while Dylan transported Jo to the emergency room.

"They've taken Jo for another CT, and then she's going to be admitted to the Neuro Intensive Care Unit. And I'm sure you don't want to hear this, but Alex called and wants us to return to the hospital. One of the electrical linemen fell and needs to be transported to a trauma unit," Dylan said, meeting him at the emergency room entrance.

"This day feels like it will never end," Casey said. He'd managed to grab a sandwich from the break room before they'd left Key West, but eventually he was going to have to stop and sleep. Besides, he didn't want to leave Jo until he made sure she was okay.

"Alex said to let you know that we could bunk at the hospital tonight. Hopefully, this will be our last call for a while," Dylan said.

"Okay, but I need to get the number to where Jo's going to be before we leave."

"I've already got it and sent it to Alex. He's going to call and speak with the neurosurgeon himself, and he said he'd call if there is any change."

Unable to find any other excuse to stay, Casey followed Dylan back to the helipad.

* * *

Jo awoke to the sound of monitors beeping and voices outside her room. She'd been woken up every hour during the night for the necessary neuro checks, and she could still feel the effects of the headache she'd had since her fall.

Her hand went to the bandage that covered the stitches on her forehead. The doctor had assured her it would heal with very little scarring. Not that she was worried about the scar. What was one more to add to her collection?

A soft knock came at her door, and a young woman dressed in scrubs, with a badge that read Case Management, walked inside.

"Hi, Ms. Kemp, I'm Cheryl from case management. Do you feel up to talking to me right now? I just have a few questions," the woman carrying a clipboard and pen asked as she stepped up to Jo's bed.

"That's fine. What can I help you with?" Jo could tell the woman was nervous, which didn't make any sense.

"I'm really sorry to disturb you, but the doctor requested that I speak with you about some of the findings on the CTs they performed last night. I understand you fell and injured your head."

Had the CTs last night shown the bleed in her head was expanding? If so, wouldn't it have been the doctor who would have spoken with her about it? "What is this about?"

"I'm sorry. I don't want to upset you, but it seems there were some other injuries, old injuries, that were seen in the X-ray and CTs that were done when you were brought into the hospital. It's our policy to follow up with the patient to make sure that when they are discharged they are going back to a safe environment," the woman explained.

Jo blinked up at her, stunned that she had never thought that her injuries from when she had been abused by Jeffrey would follow her through her medical care.

"It's okay. I'm quite safe to go home. The danger I was in, what caused those injuries, it's in the past."

The woman smiled for the first time since she'd entered the room then looked at her clipboard and jotted something down. "I'm glad to hear that. The only other thing I need to ask is concerning your next of kin. It seems they left that empty when you came in."

Jo started to give the woman's Casey's name then corrected herself, giving the woman her parents' names and number instead. Casey wasn't her next of kin. He wasn't even her real boyfriend. Had she gotten so tied up in this pretend romance that she wasn't sure what was real and what wasn't? Was it possible she'd gotten so tangled up with her own feelings for Casey that she hadn't been able to see that it was all one-sided? That Casey didn't care for her the same way she did for him?

She'd told him that she loved him only for him to try to explain her words away. Was he trying not to hurt her because he didn't return her feelings? It was so easy to see now. The way he kept returning to the fact that all he wanted was friendship, wasn't that what he had done with every other woman she'd seen him date?

She'd been a fool. He'd been trying to let her down easily while she'd continued to insist that there was more between them.

Her cell phone rang, and she looked down to see the

picture of Casey on the display. How could she face him now that she realized she'd been just one more in a line of women who had tried to make Casey love them?

Casey arrived at the hospital and went straight to Jo's room. The last two days had been busy for the Heli-Care crew, with everyone working long shifts helping out the local EMTs as well as helping with transporting patients. The residents had been allowed to return to the Keys, and there had been an increase in the number of accidents as everyone worked to repair their homes. It meant he'd only managed to stop to see Jo once and that was while he was dropping off a patient and she'd been asleep when he'd checked in with her nurse. But today he found her sitting up in the bed, only the bandage on her head hinting that she'd been injured.

"Hey," he said as he walked over to her. He wanted to touch her, to reassure himself that she really was okay. Even though all the reports from the doctors had come back good, he couldn't get that moment when he'd watched her fall out of his mind.

"I didn't expect you," Jo said. "From what Summer said about the hours you are all having to work, I didn't think I'd see you."

Her words sounded cool and detached, and the smile on her face was a little too bright.

"How are you feeling?" he asked. "Alex said you should be discharged soon."

"I'm discharging today. I'm just waiting for Summer to get here to take me home." Her voice cracked on the last word, and he reached for her hand. Something was wrong. Jo had never acted this way.

"I'll call Summer and let her know I can take you home," he said, pulling out his phone. "If I'd known you were getting out, I would have gotten off sooner."

"Don't," she said as she pulled her hand away from his.

"What's wrong, Jo?"

"I'm not going home with you. All the utilities arc back up at my apartment, and Summer is going to pick up Moose for me."

He pulled up one of the chairs and sat. What had changed in the last two days that would cause Jo to not want to return home with him? "I don't understand. Did something happen with Jeffrey?"

"I don't know. I haven't heard from him, but I don't think he'll turn up in on an island that has just been hit by a hurricane." She took a breath as if gathering her strength then looked him straight in the face. The smile she'd pasted on earlier was gone, and her eyes only held sadness now. "It's time we quit playing this game. I need to go home and get back to my real life and you do too."

"But Jeffrey…" he started.

"If Jeffrey shows up, I'll call the police. I won't let him in the apartment, and I have a lot of neighbors around if I need help. I appreciate everything you did. You've been the best friend I've ever had, but I want to go home now."

The finality of her words and the grave tone of her voice sent a streak of fear down his spine.

"We need to talk about this." He felt like he was poised on a tightrope and one wrong word could bring him crashing down.

"Isn't that my line?" she asked, her lips twitching up. And for the first time since he'd entered the room, he thought he saw a hint of the Jo he knew. "I've had a lot of time to think while I've been in the hospital, and I've decided that you are right. Pretending to be something that we're not isn't good for either of us. It's too easy to get the role-playing confused with reality. It's best that we stop things now."

He wanted to argue with her, but how could he when he'd been the one to blame all the changes in their relationship on their just being confused by the roles they were playing. She'd used his own words against him, and now he had to respect her wishes.

As a nurse walked in and started taking Jo's vital signs, Casey walked out of the room. He knew it was rude to not stay and tell Jo goodbye, but he couldn't bring himself to say the words. Everything about their conversation had seemed so final.

He'd known Jo would return home someday—it had only been a temporary arrangement—but he hadn't known it would hurt like this.

CHAPTER FIFTEEN

JO SAT IN her apartment, Moose draped over her feet, waiting for Summer's reaction. It had been over two weeks since Jo had left the hospital.

"I still can't believe it was all a sham," Summer said, sounding almost as disappointed as Jo. "And you did it all just to keep us away from your ex-husband who should be in jail instead of tormenting you?"

"Don't even think about getting involved. Jeffrey will find a way to hurt you, even if it was just your reputations. He's not worth it. And as far as the courts are concerned, he served the time he was given."

"You underestimate the power of the press. Alex's mother is an expert in controlling the media. She'd send him home looking like the abusive jerk he is," Summer said. "And no matter what you say, I don't believe that you and Casey were faking everything. There was definitely something happening between the two of you the night you babysat for me and Alex. Don't tell me there wasn't."

"Well…" Jo had to tell someone, and since she no longer had a best friend to confide in, Summer was the closest thing she had. The two of them had been close for years. And with Summer's own struggles with an unexpected pregnancy and Alex hiding his life as the son of the king of Soura, she would understand how confusing Jo's life had become.

"We both agreed that we wouldn't let anything come between our friendship. Then there was the night on the beach."

"You mean the one when you kissed Casey like he was one of those juicy Georgia peaches and you were trying to slurp him up? I heard about that. Don't tell me that was faked," Summer said, a smirk on her face as she took a swallow of the fresh lemonade Jo had just made.

"No, I'm not that good an actor." She ignored the flush of heat that traveled down to places better ignored right now as the memory of that night came back.

"So, was it good?" Summer asked, moving closer to the end of her seat.

"Oh, yes," Jo said. "It was very good. At least it was until Casey started acting weird."

"I can't imagine Casey acting weird about sex."

"We didn't have sex, at least not that night. It was the thought of having sex with me. He just doesn't think of me that way." Jo still didn't understand why he saw every-thing between them as black-and-white. They could be friends but not lovers, yet they'd had a beautiful night together. How did he explain that? Going from friends to lovers had felt natural to her.

"Are you sure? I saw the way he looked at you that night at the house. There was something there. He couldn't take his eyes off you. I would have sworn he was falling in love with you that night."

"One problem with that—Casey doesn't believe in love. He thinks love is just an unnecessary emotion that he can live without." It hurt her to think of him going through the rest of his life never knowing love. Even though he didn't return her love, she'd not been afraid to tell him how she felt. She'd embraced the love she felt for him while he had tossed it back at her. Unwanted. Her love had been unwanted.

"He can't be that stupid. Hasn't he ever been in love?" Summer asked.

"There was a fiancée once. She apparently told him that they'd confused their friendship for love before she broke up with him. He was just using the experience as an excuse to keep all women at a distance."

"I heard something about that. She left the island just before the wedding with someone else. It sounds more like she was trying to excuse her own behavior to me. Surely he's not still hung up on her."

"On her? I don't think so. It's more he blames the situation on what we mortals call love."

They both sat there a moment, each sipping her drink. Men were so hard to understand.

"So you're just going to let him go? If you're in love with him, you should fight for him," Summer said.

"Says the woman who refused to accept that she and the father of her babies could have a future together," Jo said, remembering how heartbroken Summer had been when Alex had left the island without an explanation.

"But Alex didn't give up. Just think what could have happened if he hadn't convinced me that he loved me."

"It's hard to convince someone of something they don't believe in," Jo said.

"Maybe it's not so much that he doesn't believe in it as much as he's afraid of it," Summer said.

Casey afraid of something? It was hard to believe, but Summer could be right. It did seem he ran whenever he heard the word. Could he have been hurt so bad by the things his fiancée had said that he was afraid to trust someone enough to love them?

She shifted on the couch as Moose jumped off her feet and headed to the front door. She stood to follow him even though she wasn't expecting anyone. Her dog was better than any doorbell. Stepping around the big dog who'd planted himself in front of her, she opened the door at the same moment her ex-husband reached for the bell.

She stepped back, putting Moose between them. "What are you doing here, Jeffrey?"

"I came to make sure you're okay, of course. I was worried about you when that hurricane hit." He flashed her that overly bright smile that she knew was mostly cosmetic. She'd once dreamed of punching every one of those capped teeth out of his mouth. "Aren't you going to let me in?"

She waited for the panic to set in, that heart racing, breath stealing terror that had filled her days and her nights whenever she had thought of this meeting. It didn't come. It was only anger at having her life turned upside down by this man that filled her now.

"I don't think so. You can say whatever it is you came to say right here." What kind of fool did this man think she was? Let him inside her home? No way was that ever happening. Especially not with Summer inside.

As if she knew Jo's thoughts, Summer came up behind her. "Is there a problem?"

"No problem. My ex-husband is just going to explain to me why he felt the need to come visit me when he knew he wouldn't be welcomed." Jo wasn't sure where the courage to stand up to Jeffrey was coming from, but she liked it.

"Is that any way to treat someone who was worried about you? And in front of a royal guest? Princess Summer, I apologize for my wife's bad manners." If the man's smile got any stiffer it would crumble. Jeffrey wouldn't like the fact that Jo was embarrassing him in front of someone as important as Summer. Well, that was too bad. Jo had been preparing for this visit for weeks.

"Summer was just leaving," Jo said as she nodded her head toward the door. Summer didn't need to get involved with any of this.

"Oh, no. I'm not in any hurry. Besides, I want to wait until Casey gets here. He's on his way."

The sickly sweet smile on her ex-husband's face disappeared. "Casey? That guy who had your phone?"

"There's only one Casey. Right, Jo?" Summer's smile was genuine. She'd be a vicious poker player with that smile that gave no hint that she was bluffing. Did she have a plan for what to tell Jeffrey when Casey didn't show up? Or was she just hoping he'd leave before realizing that there was no one coming to their rescue?

But she didn't need Casey to save her. She wouldn't cower in front of this man ever again. He was on her home turf now. She was going to stand her ground. She wasn't the woman he remembered. She'd fight for the life she'd made here in Key West. She would never be that woman again.

"Why did you come here, Jeffrey? Did you think I'd just let you come in and take over my life again? Did you think I'd be too scared to fight you? I'm not that frightened girl anymore."

He started to take a step toward her and then hesitated when Moose let out a low growl of warning. "Don't be so dramatic, Jo. I don't know why you say things like that. There's been a misunderstanding. We need to talk. Alone."

"Dramatic? Me? I'm not the one who put on a show for the lawyers. That was you." She was so tired of reliving that nightmare. "But yes, let's cut the drama. Whatever it is you came for, you're not going to get it. Just leave. Go home. I don't want you here."

"You can't talk to me that way. Who do you think you are? I can make your life miserable, Jo. I came all this way, and you're going to talk to me. Get rid of your friend and this mutt unless you want me to call the police. It wouldn't look very good for your friend when the media hears about her ordering this dog to attack me."

"Don't threaten me," Summer said as she tried to step past Jo.

Tires screeched in the parking lot, and they all watched as Casey rushed out of his truck, heading toward them. What was he doing here?

He'd been on his way to see Jo when he'd received Summer's call. He'd spent the last two weeks alone and miserable, and he was done with it. He'd played over and over in his mind every kiss, every touch he'd shared with Jo in the time they'd been together. And he'd remembered every time he'd denied that there was more than just friendship between them. He'd been so wrong. The weeks they'd shared together hadn't been pretending. They'd shared a home...they'd shared their time together. They'd laughed and danced. And they'd loved together. They'd been happy. Together. He finally understood how the old man with the RV, Jack, had felt. Casey no longer felt whole without Jo beside him.

He wanted to explain all of this to her, but first he had to get rid of her ex-husband.

He'd imagined all kinds of scenarios on his way to Jo's place, each ending with her injured by this dirt bag that once called himself her husband. Now, seeing her safe, he could finally take a deep breath.

"Is there a problem?" Casey asked as he stepped up to the door, pinning Jeffrey between him and Moose. Let the guy try to get around him. He'd been spoiling for this fight ever since he'd seen Jo shake from her fear of this man. Now he just wanted to get rid of this creep so that he could tell Jo he understood. He believed her now. They could be friends and lovers.

"Not anymore," Summer said as she stepped back from the door.

"This man is confused. He seems to think that he can come here, to my home, and threaten me and my friends. He even had some delusional plan to accuse Summer of ordering Moose to attack him," Jo said, her eyes never leaving the man between them.

"Really? And just who are you planning to call? If you need the number to animal control, I have them on speed dial as I volunteer with them at least once a week. Or maybe you'd like to call the local police? They're a great group of guys, though I don't think they're going to believe that bit about Moose since he's pretty well-known around the island as a big old softy."

"This has gone on long enough. I want to talk to my wife. Alone," Jeffrey said. The man's voice never wavered, but Casey could see the bead of sweat that had formed on his forehead, just below that perfect, every-hair-in-its-place haircut.

"That's ex-wife, Jeffrey. And you lost the right to tell me what to do the first time you laid a hand on me. If you came here expecting to find the same woman that you married, you're going to be disappointed. I'm not scared of you anymore. You've done all the damage to me that you could possibly do. I lived. I survived." Jo stepped around Moose and headed forward.

Casey didn't move when the man stepped back. By the time the man's back hit his chest, Casey was smiling with pride. His Jo had the man on the run. "I think it might be best if you leave now. As you can see, there's nothing for you here."

"You think you're something, don't you? You could have come home and lived like a princess. Instead, you'd rather live here in this dump with this mutt, and this…" The man straightened and adjusted the collar of his polo shirt while Casey waited to hear what insult he planned for him. "Well, I hope the two of you live miserably ever after. You deserve it."

Casey stepped back and watched the man as he headed

toward the rented sports car sitting in the parking lot. "Well, he told us, didn't he?"

Summer began to laugh until she saw the way Jo had begun to tremble. "Let's get you inside."

"I'm okay. I'm just so mad," Jo said, her hands fisted by her sides.

"We could tell," Summer said. "I was afraid I might have to come up with bail money for you for a moment there."

"It's not Jeffrey I'm mad at. It's me. Why didn't I stand up for myself all those years ago?"

As Moose headed back inside, Casey followed him and Jo before she could come to her senses and slam the door shut in his face.

Summer turned back and studied Casey's expression. When he nodded to the door, she smiled. "If you're okay, I'm going to go. The babies will be waking up from their nap soon."

"You can go too. I don't think he'll come back," Jo said, collapsing onto the couch as Summer left.

"You did good. I was proud of you," he said.

"You're not disappointed that I got all emotional?" she asked, a touch of bitterness in her tone.

"No. I started to get a little emotional myself. I wanted to knock the guy out."

"How did you get here so fast?" she asked.

"I was already on my way here, though I broke all the speed limits once Summer called me."

"You were coming to see me? Why?"

He didn't know how to do this. He was as experienced with women as any man could be, but talking about his feelings? That was hard for him.

"I needed to apologize. I didn't listen when you tried to tell me that there could be something more than friendship between us."

As he talked, he began to walk, the movement calming him as he tried to come up with the perfect words to explain how he felt. "I excused everything that happened between us with the fact that we were pretending to be a couple, when the truth was, we were a couple."

"I don't understand," Jo said, looking up at him.

He stopped pacing and sat down beside her.

"Don't you see? It's always been the two of us. We had this great relationship as friends, but I was always afraid to let there be more. I was always afraid that I'd lose you. That we'd lose the special connection we had. But when we were pretending to be romantically involved, things changed. It gave me the chance to see what it would be like to really be a couple. To share everything. And it felt right. I was just so scared that it wouldn't last, that I denied what we had could be real."

He looked over and saw the confused look on her face. He wasn't doing this right, but all he could do was tell her how he felt. What he now knew was true. "Looking at the two of us, someone would think that I was the strong one because of my size, but that's not true. You stood up to Jeffrey even though you had every right to fear him, while I was too afraid to admit to you, my best friend, that I was in love with you."

"Do you really believe that? That you love me?" Jo asked, her eyes searching his.

"Yes, I know it," Casey said, his eyes never leaving

hers. He'd missed this. The way she made him feel complete. He'd never known that was what love felt like.

"Can you say it again?" Jo said, moving closer, taking his face into her hands.

"Of course, I can." He cleared his throat then frowned when Jo laughed. "This is not funny. I'm trying to be serious."

"And I seriously love you, Casey Johnson. See, it's not so hard," Jo said, throwing her arms around him.

"Of course, it isn't. I love you, Jo. See, I can do it. And I don't care what that jerk Jeffrey says. I will never be miserable as long as I have you. You are my happily ever-after."

EPILOGUE

GIRLS DREAMED OF fairy-tale endings with their very own Prince Charming while wearing long, white lacey dresses. Once, Jo had given up on those dreams. But now she waited for her turn to walk barefoot down to the sandy shoreline where the man she'd always dreamed of waited for her.

Maybe her Prince Charming was dressed in a white button-up shirt and navy dress pants instead of the standard tux and maybe her dress, though white, didn't have a touch of lace. That was okay. This was her fairy-tale wedding. She could wear whatever she wanted to.

"Are you ready?" Summer asked from beside her.

Jo looked in front of her where a small group of her friends sat in chairs lined up to face the water. She could see her parents among the group. Were they comparing the fancy wedding they'd given her years ago when she'd married Jeffrey to the simple one she and Casey had chosen to have here among their friends? Could they see the love in Casey's eyes when he looked at her instead of the possessiveness that had always been in Jeffrey's?

"Okay, Violet," Summer said as she motioned for Dylan's daughter to walk down the deep blue runner that ran down to the beach where Casey waited.

Summer squeezed Jo's hand before turning and following the little girl. Then it was Jo's turn. She took her first step, and Moose bumped against her side.

"You're doing fine," she told him, giving his head a rub. He was taking his job of escorting her down the aisle very seriously.

Reaching Casey's side, she turned to see her friends and family gathered behind her as he took her hand and they stepped forward to commit their lives to each other while the sun began to set behind them.

Later, when the toasts had been made and the DJ took requests, Jo wandered down to the beach alone. Laughter drifted down from the pavilion where everyone was dancing, but she could still hear the soft footsteps behind her.

"Are you already trying to sneak away from me?" Casey said as his arms came around her waist.

"Or maybe I'm trying to sneak away with you," she said, leaning back against him.

"I like the sound of that. Happy?" he asked as his lips skimmed down her throat.

"I've never been happier," she said, turning around in his arms. "I have you, my friends and this beautiful island. I think I might have the very best happily-ever-after a girl could ever dream of."

* * * * *

COMING SOON!

We really hope you enjoyed reading this book. If you're looking for more romance be sure to head to the shops when new books are available on

Thursday 11th May

MILLS & BOON®

Coming next month

THE BROODING DOC AND THE SINGLE MUM
Louisa Heaton

Daniel couldn't stand still. He tried to. But his mind wouldn't let him settle. He felt as if his body was flooded with adrenaline and this was either a fight, flight or freeze response.

Most likely flight.

I thought about kissing her.

That was what he couldn't get out of his head. He'd been having such a fun time. A relaxing time. Playing football with Jack. He'd used to play football with Mason all the time, so the opportunity to play with Jack and remember what it had been like had been awesome! In a way, it had been almost as if Jack was his son. He'd been helping to guide him. Showing the little boy that he was interested in him. That he wanted to spend time with him. That he was important.

And then Stacey had joined them.

Penny had never joined in their football games. She'd always watched, or used the time that Daniel was with their son to get a few jobs done around the house. Daniel hadn't minded that. It had given them a little father-son bonding moment.

So when Stacey had joined in he'd been amazed, and then delighted. They'd had a fun time. It had been relaxing, the three of them together. Nice. Easy. So easy! He'd almost not been able to believe how easy it was for him to be with them.

And then the tackle.

They'd all gone for the ball at once and somehow tumbled into a tangle of arms and legs. And he'd landed on top of Stacey. Not fully. His hands had broken the fall, and he'd tried to avoid squashing her. But she'd been lying beneath him, red hair splayed out against the green grass. Her laughter-filled eyes had looked up at him, there'd been a smile on her face and he'd been so close to her!

He'd felt her breathing, her chest rising and falling. Her softness. Her legs entwined with his. Their faces had been so close. Mere inches away from each other! And the thought had risen unbidden to his mind.

What would it be like to kiss her?

Continue reading
THE BROODING DOC AND THE SINGLE MUM
Louisa Heaton

Available next month
www.millsandboon.co.uk

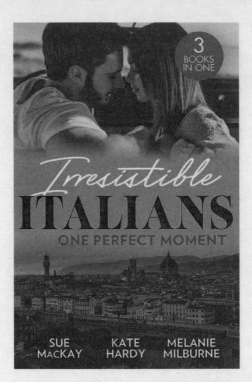

LET'S TALK

Romance

For exclusive extracts, competitions
and special offers, find us online:

 facebook.com/millsandboon

 @MillsandBoon

 @MillsandBoonUK

 @MillsandBoonUK

Get in touch on 01413 063 232

For all the latest titles coming soon, visit
millsandboon.co.uk/nextmonth

MILLS & BOON

THE HEART OF ROMANCE

A ROMANCE FOR EVERY READER

MODERN

Prepare to be swept off your feet by sophisticated, sexy and seductive heroes, in some of the world's most glamourous and romantic locations, where power and passion collide.

HISTORICAL

Escape with historical heroes from time gone by. Whether your passion is for wicked Regency Rakes, muscled Vikings or rugged Highlanders, awaken the romance of the past.

MEDICAL

Set your pulse racing with dedicated, delectable doctors in the high-pressure world of medicine, where emotions run high and passion, comfort and love are the best medicine.

True Love

Celebrate true love with tender stories of heartfelt romance, from the rush of falling in love to the joy a new baby can bring, and a focus on the emotional heart of a relationship.

Desire

Indulge in secrets and scandal, intense drama and sizzling hot action with heroes who have it all: wealth, status, good looks…everything but the right woman.

HEROES

The excitement of a gripping thriller, with intense romance at its heart. Resourceful, true-to-life women and strong, fearless men face danger and desire - a killer combination!

To see which titles are coming soon, please visit

millsandboon.co.uk/nextmonth

GET YOUR ROMANCE FIX!

Get the latest romance news, exclusive author interviews, story extracts and much more!